The Native Boy

An Autobiography of a man from Nyaake

By William K. Reeves
Edited by Nicholas Bayard

First Edition 2004

Publisher:
The New World African Press
1958 Matador Way Unit #35
Northridge, CA 91330

ISBN 0-9717692-7-3

ABOUT THE NEW WORLD AFRICAN PRESS

The New World African Press evolved over a period of fifteen years. Originally, it began as Elsie Mae Enterprises in honor of my own special guiding light, my late mother Elise Mae Holloway. Later Elsie Mae Enterprises was changed to the Boniface I. Obichere Press. This new change was in honor of my mentor, friend, and colleague, who passed from this realm and made his transition to the afterlife in the world of ancestors in 1997.

Finally, the Boniface I. Obichere Press metamorphosed into the New World African Press in 2000. While the name of the Press has gone through several name changes, its mission and purpose have remained the same: to fill the void and neglect left by the major publishing houses; to publish manuscripts that focus on the Diasporic experience in Africa, Europe, and the countries of the New World. While the press is primarily concerned with diasporic issues, it is also committed to publishing non-Diasporic manuscripts and literature such as *Bach: A Fictional Memoir* by Dr. Paul Guggenheim, and *Space: A Journalist Notebook* by DeWayne B. Johnson.

The New World African Press list of books includes the following. Clarence E. Zamba Liberty, *Growth of the Liberian State: An Analysis of Its Historiography* is the first in our Diasporic series. Others include: Herbert H. Booker, *The Noble Drew Ali and the Moorish Science Temple Movement*, and Joseph E. Holloway, *An Introduction to Classical African Civilizations, The African American Odyssey: Student's Manual and Study Guide with Text Combined Volume*, and *Neither Black Nor White: The Saga of An American family.* Sakui Malapka's *The Village Boy* is the first in the series of novels about Liberia. The other books in this series are John Gay's *Red Dust on the Green Leaves, The Brightening Shadow*, and his latest novel in this series on the Liberian Civil War, *Long Day's Anger*, and now his memoir covering fifty years of experiences in Africa, *Africa: A Dream Deferred.*

The New World African Press is proud and honored to publish the memoir of William K. Reeves, entitled, *The Native Boy: An Autobiography of a Man from Nyaake.*

Table of Contents

Preface

It has been an honor and a privilege to work with Mr. William Kamma Reeves for the three years leading up to the publication of his extraordinary and telling autobiography, *The Native Boy: An Autobiography of a man from Nyaake.* This book is a truly unique piece of work that documents both the life of an extraordinary man, and the day-to-day aspects of native Liberian culture, a culture that has been transmitted primarily in the oral form for centuries. Much of this history has been lost in the time since the first murmurs of civil war rumbled through Liberia in the latter part of the 20th century. The Native Boy is a testament to the hope and resilience of the Liberian people, and to the importance of education and good works in the present reconstruction of the country.

The story of the production of *The Native Boy* is an unusual one. Professor Beth Bryan of the English Department at Brown University and a former colleague of Mr. Reeves, presented me with the unedited, 700-page manuscript in the fall of 2001, along with the challenge of serving as copyeditor of the text. The idealistic undergraduate that I was, I underestimated the challenge given and threw myself headlong into the project to learn rather quickly that the manuscript itself contained a unique tale. Mr. Reeves had typed his memoirs out on a manual typewriter, from which a number of (rather careless) assistants copied it onto a computer disc. The data on this disc fell victim to an electronic virus that captured random portions of text and switched them around in a crushing blow to all chronological sensibilities. Adding to the confusion were the hundreds of Liberian expressions that laced the text. As fate would have it, the original typescript of The Native Boy: An Autobiography of a man from Nyaake was then entirely destroyed by mildew.

What lay in front of me was not only a sizable challenge, but an unprecedented opportunity to both immerse myself in Liberian culture from afar, and to gain the friendship and respect of a man whom I consider to be one of the greatest mentors and educators alive today. In the year 2000, Mr. Reeves, at the urging of his daughter Felicia, moved from the war-ridden Liberian countryside to a small apartment in the suburbs of Philadelphia. During the editing process, I visited Mr. Reeves a number of times in this apartment, a dark, musty place that stood in stark contrast to the community-based living situation he describes spending most of his life in. Cataracts and old age had ravaged Mr. Reeves' eyesight, making it impossible for him to read for extended periods of time. It was to be my task to make his text readable for an American audience while also preserving the original Liberian phraseology.

My first meeting with Mr. Reeves was less than promising. As I walked up to his door, I found myself nervous to be in possession of the memoirs of a wizened old man whom I had never met, a then nineteen-year-old child who had somehow been granted the power of the copyeditor's blue pencil. Mr. Reeves was admittedly doubtful of this college boy who had never traveled east of Rhode Island. But as we worked side by side, communicating by email and over the phone, all pretenses slowly ebbed, giving way to a bond of friendship. Mr. Reeves began asking me about my love life, giving me tips on how to "claw" myself a "je bor dor" (girlfriend), and I offered him my advice on how to conquer his newfound bouts of asthma, as I had suffered from asthma as a youth. He grew into a sort of father figure for me, and to this day I consider him one of my dearest friends. Throughout my work it became clear to me that everyone who has ever known Mr. Reeves has similar sentiments because of the way that he touched their lives.

I set out to finish my work on the text in the summer of 2003 under a grant from the English Department at Brown University. This was at the very same time that the Liberian civil war exploded under the eyes of the international media. During the events of what Liberians referred to as "World War III," hundreds of civilians were killed in rebel attempts to overthrow the regime of Charles Taylor. International pressure mounted for the swift exit of Taylor from Liberia, which came about in August. Mr. Reeves sent me an email the very day that Taylor fled to Nigeria, proclaiming that the "old devil" has finally left and that once again refugees like him would be able to return home.

All of these events pushed me to work fervently and tirelessly to put Mr. Reeves' autobiography in working order for publication. Mr. Reeves was patient, and sent me letters of appreciation for my work time and again. By the opening weeks of 2004, the text was sent out in its complete and chronological form to the New World African Press.

Mr. Reeves once told me to hit the iron on the head while it is red. He, no doubt, learned this lesson from experience. Had he not seized the opportunities that he did, both as a student and as an educator, there would now be countless more young Liberian men and women who turned to violence as a way of life during the years of the civil war. Education has been and will be the saving grace of the once-great nation of Liberia, and William Reeves carried the torch. The mortal form of William Kamma Reeves will one day pass away, but through the steadfast and selfless work of those he led and those who loved him, his words and his soul will live on forever.

-Nicholas Bayard

May 2004

Acknowledgement

As an asylee, a refugee, in the United States of America, it was completely unconceivable that a traumatized old man like me lost in deep frustration and heartbreaking disappointment about the wanton annihilation of my country, Liberia, the gem of West Africa, where once Freedom raised her glowing form, I was going to be able to pen together some thoughts about my obscure life and put them together in a form of a book without the genuine friendship and willing help of Mr. William L. Bates, a retired editor of Snohomish Tribune, Snohomish, Washington State.

A married couple, Milton and Eleanor, who served as US Peace Corps volunteers at St. Philomena Catholic Elementary and Junior High School in Zwedru, Liberia, introduced the Bates family to me and requested them to host me at their home in Snohomish during the Christmas of 1969. Milton and his family were in Pittsburgh, Pennsylvania, while I was auditing courses in the methods of teaching English on both junior and senior high school levels at Indiana University, Bloomington, Indiana.

From Eigermann Hall I exchanged greetings thru the magic of the telephone with the Bates family, which dramatically established the lifelong friendship. After a seventy-two hour train ride, we landed in Seattle that Christmas Eve, from where Mrs. Bates collected me for a thirty mile drive to Snohomish, northeast of Seattle.

After about thirty-three odd years, sad changing time brought me back to this hospitable country and at once I got reconnected with my namesake. As soon as the fire of friendship was rekindled, I appealed to the retired Snohomish Tribune editor to proofread my manuscript. He accepted and hence this book.

At Tubman – Wilson Institute, a public high school in Zwedru, Liberia, was one Elizabeth Bryan, a young US Peace Corps volunteer. Beth and I served as instructors at this rural high school. The carnage and mayhem raging caused by a senseless, so-called civil war in Liberia, I sought a safe haven in the United States where I landed on May 21, 2000. Many of my former students of Bishop Juwle High School, a Catholic high school in Zwedru, where I served as principal for twelve unbroken years, were in close touch with each other in the Americas. They formed and run what they call "The Alumni Association of St. Philomena School and Bishop Juwle High School." At one of their reunion annual conventions held in Massachusetts, Beth, Olwyn and Karen, former US Peace Corps volunteers to Zwedru, Liberia, having gathered from reliable information that I their former principal and US Peace Corps Site Administrator, would be in attendance, came to welcome me. The reunion remains the happiest in recent memory.

Later, I humbly requested my former US Peace Corps volunteer and my former colleague, Beth Bryan, now professor of English at Brown University, Providence, Rhode Island, to help me put my story together. Willingly she accepted the onerous task of proofreading the manuscript. From her English Department she carefully selected a dedicated education student, Nicholas M. Bayard, to do the proofreading under her close supervision. Tirelessly and diligently they edited the work of the amateur writer. The publication of this story is the handy work of their service. All of these willing hands I sincerely, gratefully and appreciatively acknowledge.

-William K. Reeves

Dedication

This book is dedicated to my parents: My father, the village chief, member of Gbor militiaman and village farmer; my mother, the devoted African housewife and a devout Christian and my daughter Felicia Quiadae who saved my aging life from the carnage and mayhem, a horrible situation caused by the senseless, so-called civil war that has devastated Liberia almost beyond repair.

INTRODUCTION

Every day I wonder whether writing a book, a novel, biography, history, or autobiography is a calling or not. The idea of writing a story about my obscure life came to me since my high school days.

The protruding, embarrassing, and defiant question is why I have not written the life story up to this time. I have a world of excuses if I would be compelled to answer it.

But, as I know it, no excuse is worth listening to. Forty long and unbroken years have come and gone since those hard but blissful high school days of mine. As a poet puts it, "Except a living man there is nothing more wonderful than book." I guess then, the time to produce a book or a story about a man is never late. Literature is timeless. Here I am to make an earnest attempt.

Over the years of my long stay in the classroom my erudite students have consistently and persistently requested me to put together some writing which would serve as my 'evil deed' that would live after me, since the good is often interred with the dead.

To me, the writing my pleasing trouble (students) is requesting is not just a story but a true life story about or from the man of Nyaake, a township nestled on seven scenic hills. In short, this attempt is to write a genuine and factual story about my obscure life, entitled, *The Native Boy*.

As you will observe in the story, if you will, the early events say nothing about dates and years. During the time my life was unfolding I had no memory; I was still a raw unlettered village boy, and since the number of years in a man's life does not matter but what he has actually done with those years, my story will be told as I know it.

In this whole narrative, I made many and varied blanket statements, statements not intended to tarnish or ridicule any person, group, or ethnic group, etc; it is just to tell it the way I experienced it.

1

CHAPTER 1 "Christmas In Tenzonke"

It was Christmas, and the Reverend William Taylor White, presiding elder of the African Methodist Episcopal Church, Cape Palmas District, had come to a forrest village called Tenzonke in Gedebo, then a chiefdom in the then Eastern Province of Liberia, to celebrate the feast of the birth of Christ with his flock of worshippers.

In that section of the vast Grebo ethnic group, Christmas is the most celebrated of all annual festivals. During this season every family (household) prepares special meals and special attires to wear too. Non-Christians as well as Christians jubilantly observe the day in many colorful performances.

The local pastor of the African Methodist Episcopal Church had personally invited all of the people of the surrounding villages to this particular celebration at which his presiding elder would physically be present. The local village which was hosting the event attracted the young people because of the bulging stream of water with its falls. Food was another tantalizer for all. And so the invitees came in large numbers. For this special occasion the usually nude village children were neatly clad with their deep interest, basking in the creek, hidden. As the guests were being traditionally received by Pastor Moses Challaba Jasay, the young people sneaked away to the creek. The Reverend White, who wanted the children to come to him, noticed them rushing off to the waterside, but waited patiently.

After some time with the people who favorably honored the invitation of the pastor, the presiding elder decided to take a walk with Pastor Moses to meet his little ones at their happy spot. This time, the swimmers were returning in their birthday suits to the village, where they had left their special Christmas wears with their parents.

Encountering them, the reverend gentleman stepped aside to give free passage to the youngsters. Smiling, the energy-filled boys (most under ten) began to pass in front of the holy man hastily in single files.

"Come to me," Reverend White beckoned to the little ones. One after another the timid children stopped by their smiling friend. Graciously holding out the box of candy and speaking through Pastor Moses, the reverend gentleman said, "Here are candies for each of you if you are willing to attend school here in this home village of yours." Without one single thought I eagerly accepted as I willingly nodded to his solicitous offer and condition. Few of my friends grasped the sweet candies and the opportunity of attending school.

Later in the village, Pastor Moses informed the parents of the children who unconsciously accepted Reverend White's gracious offer and the condition attached. Seemingly, the reverend gentleman had tantalized the little boys in accepting the candies for school. Besides education, Reverend White wanted to bring his children to Christ. During the long Christmas worship service that followed that afternoon, the students to be were Christianized. At the baptism Reverend White spoke to me through my father. Among other things, the baptizer asked my father whether my parents had given me a Christian name. "No," my father replied, but added, "we called him "Kamma." In a fatherly tune, Reverend White requested, "I want him to be like me and so I now name him 'William.'" I was now a baptized African Methodist Episcopal Church Christian. But did the name 'William' make me truly the Reverend William

2

Taylor White? From the first encounter with the holy man (that time I guess I was less than ten years old) up to the time I got to know him personally in the 1950s, Reverend White was still unbelievably handsome. In no way am I like him physically. But one thing is certain by which I am gladdened, and that is that I don't think that when he remarked that he would like me to be like him, he was talking about my physical constitution. I was invited to attend school and to be a Christian. To a very satisfactory degree, I am a Christian and acquired some education. Thus Reverend White's request, like prophesy, has come to pass.

On returning from the bulging stream with its torrential falls, I unconsciously made my lifelong commitment upon accepting the candy from the smiling holy man. Long before my father had told me that I would be sent to school. He set the path.

In the village, the women and their children (including boys and girls) eat with their hands. I was the only exception. As I was growing up one day a Mandingo trader came to our village and my father bought me a silver spoon from him. "Here, student in waiting, you must begin to live like the people in school by eating with spoon everyday." Grinning, the old man proudly presented the spoon. Having accepted the candy and received baptism and now the cord that tightly tied me to my tree of commitment, was I on the proper footing? The future would tell. School I must attend.

How soon would the presiding elder send us the teacher? For us, the students to be were in no way worrying about the time for the opening of the school or when the teacher would arrive. Of the many boys in my village who were in company with me when we were returning from the water front only I alone accepted the candy with its condition. Alone I could not talk about school. One day Pastor Moses sent a bearer to inform my father and his villagers that the teacher had arrived. One evening, teasingly, my father broke the news, "My friend will sooner or later not eat big bowls of rice each day or cold rice early morning." "Ha, does this mean that our teacher is here?" anxiously I inquired. "Yes, Pastor Moses said that your teacher came in the other day," the village chief declared. "Soon or later I will clear you off to her," my father added. Off I was sent in no time! Had the dice been cast?

CHAPTER TWO "Three Neighboring Villages"

Three neighboring villages, Tenzonke, Kablake, and Baweake, traditionally called 'Suwroke,' are the scene of this story. Tenzonke, the largest of the three, is the home of Pastor Moses and also the home of the African Methodist Episcopal Church in Gedebo, Eastern Province, Liberia. Kablake, centrally located, is the administrative headquarters of the trio villages and the home of my solicitous father. Baweake, the village that molded aluminum pot in which well seasoned Grebo palm butter, the subject of this story, was cooked, is the home of my contagiously-smiling mother.

The founders of both Tenzonke and Kablake were converts to the Christian faith. The two gentlemen, Myer Kamma and Weagbah Challaba, had gone to the Gold Coast to work for their livelihood when the Kaiser War, the First World War, broke out in 1914. Myer Kamma, the founder of Kablake, was a recruiter and headman for a cocoa plantation company in Accra, Gold Coast. He had returned from Liberia with his new laborers, and about a few months following his arrival in Accra, the world's first insanity began to unfold rapidly. Like a trauma from earthquake, Accra was terrified by the sound of an explosion heard from neighboring Togo. Alarmed, the executive of the cocoa plantation company mustered the entire people of Accra to their churches to fall upon their knees to implore God Almighty for His saving grace to spare them and people the world over from the plight of war. Some days later, headman Kamma and his recruits were repatriated.[1]

The outbreak of World War I also brought Christ to Steward Challaba. The Gold Coast was Mr. Challaba's second home. At various times, he had served as a steward for the Cocoa plantation company in Accra. The impending war in 1914 reversed his fortune. He lost his lucrative job and was compelled to return to his native land, Liberia. But Challaba got a more lucrative job. The earth-breaking sound that horrified Accra in particular and the Gold Coast in general landed the steward in Christian Church for the first time. Gazing at the multitude of terrified worshippers, the African native wondered what good would come out of praying to someone or something called God. Seriously he read the faces of the praying congregation, especially his masters' (employers) faces, who had caused the emotionally stricken inhabitants of Accra to assemble in the churches. Since the white people were kneeling before someone or something they thought and believed would secure their lives, including the lives of Africans, it was notably convincing that even the white men and their women had knelt before to this unseen power. The experienced steward, who because of his many years spent at serving his masters in the Gold Coast [Ghana], was nicknamed by his indigenous people "Kuwotapeh," (meaning a person who had traveled and worked many years in the land of British or French colonies, which they referred to as "Down the Coast") was spiritually moved. Challaba met his Savior face to face and he wholeheartedly embraced Him. The steward's stewardship silently won new dimension. He was now a steward for God the Almighty: a convert, a new creation. He was repatriated. This time his material need was not satisfied but undoubtedly he was spiritually a rich man.

With his newfound faith Kuwotapeh returned to his home village, Numapso, in the Gedebo country, a sub-group of the vast Grebo ethnic group sprawling in southeastern Liberia. At home the new convert fearlessly began to lead prayer service with some of his crowd of people in the village perched on a very towering hill. Soon or late the elders of the village noticed their Kuwotapeh behaving in ways they called "strange ways." One evening, Challaba was summoned to the town center, where the elders questioned him for the so-called strange ways in and around the densely populated village. In a straightforward move, the children politely replied. "In Accra, Gold Coast, I received the most precious gift of life; I converted to the Christian faith. I promised my Lord and God there and then that I would share this rich experience with you the villagers. This is my mission," the young convert explained. "To us you appear mad when you are with your group," the hoary elders asserted. "You are mistaken; I am not mad in the least," the new steward said emphatically, denying the made up accusation of the hard village dwellers. "Young man, simply we want to inform you that the village and its inhabitants will no longer tolerate you and your group kneeling here and there and if you wish to continue your strange behavior then we must ask you now to get out of our village," the stern elders pronounced. "Since you came back with your funny way of life you have deliberately and flagrantly violated our village norms, thus setting our ancestors against us," the angry elders added.

It is sad to say that Elder Jasay, a prominent member of the elder council of Numapso, is father of Weagbah Challaba. His wife, Challaba's mother, is the spokeswoman for the women of the village. But even with his highly placed social status, Challaba was evicted from his home village. If it is true that silence means consent, then Challaba's parents, both of high social standing, acquiesced to the eviction of their son. From your mind's eye, I guess you can see the marked frustration and disappointment that seeped through his now traumatized self.

"Years before, when I came from Down the Coast, everybody, including the iron-hearted elders of the village, heartily welcomed me because of the material things I brought and generously shared with them, but today I came home with my hands tied to my back because of the wind of change and the war that drove us from Accra," Challaba lamented. "Not knowing that I am richer now than ever before, my village elders and silent parents blindly refused to get a wholesome share of the good news that propels me to move bravely about the village the way I do." Challaba narrated exasperatedly. Dejected, Challaba went to answer his new call by going to establish his own village where he would be free to kneel here and there.

In the other village, Kablake, Myer Kamma was going through the same bitter experience Challaba was wrestling with in Numapso. The elders of Kablake declared Kamma strange, and he was threatened to be ostracized should he continue to practice his strange behavior. "There is no turning back on the gift I received from the Lord God Almighty in Accra," Kamma defied. "I would rather live a solitary life in a village of my own than to remain here and get my soul spiritually denied and deprived," Kamma angrily concluded. A solitary life he chose, and he established his new settlement about a quarter of a mile from his home village and called it "London." I don't know London, the British capital. At the time it was believed that London was but the largest city in the world. So a one-hut settlement called London in southeastern Liberia of West Africa evokes question. However, convert Kamma had for many years worked for a British cocoa plantation company in Accra, Gold Coast.

No doubt he enjoyed his job and his personal association with his British employers, perhaps Londoners, but he thought to live with his London friends away from them. In the meantime, Challaba called his village on the bank of a bulging creek "Tenzonke."

This is an English word, "station," and is here Gedebocized. Station, like railroad station, is a place or building where passengers wait for a train to take them to their destinations. And so our new convert founded his new village, the place for sowing the seed of the Gospel and waiting for his Lord.

Would Challaba and Kamma get followers? The answer is an emphatic "yes." As we know already, the young men were charismatic. Kamma, a former labor recruiter and a British cocoa plantation company head, was the symbol of employment for the young men in the village and in the group. Kuwotapeh Challaba, on the other hand, had immensely earned an enviable reputation for his generous handouts when he came from Down the Coast.

Despite the stern warning the parents of the young people of Numapso and Kablake rained on them, the obstinate men visited the new settlements frequently. Three men, Baina Twapei, Hokona Tugbeh, and Worsolur, were some of the Down the Coast elites in Gedebo. All of Them, including Challaba, had worked together at one time or the other in the Gold Coast. No doubt, they had seen the Christian churches in action in Gold Coast but made no point of theirs to visit or become part of them. But when Kuwotapeh, inflamed with the spirit of conversion, returned to their home village, the three men were inspired and unyieldingly left the old village with its conservative, quarrelsome elders. In his, the years following, more people poured into the waiting village. This time the members of the new Christian community took on western Christian names. Challaba, their leader, was now called Moses. During his long employment in the Gold Coast, our Kuwotapeh was officially known as "Pusey," a Gedebocized word for purse. The others became known as Peter, Samuel, etc. Before Moses left the old village he took as his wife a village maid. Tarweh Jobo now became the mother of the striving community.

Kamma, with his only family in his community, was fighting an uphill battle. Kablake, his old village, was by far less populated than Numapso. As the conservatism in both villages spoke defiantly it had more grip on the young people of Kablake because their number was proportionately smaller. Yielding to the spiritual call by Kamma was impeded. Many years following his establishment of his London, Kamma's camp remained lonely.

Unlike Challaba, Kamma was still living in the past, a typical African village dweller. He was always flanked by his two lively young wives. Of course since Challaba was much younger, as a try-and-see game, he had taken only one wife. In this case, the barrier would have been at Challaba's gates. By nature and tradition, the African wants to live a kingly life in a compound of many wives. Challaba's followers were his special group from Down the Coast, and were experiencing marriage life in the African style for the very first time too. Were there people in Kablake, who went and came from Down the Coast?

A year or two before the outbreak of the Kaiser War (the First World War; my indigenous people call it the Kaiser war, Kaiser the official title of the ruler of

Germany before 1918) in 1914, the famous labor recruiter of Kablake had returned from the British cocoa plantation company in Accra to the Gedebo country in Liberia. This time among the many recruited were two minors, Hiebe Toe and Nyanweju Hinneh. Following the preliminary arrangements to travel abroad, Kamma and his new recruits embarked on board a sailing vessel for the Gold Coast. Sailing on board a ship on the vast treeless ocean excited the two youngsters. The excitement was climaxed when they arrived in Accra and were given their first chance to work for pay.

At about twelve years old, the minors were not ready or old enough for any hard manual labor. They were hired, therefore, to pick foreign objects from cocoa beans spread in the sun by some strong arms every day. At this the playful workers worked steadily several hours each day.

When the impending war depressingly drove them and their elders back to Liberia, the boys, still minors, fell back into the nests of their respective mothers. It took them time to grow into their majority. Nyanweju Hinneh, closely related to Kamma, was a member of the Kablake village family. Seemingly all Liberian employees of the British Cocoa plantation company in Accra caught the contagious fever of Christianity on that woeful day. Hinneh got his share of the lifesaving fever. In reality Hinneh was a convert but in practice he had no choice as the disobliging and arrogant elders of Kablake clung absolutely to power. However, Hinneh had the burning desire of joining his relation in London in the Gedebo country. "One day I will be old enough to do what I want with my life," Hinneh yearned.

Long years following their return from the Gold Coast, and after the devastating First World War, Hinneh went on his second fortune-seeking trip to the Gold Coast. But this time his employment took him to Kumasi, where he was employed by a logging company. After spending two long years as a cook for the laborers, the overseas worker sailed back home, with his tightly packed two large wooden trunks. It seemed that the time spent in Kumasi, looking as he was, ushered him into the waiting hall of the young, enticing, and beautiful women hunting for future partners. Kumasi had groomed him. In no time after arriving, the Kumasi-groomed villager found his heart's desire in a charming young village maid named Tarnu Kpaye. "I get no time to lose; I must get my charming pleasing trouble under the roof of my parents soon," Hinneh inaudibly prayed. Without the usual traditional wedding ceremony he openly kidnapped his wife-to-be with the help of his Down the Coast life companion, Hiebo Toe, a close relation of Tarnu Kpaye and both of the Baweake village family. Married and a man in his own right now, Hinneh left the old establishment to join his former headman and the Accra-converted Christian, Kamma.

It was all paved for Hinneh with his newlywed wife to move to their chosen Christian community. But how would he leave his dangerously ill mother and his aging stepfather? No doubt, he took it to the Lord in prayer and a surprising answer came in a jiffy. "My son, I want you to live your life the way you want," Mother Nyanweju, in a shrill audible voice, unbelievably declared. With that settled, Hinneh marched briskly with his wife to the land of the Christian converts. One Kien Twapei joined the bandwagon. Kamma's London was taking on new dimensions. Some surprises were brewing somewhere in the old villages, however. Over the years the iron hand rulers-the elders of the Kablake and Numapso- gradually lost touch with reality.

They lived in a changing world but obdurately refused to change with the world. Nearly all the villagers were chanting "right, right, right," while the old conservative papis shouted with their age drowned voices "left, left, and left." Living in very slim minority and their ages having tolled on them the village masters and their consuming power rapidly dwindled into oblivion.

The majority of the people now determined never to observe the lunar sacrifice the high priest of the village prepared and offered the spirit world. As the villagers were guarded and guided with "don't, don't, don't do this," from the cantankerous elders. At this chorus the young and the middle-aged had their own litany which was sung defiantly. Soon or later the marked disagreement shattered the one-time solid village base for law and order. Numapso and Kablake were disintegrated and depopulated rapidly as the villagers took refuge in Tenzonke and Kablake. Subsequently, the hamlet London in the Gedebo country was renamed Kablake as our new London was being inundated with the people seeking comfort away from the old Kablake village. In another way, reasonable defiance had its grip on Challaba in Tenzonke, where he absolutely refused to yield to the call of the people fleeing Numapso that the young village take the name of old village that kicked him out because of his newfound faith. Challaba did not budge; Tenzonke remains Tenzonke!

Those men and women, who were still finding Challaba's so-called "strange ways" unbearable, could not compromise but to establish their safe haven called Welleke, centrally located between new Kablake and Tenzonke. Would it be correct to say that the old Gedebo conservatism and the Challaba Christian wind of change had silently clashed and shattered the two village towns? Unfortunately, the 'old papis' were unceremoniously robbed of their totalitarian power based on the solid Grebo traditions clothed with disobliging and hardened conservatism. For us, Challaba's truth had unreservedly triumphed! Bravo for the Christianity and its wind of change!

As time would tell, the inhabitants of Welleke wavered for a brief period between keeping the old order and merging with Kablake or Tenzonke. As each saw it, they made their choices between the Christian communities, which had spontaneously stretched out their receiving arms. Old Kablake and her founder did not seem to be well at home with their new faith.

The inundation of London by the unsaved people of old Kablake rolled all the wastes of the old village on London. Convert Kamma clung onto the Christian faith when he saw it in action in the Gold Coast, but unfortunately, his two wives were no active parts of his faith. As you can readily see, Kamma alone could not withstand the grossness of the nature of the many disbelievers. He wavered and crumbled beneath the grossness. In the process, Kablake went totally blank in the Christian faith. The old power emerged again and seized full control of Kablake while Tenzonke and Challaba continued to stand the test of time. Nyanweju Hinneh and Kien Twapei, who moved to London before the exodus, did not develop many roots in the Christian faith. In short, they were not yet strong men of prayer.

Chapter III "Murder and Brutality in Gedebo"

Allured by the candy and the baptism that followed, I was for lifetime unconsciously committed to both education, a long uphill process, as I later painfully discovered, and Christianity, a charge, when lived and kept according to its principles, makes one happy. The challenge is onerous on the unthinking village lad. Conscious or not, I had plunged into a swelling ocean headlong. What shall I do? This was like a crisis. In his book, *The Six Crises*, the seasoned American politician writes, "In a crisis there are two alternatives: you either run away from it or you face it."[2] Run must I? No, I cannot run away. The onus is singularly mine. I have no coward's blood in my veins. Perhaps you don't know. I come from two distinguished family lines, all with the names of celebrated warriors, who ably defended and preserved the territorial integrity of the small fertile Gedebo country, a leading rice-producing chiefdom in the then Eastern Province. Time would tell.

The everyday questions asked by many people I encounter from time to time are: (1) where was I born? and (2) when was I born? I have a ready answer for the first question. Creditably and reliably I know I was born in Kablake. Frankly I don't know when I was born. Here I take one consolation from one writer who says and I say with him, "It is not the number of years that one lives that matters but what he has actually done with those years." I would request my readers not to bother themselves about dates from this village lad whose parents lost count of time when their rice farm didn't yield much rice in a given farming year. But be assured that I was born one day, and live. No doubt too, and inevitably so, I will die one day. If you find something readable in this story, please relax and live with me vicariously as I unfold my obscure life stewardship.

Two events devastated the lives of the people of Gedebo in the 1920s. The forced labor recruitment carried out brutally by President Charles D.B. King and his miscreants, coupled with the savage killing of Yeai Nyenu, a distinguished son of the Gedebo, shattered them.

Long before what is now called Liberia, the people who happily inhabited the so-called Grain Coast [Liberia] went far out into the African colonies of the British, French, German, Spanish, and Portuguese to work for their livelihood of their own free will, rather than being explored and exploited by those colonizing powers. When the Liberian nation came into being, the people continued to go out to those colonies, especially Gold Coast and Nigeria, where they were gainfully employed. The Liberians who distinguished themselves at their jobs by being diligent and industrious were made headmen and given other higher positions in their respective companies. In due time, these trustworthy headmen were empowered to go back to their respective communities in Liberia to recruit laborers for their individual companies. This biannual recruitment was democratic, as it was purely voluntary. Happily the young indigenous men which the recruitments were conducted steadfastly seized the opportunity to work overseas for their personal lives and the care of their extended family members.

A year or two following the timely arrival of the Firestone Rubber Plantations Company, a cocoa plantation company located on the Island of Fernando Po, off the coast of Nigeria, officially petitioned the Government of Liberia to supply the company with a large manpower for the running of the plantation. No doubt, the government accepted the request and began at once to forcibly and brutally recruit the laborers. The recruiters were the armed men of the Liberian Frontier Force, the immoral suppressors of the people (whom their government officials called "Native People"). While recruiting, the armed men of the Liberian Frontier Force vandalized the villages and looted the villagers' scanty food and clothing. This brutal exercise left the Gedebo and others of the vast Grebo people frustrated and bewildered. Here minor events like births of babies and harvests did not matter—they were completely ignored as ever before.

The Gedebo country was waxing cold as they began to build up political camps. The major factions were the Wrea Musu and GeGeju Karbeh camps, all vying for the paramount chieftaincy for the Gedebo Chiefdom, a chiefdom of the Webbo District with headquarters then in Nyaake. As it is always the case, each camp had its staunch supporters. Pastor Moses Challaba Jasay of Tenzonke got secretly involved as a camper for the Gegeju Karbeh camp. Seemingly he had lost his sense of direction. Already many people of Gedebo, including the bitter elders of his original village, hated him (and even the very ground he walked on) for his 'strange ways,' aggravated by his giving or allowing the women to eat male bush goat meat, the meat exclusively eaten by the fighting men of the Gedebo.

The Wrea Musu, based in the largest town in Gedebo and supported by the most powerful and eloquent spokesman of the elders of the people, the venerable Hiedo Kesigbo, mounted a vituperatively vocal campaign against the other camp. Gegeju Karbeh, with headquarters in Joloke, Gedebo, had many followers but they were not of good standing in the Gedebo. On both sides of the creek Nipli, trouble was brewing. Some kind of showdown was in the making. As different ethnic groups grew hot in faction, the small group was markedly divided. The tension moved at a breathtaking velocity in the Gedebo country. A well known man from the Bodioh family line was slain with a sharp instrument believed to be a cutlass by an unknown man. Yeai Nyenu was brutally slaughtered in cold blood. He was of the Wrea Musu camp and a member of the Musu clan. Yeai Nyenu and his wives and children were asleep in their hut on the outskirts of Worteke, the largest town and the seat of the high priest of Gedebo, when all of a sudden his bamboo door was snatched open and what appeared to be a flash of light lighted the one-room hut. The light appeared like dust and was dotted like fireflies briefly. The light struck him like lightning and horrified him and he shouted, "Mo Yeai Ke!" He grabbed his man cutlass and leapt outside in hot pursuit of the intruder. A few yards away from his hut, Yeai Nyenu met his fateful end; he was gashed across his abdomen, slashed almost in two pieces. A short time later his wives and children came outside to see why they had not heard or seen their husband and father. They looked around the hut but to no avail. Searching further on the path leading from the hut into the bush they suddenly stepped into an ocean of blood in which their slain husband and father was lying. Wailing and yelling erupted on seeing the lifeless body in the ocean of blood.

Nothing moved in Worteke (as it was completely asleep) except two men who were on loving visitation with their paramours that dreadful night. The young men, Barbi Klaye and Geadi Toe, heard the wailing and rushed there where their

10

sights were destroyed, as Shakespeare puts it. As the wailing intensified, the whole village was woken and in no time the wailing spread like a wildfire and the village was drowned in commotion and emotion. The alarm drum was sounded and unusualness had befallen the Gedebo already in disarray.

Regardless of faction affiliation, the grieving gathered in large numbers at Worteke, the nation's capital, where the untimely death had occurred. Upon arrival and on knowing what the alarm was about, in a united move, the indigenous people began to probe into the cause of the brutal murder. The Gedebo's soothsayers, sand cutters, and other nocturnal workers were set to work. The highest and most famous herbalist-doctor, Koka Nagnen Pawah of Kablake, Gedebo, was summoned to come to examine and hand stitch the mutilated body of the fallen Yeai Nyenu. Every able-bodied man who came to Worteke willingly and spontaneously made personal inquiry here and there. Surprisingly, Barbi Klaye and Geadi Toe were arrested for being the first people who visited the bloody scene besides the immediate family. They were the prime suspects and were taken to Nyaake, being the Webbo District Headquarters and Gedebo Chiefdom and integral part of the district.

Although emotionally ablaze, soberly the people of Gedebo set their investigative machinery at work. At the gathering in the Jegbadio council square, a man was found with a fresh blood-stained cutlass. Luckily for him, the man who saw the blood on the cutlass was a closely related relative. At once he advised him to leave the gathering. He acquiesced and sneaked away from public notice, saving him from being a suspect in the hideous crime.

In Joloke, a village about three miles from Worteke, when dawn was peeping through the walls of the huts of the village, a tall slim man named Tarley from the Twapo clan was overheard calling his wife to bring him water and salt outside of their hut, where he was standing, shortly before the sound of the alarm drum struck the ears of the waking villagers. These glaring pieces of evidence as seen and heard by some people were never made public. Close examination of the body showed that the assailant was a left-handed man. Other sources revealed creditably alleged that the brutal killer was not a Gedebo man. From another source it was revealed that the assassin was on the run. Truly on the run he was! Could a man fight a dozen odds, a large gigantic fighting force, all by himself?

Mobilized, the Gbor, the fighting men, began to comb the villagers living in the neighboring towns. Every neighboring group was as sympathetically concerned and as mystified and threatened. One neighbor, the Webbo, reliably informed the Gedebo people the whereabouts of the heartless killer. Like hounds, the fighting men of Gedebo unhesitantly combed the Webbo country with the help of the brotherly people of Webbo. In no time, Tugba, Konobo Krahn, was apprehended and brought back to Gedebo. Truly he was not a Gedebo man. Left-handed he was. Upon interrogation the now-detained killer admitted into evidence that he slaughtered Yeai Nyenu, but added in a blushing way that he was hired by some people in he Gedebo country. Stubbornly he refused to give names. Barbi Klaye and Geadi Toe were still languishing in the Nyaake jail infested with fleas and mosquitoes. They were charged with the murder of Yeai Nyenu. Nothing linked them with the callous murder except that they were the first on the bloody scene when the alarm was raised by the family.

The nocturnal lovers had no day in court. Tarley was not arrested for calling for water and salt, obviously to wash his hands, which, in itself, was an explicit uncoerced revelation that he had done some ugly deed that woeful night.

That beautiful piece of evidence for the prosecution, I presume, spoke defiantly, glaringly, and stupefyingly at the Gedebo justice system. The most powerful of the Gedebo, Chief elder Hiedo Kesigbo, and his elders with their strong fighting men tightened their security. The search for the alleged culprits unabatedly continued. No arrests were issued or effected. But according to their system of justice, as they discovered the would-be assassins, in an impersonal way, turned them over to nobody but the God of their fathers, who usually, in what we humanly call his slow way, prosecuted them individually. At death each of those miscreants confessed openly of their nasty deed.

In the Gedebo country, only members of Gbor, the fighting men, men who had reached their maturity, married, and initiated, ate the meat of the bush goat (antelope). When Pastor Moses gained his autonomy and established his waiting place with his 'strange ways' people in the Gedebo country, he thought that was a license to personally and arbitrarily abrogate the traditions and customs of the conservative Grebo. "In our Christian tradition we and our female counterparts share unreservedly every meal and other things in common," Pastor Moses proudly declared. "Hereafter all alike will partake in the eating of male bush goat meat," the brave pastor added, smiling broadly.

When the news broke that Pastor Moses flagrantly violated the long standing traditions and customs of the Gedebo, their authority detailed a group of well-built men from Worteke to arrest the body of Weagbah Challaba, bringing him alive or dead. Accordingly, the arresting officers proceeded to Tenzonke. In Tenzonke the squad met the pastor in the bathroom. They rushed there and seized him without a piece of apparel on his body. He was then roped on his waist and drag away. The trio villages known as 'Suwroke' reacted courageously and positively. Members of the trio villages, led by Nyanweju Hinneh, raced to Worteke. Still ablaze with anger, when the daring men of Suwroke arrived in Worteke they saw their pastor roped and harnessed to a tree in the Bodioh quarters. Nyanweju Hinneh grabbed the rope on the waist of Pastor Moses and with sharp man cutlass cut of the rope from the pastor's waist, without a word to anybody. A piece of cloth was tied on the pastor's waist and was whisked off. The rats had smelled the cat! Suwroke had done it unilaterally and challengingly. Worteke could not temper further with Pastor Moses, the pride of his people. Worteke remained surprisingly silent.

Wounded by inhuman treatment meted to them when the Americo-Liberians and Government of Liberia (with their armed men) forcibly and brutally recruited their young men and sailed them off to Fernando Po, the people of Gedebo grieved. The grieving coupled with bitter frustration was aggravated by the willful murder of their charismatic son, Yeai Nyenu, a staunch supporter of the Wrea Musu camp. This bitter series of dreaded events literally destroyed the memories of those village dwellers. The world continued moving, while the seemingly lifeless people of Gedebo stood still. These ugly events occurred between 1928 and 1932, according to a source from a neighboring African group.

12

Chapter IV "A Man is Born, A Man Lives"

"Tell me your company and I will tell you who you are," propounded the Very Reverend Father Joseph Alfred Love, of sainted memory, principal of Our Lady of Fatima High School and president of Maryland College of Our Lady of Fatima, a Catholic institution located in Harper City, Maryland County, Liberia. The venerable Catholic priest explained the quotation mentioned supra as follows: "Man is a social being. He loves to live in his chosen group and because of this unimposed association he is most likely influenced by it. If the group, that is, members, is bad, it goes without saying that he is bad too."

Very often people want to know these social data, such as family, ethnic, education background. Out of inquisitiveness, they further inquire about when and where was one born every now and then.

Over the years I face these monotonous questions about those particulars from people I come in contact with each day, especially my curious students. Even some days when I have my inspired teaching spell, the rapt listening students cautiously interrupt me: "Mr. Reeves are your parents educated?" Grinning, I snapped the answer: "No, my parents have no formal education," No doubt, knowing these things about people in one's group enhance one's relationship, and obviously that knowledge is indispensable for buttressing the relationship further. For me, it does not matter much or at all when the time of a man's birth is not known. Once he lives, truly he was born one day. In this case, I think, he should be held singularly responsible to account for God's precious years he is spending in this turbulent world. In this brief account of my stewardship of my obscure life, I would ask those who might find this story readable not to worry about when I was born lest they will lose interest as the story slowly unfolds. Here I am not suggesting that you part with your birthday because I don't have one, like an old fox that requested her fellow foxes to get rid of their tails because she lost hers when she was caught in a trap.

The WHERE of my birth is perfectly plain and indelible. Kablake, an undeveloped forest village nestled among high evergreen trees, is the scene or place of my nativity. Both my parents are indigenous of the Suwroke trio of the Gedebo, a sub-group of the vast Grebo ethnic group lying in southeastern Liberia. Before me, my parents were blessed with two boys only to be disappointed as each died in his infancy. Then I came, and as you can readily see, I am yet to flee this troubled world. I was never sturdy from the time of my birth and have remained a sickly person. I am told that this early sickly condition of mine was the bitter source of anxiety for my mother, an African woman eager to bless her marriage with children, which, African women think, are the essence of marriage. Gradually, the anxiety of losing her third son eroded, and although sickly, I steadfastly stood the test of time. Yes, I live.

While talking about my birth and who gave it, let me briefly introduce the young woman through whose wedlock brought about the pleasing trouble on herself and her husband. My mother, the only child of her parents, was born of Targba Seebodi, of Yejake, Gedebo and Tarju Tarnu of Baweake of the Suwroke trio in Gedebo. My father, a distinguished member of Gbor, village chief, military man, leading rice farmer, etc., etc., was born of Twapei Nyenweju of Heweke, Gedebo, and

13

Belloh Chowah of Kablake, Gedebo. Their marriage was blessed with two sons: Nyanweju Hinneh and Nyanweju Cholee. Happily the young couple was gradually building up the numerical strength of their African family when a tragedy hit the family following the birth of their second child: The Gedebo nocturnal workers were snatched away from this turbulent world to be with the Lord. The granny, according to tradition, was compelled to marry to another in the family as her husband.

This time, the pleasing trouble was gladly received by Nagneh Pawah, the highest herbalist-doctor in the whole of the Gedebo country. My paternal grandmother's second union was blessed with a boy, Nyanwejy Poloe, and a girl, Pawah Nagneh.

Belloh Chowah in his brief life distinguished himself as an outstanding scout of the fighting men of Gedebo. "Scout" in this context carries the same meaning Webster or Thorndike gives: a person sent to find out what the enemy is doing. The African scout, a Grebo for that matter, has the same mission. However, a professionally trained Grebo scout performs his secret duty without the help of instruments: no means of transportation, air or land. And yet he frequently reconnoiters and his surveys are surprisingly reliable.

In Gedebo country, a warrior is trained before he is born. Tarju Tarnu, my maternal grandfather, was born a warrior. Tarju Tarnu was a warrior in waiting before he was born and slowly but steadily he grew up to reach his majority in latter years. I cannot exactly unearth how a warrior is trained before he is born. It is mysteriously held that when the Gedebo in time of peace gets concerned about its internal security it would seek means to secure sovereignty. A strong, high power delegation, meticulously selected from among the leading men and women of the Gedebo, with rich gifts is sent to Koo Je, the shrine of the highest herbalist-doctor, who is unquestionably believed to possess the power of incarnating. Upon reaching the shrine, the delegation breaks word: "Our group is not threatened but we want to make sure that things remain secure all the time within our borders. We want to put into reserve some standby warriors for some unforeseen eventuality. We come to you; we are your strangers," the delegation presents the case.

In his own way and time the man who looks into the seeds of time can tell which ones will grow and which ones will not grow over a period of time. He prepares his package and delivers it to the eagerly waiting people's delegation.

Arriving back to the group, the delegation was accorded a befitting ceremony. The herbs brought from the herbalist-doctor, according to strict direction, were mixed with well-cooked rice and other herbs seasoned in palm butter and were blended together for the consumption of the would-be bearers of the warriors-to-be. The selected women ate and drank the concoction brought from the superman. All was set. Their high hope ushered them into silence. Soon or late the hope for miracle germinated and ripened; the women became pregnant. Successfully our warrior-bearing women gave births and an appropriate ceremony was held in honor of the newly arrived by fighting men and the leading men of the Jegbadior, House of Gedebo. Surely, the group had in its reserve a strong young team of warriors in waiting.

My paternal and maternal parentage played enviable roles in the affairs of

14

Gedebo. My maternal grandfather, Tarju Tarnu, actually did not see or participate in active action as he was growing up. The interethnic feuds gradually abated and finally withered and died to beget interindigenous brotherhood. But his presence during the years of his majority gave the people of Gedebo assured and secured peace and freedom of movement among the Gedebo.

On the other hand, my own father, the leader of the Gbor in his village, earned himself an unforgettable reputation, buttressed by his stepfather, Nagneh Pawah, the highest herbalist-doctor in the Gedebo land, crowned with the highest place obtained and sustained by his younger brother, Nyanweju Cholee, in the soothsayer's circle.

In my ethnic group and in any social setting, my background is solid ground for a youngster to grow steadily but still be an individual unique in himself. As an individual, I don't make my father's glory mine. I am a free thinker.

Chapter V "My Fate is Decided"

"Pastor Moses announced that our teacher is ready to receive you the students," my father, smiling broadly, revealed. And then he, with a grin, said, "Your mother and I decided last night that this Sunday I am going to take you over to Tenzonke, where you will live with Myer Klaye and his wife Porley Yessay to attend the school." The choice was not mine. My parents met behind closed doors and decided my fate.

The next day, with my little cutlass, mat, and fishing hook with its tackle handy, my loving father and I walked silently to Tenzonke, a distance about a mile long. Myer Klaye is the younger brother of Myer Kamma. They and my father are of the same clan, what we call family in the African parlance. Myer Klaye and Porley Yessay's only child, a boy, Nyapee warmly welcomed me. Klaye and his wife promised that they would always ensure my happiness so that I would securely feel at home away from home. My father said to me, "This is your home, it belongs to our family. You must behave well by obeying your mother and father here." With that last note of warning, my father left behind his only son and went to a wife without a child in their home. What a depressing experience my parents bore!

School at last; I am here. Every journey, short or long, begins with a single step. Not only that, but the journey to the land of education is long, exciting, and challenging; my teacher, Mrs. Helen Young, an old woman probably in her late sixties, introduced the alphabet to us the students by calling out each letter and we repeated after her in unison. The recitation of the letters of the alphabet by the nearly nude village boys was exciting and inviting. After leading the repetition of the letters of the alphabet, the teacher would point to a student to lead. Many ventured while others simply blinked. For the first time when she pointed to me to lead the naming of the characters of the alphabet, I called out from A to Z without hesitation or error.

The poor granny (Mrs. Young) was mystified. Without saying a word, she held me by my arm and took me away from the group. Inaudibly I asked, "Does this mean that the teacher does not want me to learn the ABCs?" While I was outside of my group, our teacher called in Pastor Moses to inform him, I guess, what seemed strange to her. After their brief conversation, Pastor Moses, grinning, walked to me in my corner and proudly said to me, "Or wane po li kle le han kan." (Your teacher says you surprised her; you tried plenty) Wildly I stared at him!

The next day, school found me alone in my group. I reviewed the names of characters of the alphabet in order. That was completely done without a single mistake. With a pointer, the teacher pointed to the characters at random and asked me to name the letter pointed at, the way the modern teacher does it with her flash card. As the day's lesson went smoothly and satisfactorily, I questioned myself to the hearing of nobody, "This book learning must be a sweet thing." Word reached my parents that I needed a slate and a pencil. "Your son must learn how to write the letters of the alphabet," the message urged.

Progress was on my side as my third day found me learning how to write the ABC. I chewed A, B, C, and D in my initial attempt. In a while, the teacher checked my work and found that I had correctly formed each letter, that is, A, B, C, and D. Beaming with smiles, Ma Young urged me to continue to the other letters in the series. I took hold of my slate pencil, and hoping that the letter E would fall, my camera did a poor job. I experienced my Waterloo when I made the attempt to write the letter E. The battle with E lasted about twenty useless and painful minutes without success. I made some kind of a stroke and continued to write the other letters with an astonishing correct form to each of them. On the fourth day, battle with E brought a disheartening defeat in writing E again. For all of the succeeding days I struggled without hope. On the fifth day, the Honorable Geadi Toe, Clan Chief of Gedebo Chiefdom, Eastern Province, Liberia, was on his official visitation of his villages. Tenzonke was the first leg of his visitation. He met us in school. Shortly following his arrival, Pastor Moses escorted the chief into the school. The chief and Ma Young were not strangers to each other. His son, Wlebe Klaye, was with Ma Young's grandson, O. Natty B. Davis, attending school in Harper City, Maryland County. Warmly they exchanged greetings. The chief was seated in our narrow benches (or desks) in the classroom.

Glancing here and there the chief recognized me, the son of his nephew, struggling at the blackboard to form the letter E. "Let me help you," the old chief offered. Without waiting for a reply, the obese chief held my hand holding the chalk and said, "It is simple, I'll help you to form the letter E." He did by tracing my hand to form the letter E. After a few minutes of the help by the old chief, I decisively defeated Mr. E. "Bravo!" I exclaimed. In every respect and detail I was then the master of the alphabet.

On my mastery of forming correctly the letters of the alphabet, I was promoted to So. That posed no problem. I consumed it like wildfire and went on to Primer One. Alone I greedily and steadily ascended the preparatory ladder of education. Was Primer Two a challenge? I don't know, but in no time my old teacher would tell me, "William, you need Primer Three." "What would that mean now?" I whispered to myself. In any case there was nothing more to learn in Primer Two. I guess I urged myself, "There is no time to lose. The die is cast and the command is forward march!"

I was well at home with Baa Klaye and Ayee Yessay. After about a year's stay with my adopted family, I proved myself worthy of their love. But stinking trouble was brewing somewhere. Their only child was a very slow learner. Although he was far ahead of me in school and older, his daily recitation in school showed negligible success. He began to be crabby in and out of school and home. Begrudging Nyapee began to pull things apart everywhere. Obviously he appeared to be terribly envious of his younger adopted brother's success in school. The little boy himself was getting too top-heavy.

Openly Nyapee abused and in some cases aggressively assaulted me Although I was no match physically yet to restrain him one way or another I was more than aggressive and loudly abusive to him and all the members of the household, including our parents. The only thing that pleased me in the home then was my fat dish of palm butter rice. Obstinate, my whole home life narrowed almost to a zero point.

17

My father and his life friend, Sualo Toe, with a group of carriers of bags of cocoa, left the group for a long tedious trek to Cape Palmas, about fifty straggling miles away, where they would sell their produce to Frey and Zusley. Before leaving, my father was informed and requested by Ma Young, as our teacher was popularly known in Tenzonke and the surrounding villages, to buy his son a new book called Primer Three. "In no time your son ate the book up that you bought recently," Teacher Young happily narrated. "No doubt, he needs something higher and harder," Ma Young emphasized.

The village Chief went on his business trip, ruminating on the elating news of his son's successes at the village school. The Primer Three led his way back home. The grateful and hopeful father presented the newly bought Primer Three to the village school mistress. Looking through the pages of the book, Ma. Young with a coy smile observed, "I think this little mischievous boy will be challenged seriously this time."

We were two in our class. Yanwen Klaye, a boy far older than I, was now my classmate, since I had caught up with him. The first assignment from our new reader, following the introduction of the book by Teacher Young, was like a calculated assault on the two village learners. Two long pages were assigned for reading comprehension and with almost an endless list of words to learn by heart and spell the next day in class. To me this was the first all out challenge since I entered into the walls of the village school.

With nobody to go to for help with my lessons, I wondered why the teacher was so uncaring. When they say in Grebo that war killed your mother, there is no need to ask for her head as the head is the thing the killer must show to prove his manly feat. My teacher in earnest was trying to see whether I had the sustained ability to grapple with my lessons. With a bit of assistance on the pronunciation of the endless list of words, I resolved on: "Forward March!" The task of reading and spelling the next day rested on my shoulders as Yanwen Klaye unilaterally quitted school. The youngster realized that it was practically impossible for him to learn. He had on his Grebo thinking cap. "Pull off your white shirt before you eat your palm butter rice, if you know that eating the palatable dish will stain your shirt." In this way you will save yourself from staining your shirt, which is considered as a sign of greediness. And so Klaye left the school to spare him from being thrown out of the school. Lonely I was in class. Competition existed no more. Actually, was there any outward competition? If there was, the effect was negative on this young ambitious isolated village learner. I continued to myself since in truth, there was never any meaningful competition.

A handful of the little boys who unconsciously accepted the candies from the reverend gentleman were now busily engaged at the Tenzonke school. Pastor Moses was at the helm of control of the welfare of Ma Young. An experienced hunter, Pastor Moses and the other hunters in Tenzonke made sure to get fresh meat for Ma Young every day so as to rejuvenate her. Besides this, Pastor Moses had taxed each big boy in the school to cut frontess to make baskets to catch fish from the fresh water creek, making available fresh fish every morning for a palatable dish each day for the village school teacher. With fish and meat adequately available, if not abundantly, for the Sexagenarian, what would the old woman eat with the meat and fish? Generous, hospitable, and fatherly, Pastor Moses stored up a warehouse of nutritious Gedebo rice and other foodstuffs as the villages contributed lavishly to these coffers. These were only the everyday income, I must say.

The Suwroke Trio, Tenzonke, Kablake and Baweake, drew up a master plan for the annual support of the African Methodist Episcopal Church Missionary teacher. According to the plan, each married man of the Suwroke Trio would deliver annually three bunches of rice, each weighing about twenty-five pounds. Without any problem, the contributions came through each year as expected. Instead of his annual quota only my father spontaneously and willingly added three more bunches of equal weight to his yearly contribution. Occasionally, my parents sent meat and fish to Ma. Young. I guess your mind's eye tells you that the old village teacher lived a wholesome village life. With Pastor Moses around, that was always assured! Ma Young, the African Methodist Episcopal Church Missionary teacher, was the true torchbearer of Christianity and education to the local villagers and the Gedebo people. A mother and grandmother, our teacher had us students excited each day to learn more. Although English was the only means we could communicate with her, that did not impose any barrier in any way; patiently she listened to us struggling with our Gedebo English, sometimes calling in Pastor Moses to help translate what we were trying to say to her. Of course, the pastor's English was not better, as time would tell. My steady march toward the precious ladder of learning went into higher gear. Fiercely I waged a winning battle against Primer Three. It was a lonely but resolute assault. In the new primer I was progressing enviably. Sometimes I am an introvert. I became more isolated being the only student in my class. Once my lessons were done I had time for nobody, including Ma. Young. I was very obnoxious. Soon or late, I was the talk of the village. "The little boy is clever but he is hardheaded," the village complained. I left the village several times without permission from Baa Klaye or Ayee Yessay to visit my parents in Kablake. "Why are you here?" Without giving me a chance to answer her question, my mother questioned on, "Did your father invite you here during the school time?" my mother sternly demanded. "Au...au...da. I came to say that I don't want to live in Tenzonke anymore," I let loose the crocodile poopoo in the open. In that time the commander-in-chief of our family arrived. He was no other than my no-nonsense father. With his angry look nowhere around, my father seasoned me up with his usual fatherly, this time ironical, greetings. He began: "Twui, Nyanbeyu, you must have come on an important mission here during the school hours, isn't it?" The young village chief palliatively inquired. Scratching my head I hesitantly said, "I don't want to stay with those people anymore." "Hush! Nonsense! You are going back now," my father silenced me. Aggressively, the militiaman began to push me and grabbed my right arm and led me away to Tenzonke, while he hauled abusive names at me.

I did not say a word, but torrential tears flooded my breast during the journey. But my father, being so abusive, did not cause me to budge from my stance. However, my father had both the power and the might. I had none of them, comparatively. Coercion was the absolute right for the parents of old while acquiescence must have been the total embodiment of their children. I was no

19

exception.

Upon reaching his family man Klaye, my angry father told him that he had brought the 'fool' who left the village and the school without permission from anybody. "Next time, which I don't hope for, I will lay you and give you twenty-five hard lashes on your bare rump. You must remain in the fatherly and motherly care of our brother and sister in Tenzonke," my father ordered.

In Tenzonke I remained, but my incorrigible attitude did not change at all. I did not lag in my pursuit of knowledge. Voraciously I embarked upon the study of my new Primer Three and subsequently I completed it at the end of what appeared to be a school year. I was promoted to the Infant Reader. Old age was on its unabating haunt of Ma Young. The attending problems of old age heaped on Teacher Young. In all indications she needed close family care. Our teacher, a mother and grandmother, had a daughter who was also an African Methodist Episcopal Church Missionary teacher in Heweke. Ma Charley, as she was known in Heweke, a Gedebo village much larger than Tenzonke, visited her mother frequently. But this visit that brought her early that morning did not seemingly have the same mission. When she arrived in Tenzonke she summoned pastor Moses and his leading villagers to a meeting. In the meeting she informed them she thought it was time for her mother to return back to Harper for close family care of our now aging mother. Saddened by this news, Pastor Moses and his village dwellers pleaded with the Heweke teacher not to take Ma Young away now, as they would do all in their power to take care of her ailing mother. Sincere as she knew the people were, she said a no without a compromise.

Ma Young was taken away. The village and the students were left without a teacher. Heweke too lost its teacher. From what I saw, I think Ma Charley was the only living child of Ma Young. Ma Charley, Mrs. Chaldonia Davis, the Heweke teacher, was the mother of an outstanding Jurist O. Natty B. Davis and Municipal Commissioner Alfred Davis. Jurist O. Natty B. Davis was popularly known in Liberia as 'Law Tree.' It was about time, in her old age, for grandmother Young to enjoy the enriching atmosphere of the family circle. At home she was at last.

The Reverend William Taylor White, presiding Elder of the Cape Palmas District, African Methodist Episcopal Church, won the consent of the mother and daughter to share their love and education with his new flock in Gedebo.

After some time during the smooth operation of the schools in Tenzonke and Heweke, Reverend White would peep once in a while. On each visit he seemed to want to do something more for the education of the young people. Gradually he encouraged some of the bigger boys to go with him to Harper for school. My brother Nyapee was one of those who received the blessing. Because of ill health and old age, Ma Young unwillingly and painfully departed Tenzonke, leaving us students wanting. Long before, my teacher had whispered to me one night that if she decided to go home for good she would take my cousin Kledi Kamanu and me with her to Harper, where we would have the privilege of continuing our schooling. All of us awaited the day! When my father was told that the old teacher was retiring, he came running to Tenzonke to see whether Ma Young would fulfill her promise. "I had wanted to, but I cannot house two devils together. I would rather choose between them and take one. Yours is not the choice, I am sorry," Ma Young broke my father's yearning heart.

I had no barriers on my smooth path to Kablake, where I would once be with my caring parents. This time there were two children in our family. The second boy was born during my sojourn. In my role as a big brother, I became abatedly refined and my hostile attitude toward people dwindled to gentlemanliness. My academic engagement vanished. I appeared misplaced! I was lonely! To ease my loneliness I read my old book, Primer Three, and once in a while tried to read beyond what I had covered in the Infant Reader.

Long before I left the administrative village of the Suwroke Trio for Tenzonke, I played many of the children's games with my crowd of boys and girls. If we were dramatizing the story about the militiamen in Nyaake, a thrilling story my father often told us, my friends would choose me as sergeant in charge of writing the names of our supposed soldiers. I was also chosen to be the clerk of our imaginary chiefdom and its people would come around me in my make-believe office, where I would write on the plantain leaves as paper and a bamboo as pen to convey their greetings and message to the Honorable District Commissioner in Nyaake. Copiously I wrote without being able to read or understand what was so written. However, I was exclaimed and accepted as their Honorable Paramount Chief's Good Clerk.

During the long process of learning, when I was studiously, diligently, earnestly, and courageously struggling to place my feet on the first rung on the ladder of education, I discovered to be true the old Latin saying: Vox populi, Vox Dei. My crowd of boys and girls nominated and appointed me from their midst to go to school in order to become educated. There is no gainsay about it, certainly the voice of the people is the voice of God. Glory be to His Name!

Chapter VI "A Boarding School Proposed"

After old age and poor health deprived us of our teacher, I had no idea that I would ever go to school again. Somewhere in Nyaake, the vast Webbo District Headquarters of Eastern Province, Liberia, a group of leading citizens, some business executives (Messrs. Henry P. Collins, Gabriel C.H. Gadegbeku, Joseph Itoka, Joseph W. Andrews, Daniel P. Derrick, Thomas G. Bohlen, Harry Carngbe, Charles T. Nawah, to name a few), in a conference with the paramount, clan, and town chiefs and people of the district, proposed a founding of a district-sponsored boarding school for boys. As illiteracy was laying waste to the whole of the district, with a large land area extending from the Creek Hielo in Dedeabo in the Southeast to Killepo in the North, densely inhabited in some places and sparsely inhabited in others, the proposal received cool reception as ninety-nine and a half percent of the people in the meeting were old chronic illiterates. But the men who requested for the meeting with these people were formally educated in their own right. With this strong background they were prepared to sell their wholesome proposal well to the common good of the young people of the district, especially people of the school-going age. "Many untold benefits will be accrued to those who will seize the opportunity to attend the school," Mr. Gabriel Gadegbeku, who later became chairman for the school committee, asserted.

Each of the men advancing the lifesaving proposal elaborated. The idea was thrown around and individuals interested in the project received amazing approbation. Wholeheartedly the chiefs and people of the district accepted the proposal. A technical committee was appointed to work out the details of the proposal.

In a short space of time (as the committee did not lose any time), having worked out the details, each habitable hut in the district would be taxed twenty-five cents annually for the maintenance and sustenance of the school and students. A minimum of five students was required of each chiefdom in the district. The larger chiefdoms of the eight chiefdoms of the district would send more. A number of kinjahs of rice would be collected from the chiefdoms according to the numerical strength of each chiefdom annually. The chiefdom would send the labor force for the construction of the boarding campus in the meantime.

Through the district commissioner, the committee informed the chiefs and people of the district to meet in a general meeting for the submission of the committee's report. In no time, the prominent citizens of the Webbo District hurried at their usual rendezvous. At the meeting, the plan of action as submitted by the committee was overwhelmingly and enthusiastically accepted. In unison the people urged, "The school must begin early next year." Each paramount, having returned from the Nyaake meeting, assembled his elders and people and announced the good news to them: "A glorious opportunity for our children to be educated has finally dawned on us. When educated, our children will be Mleyaun too," the paramount chief declared to the people. The honorable paramount chief informed then further that only boys would be required to be sent to the district-sponsored boarding school. "We need the children of the parents who can buy pieces of clothes for their children while they attend the school," the chief explained. The Suwroke Trio was taxed one student.

The Suwroke elders converged on Kablake to plead with my parents to give their son Kpaye Kamma to attend the newly established Webbo District Sponsored Boarding School. Behind closed doors my parents conveyed the elders' request to me. "Baa, they say all children who will go to that school will not come back to visit their parents again and so I don't want to go there," I painfully in a weeping tune told my waiting parents. Surprisingly, the village chief, without altering a word, sneaked out of the door. What happened to the no-nonsense village master that he did not say a word about his little son's obstinate reply? From all probability he was stunned as the reply appeared to pull his nerve center of love for his son. The privilege of sending his son to school then fell to the lot of his friend Sualo Toe of Tenzonke. Tarlee Kuaye was the second choice of Suwroke.

In a district council meeting, the honorable district commissioner suggested to the chiefs that it was about time that they add more dignity to their respective chieftaincy by erecting for themselves residential quarters at Nyaake, where they usually meet the official visitors at the district headquarters. Acquiescently the suggestion was accepted. This was a self-help endeavor. Work began almost immediately.

The chiefs were directed to dispatch to Nyaake all the town chiefs and the able-bodied men of the villages for the construction of those structures. The orders spread far and wide. Laborers, as well as the village chiefs, flooded the construction site in Nyaake. My father was among the number. Two weeks following his going to Nyaake, my mother told her mates (my father boasted of three wives) that they should prepare some foodstuff to be taken to their husband laboring in Nyaake. In a day or two the food was gathered and their youngest was requested to take the food to their hungry husband. Happily the third wife accepted the responsibility of carrying the collected food to her husband but could not travel the road alone and so I was honored to journey with her to Nyaake. It seemed that my father needed his food replenished, as he looked haggard when we reached him. Warmly he exchanged greetings with us and soon or late we pulled off back to Kablake.

On our way from Kodeke Number One, a suburb of the hilly Township of Nyaake, where the chieftain compound was being built, we saw that the District Sponsored School boarders were housed on New Road, another suburb of Nyaake. A life friend of mine, Chanagba Kumah, one of the boys from Gedebo chiefdom, rushed out onto the road and shouted, "Ma-O, here we do the same little things we do in the village; we fish, set our snares for birds and rats, and play!" My friend pulled my legs. He added, "Come and join us; we are happy and no doubt you will be happy too." Completely I was convinced on that spur of a moment and told my father's third wife that as soon as my father would return to our village I would beg him to send me to the boarding school.

About the following day or two following our arrival from Nyaake, the polygamist came home. My mother was briefed about my surprised dream and expressed my burning desire of attending school in Nyaake. "My friends at the school in Nyaake say I must go there so that all of us will attend the school, and I want to go," I openly declared. With a cautious smile my father in a surprised mood asked, "Are you ready now to go to school this time?"

How would I go to school when I had practically nothing to wear? My parents managed to get me a little shirt, but no pair of trousers, which I could not do without. My father gave me his pair of trousers. I needed to be twice my size to wear those trousers. I had no choice as my parents had no money to buy me a pair of trousers of my size.

It was June 16, 1942. I was on my uphill trek for education in Nyaake. Truly my friends had greatly influenced me and here I was on the district sponsored boarding school under the principalship of Reverend Henry Bagbo Wilson, of sainted memory, rector of the Protestant Episcopal Church in Nyaake. Amidst sixty-odd village boys in the boarding school, with my Lappa trousers wrapped around my waist, I joined the line of students to march to the school.

In school that morning, with thick mist covering the towering peak of Mount Chelo on the western bank and that of Mount Pah on the eastern bank of River Cavalla, as she cascades between them, I was placed in the ABC group. The student teacher, Henry Tawoli Cooper, began to call out the letters of the alphabet and we students were required to repeat after him. He noticed that I was not repeating after him. A tall, slim young man, Henry stooped over me and asked, "Why are you not repeating after me?" "I was in the Infant Reader when I was in school in Tenzonke," I asserted. He then led me to the principal. The student teacher narrated what had happened during the recitation period in the ABC group. "If he said he was in the Infant Reader, put him in that class," the principal directed. Would the village Infant Reader student cope well with the town students? This time I was highly challenged and the competition was bracingly keen as I met such razors like Peter C. Nyepon of Gbeapo. At the end of that school year I was numbered among those who were promoted to the First Grade. As a war consists of a series of bitter battles, when a battle is won, especially decisively, one feels justified and confident and his hope to fight on is enlivened. "With my armor girded, and God being my keeper, I shall fight to the end," I assured myself.

Perhaps it would be interesting to get some glimpse of this historic site called NYAAKE! Nyaake is situated on a strip of land on the west bank of Liberia's largest and longest river, the Cavalla. This piece of land was jointly owned by three neighboring groups: Karbo, Gedebo, and Gbalewrobo. During the long interindigenous feuds, these joint-owners lost the strip of land to the Webbo. Some historians or griots say that the name Nyaake has its origin in the word Nyanna, which in Gedebo means a place where people ease themselves (feces are discharged). Others hold that the town took its name from the name of an old Webbo chief called Dockonyan. Whatever it is, Nyaake is a place worth claiming.

As early as 1905, Nyaake was established as a trading post. Portuguese, German, British, and other European traders found their winding way up the mighty Cavalla River to Nyaake, where they established their lucrative businesses. Foreign Christian Missionaries rowed up the torrential Cavalla river and found Nyaake as a gateway from where they could spread their Gospel in the interior of the country. The remote Liberia Government, living luxuriously on the taxes paid annually by the isolated villages living in dehumanized conditions in the countryside, through its

24

instrument of brutality, suppression, oppression, and sometimes wanton killing, the Liberian Frontier Force, acting on a lie fabricated against the people the officials of the government called "Native People," moved up the Cavalla river to exert its authority on the impoverished people. Some members of the force not meeting the men at home in the villages along the Cavalla River, singularly commissioned themselves to rape the women and to loot the poor hungry people's food and scanty clothing. On returning from their daily drudgery, the men found the villages vandalized and looted and their wives and daughters raped. Impulsively the village men went in hot pursuit of the marauding Liberian Frontier Force. In personal contact with the escaping soldiers, the enraged village men savagely employed their cutlasses and used them manfully. Under this cover, the Liberian Government waged war against the defenseless of the hinterland.

This started the so-called Grebo War of 1910. Mobilized, the Frontier Force sent a fifty man contingent, under the command of Major William Lomax, to Nyaake. At once following their arrival, a military post was erected, where the St. Mary Catholic Church stands today. Evangelist William Wede Harris and other high-ups in the country were openly accused of stirring up the "Native People" against the government that gives no protection. Since that time, Nyaake has been the "gateway" to education, civilization, commerce, trade, and so on.

Chapter VII "Success At Boarding School"

My half school year at the boarding school crowned me with unprecedented academic success. Our annual vacation was at hand. Up to this time no dormitories had yet to be constructed. In a privately-owned house, the sixty-odd students and their principal were jammed packed. The living conditions were worse than those in any normal village. We slept on naked floors, not cemented, in rooms without doors and windows without shutters too. Every morning, a senior boy in the true sense of the word in the dormitory (he was not a senior rather than an older boy, actually a young man in his twenties), would take us to the creek to bathe. Each of us willingly plunged into the running creek and rushed out, as the water was extremely cold at that time of the morning in the country. In one way or the other, the quantity of our daily meals was adequate but the meals were poorly prepared.

More than half of the boarding boys were in their twenties. Because of their ages and physical strength they claimed seniority over us, the minor ones. Some of them, like the one who took us to the creek every morning, was my classmate in the Infant Reader. At the end of the year our instructor at the creek failed miserably. As a result, he never returned to Nyaake or to the boarding school. A very small number of the older boys were in the upper classes while a substantial number was below the Infant Reader. In some cases these so-called seniors drove us minors out of the kitchen to eat our food and give us crust. This selfish attitude of our older brothers deprived the younger ones of their equal share of the meat. The little boys were maltreated. In order to get an adequate meal, the minors gathered leaves to cook and eat, supplementing their scanty meals.

The battle against the bloodsucking fleas called jiggers was fierce and threatening. In no time the boarding boys were emaciated except a few, including me. I don't know why. Although I was not fat or plump, for this is an alien language, the food and blood sucking jiggers were no problems for me. What bothered, not disturbed, me most, was the sleeping place, the room in which I slept. I came from a well cared-for village hut, with a warm smooth floor, where food was enough every day. In the midst of plenty of food I ate and eat little. After I spent a few months in the boarding school, while my mother in the memorable well established Gedebo tradition came to Nyaake to trace the whereabouts of their growing son. With a very large pot containing well-seasoned Gedebo palm butter, my mother found me at the boarding house on New Road, the first part of the town a visitor meets from Gedebo. She delivered her kinjah to the principal, himself a Grebo from another sub-Grebo group. She brought greetings from her husband and the entire village of Kablake to the principal, teachers, and their missing fussy boy, Kpaye Kamma. Reverend Henry Bagbo Wilson, chuckling, extended his hand in deep appreciation to the Gedebo woman with her contagious smiles.

The old man called in his cook to take out his share of the food. With his stomach sending gastric juice to his mouth, seemingly to arrest the palatable dish, Reverend Wilson made sure (by looking on) to get a lion's share of the palm butter and its contents, the odor of which were appetizing. My indigenous boys took charge of the remaining food. Every boy in the boarding school got a morsel. The boys showed their gratitude to the visiting mother by second handshake from each of them. For them it was strange for a mother to carry prepared food from such a distance, a distance about twelve miles long. This earned my mother their filial affection.

The next day, when the visiting Gedebo woman arrived at the boarding house to say good morning to Reverend Wilson and the boarders, the beautifully dressed village woman was ushered into the suite of the principal. I stuck at her side.

In his native tongue, Gbolobo, Reverend Wilson accounted, "On June 16, 1942, this year, your son arrived here, and next day he was off to school, the place he yearned to be, and hence his painful separation from you. I am happy to say what he has earned for himself, the school, and his dear family! I am proud to tell you that at the end of this school year he was promoted to the FIRST GRADE," the smiling principal added. He shared his breakfast with the visitor. The young woman graciously thanked the reverend gentleman and asked him to keep his watchful eyes on her growing son. She then bade him good-bye.

Our first ordeal at the boarding school ended when we broke away for the annual vacation. I was back to my old friends (still wearing their birthday suits) around the village, in a festive mood, preparing for the ensuing Christmas. This was my first long absence from home with my loving parents since I knew right from wrong. The next day, a rooster lost its head to welcome the bookman-in-the-making home. In one corner of the lively village, two young women pretending they were whispering to each other but quite loud to my hearing surpassingly: "Kpaye Kamma looks different among our village boys; he looks meditative and\refined."

There was a glowing feeling that some useful change had captured me during my six month stay at the boarding school. For the first time in my young life, I was given a heap of DON'TS. Willingly I accepted them, finding myself alone in the midst of many boys in my age group.

For about three short months I enjoyed being with my parents and my fussy crying little brother. Happy as I was at home, I felt I was misplaced and I longed to get back to the place where play was not the orders of the day.

I gathered early that the coming academic year was going to be highly competitive, and it appeared to me that I should clothe myself now for the envisaged struggle for academic excellence. In the village, it was clearly seen and known that the help I needed would never erupt from anywhere. My stay in the village appeared meaningless and endless. "For heaven's sake, get me out of here," I shouted. The morning of my mother's visit with Reverend Wilson when he told her that I arrived at the boarding school on June 16, 1942, besides being indelibly written in my photographic memory, was when I learned to count the years, months, dates, weeks, and days. Now I should begin practicing them. "Baa, I would like to be in the boarding school in Nyaake by March 1, 1943," I requested the village Spartan. Although the old people would miss me for another breathtaking period, they were gladdened that the school business was now my priority number one.

The first of March 1943 found me treading my way to the Webbo District Sponsored Boarding School. Does the stone that rejected the life-giving offer to attend the then proposed boarding school want to be accepted now?

Chapter VIII "Boarding School Life"

When many of us returned for the school year, the old rambling boarding house on New Road was dilapidated beyond repair. The school committee, under its chairman G. C. H. Gadegbeku, a scholar, musician, striving businessman, and father of many children, perhaps arranged with the office of the district commissioner to house us in some of the finished houses in the chieftain compound. We moved into the so-called new structures. In reality, and under normal circumstances, those village huts were not habitable. In fact, they were worse than previous privately owned houses. The few available huts had no doors and no shutters. With no other way, the boarders were obliged to make their abode with hordes of blood sucking fleas called jiggers. Each household improvised oil palm frontess shutters.

The whole spirit of boarding was broken as the students grouped themselves in those houses according to chiefdoms in the Webbo District. There was no central control as we knew the year before. Our meals, hunted for ourselves, were prepared separately and served separately. Every household was on its own. One thing we did together was the lining up and marching orderly to school each day. The district and its members committed gross negligence against the good of the people. The 1943 school year was bitter. The district failed flatly to meet its duty and obligation to support and maintain the school and those poor village boys, rounded up for a future better life in education. Throughout the year we did not get one clean cup of rice. One of the teachers in our school, Thomas G. Bohlen, an elderly Webbo man, sympathized with the dehumanizing conditions that plagued the boarding boys. In order to minimize our humanitarian problems, grandpa Bohlen offered us his orchard of breadfruit trees ripe with circular shaped fruits at Bohlen Station, another suburb of Nyaake. On these fruits we had breakfast, luncheon and dinner throughout the long weary year. One blessed thing of the year was that our school or classes met regularly for recitations uninterruptedly. On our breadfruit-fed stomachs we studied diligently, industriously, and earnestly. Our lessons were in the open afternoon breezy light, as we had no lanterns at night to light up our clumsy houses or to study by.

As youngsters we were always in high spirit as we helped ourselves to our respective lessons. We, the First Graders, ably distinguished ourselves in the study and mastery of the multiplication tables. Every Friday of the school week, all the students competed in the multiplication contest. In most cases I led my class to victory.

With all of the sufferings the boys experienced collectively, I had my personal trouble. All of a sudden, an abscess appeared on my right leg, just below my knee. It was so painful that I found it almost impossible to walk to school each day. However, with the excruciating pain I hopped to school. This time I was excused from marching with the boys. After some time, say a week, pus erupted and left me with a sore about an inch deep. "Why has this happened?" I wept silently.

There was a legend in the Gedebo country that a foreign white missionary, a Methodist (old), was maltreated and the cruel treatment left him with sores all over his body. Because of this, the legend alleges that anybody from a one-hundred percent uneducated indigenous groups, seeking Western type of education, would fall victim to sores. Recalling this, I cried, "My God, am I going to suffer from sores? What shall I do?" Inaudibly I questioned myself. "If the story is true, then I am finished," I grieved on. According to the legend, this was the punishment the man of God meted out to some wicked and selfish people of Gedebo, who brutally handled the Gospel bearer because he killed and ate meat they claimed belonged exclusively to the elders of the village. Of course, according to the legend, there was a hidden motive behind the merciless flogging of the foreign missionary. The truth is that those pagans did not want to hear anything about the Risen Lord. But as God would have it, as it was an isolated case, if it really happened, my parents, their parents, and their ancestors, I believe, were no part of that gross nonsense.

My namesake, John Kamma Farr, a fifth grade student and the most senior at the boarding school, gave me his timely attention by giving me some herb to treat my pus-running sore. In about a week, after giving the treatment, the sore was completely healed. Up to this date I have yet to suffer from sore, let alone sores, except wounds from cutlass or motor accidents. Thanks be to my God who spared me from such a devastating disaster!

At the close of the school year, many of us hilariously reaped the benefit of our labor and sufferings. With others, Peter C. Nyepon, the razor, and I were promoted to the second grade. Reverend Wilson was now my intimate friend, following my mother's visit with us. Frequently I went with him to hunt at night. Hunting was his hobby. The school year was indelibly written in our young memories as a year of many and varied hideous odds we encountered.

Chapter IX "Hitler's War Penetrates the Bush"

The dehumanizing effects of the Hitler War seemingly hit every corner and nook in the world without exception. International as well as national trade was blocked as people around the world were coercively demobilized. Were the remote villages, living in their archaic state, and a part of this global madness? A poet says and I say with him, "No man is an island, and no man stands alone." If this holds true with you, then the question above must be answered in the affirmative.

Remote, primordial, and unlettered as the villagers are, they are quite abreast with major events around our one world, for the rulers of many of the leading countries of the world were known by these villagers. As a darling nation, and its people highly esteemed for their high quality commodities, the Gedebo keep track of the names of the respective rulers or leaders of Germany. The two World Wars, for instance, are named respectively after each incumbent ruler. The 1914, or First World War, is remembered as Kaiser War and the 1939 War or Second World War is styled as Hitler War. They are remote but not necessarily isolated from world politics.

The world catastrophe, the Second World War, appeared to have reduced the "haves" around the world to ashes. I am wondering what happened to the "have-nots," who unceasingly gasped for help?

Truly, this time, as the poet puts it, "The naked Negro panting at the line boasts of his palm wine." No doubt, he enjoyed a satisfying degree of peace but the biting and killing poverty hovered around him. My parents, unlettered, village dwellers, were no exception during this bitter world crisis. But poverty has no sweetness. Poverty is the worst killer disease in the world. Poverty destroys ambitions! The 1939 war, called Hitler War as it is widely known in the Grebo Country, hammered the already poverty-stricken people to the ground. My father had two patches of cocoa and coffee. During the war years, he regularly harvested these cash crops but found no market to earn the fruit of his drudgery. With his earning power completely waning, the onetime village farmer had lost all.

The Lappa pair of trousers I had for the past two school years was now tattered. While our annual break from school was on, my parents mustered all their efforts to pay for a pair of trousers and a shirt, but to no avail.

The vacation slowly ended in February of 1944. By March 1, it was the time to return to school in Nyaake. March came and gradually drifted away. And so it was until July. At last my parents raked two shillings and 2/6 pence from somewhere and bought me a pair of trousers and a shirt. Finally Mr. Poverty cut me loose from Kablake to Nyaake in early August that year.

Webbo District was a vacuum, like the rest of Liberia, as outside information scarcely came in. I had no idea in Kablake what had transpired in Nyaake about the elevation of our principal, Reverend Henry Bagbo Wilson, to the position of supervisor of schools, Eastern Province, Liberia. Even the boarding school had moved to a new location in the heart of Nyaake. The Eastern Province supervisor of schools, Reverend Wilson, gave his blessing to Mr. Randolph Harmon as principal of Webbo District School. The boarders were now housed in Mr. Harmon's own house, where his immediate family resided also.

Upon my arrival in the hilly breezy town I was directed to our new residence. Everything there was strange. The boarders were now residing in a most conformable house comparatively. The boys' sleeping place was a long hall, well-cemented and the roof covered with German-made zinc.

The new principal, Mr. Randolph W. Harmon, a former store agent for one of the European trading companies in Nyaake, a middle aged man and father of many children with a nagging wife, was entertaining, jovious and loving. He told endless stories, which we enjoyed immensely. But his wife was the extreme opposite.

The devastating war had uncompromisingly driven these traders out of their lucrative jobs. To me, this did not change his good humor and nature. He had recoursed to the noble but sacrificial teaching job. Would he be supported in his new position by his termagant? She hated the very ground the boarders treaded on. With her lips pushed to her nose she called us, "these native or heathen boys." To her, I think, we were less than human beings, except her friend, Peter C. Nyepon, among us.

When I met her for the first time, she looked at me in such a way that I was not in the usual human form. Inside myself I decided never to go to the section of the house in which she and her husband with their children lived.

One day, I ran into her. Suddenly she asked me, "Where have you been?" "Nowhere," I shouted back. Because I did not add the word "Ma" to my answer, "No where," it was an insult to her. I underwent a one-week punishment, cutting and hauling wood in torrential September rains. This was my second week in school, a school year half gone, when I was snatched off. This almost crushed my burning ambition as frustration seeped through my cold body. Acquiescently I cut and hauled the wood to the house.

The teachers and new principal said that they had accepted me that time of the school year because of my outstanding grades scored the year before, and they were of the strong conviction that I would make a successful pass to the third grade. I was as appreciative as I was deeply challenged. Would the God of latecomers have His ever-ready courage and enlightenment showered upon me? Let us look up to Him to see what will the broken school year bring me for my ambitious soul.

The 1944 school year left me very repulsive about Mrs. Harmon. In Kablake, the bitter memory of her nasty ways haunted me. One day, it occurred to me that it was about time I should ask my God to let me forget and forgive her. Only Mr. Harmon's fatherly care for the boarders hovered about each day.

What would the 1945 academic year have in store for the rolling boarders? I was experiencing conflicting thoughts. In early February that year, my life friend, Challaba Kumah, now called John K. Davies, sent me words saying that school would be opened on the 16th of the month. This year clothes spelled no problem for me, as the pieces my parents bought in the middle of last year were still intact. My parents were duly informed and some foodstuff was gathered. One Sunday afternoon I gladly left the village and my anxious parents to join my friends in Nyaake situated on seven scenic hills. Our reunion was the happiest in recent memory as we thought we would meet our new charming principal, Mr. Randolph W. Harmon, not his mean wife.

By the time we reached Nyaake, Mr. Harmon was ready to pull out of town. We were distressed and disappointed. However, he was succeeded by another business executive, Mr. Joseph Andrews, a former store agent, a former bookkeeper for W. D. Wooden, a British Trading Company based in Harper, Maryland County, Liberia, an African Methodist Episcopal Church preacher, and general secretary of the citizens within the settlement of Nyaake.

In March, 1945, Reverend Andrews took charge of the school, at which he was already a teacher the year before. In a school ceremony, Mr. Harmon turned the school over to his successor. In his farewell statement, the departing principal noted with tears draining from his eyes, that he was leaving with heavy heart. "It is hard to take my leave of absence from these lively friends of mine," he averred. "I thought I would be here working among you to achieve the meaningful living through education, which you are seriously pursuing," the leaving principal emphasized. "As my hear is with you, I shall pray for you daily," *can't help*, as our ex-principal was popularly hailed among the students, added. On behalf of the students and teachers, Mr. Bohlen said, "We are sad because you are leaving us. On the other hand, we are happy because you are called for a job in your home, a principalship for St. Mark's Parish School, a Protestant Episcopal Church institute in Harper, Maryland County," Old Man Bohlen assured the gentleman.

Under the new principal, the boarders lingered to a rambling old house located near a place known as Nyaake Proper. Its general condition was not better than a large village hut except that it had rooms. In this dusty house we continued to battle for means to support ourselves in every detail and the increasing lessons.

Up to this time the district appeared divided about where to build the campus for the boarding school already in full swing. The school was not promising. But the news that the President of Liberia would be traveling through the interior the next year to Nyaake excited every inhabitant of the district headquarters, including the young and the old.

The eye servants, the officials, and people of the Webbo District, who seemed unconcerned about the plight of those village boys collected from around the vast district, caught the burning fever of what would happen to them if the president met the adaptable boys in those dehumanizing conditions they were ushered in by the one-time goodwill people. All the labor force of the district was summoned and work was begun on the boarding campus. In less than ten calendar months the campus was ready for habitation.

Reading the school schedule, we found that our Third Grade Reading, Spelling, and Useful Knowledge were scheduled for Teacher Thomas G. Bohlen, an old man in his 70s.

Everything seemed contrary to all the information about how the boarders would be housed and be provided with their immediate and necessary needs. For the three succeeding years, we received an irregularly scanty supply of rice. Nothing was given for meat, fish, salt, cooking utensils, let alone beds. The boys braced themselves up against the impending dehumanizing conditions. Worst of all, we had no dwelling place for our own. We rolled about the hilly town.

In the open District Council Hall without doors and shutters, with winds drilling though it, the school was conducted daily. The few wooden benches the school had were without backs. For desks, they were known on the printed pages as we read. In reality, there were none. For the long nine years I stayed in the school I did not see any until I went to Our Lady of Fatima High School in Harper, Maryland County.

Each of our teachers selected his own corner for his class in the open hall. All the classes were conducted with all the students standing during each recitation period.

Deprived of our warm and loving parents, we were very supportive of each other. We readily shared with one another whatever we had. Deep down in our hearts, we were quite aware of what we were seeking-education by all earnest means- which, with God on our side, we would get!

For us Third Graders, joy and sorrow resided in Old Man Bohlen's class. In a rotational way, a student read for the class each day while the rest were required to listen attentively. Picking his teeth with his homemade toothpick, he focused attention on pronunciation, accent, and punctuation. After the reading was done, comprehension questions were asked. Sometimes it was smooth; at other times, it was rough! Following the reading was Useful Knowledge. The questions for the day were listed below the page or pages read. But they were not found in the reading. Interestingly, each question was followed by its answer. The only thing one had to do was to memorize the answer of each question. For example: Why are some musical instruments called horns? Answer: Because the first musical instrument of that kind was the horn of an animal. All was left with the student to apply himself fully. I enjoyed Useful Knowledge!

If the words were dictated to write, it was another source of pleasure for me. Spelling in syllable was funny to me. With some words I tried. One day the class lined up for spelling in syllables. The word to be spelled was BUSINESS! Bus'- I- ness. The whole class tried but lost every earnest attempt. Finally, the class humbly appealed to the teacher to spell the word Business in syllables. Listen to the fun: Bus- , I- Bis-a, Ness'- ness, Bus' - I- ness'. The students burst into a thunderous laughter that almost tore the roof of the old rambling district council hall. This was the second phase of spelling. The third one was like a spelling bee; a student was asked to spell a given word such as TAUGHT. The student spelled the word t-a-g-h-t, taght. He misspelled it. The next student would take the challenge and correctly spell the word TAUGHT! Then the teacher said "d-o-w-n," and the class called the word DOWN. Again the teacher said "u-p," in unison the class said, "up." Finally the teacher would say, "cut him down." The student who spelled the word correctly would take the place of the student who missed it. The student losing would receive his award, a lash for each letter in the word TAUGHT. Wailing was the order of the day in our spelling class. Nobody enjoyed it!

Progressively, classes went on each day at the school. On the whole, the school year was dull and unimpressive as the administration was not communicative. At the end of the uneventful year many of us undeservingly earned our promotions. Nine went to the fourth Grade.

This year the school authority was tightlipped. Would there be vacation for the hungry boarders? Yes, but the uncertain reply hit us. "What does that mean?" the anxious boys worried. One evening in late December, the principal, Mr. Andrews, popped in to say that the boys would leave for vacation tomorrow and be back in school by February 1, 1946. "We are going to be located on our own campus with a boarding house, teachers' quarters, and a school building," the Reverend revealed. "The President of Liberia will pay us his official visit sometime next year," our principal speculated. We had reunion with our respective parents and relatives as we left the day according to the directive of the principal. In my mother's house, I met both my parents sitting close together like two peas in a pod. My father jumped on his feet and shouted, "Tuwi, Nyanbeju, your mother and I were just wondering why you did not come for Christmas," my father inquired. I then presented my credentials to my anxious parents (I mean my promotion statement).

As a thank-you treat, chicken in butter beans palm butter was prepared for me by my parents. The dish was so palatable that I forgot the many months I gasped for food.

In previous years, vacation periods lasted much longer than the 1945 vacation time. Late January, 1946, hastened the boys back to school because of the impending first official visit of the President of Liberia to the Webbo District. By now the construction of the boarding campus was completed. But when we arrived in late January, we were ready too to take possession of our new home, hopefully thinking that a permanent place for our abode at last had been established. The needed finishing touches, as the principal indicated, to the eagerly waiting students, were still hanging.

Sometime in April that year we took possession of our ill-prepared campus, containing three structures: a two-large room dormitory, a rectangular shaped long house with a hall throughout, intended to house the school, and a large building containing several rooms for the accommodation of the teachers and principal.

The appearance of the buildings did not show any sign that those houses were actually ready for human habitation. Ready they were, according to the school committee, fully in for the construction and operation of this school, already a strong, growing school academically. We accepted the campus in good faith, knowing that we would not be rolling about again in the coming years. But before we left for our permanent quarters, something serious happened to Charles and me at our dwelling place near that part of the town called Nyaake Proper. A young miss with a large pan on her head, passing in front of the boarding house, arrested my attention and suddenly I asked, "what are you selling?" "Fish," she said, smiling. I leapt over to her and helped her down. "How much?" I inquired. "Six pence," the seller announced, with a coy look at me. "Your fish is too dear, I cannot buy it," I snapped at her. She grabbed her pan to go and then she said, "Why waste my precious time when you poor mission boys don't have money always?" Hearing her scorn of us, I grabbed her by the arm and gave her a violent push, knocking her to the ground. The next thing I saw was her full weight leveled on my thin body. Certainly, the going was tough for me. Seeing my predicament, Charles Jackson, a boarder, who had been looking on, rushed to the scene to save his friend from the overpowering weight of the young woman venting her blazing anger on his skinny friend. His intervention was very timely. He freed me and I breathed relief. Then together we beat her fine.

She ran toward her home in Nyaake Proper, where the early European traders first established their stores. One of the oldest men of the settlement, Old Man

Peppeh, a professional fisherman, was still around, doing his own thing.

It was not long when her very stout father came galloping towards us. We ran into the house, thinking that he was coming to avenge his daughter. Of course, surely he was, but indirectly. He went straight to the principal's home to complain us. In no time, our quick-tempered principal, leaping, arrived with a bunch of kwa-wa branches in his hand, to pounce on his culprits." I understand that you, the strong boys here, wiped a passing girl, is that true?" the shuttering principal demanded. "We wanted to buy some of the fish she was selling but when we got to know the price, we told her that we were very sorry because we could not afford the price," we narrated. "Au .... Au ... waka to say, you beat the commissioner's messenger's daughter?" the already angry principal pressed on. Hesitantly, we answered, "yes, but ... E." The aggravated principal shouted to the boys standing by, "Lay him!" Those rascals seized me by hands and feet and laid me on a bench. The middle-aged, and who appeared to delight in brutal flogging, began to lash me severely. He quarreled as he lashed me, saying that my parents had deprived themselves of my service by sending me to school, where I was now practicing boxing instead of studying my lessons. He counted up to ten and then he started from one again. I exclaimed loudly, saying, "Mr. Principal, you are killing me!" This enraged him more, and laughing derisively, he said that he went to school in the night, and so he did not know how to count in the day. He flogged me until he was satisfied, brutalizing me with his twenty-five-times-two lashes. I was torn into pieces. It was Jacksor's turn. In the same vein, Charles was brutalized. At last, the battle crushed us.

The structures on our campus depicted a "don't care" attitude on the part of those who were in charge of the operation of the school, coupled with the day-to-day feeding and other supplies for the boarding school. According to their master plan, there were eight chiefdoms with an estimated population of fifty-thousand and four-thousand eight-hundred and eighty habitable huts. The plan said each hut in the district would be taxed twenty-five (25) cents annually and ten or more kinjahs of clean rice from each chiefdom, depending on its numerical strength, per year. Each kinjah would contain sixty government cups of rice. For the construction of the school, the full labor force would be supplied by the chiefdoms in the district, labor free. Only local materials, except cement and nails, would be used, with these at the disposal of the people charged with the responsibility of construction and other arrangements for the smooth running of the school, with its boarders the people for whom the school was being instituted.

According to the understanding, the boarding campus would be ready and equipped before the boys would arrive for the first year.

When the boys arrived in March, 1942, no place was made ready for the boys. As a result the boys stayed around Nyaake until Reverend Brewer was begged to give his old rambling house on New Road to house the boys. The house was without doors and shutters. It was impossible to shelter adequately sixty boys in such a broken house with floors being pulverized by jiggers.

What happened to the money collected over the years before and after the school came into being? The boarding house was scantily supplied the years before until after the first official visit of the President of Liberia to the district.

35

Of course, when the school authority knew that perhaps some dissatisfied chief or the students would complain to the president, they issued the boarders for the first time some crudely-tailored blue denim short trousers and short sleeve white shirts. The years following the president's visit, we received an adequate supply of rice frequently. A short gun was placed at the disposal of the dormitory boys. Many of us boarding boys seized the opportunity to help ourselves while helping the whole household. Our housing was never improved, though; we remained in the dusty dormitory infested with blood-sucking fleas. Since the sanitation of the campus was poor, the barefoot boys, sanitarily unarmed, experienced many casualties from day-to-day fierce battles the wingless fleas waged. Because of no care, many of our victimized brothers were irately obliged to quit school. By this, our number dwindled each year substantially.

Despite the conditions prevailing on the campus, the 1946 school year was memorable. The first three months of the year saw massive preparations for the first official visit of President William V. S. Tubman to Webbo District and its people.

A week before the president arrived, the whole district had congregated at Nyaake, Webbo District headquarters. From Barroba, the largest chiefdom in the district, came an Assembly of God Church School boarders to honor the presence of the president. We hosted them in our dormitory. The reception for the president was massive and colorful. Mr. Flo F. Page, a small skinned arithmetic teacher of the Webbo District School, delivered the welcome address. The president, in response, among other things, said, "Opportunity is like a baldheaded man with only a little yank of hair right at the top of his forehead! If you want to seize his head," he continued, "grab the yank. Grabbing the bald head would make you a loser."

The use of the English Pound Sterling and English Royal textbooks gradually came to an end in Webbo that year. American currency and textbooks were now in vogue. During the school year before, the school introduced the American textbooks in the second semester. One day the principal broke heartbreaking information to the school to the effect that all promotions would be stilled because of the late introduction of the voluminous American textbooks. The information was outrageous, destructive, and dehumanizing. Peter the Great of Gbeapo and William the Conqueror of Gedebo, the little boys who had industriously, studiously, and strenuously prepared themselves for well-deserved promotion felt inhumanly degraded. However, this was from the power that be. We were compelled to share the bitter and unusual information of no promotion for the year with our awaiting parents. For me, the 1947 school year was the most eventful year in all my elementary school days experience. Although we were retained in our previous grades, the year showered on us many and varied rich experiences. Our Royal English textbooks were few and concise. For the American textbooks, one needed a dump truck to carry his regular textbooks to school every day. Space was another problem for them. But what did they really have to sell? As we skimmed through the pages of the main textbooks, our eager hearts ran pit-a-pat. Nothing much was in them except the strange American-Indian names. The arithmetic on fourth grade level, the level of my grade, was far below our standard. We had chewed up complex fractions and other complex problems in the English arithmetic, called "shilling Arithmetic." The fractions we found in the American English text were like the ones we did in the third grade. The American English text was nothing comparable to what we had gathered when we paraded through the pages of the Royal English grammar called Davidson and Alcock. On the whole, the contents of our new American textbooks were disgusting and disappointing as they were frustrating.

We began to whisper among ourselves, "Did the principal and his teachers have time even to skim these huge volumes?" They simply shrugged when they overheard the whispering students. By myself, I pondered the question of whether it was necessary for retaining the whole school. The whole issue was eating me up. Without thinking of the consequence that would likely befall me if I should directly question the administration or a teacher, I unequivocally challenged Teacher Peter W. Kun, a Gold Coast-educated man who taught arithmetic and English to the fourth grade. "From your own judgment, was the faculty's decision logically based on their comparison of the two different textbooks content-wise, for retaining or stilling the promotions for all the students of the school?" "Well, it was the decision of the majority," Teacher Kun sighed.

Peter and I felt that we should be doubly promoted because the contents of our new American textbooks were far below what we had already achieved. Arrogantly, the Administration and the teachers kept tightlipped. In those days the teachers had absolute authority. We could not press the question "why" any further and so we languished in the fourth grade, for four long semesters, doing one thing over and over again.

Chapter X "The Election of President Tubman"

Following his inauguration in 1944, the eighteenth president of Liberia, former Senator of Maryland County and former Associate Justice of the Supreme Court of Liberia, Mr. Tubman moved with alacrity and agility to implement the many and varied plans of his platform, on which he vigorously campaigned and elected overwhelmingly. Included in the platform, among other things, was the inclusion, for the first time in the history of the country, of aboriginal representation from the provinces to the Liberian National Legislature.

For the Eastern province, Mr. Daniel P. Derrick of the Gedebo in southeastern Liberia, was elected on the majority ticket by the people of the province.

Having been inducted into the House, as representative of the people long-denied, Honorable Derrick sponsored a bill to grant the settlement of Nyaake a township status. The Honorable body wasted no time in granting the charter of a township status to Nyaake and its politically matured people. On May 4, 1947, with pageantry and colorful ceremony, the charter was presented to the citizens of Nyaake.

As prescribed by the status creating the township of Nyaake, the highest officer, township commissioner, for the governance of the township, is nominated and appointed by the president of Liberia. Accordingly, the citizen's chairman, Mr. Henry P. Collins, was honored by the president with his appointment as township commissioner for the Township of Nyaake, Webbo. In accordance with governing status also, the rest of the officers of the township were elected by the citizens as follows to wit: citizen's secretary, Mr. Joseph W. Andrews; secretary, Mr. William D. Farr; treasurer, Mr. Isaac S. Diggs; chief constable, Mr. Benedictus A. D'Almeida; general road overseer, etc. With the administration in place, the young and hilly township began its arduous task of organization.

The visit of the president of Liberia with the Webbo District and its people appeared to have opened up new avenues of political, social, and economic awakening. Nyaake was not spared by the bitter effects of the ugly Second Global War. Everything had fallen apart in every corner and nook of our one world, and resuscitating from those effects, which had devastated and dehumanized the world over, was now the fervent prayer by all the people of goodwill, Nyaake Township and the people of Webbo District included.

As we were moving along the King's Highway, the wind of change for better was engulfing us. The boarding school was finally housed on the rudely-built campus and the school as a whole was in full swing. The boarders were frequently and adequately supplied their necessities by the school authority. Happy were we!

After the first semester, 1947, just before the school left for the July 26th Independence Day break, the principal, Reverend Joseph W. Andrews, proudly announced that our eighth-grade students, three in all, would be graduating. That was a strange language within the walls of the Webbo District School. The word 'graduation' tickled and animated us to return to school as soon as the break wore out.

The idea that the world insanity was over gladdened people worldwide, I supposed. Peace at last had known the face of the globe. Things seemed golden, but as you are aware, all the glittering things are not gold. Many of the most-needed commodities, such as kerosene, salt, and other necessary items, were scarce in the countryside or not found at all. Like everybody in the countryside, the boarders needed these things so frequently the principal would send a pair of boys to Pleebo, near the Firestone Rubber Cavalla Plantation in Maryland county, to buy some. This time Charles Jacksor and I were dispatched in our Mandingo trucks to Pleebo.

From Nyaake to Pleebo was about a twelve-hours-long journey through Biabo and Gedeabo on the southeast. In Pleebo we bought few gallons of kerosene and other needed items. When we bought our commodities, instead of the regular route, we decided to go back to Nyaake by way of Tuobo through Gedebo, on a new road being constructed on a self-help basis by the two districts, Webbo and Pleebo, the distance about forty miles. Without thinking, early that morning, we began our unknown road from Pleebo. By six o'clock that afternoon we landed in my home village, Kablake, nestled under towering evergreen trees off the main road to Nyaake.

After a brief introduction of my friend to my parents upon our arrival, we were now the uninvited but welcome quests of my loving and solicitous parents. Generally the month of May was always a month when food was scarce or not found in the countryside. However, our generous host and hostess adequately fed us that night. As time was against us, after my mother served us with palm butter with pumpkin and the nutritious Gedebo rice the next day, we rushed out of the village to begin our three hour trek to the Township of Nyaake, Webbo. On our way that afternoon, just between two large villages, Joloke and Worteke, we were struck by unusual darkness. Night falling at about two in the afternoon, what has happened? Surely, some form of night had fallen. It was no mistake. We groped about. In about ten minutes there was dim daylight. Charles, being older, took from me the container of kerosene, even though it was my turn to carry it. Groping, we trampled the snaky path to Worteke, where we saw in the sky, in twilight, the sun and the moon sitting side by side in the heavens. This was one of the wonderful events of the year, 1947. The memorable event was on the 25th of May.

Chapter XI "A Father Celebrates His Son"

The end of the academic year was marked with our first graduation festivities. The three young men, Thomas K. Z. Ireland, John K. Farr, and Edward W. Farr, were awarded their laurels. This grand and unique occasion fired my aspiration and inspiration in my academic pursuit. Our long-delayed promotions this year were no hard question at the four-semesters marking time in one grade. I made it to the fifth grade double flying colors. Steadily I was ascending the elementary ladder of education. It appeared, as we gained entrance into the world of educated, that we were being brought to the gratifying attention of the township populace. "These energy-filled young men can be of some immediate help and benefit to us," Honorable Collins observed at one school program.

When I arrived in my clan circle, Kablake went wild when I broke the news of my promotion to the fifth grade. Nobody was more elated over the heart-warming news of my step made forward than the village chief, my stern but flexible father.

Greeting me, my father called me, "Ali!" Cautiously I answered my broadly-smiling father, the village strongman. Why did I answer my dear father cautiously, one would ask? In our vernacular, 'Ali' means an intimate friend, not an ordinary one but one close, if not very close to your heart. Why did my father choose to call me Ali, his first living son? Throughout that day, conflicting thoughts fought continuously within me.

After our evening meal, before I joined the boys waiting outside for our usual evening storytelling, my father said to me, "Tomorrow is a feasting day in our home with the whole village in attendance. The six taebedu and the bush goat dried meat, plus the huge three roosters with the basket full of dry red tail fish that go into the making of the palm butter dish. "The thing I longed for for these countless years since I came from Down the Coast shortly before I married you, is being gradually realized. My son, I mean our son, is getting educated. As we readily see and know, three short more years are left for him to finish school," the yearning father glorified in his son. I was confounded and dumbfounded. What had gotten my father so excited about this book business?

Gedebo, now called Kablake, led the villagers to our home for the palatable dish treat. Jubilating, the village celebrated their son's promotion to the fifth grade. I was deeply surprised but greatly encouraged by my clan's overwhelming expression of their moral support of me.

It was painful to leave the village and its robust boys and their sagacious village elders who had willingly and spontaneously showered me with their love during vacation. No doubt, knowing that all of them were wishing me continuous success in my earnest endeavor propelled me. Under the galloping escort of the singing village boys, I lingered out of the smiling village. As vision without courage perishes, may my hoping villagers pray with me to manfully gather and harness the courage. My father's underlying hope was that I should graduate one day from school. But as Scripture says that hope is not hope if its object is seen; how is it possible for one to hope for what he sees? And hoping for what one cannot see means awaiting it with patient endurance. Since I have the vision and hope, may the God of scholars endow me with the courage and endurance for this worthy pursuit of mine.

The boarding boys from Gedebo Chiefdom were late. For the first time we were not punished by the principal as we told him some pleasing lies that sounded like truth. As usual, we received a warm, noisy reception from our friends who had arrived earlier. Mr. Henry P. Collins, Nyaake Township Commissioner, one of the sagacious founders of the Webbo District School, was special to all the students in the town. Mr. Collins ran a small shop where we could buy almost all our required school materials, such as slates, slate pencils, copybooks, fool caps, etc., etc. Any time a student buyer would come into Mr. Collins's shop and ask, "Do you have slate pencil, for instance?" in an amusing way, Mr. Collins would ask, "Are you ready?" What did Mr. Collins mean when he asked the question? Every item the student wanted to buy must be spelled correctly before he would sell it to you. By this I was amused and challenged and made ready to visit Mr. Collins's shop as frequently as possible just to spell, even if I had no money to buy. He extended me an open invitation to visit his shop as my school time would permit me. I was there nearly every day, as the shop was less than a stone's throw from our school. No price was awarded me for the visits, but the exercise made me a master of the words used to spell the school materials sold in his shop.

Truly the energy-filled boys would be of some help in no distant future to the people of the young township: I was singularly honored when, through the principal, the Honorable Township Commissioner requested me to take census of all the lepers found in and around the town. For about three weeks, after school each day, I searched all in and around the town to locate and list the victims of this ancient disease. I gathered many names and presented the list to Mr. Collins, who thanked me immensely. I was glad that I could help, in a comparatively small way, the town whose wisely-thinking people were providing us with life through education.

Mr. Peter Kun, our fifth grade arithmetic and English teacher, finding that the American arithmetic and English were not challenging the ambitious students as before, discontinued them as textbooks for so progressive a class. Our old shilling English arithmetic and Davidson and Alcock Royal English grammar were reintroduced. This set the brilliant class ablaze again.

"The principal wants you just now," Bennie Wean told me. I left for the principal's quarters without delay. Bennie said that I gave him rice crust when I shared the food for the boys that day. "Au...au.. waka to say you gave rice crust to a senior boy, cha..hm..waka to you are bad of .. Au..au. Is it true?" the principal caught his breath. "If it is that I gave him rice crust, it was not done intentionally." I sincerely and apologetically pleaded with the unyielding principal. "Tomorrow, in the school, you will receive twenty-five lashes on your buttocks," the principal pronounced his prejudicial and rash judgment. The next day, the principal's strongmen were ready to lay me on the bench.

The cruel punishment was meted out to me by him in his usual brutal way. The skinny boy wailed, wailed, wailed, and wailed, saying loudly, "My mother, will I ever know this book?" The torrential tears from my wailing eyes inundated the campus towering over by Mount Chelo. Everywhere I went in town after that day of my agony in that jiggers-infested school, people would scornfully ask, and quoting

41

me, "My mother, will I ever know this book?" No doubt, scornful as they sounded, they would like to get the answer to that painful question. Probably time would answer it either negatively or positively. Listen out!

The 1948 school year crowned me with a successful pass to the sixth grade. The climbing was slow but steady! But all was not well. Our new and energetic supervisor of schools for Eastern Province died in a Harper hospital, following a brief illness. It seemed he had big dreams for the schools in Eastern Province in general, and Webbo District School in particular. As soon as he made his maiden visit to our school, Professor Wesely placed the teachers names on the official government payroll for regular monthly salaries. Before, the meager salaries the teachers received came from the district. From the district, it was reported that Principal Andrews earned a monthly salary of fourteen (14.00) dollars. The early and untimely death of the supervisor of schools for Eastern Province, a province with rampant illiteracy, dissipated all the indulgent efforts of the teachers.

As the school was developing academically, many extra-curriculum activities began to spring here and there. Added to the emerging programs was our promoter and booster, our new supervisor of schools, Eastern Province, Professor Isaac Himie Wesley, a young graduate of Liberia College and son of Henry Too Wessley, former Vice President of Liberia, the only Grebo man up to now to hold such a very high office in the country. Young Wesley replaced Reverend Henry Bagbo Wilson who had gone to be with the Lord.

Two of the many extra-curricular activities were: (1) Itoka Literacy Union, chiefly a debating club and a dramatic club. On organization of the debating club, elections were held and the honor of the secretary fell on me. A teacher was elected its president. At our first meeting of Itoka Literacy Union, we agreed to stage our first debate on the proposition: Iron and Rubber, which is more useful to humanity? Pro-Iron, Con-rubber: The pro team was ably and proficiently led by me against the razor, Peter Nyepon. Each team grouped every day to prepare their points of argument. Finally the day for the debate was announced and a circular letter was sent around informing the public about this debate, the first of its kind by the school and in the community. The night of our maiden show, the old rambling rectangular District Council Hall was jam-packed with about five-hundred people. Mr. Gabriel C. H. Gadegbeku, our school committee chairman, a scholar, and business executive, headed the panel of judges to decide the issue. After arguments were heatedly and elaborately presented, the unbiasedly attentive judges retired to their room of deliberation. A few minutes later, the smiling judges returned. The spectators, including the novice debaters, were excited. "To every argument or fight there must be a winner or loser. In this case, there is no exception," the shrewd panel leader alerted the attentively listening audience.

The judges were unanimous in their decision, and I am privileged and singularly honored to present on their behalf and in my own name to you the result of the thought-provoking arguments so ably delivered by our children, steadfastly craving for education. "The victory for tonight creditably falls on the Pro-Iron," Mr. Gadegbeku concluded. The rousing and thunderous applause from the people of the overcrowded hall almost knocked the roof of the hall off, and no doubt, the resounding sound caused the mighty Cavalla River to tremble beneath her banks.

(2) Still making of our newfound opportunities, a drama entitled, "Girls Boarding School," was staged. Our school was a co-ed institution but it was markedly almost without girls, especially in the upper and intermediate classes. The drama required only girl characters. However, the principal decided to use boys and one or two girls found in the school for the cast. The girl characters included Mrs. Caroline Bohlen (Madam Ruskine), principal of the girls boarding school, Alice Gadegbeku (Cora Greens), senior student, Teletha Young (student and Sarah Labor, student). The boy-girl characters included William Reeves (Jenny Jones), Peter Nyepon, etc.., etc. The boarding school was informed that smallpox had broken out in all of England and everybody was required by necessity to be vaccinated. Because of this information, the principal told the girls that she was laying their going home for vacation until a medical practitioner came to her call to vaccinate all the girls against the killer epidemic. Disobligingly and rowdyishly, the young ladies refused to listen to reason. "If I am to be vaccinated, it must be placed under my foot!" one cried. "Knife will not touch my smooth body!" another snarled. "Unless the doctor in question is a female, we are not going to expose ourselves to those frisky, women-hunting hounds," the girls in unison asserted.

With anxious expectation, the girls waited for the arrival of the undesirable medical practitioner. We, the girl-boys, got ourselves ready in ladies' fashionable dresses, the types women wear to entice and tantalize their men visitors. The girl-boys wore iron titis (breasts).The fruits of a wild tree resembling woman's breasts, and wigs were woven from dyed raffia palm. The young lady, Jenny Jones (William Reeves), was the talk of the town for her beautiful make-lady performance, weeks and months following the show, the first of its kind in the sprawling growing town perched on seven scenic hills towered over by Mount Chelo and the torrential rolling Cavalla River in her concave banks.

Chapter XII "The Rapid Winds of Change"

The rapid wind of change was whirling in every corner and nook in the Webbo District School. Both the school and its students were advancing academically and chronologically. The boarding boys' constant visitor and chairman of the school committee, Mr. Gabriel C. H. Gadegbeku, who, in a fatherly way, shared new ideas with us frequently, and subsequently was popularly nicknamed New Idea (for short, NI), advised the boys to get engaged in activities from which each of us would earn some money to take care of our immediate needs. Without reservation, the whole suggestion was readily bought from the experienced man.

All of us busied ourselves cutting palm nuts every week to sell, or sometimes we made oil from the palm nuts also to sell. Soon or late, we found out that the undertaking was straining and earned nothing for us in cash. Mat-making for roofing houses was the next project we thought could bring us more and fast money. This project proved more strenuous and straining, and more regrettably, brought in no appreciable income. Charles Jackson, Nathaniel Andrews, and I, styling ourselves Future Farmers of Liberia, chose gardening. Done as a hobby, the gardening, while we sometime tried the palm nut cutting and mat-making, occupied our time regularly as it brought grease to our elbows. Frequently we gathered pennies from here and there.

The next thing Nathaniel and I actively got involved in was game hunting. Since the school had one single-barreled shotgun, Nathaniel was the hunter and I was the hunter's boy. The two of us took great pleasure in it. Several months saw us together on hunting expedition up in Mount Chelo, or in the forest in Webbo, or in Gedebo countryside. Steadily Nathaniel became a good marksman. One day I gathered courage and went alone in the wilderness to try my luck with the gun. After my solo adventure in the bush, I came stepping briskly home with somebody carrying my first game (a bush goat) on his sturdy shoulders. The bush goat was about twice my weight and so I could not possibly carry it. On seeing the animal killed by the little skinny man, the boys thunderously shouted "Bravo, Bravo, Bravo," for their new hunter.

As time went by, the boys began to experiment with many projects. About two or more adventures went into raising chickens. As the chickens grew in numbers, serious ownership problems seeped among the poultry men. The fight over chicken ownership split the boarders into faction camps. We needed, I strongly felt, an immediate solution to the angrily growing and confusing problems. I had an idea.

The elders of my home village did it and it worked. It was to find the truth, but an ordeal:

"Let us take the bark of a wild tree called Karlo with a knife scrape the cambium from the bark, and place the cambium in a green leaf shaped like a funnel. But before this, a ritual must be performed before the bark is taken from the tree.

The two parties claiming ownership of the chicken in question must agree thus: Party A must agree that if the chicken belongs to him, when the juice from the cambium is put into the eyes of the chicken, they must remain normal. Party B must say the same in reverse," I expounded. Under my watchful eyes, the boys chosen to perform the ordeal did exactly as was directed. In the presence of witnesses of the administration of the ordeal to the chicken, the news spread like wildfire in and around the campus. Principal Andrews summoned all the boys for investigation of the matter, which he called strange and unchristian.

"Who brought about this diabolic idea?" the principal asked, with a forced smile on his wrinkled face. A long silence grappled the boys. After a while, one ventured out, "William Reeves helped us with the confusing problems." "Cha... Au..du..waka to say, that ordeal practice is beyond my jurisdiction. The school committee has the power and authority to investigate such matters and give judgment", the principal biasedly relinquished. Since William Reeves, the black sheep, was responsible again for this devilish behavior, no doubt, he wanted him out of the boarding school, I presumed. The reverend principal invited the chairman of the school committee for this investigation beyond his trial jurisdiction. A day or two later, the principal sent his official communication to the school committee as he told one of the boys concerned. Chairman Gadegbeku came on campus that sunny afternoon, strolling with his hairy hands on his back to judge the misdeed of this William Reeves boy. "NI!" the boys shouted, and silently retreated in the back of the dusty dormitory. On seeing the chairman on campus, I said to myself, "Lord, I am finished; my parents will kill me." Reverend Andrews and Mr. Gadegbeku joined us at the dormitory. The old teacher stated his reason why he sent for the chairman. Patiently, the chairman listened to the stuttering principal narrate what he considered the diabolic act of William Reeves. "The finger points to you and me," in his usual slowly-speaking tone the chairman toned in, "Naturally, children are dramatists," the scholar averred, "This silly happening here reminds you and me that we must be very careful what we do in the presence of our youngsters," the boys' New Idea expounded. "William Reeves is consciously not responsible for what happened here. His father and the other people in his village must be held liable for this act, the father of many children concluded. But as a warning, the chairman added, "Reeves, you are no more in the village. That practice is not Christian, and you are a Christian; don't suggest or propose such a thing again." Thank God for the wisdom of Old Man Gedegbeku that I was not thrown out of the school or punished.

But as Reverend Andrews always puts it, "A monkey cannot hide its black hands." It appeared also true with a naughty boy. Hear what happened again in which this William Reeves boy was intricately involved.

The place was just below the back of the hill where our campus was located. The place belongs to the Catholic Mission. Honorable Joseph Itoka, Webbo District Commissioner, and a Catholic, made Kesseh, an alleged criminal from Tuobo, chiefdom in the Webbo District, the custodian of that parcel of land. Kesseh had many chickens around his little hut with beautiful and clean surroundings.

In the boarding school, some of the boys were raising chickens. Very often, the poultry boys observed that their chickens were disappearing. Investigating, they came to a rash conclusion that it was Kesseh who was taking away the missing chickens.

One sunny afternoon, it was decided to raid Mr. Kesseh's quarters. Three wise emissaries were dispatched to Kesseh's hamlet. The mission included Philip

Johnson, Charles Jackson, and William Reeves. We planned accordingly. Philip carried a handful of clean rice as bait to call the chickens; with Reeves was the stick to strike the head of the chicken, especially the very large roosters; Charles would quickly place the struck chicken into the bag already under his arm. And so we went and the plan was brilliantly executed. We brought our prey, a huge rooster, home. The boys to cook the soup that night were at hand to receive the booty.

Meticulously the feathers were removed and the feathers were dumped into our pit toilet. The supervisor for the cleaning of the rooster made sure not a feather was dropped any place else. When we broke away from our regular night study class, the selected guys immediately went into the pleasing task of preparing the soup. The delicious soup and the nutritious Webbo rice were ready by 11:30 that night. Silently we consumed the chicken with plenty of rice. Luckily for us, the principal did not come around that happy night.

The next day, Mr. Kesseh, with his hands behind his back, walked slowly around our large compound. His first stop was at the principal's quarters, where he complained to the principal about his missing rooster. He told the principal that the principal's boys had stolen his huge rooster, which he believed no meat could catch. At once the principal hailed for the leaders of the boys, namely, Peter Nyepon, Nathaniel Andrews, and William Reeves, to his residence. "This man says our boys stole his huge rooster no meat, a fox or leopard, can kill," the principal relayed. "My boys don't steal, but to please you, let me ask them in your presence," the principal asserted. Reverend Andrews continued, "Me here, meat can kill me, and then why do you think that a rooster cannot be killed by any of those animals that hunt chickens? Boys, did you steal Mr. Kesseh's huge rooster that meat cannot kill?" the reverend derided poor Kesseh. In unison, the boys' leaders cried. "We did not steal Mr. Kesseh's rooster, and we do not steal, as principal well knows. If you say that to us again, you shall find yourself in the court of the district commissioner tomorrow," the boys threatened. Helpless, Mr. Kesseh lingered home down the hill to mourn the death of his elephant-sized rooster that meat could not kill.

It was in no uncertain terms that under the emerging conditions in which we found ourselves, we needed ready cash to take care of our immediate needs. All of the boarding school boys who had attained the required age to be enlisted in the militia were recruited into the Fourth Infantry Battalion of the Fourth Infantry Regiment of Liberia, with headquarters in Harper, Maryland County. Nyaake was like Sparta. All the leading men and able-bodied men of the town were militiamen. Our principal and teachers, including the chairman of the school committee, were no exception. Able-bodied as we the young people were, had we any tangible reason to excuse us from answering our national patriotic call to duty?

All of us living in the boarding school were village boys recruited from the Webbo District countryside. Our parents were poor peasants, who experienced the pangs of seasonal hunger every year. Money was never within their reach. Hustling to rest from the hard restrictions of the school, we rushed out of Nyaake wishing to be free again for a while, with our respective parents in the different chiefdoms whence we came.

On vacation each year with my willing and solicitous parents, I received four dollars, which the old people called one pound, using British sterling. Knowing this, should I expect my militia uniform to be bought by my penniless parents? Asking them would seem that I was demanding blood from rock. "Learn how to help yourselves," Chairman Gadegbeku often urged the boys. Unless we were properly uniformed on our first day of military duty, we would probably be found delinquent, tried, and imprisoned. To help myself was the only way, and help myself I did!

I had no other alternative but to immediately resort to serious and careful hunting. I raked around and found forty-five cents from my gardening pennies and bought three single-barrel shotgun cartridges. With these cartridges handy, since it was during the July 26th break, the early hours of each morning saw me crawling under the bushes, trying to get some animal to save me from being delinquent and from humiliating imprisonment. Luckily for me, one huge bush goat suddenly came within my reach and I levered my barrel at her and killed her instantly. I carried the meat to the town butcher's shop where it was sold at fifteen cents a pound. I gathered four dollars from the sale. At another time, God, who helps those who earnestly seek help, blessed me with another large bush goat. This time I earned five big dollars from the sale. I was ready to go to Pleebo, but I needed sixty cents more for transportation from Pleebo to Harper, where I had to go by car to and fro. A monkey would not budge from fruit it was nibbling when it saw me. I did not spare it! I snapped my trigger and my friend came tumbling down from the top of a high tree. My business was correct!

In company with some people traveling to Pleebo, I happily journeyed to Pleebo. The next day, that misty morning, I rode in an old duazet pickup truck to Day Break City, Harper, where I bought my three double-yards of khaki, the best available. Mr. Charles Cummings, the tailor, tailored well the long pair of trousers, a long-sleeved shirt, and a garrison cap. The cost and workmanship for the khaki uniform for this new recruit amounted to nine dollars. The snaky path I treaded from Pleebo to Nyaake was like a superhighway as I carried my earned military suit in my haversack on my back. A real soldier, wasn't I? This was one of the many ways I paddled my own canoe throughout my rocky school days without any substantial financial support from any source.

On the day of our first military duty, the enlisted boarders constituted one platoon, with our one staff sergeant and three corporals. Peter Nyepon was the staff sergeant, and Williams Reeves the first corporal. We were attached to Company A of the Fourth Infantry Battalion, Fourth Infantry Regiment. We were now part and parcel of the militia that forms the first line of defense of our country, Liberia.

That year, the battalion was raised to a regimental status known as and called ninth Infantry Regiment, with Joseph Itoka commanding, and headquarters in Nyaake. Our platoon in the whole regiment was comparatively elite, as all the members were highly literate. As a result, promotions sought us every now and then. By the end of that year, I was promoted as sergeant major (Master Sergeant) assigned on the staff of the commanding officer of the First Infantry Battalion, Ninth Infantry Regiment. My indigenous people, who were militiamen and made up Company B First Infantry Battalion, leaked the news of promotion to my parents long before my arrival on my annual break from school.

In the sixth grade, our class consisted of four students: Felicia Gadegbeku, Sarah Labor, Peter Nyepon, and William Reeves. These young boys and girls were special to the teachers, especially to the principal, whom the students nicknamed, "Waka to." "What made these students special?" Some begrudging students asked. "Well, the students are academically greedy. Because of the academic consuming power of theirs, every teacher concerned with them is challenged every day. This makes them special," the teacher professed.

"I want to see what I do for the Sixth Grade in arithmetic this year," principal Andrews, the old bookkeeper, apprised Teacher Kun, who taught the subject the year before. He wanted to teach us some old tricks in arithmetic that, when thoroughly comprehended and fully grasped, would eventually make us arithmetic wizards and witches of numbers. "When I worked for W. D. Wooden, a British merchandise trading company based in Harper, Cape Palmas, and the company could not balance its books that year. Something had seriously gone wrong with the accounts. An outstanding Gold Coast bookkeeper was hired and transported to Liberia to diagnose and correct the mistake or mistakes in the accounting.

When the famous bookkeeper arrived, he requested that all the books be placed near him. After perusing the accounts, he discovered the mistakes and then the arithmetical wizard began with heartbreaking speed to add two-digit numbers at the same time. In no time, the number doctor balanced the books and took leave of the company," Reverend Andrews sang his epic.

"Regular training and constant practice are the empowering source of his immense arithmetical strength," propounded the teacher to his insatiable knowledge seekers. "Here, we will develop these skills even more," the new arithmetic teacher emphasized.

Professor Andrews was an etymologist with seemingly a strong background in Hebrew, Greek and Latin. "You too must get deeply rooted in the study of the derivations of the origins and history of words," the learned man urged. These were the order of direction in our pursuit of knowledge that year and after. The going was getting very tough and rough with old Cuttington College Sixth-Form-educated in charge.

Word study arrested my deep interest and I made steady headway. My interest in arithmetic was without initiative. I did only what the teacher assigned me to do. In English, especially in the study of words, my initiative was without limit. However, I was not a poor student in arithmetic. My scores in arithmetic were already in the high eighties or sometime nineties. In most cases, I was a ninety-plus student.

In arithmetic, the old bookkeeper introduced what he called Cash Account, a debit and a credit accounting, while adding of numbers rapidly was the warming exercise every day. With this phase of our study in arithmetic, my insatiable interest knew no bounds. Immensely I enjoyed it, making believe that I was running a business that required me to keep cash account.

On his little business trip to Nyaake, Old Man Sualo Toe visited the Gedebo boys, particularly to see his son who was with us in the boarding school. After we exchanged warm greetings with our elder, Mr. Toe, illiterate but highly intelligent, asked, "What do you people do in Tumatu?" 'Tumatu' is the Gedebo word for arithmetic. "Cash Account," I told him. "What does it mean?" he quizzed me further. "In business, like in every life, one receives and expends money. Carefully you note how much money is received and expended in a given month or period of time. All the money you received is noted on the left hand side of the account sheet and is called Debit. And all money spent is noted on the right side of the account sheet and is called Credit. At the end of the period, you must check the account, both sides, to know how much you received and spent in all. Finally, you will know whether you have money left or not when you add all the amounts in the debit column. The same is done in the credit column. If the total in the debit column is larger than the total amount in the credit column, subtract the credit column from the debit. The difference is the money you have or should have on hand. But if you must subtract the debit from the credit, then recheck; something went wrong. On the other hand, if the amounts in both columns are equal, the money was spent carefully. There are many other things to this, which we cannot go into.

After listening attentively to my explanations, the village businessman decided to put it to test. He stated the amounts of money he received and spent in a given time. Carefully I worked out his figures. When I balanced his account and told him how much money he should have on hand, he shouted, "You are a wizard; how do you know how much money I have on hand?" Afterwards, he was like another African who visited a white missionary carpentry workshop in an African Village. The missionary left his square much needed that day at home. He grabbed a chip of wood and wrote on it to his wife at home, "Please send me my square," and handed it to his visitor to take it to his wife. "Carry this to my wife," he requested his friend. "What must I say to her?" The old African warrior asked. "Nothing, simply hand this to her," he replied. Puzzled, the illiterate African went on his mission, and on reaching the house, he delivered the chip to the missionary's wife who in turn gave him the square. Gazing wildly at the lady, the ignorant African asked, "How do you know that this is what he wants?" The perplexed African inquired. Politely the broadly smiling woman asked, "Didn't you bring me this chip?" Without a word, the village strongman took the square and the chip and delivered only the square to the missionary. He hung the chip about his neck and went about the large village, saying "See the wonder of these white people, they can make a chip talk."

Sualo Toe, my father's life friend, back home in Gedebo, told the trio villagers, "Your son Kpaye Kamma is true fortune teller, a wizard of no mean caliber."

In all of my school life, promotion to the next grade each year was never a problem for me, but rather, my rank in class was my greatest concern. In other words, I was sure of promotion every year, once I was in school and attended my recitation periods regularly and had my lessons well prepared each day.

The boys in that two-pair class were resolutely determined to keep their female counterparts abase, the traditional place for women. Although the young ladies were academically aggressive and progressive, they were fully aware that woman is woman- period! Unrelentlessly Peter and I fought for the first place in class, which was reverently referred to as DUX. All of us gloried in that honorable title. The wrestling was unabatingly tough!

Sarah and Felicia were the class's belles, but were Peter and William beaus? We were not, but the old traditional trick of boys, flirting, kept the lasses and the lads interwovenly and blithely together. Such a memorable class it was! In the meantime, our flirting had to be constantly subdued, knowing that Felecia was the daughter of the chairman of our school committee. Sarah was the ward of Mr. and Mrs. Gabriel P. Itoka, and Lois Grant Itoka was a regular teacher at the Webbo District School, where her husband intermittently taught singing. A stammerer, Sarah spoke freely and gave liberally to the boys, while Felecia, seemingly an introvert, was often silent and a miser, it would appear. But the two of them had their choice of the two young men. Whom could that be, since I said 'choice,' with two single boys in the class? Your guess could be the choice. Happily the two of them went in for the more slender fellow, William Reeves, whom the class nicknamed 'Rice'; Felecia was nicknamed 'Fish,' Sarah, 'Salt,' and Peter, 'Palm butter.' These nicknames added fun to our busy class activities.

Keenly I observed after a test and the results showed that I captured the first place in class, Sarah and Felicia would go wild rejoicing for my success. Never was it when my brother was rated first in class. Felecia once presented me with a well-embroidered pocket handkerchief with a heart designed in the center, her own handy work. Before that year ended, Felecia was whisked off from Nyaake for some scholarship in Monrovia. From Monrovia, Felecia, 'Fish,' sent me a letter narrating all the interesting experiences she was gathering in her new school. Enclosed in the letter was what appeared to be a gold ring for my small fingers. In early 1950, Sarah left for Monrovia, her home. To tell me her whereabouts, Sarah sent me a letter in which she vicariously brought Monrovia to me in Nyaake. "Herein, I enclosed two cents for your recess (smiles)," 'Salt' wrote. Each time I received some gift from any of the girls while in class with us, or after they left, I would make it known to poor Peter, poor No Friend.

Life is an unending battle, and as a song says, "Gird your armor on." With the guiding and protecting hand of God I have been moving steadily and steadfastly throughout these rocky succeeding school years of mine up to this time.

As the poet says, "The eminence by great men reached and kept was not obtained by sudden flight, but while their companions slept they were upward toiling through the night." In no way does this quotation suggest smooth sailing in the world in which God owes us living, but we must get out to collect it. If I had attained any height in these succeeding years, I owed it all to God who gave me the abiding strength. And like St. Paul's letter to the Romans, I say through God I am gaining access to education by trusting in God, in whose grace I now stand, and boast of my hope to continue to succeed in the glory of God. But not only that, I even boast of my afflictions. I know that makes for endurance, and endurance for tested virtue for hope. And this hope will not leave me disappointed because the love of God has been poured out in my heart through the Holy Spirit. I was abounded with the hope of successfully capturing the apex, the highest grade, eighth grade in school, in no distant future. Fervently I prayed.

Chapter XIII "Education Pays"

My father had received the information that I was enlisted in the militia and by the end of that year I was promoted to the rank of a Battalion Sergeant Major assigned on the staff of the commanding officer of the First Infantry Battalion, Ninth Infantry Regiment, under the command of Joseph Itoka with headquarters at Nyaake.

The news was inspiriting and exciting for my father. When I arrived home late December, 1949, the village chief found it hard to express his surprise for my rapid promotion, having spent less than a year since my enlistment in the military force. "Shortly before the forced recruitment of laborers by the Liberian Frontier Force for the Island of Fernando Po Cocoa Plantation, we were asked to volunteer for enlistment in the Liberian Militia and unwillingly I was enrolled," my father vividly recalled. "Since then I remained a militiaman until the villages unanimously selected me to serve as town chief for the Trio Villages," the old soldier narrated. He continued, "I could not be chief and a soldier at the same time and so I deliberately retired myself. Failure to perform military duty for practice or parade as prescribed by law, I was often delinquent and a muster-fine collector harassed me and robbed me of earned pennies and farthings frequently, not realizing that I was commander in chief of the militiamen of the villages under my chieftaincy," the town chief declared. "They forgot to know that I was the founding member of the Fourth Infantry Company, Fourth Infantry Battalion, Fourth Infantry Regiment with headquarters in Harper, Maryland County, Liberia. The Company was known as Yancy Volunteers in honor of Allen Yancy, then Vice President of Liberia. I performed regular military duty when we attained Battalion status and subsequently I was called to serve my government and country in another capacity," the village government official gave the historical background of the origin of the militia organization in Nyaake and yea the vast Webbo District. "For about ten long years I drilled as an enlisted man until in the mid-1930s when President Edwin Barclay was making his first official visit through the hinterland to the Webbo District for the first time, I was designated a corporal to go to Biabo to arrest all militiamen who had failed to assemble at Nyaake, the usual rendezvous to perform military duty for their commander in chief. Of course that was a temporal assignment; as soon as the delinquent militiamen were brought I had no non-commissioned rank again. That was long before I brought you into the world," the young father concluded.

Why were the villagers of Kablake jubilating when they learned that their son Kpaye Kamma was promoted to the fifth grade? Was it a considerably high attainment? If you were a member of the living society of Liberia then, your answer would have been a mighty Y-E-S. Many of the government functionaries had eighth grade maximum attainment in education, which they gloriously claimed "Standard Eighth." In the hinterland, it was worse if not ridiculous. Illiteracy ravaged the countryside. Some of my teachers in the Webbo District School were below Standard Three education. Their output was marvelous and puzzling.

I could not help but to think with that prolific sixteenth-century English writer, dramatist, poet, sonneteer, William Shakespeare, when in his tragedy-comedy, *The Merchant of Venice*, through a character, he declared admirably, "I have not seen so young a body with so old a head." In like vein, praiseworthily and admirably of my grade teachers I said emphatically, "I have not seen a group of people with so little knowledge of formal education and who gave such vast knowledge to their pupils." Our teachers had comparatively small formal education and no teacher education at all, yet they were masters in their own right because of their profound dedication, devotion and sacrifice for their needy brothers and sisters.

What our people feared originally appeared to be happening. Since my promotion to the fifth grade I did not like to spend much time in Kablake. "We must not allow our children to go to school because when they become educated they will not be our children again but Mleyaun, the old people cautioned.

Mr. Mle was the Grebo chief who welcomed the freed slaves from America in Cape Palmas. The freed slaves were widely called in most of Southeastern Liberia as the people of Chief Mle since indeed he welcomed them to that part of the Grain Coast. My people, whom the freed slaves ignorantly called native people or heathens, strongly held, therefore, that if their children were educated by these freed slaves they would put their own children against them, the derisively-called natives or heathens. If my parents and their fellow village dwellers presumed this in my case, the presumption was unwarranted. I love my parents particularly and my indigenous people generally. I just wanted to be closer to the book learning so that I would achieve my goal in time without faltering. Another reason was that I hated the very intruding presence of some members of the Liberian Frontier Force who frequented the villages to forcibly recruit porters to carry their cargoes to Camp King, a military installation in Wropake, Barrobo Chiefdom, Webbo District, Eastern Province, Liberia. Like the beasts of burden, these porters carried these overweight loads without pay through the long winding paths, some impassable in some places. With their old rustic Belgian rifles slanting across their backs covered with tattered khaki shirts, these armed men demanded and collected food from those who had to carry their cargoes to Barrobo.

As I was being slowly enlisted and gathering some years I came to detest the nuisances who nefariously treated their so-called native people. To avoid them I thought to stay away from my home village and get ready for my future that would earn me the power to keep those roving armed men abase all my life. Before me was Kablake always gloried as my dear home, sweet home. There is no place like home.

In early January 1950, I stole out of the village and rushed back to Nyaake to do a small vacation job with Itoka and Sons Merchandise Trading Company. Mr. Felix Michael Itoka, the manager of the business, had long caught my love and admiration for him. He was my role model. I thought working with him directly would help me to copy him, if possible exactly. I spent the rest of the vacation months with him in the store. I received two yards of cloth as my pay for my service rendered Mr. Itoka in the store.

My brief stay with Mr. Itoka gave him certain credence in his heart for me. He keenly observed my skill in arithmetic and decided to employ me during the year to take inventory of his trading posts that dotted the countryside. In July 1950, Mr. Itoka sent me on my first assignment to the Firestone Rubber Cavalla Plantations Company to deliver tens of thousands of tons of rice bought from the Webbo District.

The huge consignment was transported to Firestone by way of paddled canoes on the winding Cavalla River. I tramped the straggling paths to the plantations. When the rice arrived at the Gbolobo wharf, it was from there the company took delivery of the nutritious rice. The company issued me a receipt in the name of Itoka and Sons.

At another time in the year, I was dispatched for inventory duty to Taryake, Nyenebo, Nyenebo Clan, Gedebo Chiefdom. Dogbyou Toe, a grand polygamist with ten beautiful young wives, all in their teens and himself on the threshold of debilitating middle age, was the agent at the post. He and his wives were hospitably generous as they received me in the honorable Grebo tradition. A huge rooster was slaughtered and prepared in the most cherished and palatable dish, Grebo palm butter, for the reception. With this sumptuous reception in my honor, it would not ingratiate but rather paint me ungrateful had I conducted the inventory on the same day of the reception. Delay was, therefore, absolutely necessary. Into business we went the next day.

The only thing my hospitable host was able to do for the inventory was to display the invoices of the stock received and the receipts obtained when he delivered produce to the manager in Nyaake. He could not help himself, neither could he help me in sorting out the invoices and receipts. Patiently I went through them and posted them accordingly. The next day I found my way back to the district headquarters. Mr. Itoka was pleased again with the inventory. Both agents were in troubled water. Their inventory sheets proved beyond all reasonable doubt that they were miserably short; they sent little produce against the many goods received. Did Reverend Andrews succeed well in imparting his old cash account tricks to his student?

With Fish and Salt gone, Palm butter and Rice were lonesomely promoted to the seventh grade. We were like human bodies without life. Our sweet lasses had left us in the wilderness. Our class without our girls, our social and academic partners, would spell meaningless. Would this be a crisis? Perhaps not!

Did Principal Andrews make us wizards and witches at numbers during the year as he desired the previous year? By what standard could we be measured now? But I thought in a very satisfying degree the old bookkeeper immensely accomplished much with us. In the whole school only the members of our class had mastered the multiplication tables from two to twelve and other arithmetical tricks, which enormously enhanced our mental capacities. By the end of the year we were rigidly required to learn the multiplication tables from thirteen to twenty-five times.

On these we drilled as usual because the old teacher emphasized that to acquire rapid speed in adding numbers and other arithmetical tricks with numbers, the mastery of multiplication tables is the prerequisite, and so their mastery is a must. Must it was with that man from the old school, where the authority of the teacher entertained no argument from the students. In the seventh grade, Peter and I met three retained students.

Following the untimely death of our young and energetic new supervisor of Eastern Province schools, Professor Isaac Himie Wesley, the former Cape Palmas High School principal, Professor Henry Nyema Prowd was ushered in by the Liberian Government. According to those old Cuttington College and Divinity School young men, the college disintegrated and fell apart, leaving them uncrowned in their senior year for their many hard and long years of their academic pursuit. In our school was Teacher Joseph N. Washington, their former classmate. These old friends found themselves together again. Would their reunion in the school be a hopeful sign for the wholesome development and improvement of the school? Supervisor Prowd and Principal Andrews appeared not to have anything in common except they were human beings. Reverend Andrews tended not to hurt people and Mr. Prowd was the extreme opposite. What would this marked difference in the attitude of both men give to the school?

Frequently the supervisor visited the Webbo District School and each time he came in he heaped insults on our tolerant principal. The students began to feel repugnant about his unbecoming attitude towards our principal. He never called the principal into conference so as to discuss what he saw as wrong in the school, but rather as soon as he entered he would rap on the blackboard, saying, "Principal Andrews, you don't want to hurt anybody, yet you hurt everybody. See how your school is so disorganized." At this vituperative pronouncement from a man in a high authority the students were always terrified. Nearly all his visits were marked with this kind of unnecessary disturbance.

Realizing that the students did not honor his presence in the school any longer, he stole in every morning to teach seventh grade English grammar. Knowing how brutal he was with his mouth, I prayed to my God to make more studious than ever before. From all indications, the God of earnest seekers tripled my voracious study habits. In grammar, Mr. Prowd taught the conjugations of verbs, comparisons of adjectives and adverbs, and parsing. We had a litany of these every day. Those who did not know the tunes of these everyday songs were brutally lashed by the supervisor. All in all, his approach and angry appearance in class intimidated the slow students and inhibited the learning process.

Mr. Prowd continued his kicking of Reverend Andrews around. This barbarous behavior of Mr. Prowd towards Reverend Andrews became the talk of the hilly town. Subsequently, the African Methodist Episcopal Church, Cape District Presiding Elder, Reverend William Taylor White, visited with us his members at the Yancy Memorial A.M.E. Church in Nyaake, where Reverend Andrews was serving as Pastor. At a Sunday worship service at the church where nearly all the leading men and women, including Supervisor Prowd, assembled to hear the renowned preacher, Reverend White preached. "Touch not my anointed and do my prophet no harm," Reverend White loudly and calmly drew the attention of his eagerly awaiting congregation. Briefly he expounded and at last he said, "Reverend Joseph W. Andrews is a stout man in the Lord's vineyard. He does not carouse; he is not interested in material things; his ambitions are not vaulting; he waits for his time," the reverend gentleman enumerated. "Why should people in authority humiliate such a fine gentleman?" the presiding elder asked.

In school the next day, Monday, in his usual fiery manner, dressed in khaki long sleeves shirt and trousers, the Eastern Province school boss rushed into the open hall school building with the students grouped here and there according to grades. He took his stand on the platform and then rapped vigorously on the blackboard, calling the attention of the principal. Instead, the whole attention of the school was arrested as all at once faced where their khaki-clad supervisor was standing and calling the principal. "And so Mr. Andrews, you complained me to your presiding elder because I do my job the best way I know it?" Supervisor Prowd demanded. He continued, "And because of that he tried to intimidate me, intimidate me where, in the pulpit?" He added, "But remember, I am the only living child of my mother." With this, he burst into tears, and with head bowed he lingered out of the school. Following his exit, Reverend White walked in after receiving a rousing obeisance from the students agitated by the rude manner of their supervisor. In a fatherly tone he implicitly began, "When I came to live in Harper, your principal and supervisor were shirt tail boys. I remember when little Henry came on his aunt's errand to me for some small help. I mean they were all little boys, the old school master revealed. "If you are not a drunkard, can the public saying that you are a drunkard makes you a drunkard?" the reverend gentleman asked and then departed.

Unwillingly, Teacher Kun let go his arithmetic class with us to the principal. "You killed my spirit for teaching arithmetic when I was without this Nyepon and Reeves class. Won't you oblige me by giving the class that challenges me?" Teacher Kun pleaded with the principal. "Au..au..waka to say, .. Cha.. You bad of...au teacher, you may have your darling class," the jovial principal waived the class to his favorite lieutenant.

The American arithmetic textbooks did not promote our ambition and skill in arithmetic well. Versed in English shilling arithmetic, Mr. Kun at once plunged us into complex fractions, simple interest, compound interest, simple and compound proportions, etc., etc. With our multiplication tables at our fingertips, Peter the Great of Gbeapo and William the Conqueror of Gedebo were highly challenged and propelled. Headlong, Peter and I studied harder and progressively. The rough sailing drowned two of our mates. The mad waves seized them bodily and dumped them overboard. The academic demise of our comrades did not frighten us, neither did it deter us. But rather in unison we cried, "In the battlefield of life, be a hero." And so we girded our armors. During this excited and troubled year, William Reeves was a black sheep again. Late one afternoon, I was sitting in a windowsill, reading a Liberian history pamphlet's introductory note which said in part, "Expurgate where necessary," when Teacher Peter C. Newton suddenly entered the dormitory and said to me, "The supervisor wants you to send six benches to the District Council Hall just now." "Just now?" I unbelievably asked, because all the boarding boys were scattered here and there, studying for tomorrow's test. "I mean just now," the seemingly angry teacher replied and disappeared from my sight.

I gathered six boys and we were dispatched with the benches in no time. After the boys left with the benches I was summoned by the principal. I went over to him. "Teacher Newton told me that you gave him cheek a few minutes ago when he told you that you should send six benches to the hall, upon the directive of the supervisor of schools, au..au..du..waka to say, is that correct?" the principal inquired. "No, sir," I replied in astonishment. "Perhaps he thought that I was speaking to him, but I was reading some passage that said, 'Expurgate where necessary,' when he suddenly entered the dormitory." "Au..au..waka to say, the man said you gave him cheek. You must be punished tomorrow in school," the old teacher delivered his usual rash decree. It would appear that the principal was not convinced that I disrespected the teacher but no doubt Mr. Newton hauled that fabricated lie to Mr. Prowd, whom the principal feared, and so true or not, William Reeves must be punished. The next day I received twelve hard cuts on my rump.

A teacher performed this laborious task. Would this dissuade me from attaining the highest peak in this school? Inwardly I sang,

> Serene I fold my hands and wait,
> I fear no wind, nor tide or sea,
> I rave no more 'gainst time nor fate,
> For lo, my own shall come to me.

With these didactics, victory would come in no distant future. At the end of the year, the three of us, Peter Nyepon, Fred Toequie, and I mounted and reached the summit, but would we be honored when the sun goeth down?

Were those native boys recruited from the villages around the Webbo District being properly educated and christianized also? As a matter of fact, many of us, if not all of us, were Christians before the recruitment. Although our parents were forest dwellers, many of them were true Christians, being bright lights in the wilderness.

Under Reverend Henry Bagbo Wilson, we were churchgoers at the Protestant Episcopal Church in Kodeke No.1. Our principal was the rector and he delivered his long sermons in both English and Grebo every Sunday. As we understood but little English, we were bored. But if you nodded your head during these windy sermons you would be punished for sleeping in church in school the next day, Monday. To avoid this wanton punishment, each student smeared his fingertip with hot pepper to awaken himself by rubbing the pepper-smeared fingertip to his eyelid. This kept one wide awake.

When Mr. Randolph W. Harmon became principal, we worshipped at the same church where Mr. Harmon was a lay reader. The principalship of Mr. Joseph W. Andrews won us over to the Yancy Memorial A.M.E. Church pastored by the principal. We thought Reverend Wilson was long, windy, and boring, but Reverend Andrews, stammering, quoted passages from every book and chapter of both the Old and New Testaments. He was more windy and boring and unknowingly licensed us to take siesta during his unending deliberations. From the beginning we listened and gathered some useful lessons, anyway. At last I discovered my Tenzonke Church, where the Reverend William Taylor White baptized me and named me "William" after his own name, saying, "I want you to be like me."

One of our happiest events in the Webbo District School was our annual serenading. Singing, the students went from door to door of nearly every home in Nyaake, especially homes where we were sure we could collect some pennies from the owners. This annual extracurricular activity was always well organized beforehand. Speakers at each door were carefully selected. I was a very active participant in this nocturnal loose gathering of students, which grossly encouraged flirting. I was unanimously selected to speak at the door of one of my most outstanding role models, Mr. Edmond Bradsford Gibson, a slim, tall handsome young man with cat eyes, then Webbo District Clerk.

According to the prepared list for our uninvited visits to those homes, Mr. Gibson's name ranked second after the district commissioner. At a home, the school usually sang a hymn that was the family's favorite. Special research was done long before the execution of the program on which the school heavily relied to raise money for the annual picnic. When we arrived at the home of Mr. and Mrs. Gibson, we met him sitting with his chin resting in his left palm and his wife sitting opposite him. The widely sung Christian hymn, "Blessed Assurance, Jesus is Mine," greeted the Gibsons. It was then my turn to greet the family on behalf of the school and in my own name to tell them why we chose to visit them.

With his chin still heavily resting in his palm, strongly supported by his elbow placed on his thigh in a soft cushion chair, Mr. Gibson appeared to be listening. Briefly I charmed the honorable district clerk with few words that put him high on the school and political ladder of the district and the township of Nyaake, Webbo. In reply, Mr. Gibson solemnly asked, "Have you seen stars in the noonday?" The rhetorical question hushed all of us into an unbelievable silence rarely experienced among youngsters. After a few minutes Mr. Gibson, with his hands away from his chin and sitting erect and speaking louder and distinctly, asked again, "Have you seen stars in the noonday?" It was like a bombshell again. The question was very puzzling to us; we were standing in darkness, except in front of Mr. Gibson was a burning lantern that was dimmed almost to quench. In astonishment we shook our heads and finally we cried out, "No sir." The students were lost in wonderland. Beholding, we wanted the elder to clear the cloud of no understanding that hovered about us.

Suddenly, Mr. Gibson relieved us when he declared, "I was about twelve or less years old when my father died, leaving my mother with little children, including me. I was the second oldest of us. All needed close attention, care, and tender support, but from whom? At that tender age of mine I was compelled to leave school in order to help my elder brother, who was not much older than I was, for support of our fatherless family. Many of you are blessed to be in school at your ages. I wish I had the time like yours." Mr. Gibson concluded. I admired and envied Mr. Gibson secretly.

I thought he was one of the most educated men of the district and the most elegantly dressed man in the town. Particularly I liked the way he wore his wristwatch and the way he swung his umbrella. Up to date I wear my wristwatch and swing my umbrella in his fashion. Mr. Gibson's brief remarks were touching. In essence, Mr. Gibson implicitly told us that he had no formal education, but yet from my personal admiration and keen observation of him, I thought Mr. Gibson was well educated, at least he had some formal education. Perhaps he gathered his own knowledge from reading many and varied avenues of generating sources of knowledge. He was always with Time Magazine. With but little education, comparatively, Honorable Edmund Bradsford Gibson, after working at many odd jobs, began life as a craftsman, a bricklayer, road overseer, district clerk, assistant county commissioner, district commissioner, county inspector, member of the House of Representatives of the Liberian Legislature, and later member of the Liberian Senate and major in the Liberian militia, Ninth Infantry Regiment. (Just a bird's eye view of the distinguished background of my role model).

Nyaake particularly and the Webbo District generally provided the wholesome environment for us the country boys to grow educationally and morally well.

My friendship with the Itokas grew steadily and it nearly engulfed all the members of that large family. It began with Mr. Felix Michael Itoka, General Manager of Itoka and Sons, Inc. The fire caught their generous and gracious mother, Mrs. Elizabeth K. Itoka, popularly called Dada, Veronica Itoka-Harmon, the only girl in the family, Joe, Jr., Aloysius, a personal friend of mine, Mr. Gabriel P. Itoka and his wife, Lois Grant-Itoka, and my gracious and generous parents and teachers. These generous and solicitous friends enlivened and encouraged me to be part of them every day. My close association too with this family gratifyingly and immensely enhanced my academic and social growth in Nyaake, making Nyaake immortal and the memory outstanding and everlasting.

Jiggers had defiantly declared an all out toe-mutilating war against the teenagers of the township. It appeared that my feet were naturally immune from whatever the wingless belligerents used to mutilate toes. Seeing how fierce the war was raging, Mr. B.K. Itoka offered me a pair of saddles to help to defend my toes against the wingless bloodsuckers.

Webbo Military Brass Band was busily engaged in preparing for the second inauguration of President William V. S. Tubman. Major Gabriel Gadegbeku, the instructor of the band, wanted to revamp it by bringing in some advanced students from the school. Peter and I with other boys were selected. It was early in 1951, our senior year, eighth grade by now. For one or two months we attended intense practice. One day we went to the band practice, and it seemed the older and the most experienced bandmen were not coming that day or they would be late. They came, but were unusually late. Many of them were my father's age. The presenters each took charge of his instrument and began to tune it. In that time the elderly people arrived. Old Man Gadegbeku was blue. He ordered that one of them in particular should be given some cuts in his palm. "Reeves, give that man five hard lashes for being late," the band instructor ordered. He turned about face and disappeared. Mr. B.K. Itoka, the band master, overheard this instruction to me and he hailed me at once to go over to the place where he was sitting. "I heard the old man telling you to give that man five lashes in his hand. Don't try it," he warned. "If you lash that man, in the next few days or weeks, your skin, your whole body, that is, will be covered with leprosy. If you want it, then do it," he continued. I was horrified. In fact, seeing the old man, I could not ever gather that kind of courage to lash my own father, as it were. I did not make the least attempt. I had no intention at all. But I was grateful to Mr. Itoka for saving my young life from that destructive ancient disease. But why did Mr. Gadegbeku order me, a novice in the band and one of the youngest in the group, to lash the hoary haired man? At another time, Mr. B. K. Ikota noticed me wiping my left ear. With concern, he asked, "What is that?" "Pus. For this school business, my father slapped me once and this caused me this trouble; pus runs from my ear sometimes," I explained to my concerned friend. "Wait for me, I want to do something," Mr. Itoka offered. He left and returned in a split second with some green

58

grass squeezed with his fingers and asked me to show him the infected ear. I did, and he squeezed the juice of that stuff into the ear. This is the lifesaving and generous memory I keep of my benefactor, Mr. Boniface K. Itoka of the hilly Township of Nyaake, Webbo.

Since 1947 no student or students had attained eighth grade. This year, 1951, the school was being blessed and honored with eighth grade students, three boys in all, young men hoping to be pronounced graduates at the end of the year. In the eighth grade the principal introduced the two new ugly subjects, algebra and Latin, a dead language, as he told us when he introduced the subjects. As we saw it, algebra was another form of arithmetic, except it carried funny forms, figures and letters mating together and letters wearing figures on their heads, sometimes read squares, cubes or powers. That appeared very absurd, didn't it? We murmured among ourselves, "What do we want with a dead language? Truly, this man is an ancient teacher, a real out-of-date type," the prospective graduates scorned the poor old man. What did we expect to benefit from the newly added subjects, strange and ugly as they were? "We must apply ourselves fully in studying them understandingly," the seniors for the year urged themselves on. With our unshaken trust and high hope in God, the giver of honest gifts, the class briskly and dauntlessly embarked upon our studies for our last and most important leg on our sojourn in the Webbo District School.

Peter and I did not know how it happened. In the afternoon, one rainy day, the BIG TWO rushed to downtown Nyaake for the band practice. "Peter and Reeves, you are excused from taking part in the band altogether as of today's date. We want you to fully concentrate your whole time on your studies. Your success will surely be a source of happiness for those of us who helped to mold you throughout these laborious and sometime stormy years being spent within the walls of the Webbo District School. My committee and I wish you in advance a successful school year and may the end of the journey be crowned with victory," Mr. Gadegbeku, the band instructor and chairman of our school committee, plaintively announced. We thanked our NI sincerely and we jogged to our campus perched on a steep hill over towered by Mount Chelo. It was learned later that the supervisor of schools had intervened on our behalf to discontinue the band practice. Our grateful thanks and appreciation were extended to the supervisor for his timely intervention. The habit of reading frequently outside of my school subjects slowly but steadily took hold of me. In those days, newspapers and supplementary reading materials were non-existent in our part of the Liberian world, while even textbooks were scantily supplied. But that did not quench my reading thirst. I thought it was as true with money as it was with knowledge. It doesn't matter where the readable material is obtained, the knowledge gathered from it won't bite the gatherer. Literature is timeless. I plundered for reading materials in every corner and nook of the township. One blessed day, somebody gave me a book which was old but very readable. The book told about the various vocations and avocations of the world. Two professions, legal and medical, appealed to my appetite. In few sentences the author described the legal and medical professions and what it entailed to acquire either of them. Among other things, the author emphatically stressed that it was absolutely necessary to be well grounded in languages like Greek, Hebrew, and Latin. "Latin included?" frighteningly and inaudibly I queried. At once

I resolved to do my best in the study of Latin as I wanted to be a lawyer or a medical doctor. My ambition was set ablaze, thinking and hoping that my early exposure to Latin in the grade school would adequately prepare me for either of the two famous professions, God willing.

Reverend Andrews regularly drilled us in figures called powers placed on the heads of letters and his dead language declensions with its numerous cases, while Teacher Kun labored us vigorously with Unitary Method in solving problems in simple and compound proportions. The war was on and the battles raged day in and day out! To us the year was moving on a snail's back, dragging its feet, as it were. What happened? Can't you move? For me, it was a weary wait. Tired one night, I did not prepare my Latin lesson for the next day. The period for Latin came and Reverend Andrews crawled in. "Reeves, decline the Latin word Puella, meaning girl, singular and plural of each case," the dead language instructor directed. Not prepared and out of frustration I saucily asked one of my most well meaning teachers, "What benefit will I get from studying this dead language? You told us the language was spoken in Rome. Would I ever go to Rome?" I derided the poor teacher. For a long unusual pause, the principal painfully forced a smile and then said, "Au..au..waka to say, it is before; it is not behind you." What was the cause of this untimely obstinate behavior of mine? I regretted it wholeheartedly. I took it to the Lord in prayer and implored his forgiveness.

Over the years, Peter the Great of Gbeapo and William the Conqueror of the Gedebo had ardently and assiduously been wrestling neck to neck for the first place in class. The end of this year would cease the perennial rivalry. Utmost in my mind was this burning and protruding question: To whom will the first place in class go this last year of our sojourn? We were told that the first place in class in the last grade in the school bore a magnificent denotation; instead of being called a "Dux," it is magnificently called valedictorian. Wa-o!

In October the school began to wind up the work for the year. We were busily engaged preparing for what they happily called GRADUATION. Sources close to the regular faculty meeting, in a don't-tell-anybody tone, said that the program for the auspicious occasion was tentatively being made ready while our respective scores in each subject were being calculated to determine the ranks in class. How long would that take? For nine long years we yearned for a remarkable one. Was it loitering? We wanted it galloped! One fine day in summer, the arithmeticians of the school presented the grade report to the principal, the old bookkeeper and man versed in calculations. Needless to say, he scrutinized the report and finally he affixed his official signature, signifying his approval. The next day, the prospective graduates were arrayed in the principal's office for announcement of their verdict, following our indictment and trial. Silently we gazed at the Principal. "Au...au..waka to say, you bad of.... Are you afraid? Au.. Afraid or what?" Reverend Andrews kept us in heartbreaking suspense. At last a broad smile swept over the wrinkled face of the principal and he started to call our roll according to rank in ascending order. As we were only three young men in our class, when the principal named the first and second boys, I was very sure then that the first place was definitely and positively mine. Our race in the classroom was over. Webbo District School had breathtakingly waited for four long years to celebrate its second graduation. "School picnic will be followed by graduation on November 18, 1951," the Reverend Joseph Wodo Andrews, principal of the Webbo District School, proudly declared. A whirlwind of jubilation engulfed the countryside school.

At the Webbo District School the seniors had a distinguished place. This year it was very special for them. On the spur of a moment, seeing no teacher around, a senior boy would take control of the school. In this responsible atmosphere we were led year in, year out.

When we the seniors had our full grip on our studies and voiced openly what they called "excellent performance," the students publicly referred to us as gods of the year. Leisurely the three of us walked to school each day. As we glided up the stairway ascending into the long open hall school, on sight, a student would loudly announce, "The gods are ascending!" The students then made their obeisance to the seniors, their rich source of academic aspiration and inspiration. This was their spontaneous order of the day. Were we gods? No! Not in the least. It was only the general human tendency, ascribing or making human deity.

Our "New Idea," Old Man Gadegbeku, paid a surprise visit to give us some story, seemingly a real life situation: "A regiment of soldiers was sent into warfare. After battling with the enemy for several days, their number was considerably reduced. In the meantime, the regiment made significant gains too, and so the commander and the officers agreed to advance. In this light, the commander dispatched a verbal message to general command headquarters and the message said, "Sir, send us reinforcement, we are going to advance." After traveling by many mouths and many days, the unwritten message finally reached the headquarters to say, "Please send us two shillings and six pence, we are going to have a dance."

"Did the original message mention anything about money or dance?" NI inquired. "I want to tell you as you go into the world, a school without blackboards and teachers, don't do any serious business verbally," the prolific storyteller advised.

In the over packed edifice of the Yancy Memorial African Methodist Episcopal Church, the students and faculty of the Webbo District School, with the officials and other distinguished invitees, and the public in general, congregated themselves to witness the second graduation exercise of the school. The commencement speaker was no other than the forceful speaker, Honorable J. Richard Garnette, Revenue Agent for the Webbo District. My father was in attendance too, without my mother, who since 1942 paid her first and only visit during my stay at Nyaake. The honorees of the night, the graduates, were perched on three wooden chairs placed side by side. Dressed in well tailored light green striped blue suits, the school leavers listened as the items of the program interspersed with the items each of us had to perform were being rendered. Senior Fred D. Toequie delivered the brief class history. It was followed by the salutatorian, Senior Peter C. Nyepon, a great speaker, and then came the valedictorian, Senior William K. Reeves, who took the stand. "It took us nine stormy and rocky years to attain this height tonight. As I know as well as you do, the journey was not all stormy or rocky, it was also blissful and challenging. And challenged we were. And therefore, we need a watchword, carefully chosen from among the many useful words, a word that would propel, enliven, and encourage us daily, of the English language. PERSEVERANCE was our unanimous choice and Thorndike or Webster defines it briefly as follows: Sticking to a purpose or an aim; never giving up what one has set out to do. With God leading and guarding our way, we persevered to capture this which we gloriously claimed a noble height. My dear students, I would therefore advise you to have a cause to achieve or die for. Goodbye my good friends. Keep the torch of education burning. To the honorable district and township commissioners, our fathers, the paramount chiefs and clan chiefs, elders and people with our mothers, their wives, in the name of our graduates and in my own name, I say a big thank you to all of you. I sincerely and earnestly ask to continue to provide the means by which our brothers and sisters will get the benefit of education." I bowed and majestically walked away to my seat.

Following the introduction of the Guest speaker, Mr. Garnette moved forward to the speaker's stand. A stocky middle-aged man with cross eyes, seemingly very educated, the Honorable Garnette aired, "I want to speak to you on the theme of education on this unique, auspicious, and historic occasion. The word education is derived from two Latin stems, educo and decare, I put in and draw out."

"Another etymologist?" I whispered to my colleagues. "Depict the glory of Webbo District; I have depicted the glory of Edina, Grand Bassa County," the commencement speaker alerted his eagerly listening audience. "What have you put in, and what will you draw out?" the learned speaker questioned. He went rambling and dangling here and there for about twenty-five long weary minutes. I could not and did not get anything out of what the Revenue Agent was saying. "If this is what they call education, then I believe we have not begun learning," frustratingly I murmured to my friends. Teacher Lois and Teacher Gabriel adopted me as their son in Nyaake. Both of them were teachers at the Webbo District School. Teacher Gabriel, the husband, popularly known within the walls of the school as So-fe-la, taught singing at our school, where Teacher Lois, his wife, was a regular teacher. This loving couple made Nyaake my home away from home. I would leave them and Nyaake my home at the end of the year. For me, words were too empty to express sufficiently my heartfelt thanks and appreciation for their tender love and care lavished on me many of those nine unbroken years. I prayed that my God would thank and shower his manifold blessings seasoned with his saving graces on them. In a very small way, could I show my thanks and appreciation in a concrete way?

My parents were made abreast of this generous couple's love and care for me each time I was on vacation in the village. I got my parents involved to get something as a token of appreciation to them. They suggested a billy goat and cups of rice when I visited with them while we were winding up things at the school.

After a few days absence from Nyaake I went to greet them when Teacher Lois revealed to me that she and her husband were planning to honor me with a dinner party for my graduation. "Teacher, why should you continue to deprive yourselves of life just to help or please me?" I cajoled. "It gives us joy to do that for you for your endurance and courage," chuckling, the young lady rejected. "My parents would like to send you some rice and a billy goat. Perhaps those could help you with your dinner party in honor of your son. Don't you think so?" I pressed her. "Gabriel will decide; come later," the housewife brushed me aside. The next day, I met them at their home and Mr. Itoka sanctioned my suggestion. When my father came in for the big occasion, the things he brought according to our understanding were turned over to Mrs. Itoka. On the day following the graduation, the grand party, with a variety of palatable kwi[3] and African dishes, jolof rice not being left out, was held in the beautifully decorated yard of their home near Nyaake proper. Wholeheartedly I thanked my benefactors, Gabriel and Lois Itoka, who, over the years, tendered me their love and care, crowned with this luxurious party singularly honoring me.

It was all over for me in Nyaake. The pertinent question was, where would I go next? My going to Kablake was understood, but for how long? My next course of action was mapped out. But as I knew it, I had the will but no way. The financial support was completely lacking. My parents were only peasant farmers, who did not produce adequately to feed themselves. Some years they got nothing from their drudgery. Strenuously each vacation they gave me four dollars to take care of my school needs, when I spent about two or three months with them each break. With this in the back of my mind, I went to Kablake to mark the end of my stay at the Webbo District Headquarters and the hilly Township of Nyaake, Webbo. On my way home, enthusiastic crowds in the network of villages through which I came on the snaky paths to the Trio villages headquarters, Kablake, greeted me laudably. In Kablake, the jubilant waiting crowd lifted me shoulder high. Of course, that was no problem because the heavy weight was never there. The village loaded me with palm butter chop every day, hoping to get me to gain a few pounds in weight, but to no avail as usual. At the end of the Christmas festivities that year, 1951, massive preparations for the graduation feast in my honor went underway. The first week in January, 1952, my father and mother, the power behind the screen, in conjunction with their respective clans, contributed copiously for the graduation feast. Tarnu Kpaye's clan delivered one nanny goat, rice, plenty of dried meat, and fish; Nyanweju Hinneh's clan, headed by my namesake, Myer Kamma, gave abundantly of rice, dried meat, fish, and a huge billy goat; my parents were ready with everything that would make the occasion meaningful and successful. A billy goat was their main contribution. Old Man Kamma chaired the meeting that put the finishing touches to the arrangements for the week-long festivities. According to the elaborate plan, the two billy goats would be slaughtered on the closing day of the feast. The nanny goat brought by my mother's people would be kept for my personal property. This was the elderly advice of the founder of London in the Gedebo country. Everything was followed to the letter. Drumming and dancing began in earnest, the people from all over the Gedebo country having congregated themselves in Kablake. They danced and they ate day in and day out. Never liking to dance and then a poor dancer, once a day I took a tread on the floor amidst cheers and laughers. On the last day, which was more or less a picnic day, after eating, the multitude of spectators gathered to witness the last item on the program, to hear the honoree. Under the handkerchief-waving young men and women, the honoree, dressed in his graduation suit, was escorted solemnly to his especially prepared seat. Briefly I thanked my elders, friends, relatives, and loved ones who accepted our invitation and came to our program. "The wind of change in the field of education sweeps over our group now. For this useful change to continue, I would ask all of you to pray fervently, ardently, and assiduously, and may it touch

63

every village and hamlet of our small, fertile, rich lands. With education acquired we will be able to harness the riches of our people and country. Mleyaun, the freed slaves from America, met us here in these forests, which our great ancestors spilled their blood to obtain. The land and everything herein are legally and morally ours. But since they are the offspring of those who were actually enslaved from here, let us accept them as our own. I think their calling us Natives, a word used ignobly to downgrade us, as emphasized in one of their preambles to their 1847 constitution, "The Native African bowing down before us....", is a gross ignorance on their part, a kind of ignorance that dispossesses them of the land we would brotherly share with them. Obviously, if they are not natives of this land, then it is crystal clear that they cannot claim ownership. At the graduation, the Honorable District Commissioner, Joseph Itoka, told us that comparatively, eighth grade education is no education. We were therefore strongly urged to continue on to the high school, which I must attend and finish, God being my keeper. Thank you again, my good people. I ask you to join me in saying a big thank you to my loving parents and others whose enormous sacrifice crowned me with victory." I prayed and bowed and then without a word I waved my hands in goodbye.

When the cheering, drumming, dancing, and eating stopped, what was next? "I think it is about time I should remind you that I must go to high school this year. Do you remember what the district commissioner told you the parents?" I asked my father. "Yes, but my son, I have no money. I cannot even buy a pair of trousers, let alone a coat for the requirement of the kind of clothes you must wear in high school. I want you to spend this year with us in the village and together we will work on our rice farm. After harvest, some of the rice will be sold and the proceeds we will be able to buy you your needs for high school next year. Let's put everything in God's hands," my father pleaded. "I know you don't have money and there is no way of getting it. The situation is sickening and depriving, but what can we do when the money is not here? I think the idea of working on the rice farm in order to get the money is good but it would mean little at the end of the day. If I stay in the village for about a year, having no contact with educated people, I would be placed at the losing end. Education requires constant contact with it or with those who have it. It is like okra. It is very slippery. It goes away from you just like that! Let me go to seek employment with the little education I think I have and maybe within a year I might be able to get some of the requirement. Let us try that because whether I get enough money or clothes for my high school requirement, no doubt, I will not lose plenty from my small education already acquired." I explained and pleaded with my impecunious father.

To suggest that I did not agree with my father to stay in the village to work on the rice farm so as to generate money for my going to high school was a disobedience to his fatherhood. He rushed out of the little room where we were holding our indoor tete-a-tete. A few minutes later he returned with the head of our clan, Myer Kamma. Seated, the elder asked, "What happened?" My father narrated what he told me and my response to him. "I think what he said makes sense because he knows more about what he told you than you and I do. Let him go," the patriarch uncompromisingly directed. Reluctantly my father yielded to his elder's advice. But why couldn't his own little boy acquiesce to his father's suggestions? Was the village boy Mleyaun already because of his education, and did he not want village life again?

My mother gathered fifty cups of rice and six dollars and my parents, with eyes draining tears, bade me goodbye. With the help of a carrier provided by my parents, I lingered out of Kablake, hoping all would go well with me in Pleebo, where I was going to seek employment. The journey from Kablake to Pleebo took me about two days.

Chapter XIV "Working My Way Through High School"

When I arrived in Pleebo, a large town perched on the edge of the Firestone Cavalla Rubber Plantations, with booming commercial businesses packed with some of the plantation workers in poorly constructed and unsanitary houses, I lodged in the home of my country man, Old Man Toe Davis, one of the long service workers of the rubber plantations.

Inquiring about employment possibility, I was told that a team of surveyors surveying a proposed highway from Pleebo in Maryland County to Tappita in Central Province was in town. I thought, perhaps, they would want to employ some workers. I wrote my application that day and delivered it in person. After reading my application in a schoolboy's legible and neat handwriting, the leader of the team told me that they did not need skilled workers at present but rather people who could use well the cutlass to cut the lines on the survey trails. My first day's attempt crushed me but I was not discouraged. As I headed for my lodging place, somebody hailed me. It was Mr. Kolee Neufville, a business man from Nyaake. When I reached him, he asked, "Kamma, what are you doing here? Aren't you supposed to be in high school now?" "I cannot enter high school this year because I don't have clothes to wear in high school. I am seeking employment from anybody who may need my service. I have just returned from the surveyors' house where I delivered my prepared application in person. Regrettably, I was informed that skilled workers would wait for now," I confided to Mr. Neufville. "Try Firestone Hospital or Central Site," the businessman suggested. I hung my head for a long while without saying a word. "Well, people tell me that Firestone is good on sacking their employees. I would rather not get into such an embarrassing situation, if I may say so," reluctantly, I narrated the hearsay. "That is not correct. Firestone does keep its employees on the job as long as they behave well. Quite recently, the company awarded expensive and durable wristwatches to employees, who, for twenty-five years rendered faithful services. The man in whose house you lodge was one of the honorees. Good behavior keeps you there while misbehavior dismisses you," Mr. Neufville advised.

Convinced, I rushed to the house to write an application at once. I personally handed it to a medical doctor at the hospital, who told me to call back the next day at nine o'clock in the morning. Of course, seven-thirty in the morning the next day found me waiting in the outpatient waiting room of the hospital. At about eight-thirty that morning, I heard a voice saying, "Who is William Reeves?" I answered, "Here am I." The messenger beckoned me into the corridor of the hospital with its sparkling floors. Another applicant went in with me. Standing in the endless corridor with my letter of application in her hand, reading, was a middle-aged woman. I was poorly dressed in old short trousers and a short-sleeved shirt, without shoes or sneakers. The other applicant, well dressed in well pressed trousers and a well tailored short-sleeved shirt, presented his letter of application.

On reading the well dressed young man's letter, she discovered that the young man was a sixth grade student. "No, sixth grade people have no place here," Mrs. Petersen rejected. Then directly she faced me with a striking question, "Where is your certificate showing that you completed the eighth grade?" There was no need to fear to tell the truth. Boldly but respectfully, I said, "I don't have it with me." But how do I know that you finished the eighth grade?" the medical director's wife questioned. "Since I have here with me that which gave it to me, why not try me?" I challenged her. "Well, wait for me," she said and disappeared. In a few minutes time she came, spinning like a top. Presenting the test written on the back of my application, smiling, she said, "Here are forty-five questions to be answered in forty-five minutes." She handed me a pen and pointed to a chair on which I sat to write the test. Would Mrs. Petersen prove her case against me? Let's see. Carefully I read the questions. Inwardly I confided to myself, "If this is what I must pass to get the job, with God guiding, I shall surely get it," heavily, I breathed out. My God leading the way, I started. After about twenty-five minutes of writing the test, I rested my pen. Mrs. Petersen came over to me and asked, "Are you through?" "I think I have done my best," I sincerely replied. "Your employment here largely depends on how well you perform on the test. If not, of course, the opposite will be yours," Mrs. Petersen warned. When she left I read over my answers and still I thought I had done my best. "Well, the result will tell," I hoped.

On her second call she snatched the test paper from the table. About ten minutes later, she came and grabbed me by my right wrist and whisked me off to the chief clerk's desk. "Take down his name, he comes to work tomorrow morning," she directed. Working hours at Firestone began promptly at seven sharp in the morning. By six-thirty the next day I was in the hospital, ready to work. At seven I was issued a uniform, a pair of white short trousers and a white short-sleeved shirt with a red cross sewed on the shirt pocket. I was assigned in the male general ward with about twenty-five beds. That morning when the chief clerk arrived on duty I was summoned to his office for him to tell me what I would earn per day. "Firestone starts you with twenty-eight cents a day," Mr. Thomas N. Williams, chief clerk, informed me. "What will I get at the end of a month with this very low wage?" I questioned myself to the hearing of nobody. "Do you mean that my total monthly earning will be eight dollars and forty cents?" I prayed. I went to my assigned place. Throughout the working day in the ward heartbrokenly I pondered. Thinking with that sixteenth century prolific English writer, William Shakespeare, I said, "Things without remedy should be done without regard. What is done is done."[4] There seemed to be no hope for entering high school next year as I had envisaged. Whatsoever it was, I accepted the employment without a word of dissatisfaction expressed to my employer.

Diligently I worked for that meager wage. Training on the job was announced. Nursing school in the hospital would be opened to all of the employees in nursing area in the hospital. Books were issued and promptly we began the study of the nursing arts under the supervisor, Mr. Samuel Wodo Natt. Every trainee assigned in the male ward was assigned to a patient to nurse. Nothing in the hospital enlivened it more than this exclusive assignment given each trainee. I took great delight in it as we had to observe the sick condition of the patient entrusted in our special care. On the nurse's sheet in the patient's chart carefully one had to record the day to day condition, improving or not improving. In the meantime, we practiced routine nursing such as taking pulse, respiration, blood pressure etc. Mrs. Mary Sandy, the head nurse, an old woman, seemingly in her late sixties, rigorously drilled us in these daily procedures. The making up of beds was an every minute thing in the ward. There were many ways of making up beds in different cases: a bedridden patient, an operated case, etc.

Our shift schedule ran fortnightly. But during my first one month at the job I was kept on the morning shift. In the second month when the schedule changed, my shift sent me on evening duty at the same ward. While we were busy tending the patients one evening, the towering medical director of the hospital, Dr. Egon R. Petersen, walked in. He sat at the nurse's desk and began to peruse through the patients' charts. All of a sudden he called, "Mr. Natt, who is William Reeves?" When I heard the question I was shocked, thinking, maybe he wants to sack me. Instead of moving towards him I tried to sneak into the bathroom. The supervisor spotted me and called me at once. Frightened, I doddered towards them. The doctor looked me up and down with his piercing cat eyes, and then queried, "Are you the William Reeves?" "Yes doctor," I replied. I had mustered some courage to answer in a pleasant voice, seeing some pleasing sign on his white face. "Very good," the medical boss observed. He then got up and briskly walked out of the ward. When the doctor left, silence gripped the supervisor and I was lost in contemplation. I guessed that the doctor found my name written on one of the nurses' sheets in the patients' charts. The question was, why did he single me out? Certainly there were the names of other trainees who attached their names to their respective patients' charts. His singling me out suggested what? Anxiously I wanted these pertinent questions answered. I did not want guessed answers that could probably multiply my biting anxiety. And so I silently took it to the Lord in prayer:

"My Lord Jesus Christ, is the game over? Does this prove me right about my fear I mentioned to Mr. Kolee Neufville? But my dear Lord, whatsoever it is, please keep me on this poorly paying job as it is often said that half a loaf is better than no bread," I prayed. The doctor's facial expression on seeing my name sealed on the nurses' sheet in my assigned patient's chart augured[5] well for me. After looking at my patient's chart, the doctor sanctioned, sealed, and delivered his impression about my nurse's sheet in these meaningful words: "Very good." With this I took courage and went back to nurse my patient.

At the end of that fortnight, when the schedule changed, I was continued on the evening shift. This time I had a new boss, Mr. Robert Mensah. Our respective assignments in the ward remained intact. Each trainee was encouraged to read carefully and understandingly the nurse's Routine Manual every day at one's leisure. As reading was already my hobby I found no problem with that. The evening shift actually gave me the ample time to chew the booklet up. On a Sunday or holiday, the evening shift team was split into two teams including the nurses, trainees, and the supervisor, each working four hours instead of the normal eight hour period a day. I was alone on team two of the evening shift on a Sunday or holiday, completing the evening shift full time. The first team came for the first four hours. One Sunday, the very first time I would be alone in the ward, I came to work early enough to take over for the first team. The supervisor strongly suggested that I must follow routinely the nurse's manual. Well at home with the manual, I had no problem. On the job I did everything in line with the nurse's manual. When the full evening shift team met on

Monday, I did not know that I had done, or failed to do, something on my lone assignment on that Sunday, the day before. Without a word to me about his discovered task I did not perform, my supervisor, Mr. Mensah, complained to Doctor Petersen because I failed to do what, according to him, the task requires of the person or persons on the split shift. The chief clerk ordered me to his office to show Firestone why I failed to carry out an assigned task. "The doctor wants to know why you did not take the pulse, respiration, and temperature of each patient in the male ward!" the clerk demanded. "Sir, I did nothing wrong according to the nurse's Routine Manual," I asserted. "Do you know exactly what to do on duty during your period according to the manual?" Mr. Williams pressed me. "Certainly, I do know exactly what the manual requires of me or any other person on that split shift," I emphasized. "Can you show me your ground in the manual?" the chief clerk searched. "Yes, sir," confidently, chuckling, I replied. I went for the manual from the nurses' desk in the male ward and showed him my solid ground, which was not sinking sand. Surprisingly convinced, after my ground was shown him, that a comparatively newly employed worker had done well his duty, shaking his head, Mr. Williams said to me, "Get back to the ward and do your work." Later in the day, Mr. Mensah and I were called by the chief clerk, Mr. Mensah dragging himself with his big belly like a woman nine months gone while I made few strides to the office. "Did you inquire from this boy why he failed, according to you, to do on duty what the manual requires him or any other person on that shift?" The chief clerk interrogated. "I did not ask him," Mr. Mensah let the hog poopoo out. Mr. Williams smeared him with the stinky mess. "You shamed the hospital this morning by complaining your under worker without investigating or inquiring from him why he did not completely carry out his assigned task," Mr. Williams regretted. "You have worked for the hospital for twenty unbroken years and it seems you do not know a thing about the nurse's Routine Manual. It is with the manual that this little boy dealt you a massive blow that crumbled you to the ground. I will inform the doctor that the company has no case against William Reeves and hence the company cannot cross him two half days[6] as stipulated in the Firestone Employment Manual," the boss clerk concluded. I felt like a great hero. David killed Goliath! But back in my head I was quite aware that he was still the supervisor.

By the end of the shift, an uncle of mine died in my home in Gedebo. I requested the hospital authority to permit me to go there for a five day period. It was granted. The dead uncle, Heabi Toe, my father's life friend, who was a minor with my father when they traveled with their elders to the Gold Coast shortly before the Kaiser War in 1914, loved and cared for me. He was my mother's elder brother. When I returned on duty, the schedule had changed and shifted me to the Outpatient Department. On the eighth day of my assignment in that department, at about ten o'clock that morning, I was dressing a woman covered with ulcers, which was diagnosed to be syphilis, when I heard a call saying, "Mr. Cooper, is William there?" It was Dr. Petersen.

"Yes, doctor," Mr. Jacob Nmah Cooper, the supervisor of the department, affirmed. The handsome Norwegian medical practitioner, Dr. Petersen, ushered himself in. With masked mouth and covered head I came out of the dressing room. By then poopoo and peepee attacked me. Fear gripped me! Inwardly I said, "O Lord, help me! Does this mean my end here?" "Mr. Cooper, I am taking Reeves away from you. The hospital needs him somewhere else," the medical director informed the supervisor. Of all the Liberian employees, Nmah Cooper was one of the few people the medical director had some respect for or tolerated much. Every morning it would appear that Mr. Cooper seasoned himself with the gill of mother's milk, cane juice. The sour odor from his mouth revealed that the middle-aged man had his gauge correct. Laden with high spirit, Mr. Cooper's abusive expressions knew no bounds.

With my hand in his hand, Dr. Petersen led me out and through the laboratory into his office and to the clerk's office. The supply clerk was in his seat. "Get up," the doctor politely told the protruding and four-eyed clerk. "Leave the seat and let William sit there," the doctor directed. With William in the supply clerk's seat, the doctor asked him to go to the Central Supply Room, where he was being assigned. As soon as the young man left the doctor declared, "You are the supply clerk as of today's date and you are directly amenable to me. He then pulled out one of the stock cards. Handing it to me the doctor asked, "Do you see anything wrong on this card?" With my thinking cap on, I looked at the card more closely and carefully and I was sure that I knew what I was going to say. I breathed deeply in and out and said, "Yes, doctor, I think I see something." "What is it?" The doctor dug. "Here, I think, he made a mistake in his subtraction," I pointed out to the doctor. "Since you really saw the mistake, your job here is to correct all the mistakes found on each of these stock cards as you are the supply clerk now," the smiling doctor announced. That whole day I busied myself, discovering mistakes on the cards. Three days following my appointment, through the chief clerk, I was told that my daily wage was now ten cents more. Well. Forty cents a day is not as bad as twenty-eight cents or thirty a day. No doubt, when I work throughout a month, my little income shall not be less than twelve big dollars. "What a blessing, my Lord; continue to help me to diligently do well my task," I most fervently and sincerely prayed.

I enjoyed working for and with Dr. Petersen. I had one problem and that was with Dr. Petersen's wife, Legate. A middle-aged woman bursting with energy, which seemingly led her to be aggressive, she was my pest. But I thought there was something else to it. She loved the glass. Mrs. Legate Petersen was the supervisor of nurses, medical supplies, and medicine in the Firestone Cavalla Rubber Plantation Hospital and. She collected the list of supplies and medicine to be used for a day in the hospital. The lists, called invoices, were matched with the stock card minus number on the invoice. This was principally my daily work as supply clerk. If she handed me these lists in the morning, there was no problem. When the afternoon fell, it meant trouble for me. During her break on a working day, which lasted about two hours, she bent her elbow so much that she made a nuisance of herself. When she returned to the hospital, she would push me with her backside to get in my seat at my desk. "Here, enter these," she would order. That broke the normal procedure. Acquiescently I would take the lists she had no authorization to send to my office that time of the day. As soon as she left my desk I would take the lists, the invoices, to Dr. Petersen. He would put a red cross across the invoices and initial it, ERP. This meant that I must not work on the invoices.

All of the employees in the nursing area in the hospital attended on the job training every day. In the class one day, Dr. Petersen worked a problem on the board. I did not understand how he arrived at the answer. "I would advise you to go back to school before it gets too late," the teacher mocked me. I was in no way offended. I thought it was an outright encouragement. Wasn't it? In our anatomy class, the junior doctor, Olesen, wrote the word 'Os' on the board. "This is a Latin word. Do you know what the word means in English?" The doctor searched for the answer. Heartbreaking silence, seemingly breathing the air of insubordination, seized me. But my guiding angel was present, putting my wit together, and suddenly I recalled what that Latin word means in English. I sat erect as others appeared to slumber in their seats. "Yes doctor, I think I know the answer," I bravely announced. "Give it now, if you know," the teacher requested. "It is the Latin word for 'bone' in English," I told the lost class. Smiling broadly, the teacher quickened his steps toward my seat and gave me an appreciative pat on my thin shoulder. My classmates enviably eyed me. In that time I experienced my inner man lashing and asking me whether I was in Rome now? Silently I exclaimed, "The Scripture says one's sin would find him out! Did I sin, and when and where?" I pondered. The inner man questioned me, "Can you remember the smart answer you gave to your elderly Latin teacher in Nyaake, when you did not do your Latin homework assignment? You said that he should not bother you with that dead language, Latin, and adding that you had no intention to plan to go to Rome, not in the least. Vividly I recalled that stupid assertion, a glaring insubordination to my teacher and principal. I had not gone fifty miles from Nyaake when I found Rome in the Firestone Rubber Cavalla Plantation Hospital, Gedetarbo, Maryland County, Liberia. Was it a wild daydream? My conscience pierced me. Here I was with the heavy head; I would study for the medical or the legal profession, in which case I would establish a strong background in that dead language. I prayed forgiveness for my rudeness to my Latin teacher.

That answer of mine about the Latin word 'Os' earned me a distinguished and enviable place in the anatomy class. As the class progressed, we began the naming of the various parts of the human body, especially the bones and the muscles, biceps and triceps, etc. I knew many of the prefixes derived from the dead Latin language and so I excelled in the anatomy class.

Everything in the hospital, as regarding my work and studies, was well with me. After work one day in Pleebo, at about five in that bright afternoon, I went strolling on the potholed and narrow so-called streets. I met three or more young men standing and intently discussing at Tendeke Square. I greeted and joined them. Seriously they were discussing the possibility of attending school next year. The fever caught me instantaneously. "Gentlemen, is there any possibility for me to attend school next year?" I queried. In unison they answered, "Yes." "Wha-o! Where?" I urged.

The Catholic Mission is asking boys who would want to attend their high school, especially those who cannot afford the tuition fees, and will teach for the mission upon completion of the high school," the young men disclosed. "I would be glad to make use of the glorious opportunity were I a Catholic," I unreservedly declared. "You don't have to be a Catholic, only express your desire by means of an application stating your financial condition," one of the young men asserted. I thanked them and excused myself from their company.

At my desk the next day, I penned my application to the mission. Shortly after I finished writing the application, Dr. Olesen, with a bundle of medical journals under his arm, reached my desk and landed the journals on my desk. "Doctor, may I have a copy to read and return?" I begged. Smiling, he said, "Give me a scrap of paper." I handed him the paper. On that scrap of paper he drew a ladder. He came nearer to me and said, "Here, this is a ladder, a ladder of education. These are the rungs. You told me that you finished the eighth grade. If it is true, then here you are standing away from the ladder. When you have finished high school, your place will be at the base of the ladder. Your foot has not touched any of the rungs yet. Your university degree will place your foot on the first rung of the ladder from the base. To read and understand the medical journals, you have to raise your feet of academic degrees onto almost the last rung of the ladder. If you wish to do so, then you must go back to school again, again, and again," chuckling, he walked away with his English, peppered with Norwegian accents.

That afternoon, immediately following the three o'clock siren cry, I hastened to Pleebo to get a ride to Harper. At the Catholic Mission in Harper I delivered my letter of application to Monsignor Francis Carroll, SMA, prefect Apostelic of Cape Palmas. After reading the letter, the Catholic clergyman told me that the only way he would accept me on the mission would be when I passed the entrance test he would give me. "I cannot give you that test now," looking at his watch, "because by the time you finish taking the test, all of the transport trucks would have left Harper for Pleebo, and you have to go to work tomorrow morning, according to you. Let me give you a note to give Reverend Father John Feeney, SMA, to administer the test to you after your working hour tomorrow," Monsignor Carroll advised.

My hope for entering high school was enkindled. Highly considered by a man who did not know me at all, I was deeply gratified. Happily I thanked the monsignor and departed Harper City. I delivered the note to the reverend gentleman. "Come here tomorrow after you quit your job for the test," Father Feeney advised. That night I got closer to my God Almighty for his strength and his grace to strengthen me with my little elementary knowledge in order to make a successful pass at the pending entrance test. At work the next day I was in high spirits the whole day, elated with the burning desire of my going to high school. From work I went on the Pleebo Catholic Mission to meet the priest for the test. After greeting him I reminded him, "I am here for the test." He hurried into his room to get the test, I presumed. When he returned, my do-or-die test was placed before me. Silently I prayed and then began reading the questions one after the other. I breathed in deeply and out. I wrote the test as fast as I could. The time it took me appeared to have amazingly impressed the priest about my ability. At once he graded the paper and intensely gazing at me, he announced, "Good boy, William, you passed the test successfully. I am going to tell the bishop to accept you. In the meantime, you must quit the job before the end of January 1953," the priest warned. This I thought was a secret and something very personal between the priest and me. I took more pleasure in setting the records straight about everything I worked at in the hospital, including the monthly inventory of Firestone property, checking the requisitions for both Harbel and Akron, Ohio, the stock cards, etc. I was very, very tightlipped on the high hope of the visible possibility of my going to high school the coming year. I prayed constantly and sincerely.

As usual, I was in my seat at my desk by ten minutes to seven every morning. Dr. Petersen was always there about five minutes later. Through the main entrance from the private wards, Dr. Petersen came. As soon as he would open the door he would greet me. I never had the chance one single morning to give him the time of the day. I thought that was amazing condescension on the part of the doctor, who was the highest in the hospital's hierarchy. I highly appreciated it. The relationship between the doctor and me was characterized by paternal care and a filial loving atmosphere. He was truly my father. The chief clerk once remarked to me, "Kamma-o, Dr. Petersen has high respect and love for you. When your predecessor was here, if the doctor needed him he would shout for him from his office. But since you took over, the doctor walks from his office just to tell you that he needs you. I think there is something special in his attitude towards you, don't you think so?" "Certainly, I think that special something was gathered over a period of time. I guess it came from my first face-to-face encounter with the medical director in the male ward. My mind's eye told me that when he introduced me to my new assignment, about a glance I took at a stock card I discovered a mistake in the supply clerk's subtraction. I may be wrong, but I think his caring and respect and love for me as you observed are hinged on the foregoing," I recollected. "I guess all is admiration. I am singularly honored to know that such a highly-placed man admires me," I added.

This smooth working relationship existed until my secret leaked out. I did not know. Mr. Punctuality glided through the big door of the main entrance from the private ward. This time he did not say a word to me but rather he made double strides, passing through the clerk's office into his. Later, he passed again with all the speed to the wards to make his early visit with patients. Back in his office, he rattled his typewriter for something. Again he moved briskly through our office straight to the operation theater. After meticulously using his scalpel blades, the doctor returned to his office and left again for his bungalow. This time I became concerned. "Why would the doctor not talk or greet me?" I questioned the air. In no time, the medical director returned. I heard the rattling of his typewriter. I went straight to his door and rapped. "Come in," a voice from within called. I slid the door off the threshold and said, "Why you have not spoken to me since yesterday?" "Because you are deceiving me. You are planning to leave me and you have yet to tell me," my friend concluded." Doctor, you like to laugh at people. I was keeping it secret until I passed the entrance test and was given the green light. But can you remember telling me to go back to school? Don't you think it is proper for your son to go back to school?" I appealed to him. "Well, we will talk about that later," the medical boss, smiling, brushed me aside. I said to myself, I think in essence he has consented.

However, I will wait but hope. I hope I will not be too late for school. Two long days without a word about my going to high school. Did the doctor mean to keep me on the job against my will? On the morning of the third day, my friend came with his left hand stuck in his pocket and his blond hair brushing his white face. "Reeves, definitely, you will be allowed to go to high school. But not now. Father Feeney told me that you passed the test and he has informed the bishop to reserve your place on

73

the mission. At the end of May this year, my contract with Firestone expires and so I am getting ready to leave, not for school, but for my home on the Scandinavian Peninsula. I want to set all the records straight before your employment is terminated, because if not, to get a new supply clerk might cause problems as I have no time now to train another person. I hope you understand. Do your work well and I will see what I can do for you. I personally acquainted the priest with my situation and he promised me that your place on the mission would be secured," the doctor promised. Shortly after I arrived at my desk that misty morning, my blond-haired friend rushed in, but as usual, he warmly greeted me, which I returned by rising, and I gave him kindergarten children's obeisance.

After his long morning rounds with his patients, he took his time to reach my desk. "Hereafter, I would ask you to report to work at nine every morning and leave at five in the afternoon until you have satisfied me with the records. Each day you work now, Firestone will mark you one and a half cents a day." Everything went smoothly and satisfactorily as the records were being set correctly.

On the ninth of February, 1953, that bright Sunday morning, while the beaming sun of February peeped through the leafy rubber trees of the plantations, at the hospital, upon his arrival, the medical practitioner walked to me at my desk and said, "You may resign now and come tomorrow to collect your pay. I will take you to the Central site myself," my father released and relieved me. At the usual time I reported to work, I arrived at the hospital to wait for my Norwegian friend to drive me to the Central site to receive my pay. When I received the money, on our way back to the hospital, I thanked my benefactor sincerely and promised to be in touch with him and Mrs. Petersen. In the hospital I met all those who in a fatherly and motherly way urged me to go back to school, including the following: Ma Mary Sandy, Ma Beatrice Verdier, Messrs. Samuel W. Natt, Thomas N. William, John Teba Wallace, and others. I bade them goodbye and implored them to continue to help me through their daily prayers. Back to Pleebo, Gedebo was my next stop.

Early the next morning found me riding on a worn-out pickup. My parents were surprised to see me early in the year. It would appear that my father was upset, thinking that I was sacked from job. "They sacked you?" my father suddenly asked. "No, baa, I seized a chance to go to school. It is all arranged for me to attend a Catholic high school in Harper. The mission will bear all of what it entails to go through the high school. When I graduate from there, then I will teach for the number of years I spent in the school. Of course, it is a four-year course. I pray that it will not last more than that. I explained this to my namesake, Myer Kamma, the clan patriarch. When I briefly told him the thrilling story, he gave me his blessing. My parents were skeptical about what I said I was going to do. They thought I had a hidden agenda.

On the third day, I left for Pleebo. In Pleebo I put my little belongings together to leave for good in search of education on the Catholic Mission, which was graciously offering me the glorious opportunity. A passenger truck landed me at the foot of the Catholic Mission hill in Harper. With my little wooden box placed on my head, I ascended the hill. This was the eighteenth of February, 1953.

The monsignor received me warmly while boarding boys yelled and screamed for the new arrival. That evening, the priest in charge of the boys, Reverend Father Albert Turcootte, SMA, a Canadian American, delivered to me twelve large copybooks, a set of textbooks, a pen, and a pencil. This was my enabling equipment for the freshman high school studies. Father Turcootte briefed me about the daily routine of the mission. Here I was a very strange person, and appeared to be lost among about one hundred percent Catholics. "But, if I felt so strange among human beings, what would happen to me among animals?" I reasoned. I joined the students the next day for school. Devotion was held in the open. The construction of the main school building had just begun. Because of this classes were being conducted here and there on the mission. Part of the boys' dining hall was used for freshmen. The first subject that morning was algebra, substituting numbers in place of letters. The exercise was given with the number of problems to be done. In earnest I began solving the problems without asking anybody for explanation. There were some students in the class who seemed to be daydreaming, lost in the process, while my head was high in the sky. Algebra was not a strange subject for me. All the five problems I solved correctly. The teacher, after examining each student's work, announced the names of the students who had all five correct. My name was clearly mentioned. This caused a big stir at me, a new student. The next subject was English. Monsignor Carroll was the instructor. It was about analyzing sentences. Analyzing was a strange word, but not a foreign language for me as doing it was almost the same as parsing. Actively I participated. Then came the Latin period. The class had just engaged in the first declension, declension of a few Latin words and translations of Latin sentences into English and English into Latin. I held my head above the water again. In the hilly Township of Nyaake, my eighth grade class had done up to the end of the third declension.

At recess, the isolation I experienced the day I arrived on the mission began to rapidly break away as my classmates hovered about me, inquiring about what school I previously attended. Of course my previous school was no other than the Webbo District School, where I graduated from the eighth grade. Back home in the dormitory, I was bombarded with questions from the dorm boys. The isolation I suffered my first day on the mission vanished. In no uncertain terms, I was their mate and a classmate of the freshmen, the most senior class of the newly established Our Lady of Fatima High School.

In the evening, on my third day on the mission, the monsignor graced the boys' study hall with his presence. "I am here to set up how you boys will be governed. We shall first appoint our prefect, who will control the boys and other officers. We will name our prefect first. Our friend from Firestone will serve." The speculation was baffling as there were four of us who came from the rubber plantation. For me, I had not the slightest idea that it could be me. I thought this was a catholic thing in which I had no share. Finally the bishop said, "Our friend from the Firestone Hospital gets the prefectship." I was stricken by a surprise that dumbfounded me. All of a sudden a voice spoke out, "Bishop, why didn't you allow us to vote?" The voice inquired. "Prefect, this rude young man's chore assignment must be in the priest's office," the bishop directed. A puny young man from Eastern Province was placed in charge of the boys. Leading boys was not a new thing for me.

But with the young men coming from all over Liberia, I needed more tact. With Liguori Segbwe Young, a well-built young man as my assistant, assuringly buttressing me, we were the officials of the year.

Somebody who would be my lifetime friend still kept himself away from me, or the other way around. "It was who?" I silently asked. There was no answer to my silent question directed at nobody. Among the dormitory boys were two or more young men from the interior. They included Harry T. F. Nayou, George Sokro, Johnson Weah and me.

As the school progressed, there appeared a heated competition among the instructors. Each of them gave homework in complete disregard of the length of time it would take to solve a problem, or translate a sentence into Latin or English. The number of problems in algebra and arithmetic for homework was extremely exorbitant as much as it was burdensome. There was hardly any leisure time for the boys on the mission that fed them poorly. The piles of homework and the daily recitation in school generated a kind of stimuli that challenged and propelled us. Aggressively we forged ahead.

But the class of twenty-seven students began to disintegrate into two separate camps - the "doing well" and the "not coping."

Arithmetic among the freshmen subjects excused Harry and me. To our great honor, our instructor, Reverend Father Joseph Alfred Love, principal, our Lady of Fatima High School, named Harry Nayou and William Reeves as assistant instructors in arithmetic. My unitary method that I stealthily collected from my Gold Coast-educated teacher, Mr. Peter Weah Kun, arrested Father Love's attention and admiration for the process when he looked over my work in arithmetic in class. "Your method of doing simple interest is sound reasoning. I would like for you to help your fellow students with it while I am gone to Monrovia for couple of weeks," the reverend gentleman requested. Between the two, Harry and me, the students chose. More than half of the class sought my help and help I willingly gave for a period of about six weeks.

Before the first semester drew to a close, the principal announced to our class that the "doing well" students, if they continued to do well, would be promoted to the eleventh grade. The pronouncement re-enkindled the fire in us to study harder. And study harder we did!

The young students who challenged the bishop for appointing me instead of holding a democratic election where the will of the majority would prevail hardened his claim. The bishop explained that all of us were strange to one another, and such an election would have given meaningless results. The way he raised the objection completely disregarded the high position of the Catholic prelate. That evening of my appointment as prefect for the dorm boys, in close consultation with my assistant and classmate, Liguori, we listed the routine chores and respective assignments we made. Accordingly, my friend, the disrespectful objector, was placed in charge of the priest's office. The next day he willingly and stubbornly dropped the fat bone, education, and hastily found his home to live with Mother Ignorance. Our daily meals were very poor in nutrient contents. Consequently, the dorm boys suffered from beriberi, sore corners,[7] etc. Those of us who were already thin got more emaciated. I remembered

I was so dry that the bishop cried out, "William, you are a disgrace to the mission. Your thin frame tells a horrible story about the mission." "Bishop, don't worry about me. The whole world knows that I was born thin, I am living thin, and I think I will die thin. Once I adequately respond to my lessons, and satisfactory results are obtained, I think that is enough to please the mission. With God I am resolutely determined to graduate from high school and teach for the number of years it shall take me to finish the course. God shall, I hope, keep me alive and well enough as long as I gratefully pay the mission in kind for giving me the chance to earn high school education. Please join me in my prayer for my survival," I implored the bishop. The mission provided farina and salt for breakfast, cassava and smoked fish for lunch, and rice with soup, greens or palm butter. The mission also hired a cook to prepare the meals. How well he prepared the food was the big unanswered question. But in order to avoid eating the salted smoked fish directly, the boys grouped themselves to gather some leaves to be cooked and seasoned with each group member's piece of smoked fish. Each group was styled or called Green Grass Society, or Put and Take Society. This simply meant that when their greens pot was cooked, each contributor would take out the piece of smoked fish he put in. In this case you had to take out exactly what you had put in. By this, the itch and other skin rashes were minimized.

During the week, each person did or failed to do his work. At the weekend, those who failed to carry out their assignments were delinquent and sent to the grievance board, presided over by student Harry Nayou that year. Here justice was colorlessly displayed.

All our high school teachers were Catholics priests, Irish Americans, Irish and British. In such a highly Christian atmosphere where the teacher was clothed with almost absolute authority, a student earnestly seeking education would readily be on the acquiescent line. A vast majority of the students acquiescently adhered to the school rules and regulations.

The priest-teachers were often on the move for their pastoral work, especially the math teacher, who was frequently helped by an Indian math wizard called professor Laksmana, a UNESCO-employed instructor for Cape Palmas High School, a Liberian Government institution. As soon as the wizard was informed that our math teacher was not in, the tall slim wizard with a tight short coat and a flimsy necktie would immediately substitute for our absent math teacher. Helpful he was, but his embarrassing English pronunciations with high Indian accents baffled us, for instance, a word like DIVIDE with the letter V in the center of the word. He would pronounce DIWIDE, sounding like the letter W. This left us in space. However, we highly appreciated his willingness to help always. His solutions of mathematical problems were very much easier than those of our regular math teacher. Was it students' wistful thinking?

Mosquitoes took a toll on us. Located on a hill a few hundred yards from Lake Shepherd, the Catholic Mission in Harper city housed the monsignor and his priests, including the dorm boys.

Bishop Carroll and the priests lived in one-story building and the boys were domiciled in two small rectangular buildings with windows without screens. Here the blood-sucking and malaria-infesting insects brutalized us highly.

Although mosquito nets were sold here and there in town, the impecunious position in which many of us were placed sold us to those nagging insects. Frequently, many of the dorm boys visited the government-run clinic perched high on the Cape of Palms. Treatment there was absolutely free. I had my turns there too, but not for skin rashes or malaria. What it was one time, I did not know. One morning I reported sick and was directed to join other dorm boys for a visit to the clinic. At the hospital we were separately placed with the clinicians, who administered medicines accordingly, I supposed. My medicine (tablets) was given me and I was asked to take two tablets at once when a glass of water was handed me. I took the tablets and I found my way home. On my way home I began to feel dizzy and so I made a stop at one of my schoolmate parents' house. I knocked at the door and luckily for me it was the mother who opened the door. Looking at me, Mrs. Elizabeth Tweh, my mother, cried, "Did you take medicine?" "Yes, mom, I did." With this she rushed out of sight to return in no time. "Here, take this glass of milk, you are dying," she said, and pulled me away to a room where she rested me on a soft-mattressed bed. After about an hour's rest, which dozed me to sleep, I awoke. The nurse came in. "You must be feeling fine now, aren't you?" She queried. "I am fine, thank you." With the dizziness partly in me, I fretted to the dormitory where, perhaps, the vivacious dorm boys would lift away the unwanted dizziness. By the time I arrived, our lunch was being shared as the boys busied themselves gathering their leaves to prepare to gobble the starchy cassava meal. I joined my group while I narrated my long story of the unfortunate dizziness I experienced after taking a dose of tablets at the hospital and how Mrs. Elizabeth Tweh, Aletha and Philina Brown's mother, graciously rescued me when I knocked for help at the door of her home on Reevy Street, downtown Harper.

Following the noisy eating period was a short break that retired the boys to the dormitories to get ready for the study period that began precisely at two every afternoon, Monday through Friday. At study time I inquired about home assignments in each subject. As usual, some of my classmates were selfish as they were reluctant to oblige their absent and sick mate with the necessary information he needed. Into doing my homework I plunged at once. The Latin and algebra assignments were the longest and the hardest. Without flinching, I did all of them with the guiding hand of God Almighty.

With the dizziness gone the next day I was physically present in school and among my ever teasing classmates. The day went well with the class. The respective teachers, as they took their turns, corrected and graded each homework.

For our dinner, or supper, Fred the cook adorned the dining room tables with his sour shark soup, which I had no compromise for. Heartily and bitterly I hated the very pot in which the soup was cooked. I never ate the stuff! Once the food was not satisfactory, it was the right of the prefect to question the cook as to why the dish for the night was not palatable and markedly low in quantity. "Every day, the mission gives you seventy-five cents to buy three bundles of fresh fish, snapper or herrings, which can give each student enough fish for his meal. Instead of that, you buy hunks of shark at two cents a hunk. You bought ten hunks maximum each meal this week. This means that from the seventy-five cents allotted each day, you keep in your coffers fifty-five cents. By this reckoning, no doubt, you have in your possession for this week three dollars and eighty-five cents. Why do you mistreat the boys like that?" I demanded.

Fred the cook had no satisfactory answer or answers to offer. The boys raged and raged at him but to no avail, as he only said, "Don't worry boys." There was never any difference between Fred's palm butter, soup, or gravy but he kept singing, "Don't worry, boys." Fred's food continued to be tasteless. Of course, worried we were!

As the teachers said it would be at the end of the school, so it was. Those who stoop to conquer stood the test of time and were accordingly awarded promotion to the eleventh grade. Earners and wearers of the laurels were as follows: James O'Brien Bush, Ignatius Wesseh, Joseph Weah, Anthony J. Nagbwe, Patrick John Wallace, Edwin Snogba, Francis G. Nyaka, Alfred Togba, Harry T. Nayou, Liguori Segbwe Young, Alphonso N. Davis, Sandy Gorgla and William K. Reeves, out of the twenty-seven freshmen. Would our earnest and honest labor earn us another desired promotion and the final victory?

From the onset the mission, in no veiled terms, told us that there would be no vacation at all at the end of a semester or the year. Was the rule conclusive and was there no compromise?

Three days after the school was closed, the dorm boys were ordered to clean in and around the mission compound. Disobligingly the boys refused to work. My assistant and I went out to map out the various assignments for each person or group of persons. We went back into the dormitory to read out the names according to assignments. "Please get out to do your tasks," I requested. None of them budged. I repeated my request but it was like wasting water on a dog's back. Their dead silence left me bewildered. Could you imagine me? "Are we trying to insult or abuse and bite the hand that tends to give us the bread of life, education?" I whispered to myself. Again I pleaded with them, "Gentlemen, get out to do your tasks." This time they booed me and added, "To spoons and spoons alone our hands shall bend!" More obstinately they defied, "No vacation, no work." Without another word to them, I meditatively disappeared from the sulky dorm boys. In the meantime, I recalled vividly what I had said to myself the eventful night I was made prefect. In principle and practice, I sincerely accepted the onerous leadership, a non-Catholic in a completely Catholic setting, and with young men to lead coming from diverse backgrounds, unlike the dorm boys at the Webbo District School. Assuringly I murmured, "But leading boys is not a strange thing to me," and added, "and I need more tact this time and place." And so deep in my heart I knew that many who were my classmates admired me. I decided to go back to them to lodge another plea with them. "Here, we are seeking education to better our lives in the future. As I know as well as you do know, many of us, if not all of us, cannot get the necessary support from our respective parents, willing as they are, I presume. What our parents cannot shoulder, the mission is unreservedly, spontaneously, and willingly sharing with us— education enriched with Catholic religious life. Are we saying that education is not what we desire? Then why did we come here? We must not abuse the God given opportunity," I pleaded. Obviously convinced, my friends called me the way they did when they needed my help (William, Reeves, paramount chief, etc.), "We would like to meet the bishop regarding whether it is not possible for him to make an exception to the rule or modify it," they urged. "There is no way we can meet and plead with the bishop to change his rule or modify it when we disobligingly and obstinately carry on the way we do. Get to work now and later I will arrange the time with him," I advised. The jolly good news mustered their working mood and they rushed out to do their respective chores. We were together again. The various tasks were satisfactorily done.

After Liguori and I had inspected the tasks assigned and found them satisfactorily done I sneaked away to meet with the bishop. On a father to a son basis I told the bishop the boys' intention to meet in audience with him. He consented to meet with us "black monkeys," as he popularly styled us. Often too, one of our classmates openly called the bishop "Irish monkey." That joke was very expensive but Alfred Togba had indeed the guts, didn't he? The bishop was quite a condescending man as he gaily laughed at his so-called friend, Alfred Togba of Picnicess. The bishop intimated to me during my private audience with him in the interest of the boys that he had a close conversation about me with Dr. Egon R. Petersen of the Cavalla Hospital. Among other things, he said that the Norwegian experienced medical practitioner had revealed to him that he, Doctor Petersen, had not met or seen an honest African as honest as William Reeves, who also did his work almost to perfection. "It was because of this strong recommendation I appointed you as prefect for the boys. Please keep out of that foolishness of the boys," the bishop strongly advised.

Eight of the clock that night, we stole into the bishop's parlor. "I have no intention to change the rule or modify. However, I shall make some exception in no distant future, especially for the young men who made the big leap," the monsignor clarified. As usual, he distributed his homemade condensed milk candies among the boys. In February, 1954, Bishop Carroll granted me a two week leave to visit my parents in Gedebo, Eastern Province. This was one of the busiest times of the rice farming season. My father was trying to re-establish his coffee farm that was turned into high forest because of the Hitler War, which deprived the farmers of their annual income. Most of the time, then, my father lived on the farm with his new wives while my mother was forced into retirement and the other woman, my mother's first mate, sick, was just hanging.

In the main village, Kablake, where my mother resided with my younger brother, I lodged. Early one morning, on a misty day in February, a wild cry by a man from my father's farm terrified the villagers. He reported that a young woman suffering epilepsy unknowingly left the farm hut and went into the wilds. Since this morning when it was discovered, his farmhands vigorously launched a careful hunt for her in the green forest. By ten that morning they had not spotted her anywhere; my father dispatched this man to inform the Kablake village that somebody was missing from his farm family. The alarm talking drum was sounded to broadcast the chilly news, which arrested the attention of all the inhabitants of the Gedebo country. In the matter of one or two hours time, my father's farm was inundated with anxious Gedebo people. On arrival, the leading men on the spot suggested that some men and women be selected to go to consult some men and women in and outside of the Gedebo. Three groups were dispatched on the double. The rest of the multitude of people seriously began to plunder the forest, combing it throughout that day without getting a single glimpse of the missing woman. At sunset everybody unwillingly retired to the farm hut, hoping that the groups sent out had come with some information leading up to locating where the epileptic missing young woman would be found. The first group to arrive indicated that the young lady unconsciously left the hut and farm at the instance of nobody. The group added that the lady had just experienced the spell when she awoke early that morning because she was about to prepare the house for the arrival of some group of young men from Tupeluso who were hired to help on their rice farm. Shortly after this dubious information was broken, the second group came almost with the same message: no foul play. Unlike the second group, the first group consulted their witch doctor outside of Gedebo, whose advice would most likely be natural and unbiased.

I took cover under a tree that spread it branches around the hut, to catch a nap. In no time sleep stole me off. For how long I slept was open to the guess of anybody. But the screaming and lamenting of an old man awakened me suddenly. "What is happening now?" doddering, I asked. As I rushed to the scene, another screaming voice added and then another. On the scene I beheld a screaming and lamenting old man, Old Man Myer Kamma, an octogenarian, who was being squeezed to death. A crude handcuff made from wood was the cruel device. Instead of a handcuff it was used as a footcuff. Two pieces of wood with teeth curved on each of them served the devilish whim. The device pieces are placed side by side and one end is tied with a strong cord. The cord end is left open. The open end is hooked like a fork and placed horizontally across the lower leg, right on the tibia, a little above the ankles and the open end is brought together by means of another cord. Then tightened. From the screaming and yelling, the victim revealed that no doubt that he was experiencing excruciating pain. Done on the foot of a man advanced in age, the footcuff was bringing galloping death to the aged.

Sualo Toe, my father's life-friend, and my father were the other screaming victims of this apparent cruelty to the octogenarian and the men in their early sixties. This provoked me to anger, but I took my time to count ten before I spoke out. "My people, why are you treating these old men like this? Are they responsible for the disappearance of the missing epileptic young lady? Has the last group come and informed you that these people being so maltreated are the culprits?" vehemently I questioned. There was no answer from the huge crowd. Again I demanded, "Who took that these fathers of ours are the ones who took away the stray lady?" This question provoked an unrestrained anger of the multitude of people. They began to call me by all kinds of names. One of the young men in the yelling crowd, at the pitch of his voice, questioned me, "Is it because you say you know book—that is the reason why you are questioning the people of Gedebo?" In reply to what I considered a nonsensical and impertinent question I said, among other things, "I have the greatest respect for all of you the people of Gedebo because my parents are natives of Gedeboland, where their ancestors proudly laid down their lives for the land they loved. Why should I insult you for something that has no bearing on the issue at bar? The first and second groups sent out to consult a number of witch doctors, and having consulted them, reported to the hearing of all of us here that the young lady unconsciously left the hut shortly after her slumberous sleep following the attack of the spell. This was corroborated by the second group who added, 'No foul play.' Who told you that these old men you are mistreating took the epileptic woman from this farm here?" There was an earth breaking uproar.

Furiously the multitude dispersed and off they went. Alarmed by the wild movement of the huge crowd, my mother burst into tears saying did I question the people. Amidst this uproarious confusion, my mother, father with his farm wives and I started for Kablake. Just before we reached the village, we met an elderly man, Gbo Toe, one of the most respected men of the group and a distant relative of my mother. "What is this big commotion about?" the elder queried. My father explained the whole episode in detail. "Well, I am very sorry that the missing woman has not been found and those who came to search for her left in such a blazing anger. If what you told me is all their reason for their departure in such an abrupt and rude way, I would say that they are not true men of the Gedebo people. However, since they are the people of the country, and one single man would find it impossible to go against them, I strongly suggest that your son apologize to them. So far I understand about what happened, your son did no wrong. I will appease them by saying that your son wronged them. They will readily accept the apology, I guess," the Gedebo elder concluded.

Thinking with Robin Hood, "One man cannot fight a dozen all by himself." I accepted the advice and thanked him very sincerely for his timely intervention. When we reached the village we found it laid in ruins. The evading multitude rampaged Kablake, killing ducks, chickens, goats, sheep, etc. From the calm attitude of the throng once blazed with anger, it seemed that the old man had talked with them before he met us on the outskirts of the village. Evidently, he coaxed as they were seated, preying on the booties. "People of Gedebo, you came here to search for a woman who strayed away from the farm. You have yet to recover her. To depart without recovering your missing sister does not tell a story of a responsible people. Your action or reaction tantamount to a crushing defeat never known to the indomitable people of Gedebo, the breadbasket of the lower subsections of the vast Grebo group. Our forefathers and fathers knew no defeat or defeats in the Gedeboland. It behooves all of us to esteem, defend, and protect this land which our dauntless forefathers laid down their lives to maintain. I understand that one little boy, Kpaye Kamma, frightened you away. Is that true?" Elder Gbo Toe challenged the tense crowd. The thundering No's bellowed, and the vibration almost tore the thatched roofs of the huts off. However, the group's strong man continued, "Let me not probe into the reason of your untimely departure. I shall now ask Kpaye Kamma, whose name trickled here and there in this sad episode, to apologize to the gallant men of this noble group," the Suwasu village chief asserted. I spoke up, "I am under age and all of you know my father. In this case, I cannot speak directly to my elders. Let me speak through old man Gbo Toe, therefore whom I am humbly requesting to sincerely apologize to my fathers, relatives, friends, and loved ones." The apology was extended and accepted by the crushing and roaring throngs. Understandably, the search would be continued the next day. But late that afternoon, messengers from the paramount chief's office showed up to arrest all the people who came to search for the missing epileptic woman, Tarweh Meinde. "The paramount chief, the venerable Musu, ordered us, the messengers here, to arrest you and bring you live or dead to Karloke to answer to his court for something you allegedly did wrong," the messengers verbally revealed the contents of the writ of arrest. Obediently, the people began to tramp the three-hour winding paths to Karloke.

Just before we reached to the chief's compound, near a creek, the veteran politician, statesman, and the griot of the Gedebo country, Chief Musu, was exercising himself on his farm. We entered his compound. Some frisky fellows got hold of the compound's drum and sounded it. Horns blasted, calling and greeting the octogenarian paramount chief. Slowly but steadily the old chief glided. On reaching the compound Ba Musu in his shrill low voice inquired, "Did you Gedebo people hear the drum that bellowed when you entered my compound?" In an eardrum-breaking unison of "Yes," the arrested people cried. "Who beat the drum?" the veteran politician questioned. "All of us beat the drum," the prisoners roared. "That is not possible. Please tell me the name of the man who beat my drum after you entered my compound on these official grounds of the paramount chief of the Gedebo Chiefdom," the Gedebo Koo demanded. One Kodi Musu was finally identified as the one who beat the drum. "Messenger, collect five dollars from that man," the chief ordered. Forthwith the five dollars was unwillingly paid. "It is very late now for the court to go into the matter for which you were ordered arrested. All must report here at nine tomorrow morning, precisely," the griot directed.

But before we left, the chief told us that the sounding of the drum, raising alarm in another people's territory, is a flagrant violation of our Gedebo traditions and customs. "It tantamounts to gross aggression. Bear in mind the crime you have so indiscreetly meted out to us." He said he was sorry that most of the inhabitants of Karloke are sojourners, knowing little or nothing about the traditions and customs of Gedebo. If they had known, they were going to repel your deliberate aggression forcibly. Respectively, we sought places to spend the night in the surrounding villages that belted the chiefdom headquarters.

At nine the next morning, the veteran investigator began to critically examine what led to the wanton destruction of property in Kablake. This, he said, was another aggression against those peaceful villagers. "By the way, why did you leave the farm without recovering the missing young woman?" the chief queried. Clan Chief Charles K. Bohlen, brother of the epileptic stray, advanced to the witness stand to answer the inquiry of the paramount chief. Since Chief Bohlen was at the center of the whole scenario, and clan chief of the Gedebo Chiefdom, it was all his official duty to tell his boss what happened in and around his clan. "The traditional alarm-talking drum was sounded in the Trio villages area, summoning all able-bodied men that something had gone amiss. Accordingly, the men rallied there to find out what had happened. Told, my people began to plunder about the high forest in search of the missing woman, who happened to be my own sister, Tarweh Meinde, and for a day or so they combed the damned forest. Late that afternoon, this little boy," pointing at me, "heaped insults on us, saying nobody had the right to put sakelepede on the feet of Town Chief Sualo Toe, Old Man Myer Kamma, and his father, Nyanweju Hinneh. Since our presence was not appreciated, we decided to go away." The honorable clan chief had told a willful lie. The urge to refute that blatant lie was blazing in me. I raised my hand, calling the attention of the paramount chief. When I was recognized, I seized the witness stand. "It is very surprising and heartbreaking that Mr. Bohlen deliberately and biasedly made such a cover-up statement intended to destroy my father and his family. My father and Old Man Myer Kamma and the town chief of the Trio villages were being squeezed to death. Their wailing and screaming snatched me from my well-deserved siesta. In a respected and humble way, I inquired what had happened to cause this frail old man and other two men to be tortured. When you came to the alarm call yesterday, we all agreed that three teams be sent out to consult witch doctors in and around our people. We did. Just at about sunset, one of the three groups reported back to us, after consulting Koo Kar Krala of Yeyake, one of the leading witch doctors of our time. This team told us that the epileptic lady had unknowingly left the hut on the farm. They informed us further that she was at large and vigorous efforts were required to overtake her in the high forest. The second group, according to their traditional doctor consulted in a neighboring group, said that there was no foul play, but that we should be steadfast in our search. We are still waiting for the third and last group. Has this last group come and credibly told you that these old men took or kidnapped the epileptic young woman?" in this frame of explicit statements I finally asked.

"This huge crowd of people hauled curses at me and called me by all kinds of names. Having booed me, the multitude vanished into the forest! My parents and I with other people left for the main village Kablake, which was laid waste by the throng. At the instance of Elder Gbo Toe's intervention, the evading throng settled down. After appeasing them, the elder ordered me to apologize to the rowdy and cursing crowd. Humbly and respectfully, I sincerely apologized to them. This was a token of appreciation for their spontaneous and humanitarian service being rendered the Newean family. It was during this reconciliation period that your messengers arrived with the writ of arrest. This is the essence of the case."

Paramount Chief Musu, the Solomon of Gedebo, after hearing from his clan chief, the spokesman of Gedebo, and my family, which I represented, rendered judgment based on the conservative Gedebo tradition. "Since the missing woman is the daughter of the family called Tarloou her mother is now married to Nyanweju Hinneh and the woman was given to him by his mother's family. According to tradition, the family that pays dowry on a woman is wholly and solely responsible for any trouble she may cause anywhere. The judgment of this is, therefore, that all the expenses, including the damage done to Kablake and its people, must be paid by the Tarloou family; it is hereby so ordered."

My two week break with my parents spelled sour. All the good news I had was not fully and joyfully delivered. Unfortunately, the usual pleasantries done me on announcing or presenting my certificate of promotion were not tendered because of this ugly happening on the farm. It robbed me of the awards that attended me when such an achievement was attained in the grade school.

However, my parents were delighted when I told them that the high school course would take me three short years instead of four long years. But there was more to it. In the school, I would require an appreciable amount of money to buy myself some school outfit which would dignify the high school student. I was very sure as I noticed that my father had finally awakened from his long slumber of pecunious reverse. Thirty dollars would be enough to render me the deal. Did this willing and solicitous father of mine have that much to give to his son in need? The poor man had nobody to discuss his son's pressing financial problem with, as he had completely deserted my mother, his head wife who used to manage their meager proceeds from the sale of cocoa and coffee gathered from their old trees recovered following the end of the devastating Hitler War. I mustered my courage to tell the man the true story of my two week mission to him and the village. His desertion of my mother, his lawful wife, had nothing to do with that. His son in school, the only one at that. Most often I thought of my father as a man whose heart was always filled with the milk of human kindness. In no uncertain terms the village proudly exclaimed of him as the pride of the village. "Baa, you know, I am growing steadily in age and this book business. These days I need more money. Four or six dollars will not suffice. I need thirty dollars. Please help me," I pleaded. "I shall surely take care of your need this time. Presently I don't have that much in my coffers. I spent almost that amount for the cane juice to give kola to the people who came to search for the missing woman. You and I will go to Karloke to collect the amount needed from the Lebanese with whom I do business. No doubt, he will oblige me to pay him later in cocoa equivalent," my father assured me. In Karloke the Lebanese merchant readily consented to loan my father the thirty dollars, but on straight terms. He wanted forty bowls of cocoa, each bowl weighing five pounds net, at twenty-five cents a bowl. At that time, during the regular harvest, each five pound bowl yielded five dollars, or one dollar a pound. My father accepted the usurer's terms. But while they were putting things together, I was on the other hand tearing them apart.

As they were discussing, I was busily calculating the life-draining so-called bargain. The highway robber felt that he had concluded his deal with the poor peasant farmer. This was a wild daydream that had no semblance of reality. He was licking the honey on his lips that was not there. At harvest time he would earn from the forty bowls of the produce five dollars times forty bowls, or two hundred dollars minus thirty dollars laid out. One hundred and seventy dollars would be accrued, which he called PROFIT. Truly here was a thief in sheep's clothing. "Baa, I don't need the money. Don't take it! His terms are not only exorbitant, but suicidal when you accept the money on his usurious terms. I will go back to Harper, even if I have to walk there. Don't worry," I vehemently protested. My father appeared dumbfounded by my reaction to the usurer and his usurious and diabolical plot.

Without a word, my father led me to the home of some relatives. After pleasantries were exchanged with his kin, the village master, still surprised and bewildered, suddenly asked, "What happened?" I told him and his relatives that in October or November this year, cocoa price would rise to five or more dollars a bowl. And so the forty bowls which my father will give him for thirty dollars will earn him by October or November not less than one hundred seventy dollars net. This explanation did not seem to satisfy my father for my refusal of the thirty dollars. I explained further, "In two or three months, that heartless Lebanese will get two hundred dollars from the thirty on the forty bowls. In our way of counting that will be ten-twenty.

Thirty dollars taken from the two hundred dollars, he will be left with eight times twenty plus ten dollars. That will make him a hundrednaire at your expense because your son needs money to take care of his necessities in high school. I don't want to be an accomplice to a heinous crime against the poor." Back to Kablake we went. That evening a friend lent him a helping hand, and the next day my father put me away.

In Harper, the school year was in sight. Intensive preparations were underway for the coming school year. I joined the bandwagon. The Conditores (founders) of Our Lady of Fatima High School were warming up for academic '54. Would we get to the top at the end of the year? This was the protruding question that needed to be answered unequivocally. The thirteen-odd boys were ready to brace the academic storm as Fatima High School would shine through the years.

Chapter XV "In Search of the Hidden Gem"

Since early in the 1950s, Harper City had been besieged by young people flocking from the countryside where the masses of the Liberian populace resided. Was this a peaceful invasion, if there can be any, by these village boys rushing into this Americo-Liberian enclave? Were they coming in war? No, far from it! A wind of change for a better life through education had struck them, and so they were bravely venturing away from their anxious parents in search of this hidden gem.

For a number of years, the Cape Palmas High School authority cleverly devised a plan which banned the native boys from attending the high school. Imagine a country boy who wrapped his mother's lappa as his clothes around his neck while attending primary classes in the village mission school, and perhaps managing to get a pair of short trousers and a shirt to take him through the intermediate classes into eighth grade. He never wore a long pair of trousers, let alone a pair of shoes. In those days, a student was required under the rule to dress in coat suit every day to attend Cape Palmas High School. This was the nonverbal ban. If any country boy attended at that time, the number must have been very negligible at government-owned institutions. Of course now they fully realized that there is time for everything, as the prophet of old asserted. The tide was flowing with a mighty current that could not be abated. The die was cast and there was no turning back, and so Cape Palmas was inundated by these indigenous Africans from the countryside.

The Hitler War had ended, and slowly but steadily the whole world was recovering from the brutal devastation experienced all over, without the least exception anywhere on the globe. As people everywhere were reconstructing their countries and lives, the demand for education became the focus. Even the villagers needed a full share of that life-giving food, and so the young rushed anywhere and everywhere to fetch it. As God would have it in the fifties, Moses Weefur, himself a native, took over the administration of Cape Palmas High School. He declared that attending high school in coat suit was too costly and not practical. He then directed that hereafter all the students would attend in clean and neat clothes rather than coat suits. With this barrier removed, the native boys studiously fortified themselves for their academic pursuit.

At Fatima High School, the country boys could not afford the school fees. Only one or two mixed with the urban elites. The select thirteen promoted from the ninth grade to the eleventh grade were increased in number by two students, a James George, from Gbarnga, Central Province, and a Henrietta Bush, a Harper City lass. This year, classes would be conducted in our newly completed, long, roomy, rectangular, concrete one-story building perched on the left side of Maryland Avenue as you entered the peninsular, beautiful Harper City, partly nestled on the Cape of Palmas. Before we were engaged in the academic battle of the year, three subjects were added to our already heavy academic load. What were the reverend principal and his faculty up to, frightening us away? For us, the addition was an open challenge; head on we met it!

Relocated in our new spacious classroom, studiously we attacked our increased load of studies. Of the newly introduced subjects, for me, geometry was my source of frustration. Naturally, the coordination of my fingers is very poor. Is it because of the unusual tiny size of my fingers? At the onset, I struggled desperately with geometry. My first result in the subject graded me below my seatmate, Henrietta, the only girl in a fourteen-strong-boys class. She scored eighty-eight percent, while poor me earned eight points below a woman.

To me this was as humiliating as it was insulting to my manhood. Inwardly I resented it vehemently as I assiduously and diligently applied myself to the understanding and study of the subject. I succeeded well.

Before Henrietta enrolled at Our Lady of Fatima High School, she had an infected sore foot. After the first period test and Easter came, we left for the break. When classes resumed after the Easter break, Henrietta did not return. Her brother, one of our classmates, James Bush, informed us that his sister's sore foot was so infected and swollen that she did not dare walk on it. The class had lost its only lass in general, but the loss affected me more because she was my troublesome seatmate. (Pleasing trouble, I mean.) Sometimes she was like a pest to me. During other periods I was willing to flirt, but not when the English and literature teacher came. At that time I did not want even the innocent fly to touch me. She would constantly disturb me in face of my frequent warnings that I would have no time for any other thing in class once the English or literature was there. Always I warned her, "Mind you, I'll report you to the bishop, our English and literature teacher, one day." That did not deter her from her pranks. One day, as soon as the bishop stepped into the classroom, Betty, as she was popularly called in class, became mischievous again.

"Stop, Betty, if you continue troubling me, I shall surely report you to the teacher this morning," I strongly warned her. But that was to no avail as she kept nagging me. In a loud voice I said, "Betty, stop troubling me!" "Who is that?" The bishop, turning away from the blackboard, suddenly inquired. "Betty," I told him. In his usual jovial way, he called, "Betty, if you were a boy I would call you an ass, but since you are a girl, you are an assy." Betty could not believe her ears. When she fully understood the bishop, she wept bitterly. After that, Betty did not play with me in our English and literature class, the center of my underlying interest. The envious boys in the class who did not get the blessing of the only girl sharing their seats with them thought and wished she would desert me because of the incident. They were sadly disappointed and frustrated. Our friendship was netted more closely together than ever before. Our nickname, US TWO, vibrated in the class as well as outside of class every day. Our physics teacher was our biggest problem for the year. Reverend Father J.J. Breslin, SMA, would not explain those many formulas. Each time you asked him, he would reply, "You're supposed to know." *Know how? When was I ever taught?* This frustrated the whole class, except one or two who had deep interest in that subject. John Patrick Wallace, Alphonsus Nyenati Davis, and Harry Tilly Nayou were in love with that formula-clad subject.

Once in a while the Indian mathematician wizard would pay us a timely visit when the priest-teacher was absent. His explanation softened and sweetened the seemingly bitter and uninteresting subject. Slowly I picked up and began to sit erect for the subject in class. I remember one day after our period test in physics, and after grading the papers, the priest sent each of us a note. My note read, "Ignorant teachers ruin a community." But sometimes when he was absent and the mathematics wizard substituted for him, we were enlightened and the physics teacher never had the cause to pen any of us a note again. Our cooperative spirit boosted our efforts to succeed. We kept the bright academic light blazing throughout the year.

My grades in English, literature, Latin, and mathematics remained in the high nineties. To go to a law or medical school in Europe was still my burning desire. How would this native boy get to Germany, the European country where he was longing to pursue his life's dream?

At the end of the first semester, James George disobligingly quitted the class and the school and was placed on board a plane bound for Monrovia, from where his parents would pick him up for their home, supposedly in Gbarnga. We were now back to our homogeneous number, which made the historic leap the year before. This year crowned us with another promotion which placed us on the last rung on the high school ladder. Twelfth graders we were now for academic 1955. We asked ourselves, "Will there be any stars in our crowns when the sun goeth down?"
Together we answered, "Yes, with God and determined minds all things are possible."

1955 was the year our high toll would come to a close, meaning if everything went well we would be graduating at the end of the year. Our hope was loftily raised on high. Our senior year brought us special dispensation: the annual vacation was for all! Happily we left for our respective homes for warm reunion with our families.

In Kablake, I broke the greatest news of the year. "With everything being the same in God's holy name, I will finish high school at the end of this year," I hopefully revealed to my proud parents.

During the two years of my boarding life I tried to divorce worry for material things off of my mind. Every Sunday after Benediction, at four in the afternoon, the boys were given permission to stroll anywhere of their choosing. Of course, the boys took advantage of this weekly opportunity to visit their corners and nooks in the City of Harper. I never bothered myself for such a visit because I had nothing decent to wear on a Sunday, which was adorned with the young and old wearing expensive clothes. Would I not be part of that special Sunday outing again hopefully in my last year in the city? This would leave me not knowing anything much about the social life of so beautiful a city. Well, I comforted myself, "I think that is not important. Education is more important. I must by all means get education and all other things will be added onto me."

After our promotion was announced by the administration and our respective grade cards distributed, the class met behind closed doors to discuss what we would wear for commencement. After a lengthy discussion, it was agreed that each would get two coat suits, a pair of light green pants, a light green nylon short-sleeved shirt, and a face cap, also light green with the inscription ATINA![8] on the face. This included neckties, socks, two long-sleeved shirts (white), etc.

From my rough estimate, I needed about sixty dollars to get me my entire outfit for the pending graduation in early December ensuing. I went home to sound my parents whether there was any way they would be able to rake up the money somewhere before the purchasing of the required articles. "Long strings are tied to this graduation business at the end of the year. I need a huge amount of money to defray my expenses. Baa, will you be able to find the money by the end of the first semester this year?" I asked, fingering my father. In no unequivocal terms my father promised to do all within his financial strength to meet my need before the end of the first semester of this year. As a man without a definite source of income, his strong worded assurance was only a dim hope. But what could I do? Nothing but hope, hoping that God of the needy would redress us in time. My one month vacation with my village and parents of Kablake ran out. I left my people unwillingly for the vivacious boarding life on the mission infested with whispering mosquitoes.

From where to find the money for buying my graduation things left me completely where I squarely faced my studies for the year.

Reverend Father Nicholas Grimely, SMA, ushered in his new course called ELOCUTION for us. He started us with Shakespeare's Julius Caesar Marillus' vituperative speech to the Romans. The subject caught our immediate interest. But the reverend gentleman failed to know that he had to take us from where we were instead of taking us from where he thought we were. Seemingly he did not know that one of the greatest embarrassing problems in the Liberian school system is poor reading and comprehension; children read far below their grade level. We in the twelfth grade then were no exception. Starting us with a classic writing, to my mind, created his own frustration and disappointment. A simple prose reading would have been a good beginning. Eagerly we commenced but we were markedly short of the expectation of the teacher. The whole course was a heartbreaking failure. For the teacher our reading was horrible, as each time he listened to one of us reading he would exclaim, "Oh, no, you shame Shakespeare in his grave." Nothing did we gather from the course except the big-sounding word ELOCUTION!

In our new classroom one day after recess, while the students were rushing in, our Christian doctrine teacher, Reverend Father William J. Elliott, SMA, physically attacked student Patrick John Wallace by boxing him all over his body.

The father's unprovoked action surprised and disturbed the class beyond expression. Patrick did not do or say anything to him, so far as we knew. The priest did not say anything to the young man, but simply dealt him blow after blow and finally said, "Brother, take it. We have war." "Take the blow for what?" the class wondered. Perturbed, the class wanted to take the law into its hand by meeting force with force with the priest. Reasoning prevailed over rash action. We knew this would have been absolutely wrong on the part of the angry students. An alternative course was taken. We decided to write a note to the principal of the school, informing him of the surprising and unethical behavior of the father and requesting him to tell the priest to desist from such a wanton action or the class would throw him through the window. The note was signatured by the entire class and dispatched to the reverend principal's office. The strong wording of the note spurred the principal to immediate action. The principal came running. When he reached our classroom, he was breathless. "Who wrote and signed this note?" breathlessly the principal questioned.

He then polled the class, "Is this your signature with every member of the class?" The answer was a big yes except for one person, Francis Gbeta Nyanka, who answered in the negative. Francis said the class coerced him to sign the note. Our threat to throw the priest-teacher over the window the next time he fought any of us created a serious concern for the principal.

No doubt, behind closed doors the priests met to discuss the unpriestly attitude of Father Elliott. The next thing we heard about Father Elliott was that he was to take residence as parish priest, St. Patrick Church in Grandcess, municipality of Grandcess, Kru Coast Territory. The principal never said a word about what his teacher did to us in class. However, it was strongly believed that the faculty was unbiasedly convinced that the priest-teacher boxed Patrick without any cause. In the first place, Patrick was never a rude or sulky student. The class did not offer or express any regrets for the threat since it was not carried out.

Outside of this incident, nothing else obstructed the smooth process that gripped the class in its final year in high school. While I was well with my studies, personal problems haunted me. They showed their ugly teeth to me every day. To my great astonishment, I had not a pen or a pencil to do my homework in the ten-odd subjects. They had vanished. With no money to buy a pen or a pencil, every day I waited for my kind friend or a classmate who would lend me his pen.

One afternoon it was my time to ring the Angelus, but because of my late engagement at my homework, I was compelled to request my play son Tommy to ring the bell in my stead. This annoyed Father Turcotte. "Why did you ask Tommy to do your assignment?" Father Turcotte demanded. Late that evening Father Turcotte came to the study hall, where the students were studiously engaged preparing for the next school day. "William, why did you not ring the Angelus yourself this afternoon?" my French, Latin, and History teacher inquired. "Father, I begged him to ring the bell for me because I had a pile of homework that I needed to tackle at once. At the time, a friend of mine was willing to let me use his pen for a short period. I had no time to lose," I explained. "You bamboo, you black monkey; you have no right to ask any of the junior students to perform your assigned task," the priest named me. "Father, I am sorry. But don't you think Tommy should help me when I need his help in as much as I help him with his lessons every day?" I cried. This question provoked the father to anger. With the long stick he had in his hand, he deliberately struck my head. He disappeared at once and headed for the priests' house. I collected myself from behind the table that separated me from him and ran after him with all the intent and purpose to hit him with that stick with which he heartlessly struck me. Before I reached the priests' house he had gone upstairs into his room. I met the bishop at the door. "What are you doing with that long stick in your hand?" the bishop inquired. "Father Turcotte hit me with this and I must strike him with it too," angrily I told the bishop. The bishop asked, "What happened?" I took in deep breath and for a while I did not speak. Finally, I explained the whole story to the concerned bishop as he focused all his attention on me. "Could you strike the priest with that stick? I would never believe that you would have ever behaved like that. Go back to your study hall and at your night prayer ask the Lord to restrain you from such a temper," the bishop advised.

The following week, the Wednesday plane flew off to Greenville Sinoe County, where the priest who struck me would reside as parish priest at St. Joseph Parish.

My daily mission chore placed me in charge of Bishop Carroll's suite. Still not a Catholic, I was happy that I was steadily getting immersed but not converted. Prefect emeritus, and now presiding officer for the mission boys grievance board, I

91

was quite a distinguished person among my equals, wasn't I?

The unaddressed personal nagging problems were growing in number. I had yet to find myself a few dimes to buy a pen to do my classwork as well as my homework, which, the seemingly unconscious and heartless teachers who did not consider time limits, piled onto us. The weekly washing of my scanty clothes was rendering them tattered. This raised a grave alarm for me. In this interim, I dared not bother my father, who was struggling to rake around for sixty dollars for my pending graduation. To whom would I turn for the urgent need? This was grievous and the concern ate me up every day. During that time I heard that the Honorable Daniel P. Derrick had arrived by air and was briefly staying in Harper for a day or two with Mr. and Mrs. Samuel A. Cole. "Well, well," I whispered to myself, "I guess, when I beg Honorable Derrick, my mother's distant relative, for fifty cents he will surely oblige a boy in need!" With this I begged the priest to please allow my play son to take my note to Honorable Derrick. The priest consented on the condition that I would forfeit my right for Sunday walk, which every boarder was granted every Sunday. I had no choice but to waive it. My son handed my indigenous man the note. The boy came back with a message saying that the old man wanted to see me in person because he heard that I was in school and was doing fine.

Highly my spirit was lifted and encouraged to personally meet the honorable gentleman, and so I put in another excuse. It was granted, but would cost me two Sunday walks. When I met him he lavished all praises Gedebo elders showered on young persons they think are promising. For about thirty minutes, the man sang praises for his cousin's son. Inside myself, I was wondering what would be the end result of the praises which, deep in my heart, I knew I did not deserve. Finally I said to him, "Baa, we are not allowed to be out after six in the evening. It is about time for me to leave before I get late." He began to search his pockets. He turned all of them out. At last he said, "Oh, I have no money. Next time." Unbelievably I stole away from his presence. "But God, this is my last year in high school, I suppose. Is it going to be true with me as the poet sings, "In sight of port sank many a vessel fair?" I lamented. Almost crushed to death, I managed to go to the bishop's suite to prepare his bed for the night. In his sitting room the bishop was writing at his desk. I forgot my manners. I did not speak to him but rather I slid into his room. My work done, I was trying to steal away when the bishop's glance caught me and he abruptly called, "William, when did you get here?" Shamefully, I answered, "When you were writing I came in." "That is strange. You came in and passed by me without a word to me? Is something bothering you?" The bishop expressed concern. "Yes, bishop, I have some nagging problems. For about two weeks now I have had to borrow pens to do my class or homework, and secondly, my two good pairs of trousers are wearing out fast," I revealed my heavy burden. "William, you are a true Nyanbo black monkey. Couldn't you ask me for a pen or pencil piled up in my room? You are indeed stupid. Why worry about things you have?" the bishop questioned. The benevolent Catholic prelate then told me to get a pen and a pencil from among his pens and pencils. After I collected my much-needed writing instruments I heard the bishop saying, "Pull my drawers and you will find a piece of cloth, a double yard and a half, to make yourself a pair of trousers." My benefactor's benevolence choked me. I was dumbfounded. I could not muster any expression by which I would heartily acknowledge and sincerely thank my foster father. I turned away from him as tears spilled down my cheeks. I was rejuvenated after the good old priest showered upon me his humanitarian blessing. I was propelled in full swing again at my studies.

Gradually the first semester drew to a close. Academically all of the members of the class were in good standing. In no veiled terms we were assured that graduation would unquestionably be ours at the end of the year.

Gladdened by the shining hope and the assurance from the administration and my personal grade records, I thought it was about time to set out to arrange for my outfit for the graduation. On this urge I humbly requested the bishop to grant me a two-week break to visit my parents at the southeastern end of the Eastern Province in order to remind them of this pending momentous event. July, especially beginning in the second week of the month, knocks the virgin hunger season off in most of the interior Gedebo country. When I landed in the village the villagers were in harvest mood. Hunger had once more disappeared and the rustics were once more happy. Did this suggest too that my parents had burrowed all around the countryside for the money I needed? The reunion with my parents and relatives generated new dimensions. This built my hope on higher ground, hope of getting what I requested from the literally penniless people. "Time seems to be flying fast. Our first semester ended and this is our mid-year break. I am just here to remind you about the amount of money I need when I finish school," I reminded my parents. "Your mother has been very helpful in obtaining the money. Many of her relatives gave their widow's mites. It is from these bits and pieces we have gathered for you seventy dollars. If you need it now, we will deliver it to you," smiling broadly my father declared. My heart leapt in grateful thanks. I tightly embraced the former Trio village chief, now a village elder. I hugged my mother and sang her praises and thanked God that she was still her husband's wife (although the village polygamist literally deserted her). With my package sealed, I left with the understanding that my father would send a special emissary to deliver the package to me in Harper in mid-October ensuing.

The second semester, 1955, began promptly in early August. The thirteen prospective graduates resumed school without delay. It would appear the two week break had refreshed and regenerated the instructors.

As this class would be their first product produced from the newly established Our Lady of Fatima High School, our dedicated priest-teachers wanted the full academic endowment and Catholic religious culture enrichment enshrined in the pioneer graduates. Unlike footballers, the teachers had nothing to spare. Time was precious. They wanted their first graduates the best among many. Everything possible must be inculcated. And so it was throughout the second semester, putting finishing touches, as it were, to our academic sojourn in high school.

Having my new pair of trousers made and a pen and pencil generously given by Monsignor Carroll, I had a complete peace within and outside of me. Fully I applied myself, preparing for our final examinations scheduled for some time in October.

One sunny Saturday, the boarding boys were told to clean up the auditorium. Brooms and rags in hand, we got engaged to the task. During that work I experienced a sharp headache. I came downstairs and rested myself on the lawn in front of the school building. The rest did not help. The headache worsened and I was compelled to climb the hill to rest in the dormitory.

Instead of going to bed, I entered the mission pickup in which my play son Tommy was sitting. The driver had left the key in the switch. I turned the key and the thing kicked. Tommy said to me, "Try it again." Try I did. I placed my foot on the accelerator. I pressed my foot harder and the pickup moved backward with speed and bumped into the priest's guest house, where Father Gilmore, SMA, was enjoying his siesta. Luckily for me, the high basement before the house repelled the force. The springs of the pickup were broken and other parts damaged. Here landed a penniless young man into trouble. I said to myself, "It is true—trouble does not look for man but man does look for trouble." Would the mission demand me to repair the pickup or expel me from both the school and the mission? If they did any of them, it would be a coup de grace to my schooling and life.

Since the bishop was out visiting Monrovia when the incident occurred, everything was hanging pending his arrival back to Harper. When the bishop arrived that afternoon, he summoned me to his suite. He appeared so angry that I was afraid to go near him. He was foaming at the mouth. His anger was vented on me, which dehumanized me. Absolutely I was wrong out of gross ignorance. With all my heart I implored the bishop to be palliative and fatherly. The mission repaired the pickup without asking me for a cent. I was torn into pieces again.

In early September, chicken pox broke out in Harper. Some mission boys became the victims. At that time I had some rashes on my face that looked like the contagious stuff and so I was quarantined with the rest of the infested students. Actually, my case was wrongly diagnosed. For about a week or so we were isolated from the rest of the boarders.

The mission served us well daily within our quarantine. I was not sick and so I preyed on the sick boys' food. I tried to memorize my part of the drama the school would stage at the end of the school year. When the sick people appeared well, we were discharged. A week following the restoration of our freedom the infectious disease arrested me, about a week before our school-leaver examinations. For two long weeks I was to be confined in a room. The possibility of my taking the examinations did not exit at all. "Am I going to be left out of the examination, which when taken and successfully passed, would entitle me to graduation?" I was left wondering. Every day I was lost in contemplation about my fate.

"How are you, William?" Reverend Father John Guiney, SMA, greeted me in my isolation room. "Father, the pains caused by this chicken pox are heightened by an overwhelming tension about our final examinations next Monday. What shall I do?" I cried. "The examinations shall not be administered until you are all well." The priest assured me. This strengthened me physically and morally. In mid-October I was fully recovered from that infectious disease, which partly scarred my face.

In late October the examinations were administered, graded, and the results announced to the examinees in an exclusive meeting with Father Guiney. No doubt, with this done, planning for the first graduation of Our Lady of Fatima High School went underway.

Early in the year the class was organized. Officers were elected: William K. Reeves, president, James O'Brien Bush, vice president, Liguori S. Young, secretary, Anthony J. Nagbwe, critic etc. At the first elections of the class, Harry T. Nayou was elected president. For sure, I did not know what went wrong. But late that afternoon following the elections I received a note from Ignatius Wesseh saying that I should accept the presidency of our class. Another note followed afterwards, making the same request; in some demanding me to accept the presidency. "But how can that be, when we elected Harry Nayou just yesterday?" I asked.

In school the next day, during recess, Ignatius Wesseh called the class to meeting and announced the annulment of the elections of the day before. All the members of the class voted for the cancellation of the elections except Harry and me. The class then unanimously elected me as president. As we were not bound for lessons again, our whole business then was to select and purchase our graduation outfit. Committees set up. As soon as the selections were made and accepted, purchasing was the order of the day. James Bush, the only Americo-Liberian among us, refused to buy the local cloth or make his suite locally. The rest of us bought and made our suites locally.

One of the activities for the commencement season was a drama to be staged by the school. The drama, *You Paid in Your Own Coin*, was about two young people in love. The affair culminated in a proposal of marriage by the young man, Michael John Jackson, to the young lady, Charlotte Roberts: "Charlotte, will you marry me?" The young charming lady with a trusting heart replied in the most positive expression, "I will, Michael." Then they hugged and kissed each other.

It would appear that this heartwarming agreement was sealed, with the concerned parties hoping it would be delivered soon. Did the sweet dream come through? Certainly not, but rather unhesitantly it was shattered. Michael's father moved in and unhesistantly annulled his son's proposal of marriage to Charlotte. Heartbroken, Charlotte sought redress through the court of law and of competent jurisdiction by a suit of BREACH OF PROMISE OF MARRIAGE, having retained her lawyer.

Three of the seniors were some of the characters. They included Liguori Young, the trial judge, Anthony Nagbwe, Michael's father, and William Reeves, lawyer for Miss Roberts, the prosecutor.

For the breach of promise of marriage, Charlotte (with her attorney) was claiming ten thousand dollars damage from defendant Michael John Jackson. In our submission we claimed that "a promise of marriage was made to Charlotte Roberts and that she earnestly and graciously accepted the loving proposal. In no time, the would-be lifetime agreement was publicly annulled by her fiancée's father. With the promise broken, we had no other alternative but to seek redress through the legal means. We are claiming and demanding ten thousand dollars damage and all the costs of the court against the defendant."

The witness who was actually present when Charlotte and Michael were sitting as close together as two peas in a pod and Michael popped up the question, "Charlotte, will you marry me?" Without flinching and with a trusting heart, she responded, "I will, Michael." Our star witness recounted this tale and added that then they hugged and kissed each other. Other witnesses testified, and their corroboration was beyond all reasonable doubt in each piece of evidence adduced in the case in court. Having firmly established the breach of promise of marriage under the statute made and provided, we humbly requested the honorable court to award us our just and legal compensation of ten thousand dollars for the damage done us. We were duly awarded.

The drama scored a huge success. Many requested that it should be encored the next day. But it was not possible as many other activities were scheduled.

The morning following the staging of the drama, I went to town in order to do shopping. As I slowly moved down Water Street, I saw behind me the Honorable Allen Yancy driving slowly. I freed the way for him, but instead of passing on, he suddenly braked the car to a complete stop. He came out of the car and quickened his strides towards me. "What does he want now?" I whispered to myself. "I just want to congratulate you for your excellent performance as an attorney-at-law in the drama last night. It was super, I assure you. But that is not all; I hope in no distant time we will have you as an attorney-at-law in the Maryland Bar Association. I say again, your performance was excellent," counselor-at-law Allen Yancy urged me.

Some time in November, the administration invited the prospective graduates to a meeting. Among other things discussed were the items of the souvenir graduation program, which included speeches and other items.

Already each student's grade scores had given him his place in class. That brilliant, near-perfect student, Harry T. Nayou, scored the first place in class and was hence named the valedictorian. Second in class was Harry's arch rival, William K. Reeves, salutatorian. Senior Senator A. Dash Wilson was the commencement speaker.

Father William J. Elliott, our boxing friend, would deliver the baccalaureate homily, etc. With this arrangement, the stage was set for Our Lady of Fatima High School's first graduation. The pageantry of the graduation was spectacular!

At the baccalaureate, Father Elliott admonished us to know that everything came from God Almighty and so in all our endeavors we should always look to God and ask for his guidance. Our commencement speaker told us, "As a bamboo tree grows taller, the more it bends." He informed us that the more educated we became, the better we should understand and treat people. And so we ended to begin.

Chapter XVI "A Teacher at Last"

In the 1940s and 1950s, in order to teach in a Liberian school, the prospective teacher had to obtain from the Department of Education, Republic of Liberia, represented by a supervisor of schools in the county or province, a license to teach. At the beginning of each year, January, an in-service training program called "Teacher Institute," was conducted in each designated place, county or province, where the teachers met for some organized courses of study to upgrade themselves. The courses included language arts, arithmetic, etc.

For Eastern Province, most of the instructors were the Assembly of God female missionaries. For about a month classes were regularly conducted. Tests were administered to all, especially the prospective teachers, whose success at the exam or attendance awarded them certificates. Once a certificate was obtained and presented to the supervisor, the teacher license was officially issued and delivered to the prospective teacher, empowering him.

Knowing that I had committed myself to teach for the Catholic Mission upon completion of high school, I deemed it my bounded duty and obligation to make all necessary preparation for the onerous task. Since I was completely penniless, I thought to go the teacher institute, now called Teacher Vacation School, in Nyaake, where I was sure to get lodging and good meals from relatives and friends.

After four long years of absence from Nyaake, the second cradle of my education, the reunion there would be memorable. In mid-December, following my graduation, I departed Harper for Nyaake.

For about a week, as I patrolled the hilly township, I recollected fond memories about the Webbo District School and the social life of the township. With a place arranged for my lodging for the Teacher Vacation School, I found my way out of Nyaake to the old village, Kablake, the happiest spot in the world for me.

The twelve-hut village was bustling with Christmas activities. My father was not able to attend my graduation ceremony because my namesake, Old Man Myer Kamma, was seriously sick. But before I arrived, the old man had their agenda ready for a grand reception to go underway for me. I highly appreciated their intended honor for me but I was very sorry as I did not want such an honor anymore. I requested their indulgence and understanding for my apparent refusal of their well-thought-of honor. I just wanted them to prepare for me a chicken, well-seasoned in palm butter, as they did when I was promoted from one grade to another. My mother agreed with me and urged my father to listen. On Christmas day, the whole village lavished me with the Grebo National anthem dish, the well-seasoned palm butter. A week following Christmas, I dodged the villagers to get to Nyaake. I had learned that my crowd of boys were preparing to lavish a sumptuous party in my honor on New Year Day.

In Nyaake, the Teacher Vacation School commenced promptly the first week in January, 1956. The in-service and prospective teachers and the missionary instructors were ready for business. All the teachers attending the session were non-high school graduates except me. However, I took a language arts course with the most advanced teachers. Miss Pape, a middle age Assembly of God American missionary, instructed my group. We did disarming of sentences, which actually was a review of my first year's work in high school. My final score at the test showed that I was perfect. Perfect in people's language? Well, a one-eyed man in the village of the blind makes him a king. Doesn't it? I was awarded a certificate.

One weekend, during the vacation school, one afternoon, I strolled to one of my favorite corners, New Road, in Nyaake. I went to a house where my old je bor dor[9] lived. The reunion was the happiest in recent memory. After pleasantries, we began to recall those flirting days when I used to steal away from the mission once in a while on my noctural visit with her. As this reunion re-ignited the mutual affair, an understanding was reached that I would call back that day at about eight in the evening. At the appointed time I arrived where my treasure was. At that house was a former mission mate of mine. There was another reunion. Briefly we exchanged greetings and then I inquired about Cecelia, that young woman whose love for me had no limits. Samuel told me that Maiche was in her room. I briskly moved toward the room and knocked lightly on the door. My friend's mother rushed at me, shouting and yelling and calling me all kinds of names. "Kpaye Kamma-o, let lightning kill you, you leave in your sleep," etc., etc. Everybody in the surrounding houses was awakened by the woman's vicious wailing and evoking of all the evils in the world on me. Her brother rushed in to find out from her what all the shouting was about. "This man (meaning me) came to my house and knocked at my daughter's door. He has no business there. My daughter is being wooed by Jackson. Does this Kamma man want to decoy my daughter? This is the reason I shouted and I am shouting again, Kpaye Kamma-o, you must die if you don't move from behind my daughter! This will beat him off my daughter and my house[10] ..... Kpaye Kamma-o, leave my daughter alone! I want her to marry to a responsible man. You are not a responsible man. Mr. Joshua Jackson is a responsible man and he is the man I want, not you," the mother of Maiche declared.

"Cecelia, do you know this young man?" Mr. Neah, the uncle of Cecelia, queried. "Yes, I know William Reeves very intimately. He is my loved one since our elementary school days here in Nyaake. My mother has full knowledge of what exists between William and me. Why should she behave this way to my friend whom she has known over these many succeeding years of our love affair? William is the only man I know in this whole wide world. By the way, who is this your Mr. Jackson?" Cecelia asked. Mr. Neah suspended the investigation until the next day after I was free from school.

When the family probing continued the next day I was asked to tell my side of the story. "Cecelia and I became friends when I was a boarder at the Webbo District School. It was intimately known by many members, including Ayee Kuliju, Cecelia's mother, of Cecelia's family. Directly Cecelia's mother received from me whatever I had to give to my love. Fresh meat was sometimes part of the package. Having fostered the relationship between Cecelia and me, my mother is now saying I must die because some responsible man wants her daughter's hand in marriage. Is that the way a sincere and loving friend of her daughter should be treated?" I lamented.

Mr. Neah and a former teacher of mine, Joseph N. Washington, strongly admonished our mother never to treat anybody like that anymore, let alone her daughter's dear one. The old woman apologized to me and I thanked the men for their timely and fatherly intervention. My friendship with Cecelia never faded away. In February I went back to Harper to find out from the mission where I would be assigned. Before graduation, Father Turcotte had reliably informed me that the mission would send me to Greenville, Sinoe County, to teach there. "Tell the bishop that you don't know anybody in Greenville and so it is impossible for you to accept to go to a place where you don't know or have anybody of your own. If he refuses, then tell him that you would rather go somewhere else to work so as to pay back the mission what you committedly owe it. Sinoe people don't like strangers. *Don't go there,*" the priest strongly advised.

Bishop Carroll was out of the country. Father Breslin was in charge. When I met him on the question, he told me, "Get ready to leave by plane on Wednesday to go to Greenville where you will take up your three year teaching assignment," the priest pronounced. "I am very sorry, I don't know the place you called Greenville and so it is not possible for me to go there to teach. I went to school right here. Why not assign me here? I won't go to Greenville," I asserted.

In that time Father Love called, "Father Breslin, Monsignor and I decided that William and Harry are to teach here so that they will be afforded the opportunity to attend college. They really worked hard in high school and behaved well during their tenure with us on the mission," Father Love, OLF, principal, rescued me.

It was clearly and satisfactorily understood that I would teach at Our Lady of Fatima High School, Elementary Division. Assigned, I went back to Kablake to get ready for my first teaching year.

While I was moving up and down, the man who had firmly stood by me died. My namesake, Myer Kamma, the patriarch of our family and one of the elders of the Gedebo, was entitled to the traditional Gedebo grand burial ceremony that the elders and the high priest with fighting men would attend. I had to be part of that pageantry to pay tribute to the celebrated Kwotapei, pioneer Christian and village elder. But because the death occurred in the heart of the underbrushing for the rice farming time, only the mortal remains of the saintly man were interred.

In December of that year, the great feast was scheduled to take place. After the mortal remains were deposited into his resting place, on the fourth day following the burial, we the family shaved our hairs, showing that we were deeply mourning the death of our father.

In a meeting with Father Love, Harry and I were told by the reverend gentleman that we were assigned to teach at Fatima. Each of us would get a monthly salary of twenty-five dollars. Harry and I murmured, "A twenty-five dollars monthly salary for each of us?" Would this meager income provide adequately for each of us in the city, taking into consideration college fees, rental and food money, and other necessities of life? Since these poor country boys attended and obtained their high school education at the expense of the Catholic Mission, we had no ground for arguments or contention. We had no alternative as we were now victims of necessity. As Captain William D. Johnny of the Ninth Infantry Regiment put it, "Necessity compels a free man to be a slave."

Young as we were, we hoped to be active, not passive, in the tantalizing social life of Harper city with its conservative but elegantly daily-dressed people. What would twenty-five dollars buy for a young teacher who would be required to be spick-and-span everyday?

Just before our graduation one Sunday afternoon, Father Breslin distributed copies of agreement to be entered into between the mission and each of the candidates, students who could not afford the tuition fees and other requirements to live on the mission, and attended the high school at the expense of the mission with the understanding that after finishing the high school they would teach for the number of years it would take them to finish the school.

Perusing my copy, to my dismay, I found the terms of the contract strictly binding on the grantee with no benefits expressed or implied or inferred for him. At once I resolutely decided not to sign such a one-sided contract, the terms of which would selfishly benefit only the grantor. When I handed back my copy, the priest shouted at me, "Why didn't you sign the contract?" I told him that I came on the mission on a verbal understanding and I was committed to my promise to teach for the mission the number of years I spent at the high school until it was fully carried out by the help of God Almighty. The signing of the contract, I seriously observed, would not strengthen or weaken or annihilate the promise I made from the very depth of my yearning heart for high school education. That so-called contract never saw my signature.

After a few months of our teaching, Father Love raised the meager salary of each of us to thirty-five dollars a month. This was what each of us lived on for the four long unbroken years we taught at Fatima.

In the school I was placed in charge of sixth grade as a homeroom teacher. This meant that I had exclusive control over the class and students, teaching all its subjects prescribed. This was an open challenge to the novice teacher in the sacrificial but noble profession. The class was loaded with budding teenage girls and boys.

Just a year before, the students and I were all Fatima's students, but the winds of change made the difference. What a changing world we live in!

My skinny size and familiarity with the students tended to breathe contempt from the students. How to handle the problem was my immediate test. How well I would manage it, time would tell.

Chapter XVII "The Beginner-Teacher Begins"

My first public duty would now be rendered to my dear alma mater. As one of the founding members of the first class of graduates, the opportunity was unique and glorious. Perhaps it was going to be all true here. As it is said, "A prophet has honor except in his home." I needed all the tact to handle my former schoolmates. In order to succeed I should have the courage enough to positively draw a definite line between the students and me. By nature, I am conservative, liberal, and democratic. Characterized by these presumed qualities, I would continue to build firmly on them. It had always meant for me that my "yes" meant yes and my "no" meant no. Added to this was my literal interpretation of the Biblical passages from Genesis 3:19:

"In the sweat of your face you shall eat bread ....." In these words I would fashion my teaching lifestyle in particular and life in general. Besides that, my own hard life taught me to always have a strong will so that I would find a way. With courage and a determined mind I had reached thus far. In my profession I would not be a social welfare agent; paternalism degenerates and dehumanizes. Merit would be my clarion call. I don't believe in or behold to "give me." Everything I own or I have in life, if I have anything at all, came to me through hard and earnest labor. This meant that day that any grade a student under me would get from me would be based on his time and application of the time to his lessons crowned by his behavior. Therefore what a student earned academically would be awarded on merit and nothing else. With my objective clearly defined and my goals set and God Almighty leading the way, I plunged myself bodily into the noble but sacrificial profession.

Conservative, orderly, and disciplined, Harper, Cape Palmas, was an ideal and suitable place for a beginner-teacher. Over eighty percent of the students who attended the school hailed from well established Christian homes. At this rate, discipline problems were isolated happenings. In this wholesome atmosphere, the novice-teacher was being nurtured. Under these solicitous conditions my lifelong occupation seized me. My sisterly and brotherly students helped me as they highly appreciated and honored my academic standing.

The transmission of my little storeroom of knowledge to my eager and ambitious students was now the inward burning issue of mine. As I saw it, patience, since seemingly the subject matter was handy, I guessed, was the much needed vehicle to convey or impart the knowledge to my docile students, whose cooperation at that stage propelled me happily.

The first three months of my teaching experience excited me into action and enlightened me. The year 1956 had initiated me into the teaching profession. Would I endure?

Reverend Father Joseph Alfred Love said that he and the monsignor wanted Harry and William to remain in Harper so that they would have the grand opportunity of attending Maryland College of Our Lady of Fatima, a small but a unique teacher training institution of the Catholic Church in Liberia. The reverend gentleman was very sincere and truthful to his desire for Harry and me.

Consequently we were enrolled at the college. The college conducted its classes in the afternoon. The SMA Fathers and Benedine Sisters served as instructors while the Very Reverend Dr. Joseph Alfred Love was at the helm of the administration of the institution. It was a four year degree-awarding course in education.

Simultaneously I embarked on this course and teaching at Fatima Elementary School. Both undertakings were desperately challenging. Before long, I realized I needed to fully apply myself, without reservation, as the challenge required and demanded.

Actually I spent three short years in the Catholic high school. According to the understanding reached between the mission and me, I would teach for the mission for the number of years I would spend at the high school before completion. In view of this, I was not obligated to the mission for the four year service but for three years, which I spent in the school. But if my course at the college was a four year course that would not be completed at the time my service with the mission would have been concluded, then where would I stand? Would the mission employ me as an independent seeking a job with the mission so as to complete my four-year course at the college?

Could I not show some sign of gratitude to the mission by not seeking new arrangement of employment? Doing this would definitely suggest that I was biting the hand that was feeding me wholesomely. "I shall not be ungrateful to Father Love and the Catholic Mission," I warned myself. In grateful acknowledgement I decided to take an extra mile. I did not ask or require the mission to grant me extra understanding because my three year service had expired. I continued receiving thirty-five dollars as my monthly salary until my fourth year with the mission ended, crowning me with a Bachelor's degree in education from Our Lady of Fatima in Maryland County. The opportunity that Father Love willingly granted me to attend and obtain college education, a tool that would prepare me for a viable, perhaps lucrative future, was paramount. I did not complain. The profit from the thirty-five dollar salary was enormous at the end. My God was in control.

At the Fatima Elementary school, instructional materials were in abundance. Lesson Planning was no problem. For me, the school was more or less a laboratory. I considered it as the center of practical teaching as those instructors at the college were those under whose immediate supervision I taught each day. My professional behavior and presentation were on screening by those watchful sisters who appeared to be omnipresent. This totally imbued professionalism in me and others who were blessed to be teachers at Fatima at that given time.

Under me the sixth grade daily lessons were conducted. The class was comprised of about forty-five nearly homogeneous students, both male and female, every year of my four year tenure. Lively and studious, those greedy knowledge-seeking young people challenged me all along the way of my beginner teaching experience. Unlike many grade groups, my sixth graders were very cooperative, in terms of their daily preparation and recitation. They found their homework exercises more exciting as each was rewarded for the kind of performance put in. The homework was graded on a merit system: we had two types of stars, golden and silver. In arithmetic, those who had all correctly earned a silver star while those with one mistake received the golden star. This made the competition keen. The number of stars collected during the school week won the student a distinction, which gradually led him or her to earning first or second honor of the six week marking period. Many of the students were above average. In this number over fifty percent were female.

As I began my teaching career, my ambition of becoming a medical doctor or a lawyer eroded. One day I inaudibly questioned myself, "My God, why do I want to be a lawyer or a medical doctor? If that is all to it, then I give the ambition up! No doubt, teaching is one of the generous ways of serving humanity, " I comforted myself. "Was it poverty? You said it was your interest." I had in earnest accepted my non-fulfillment of my long-standing youthful dream. The substitute, although I never desired it, was as noble as the medical or legal profession. They all served humanity. As God would have it, I was entering college immediately following my graduation from high school. This was a special blessing for a rural helot who could not provide for himself in high school. I was going to be ever so thankful to reverend Dr. Joseph Alfred Love and Bishop Francis Carroll for the magnanimous and humanitarian consideration given me. Being trained as a professional teacher gladdened me profoundly. 1956 brought me to begin again. Accordingly I enrolled at Maryland College of Our Lady of Fatima College. The student population was comparatively small. The vast majority of the students were old teachers and middle-aged. Being in my mid-twenties, I found my early college life socially boring and academically awakening. At our studies, my classmates and I were like a child and his elder fighting over a thick Grebo palm butter dish. The old teachers wanted to enrich themselves professionally while being advanced academically, having worked for years in that sacrifice-laden profession. The competition was keen. The old and the young alike wrestled incessantly with both the courses.

As the year slowly wound down, our teaching became more animating, interesting and immersing. Already it was a daily pleasurable task for me. My rapport with my students grew. In this case, I particularly noticed a girl of about fifteen years old in my sixth grade class. From a well-to-do Liberian family, Grace Tubman adorned my desk with a bouquet of beautiful flowers every morning of the school day. She became an intimate friend of mine.

One morning, Grace, a well proportionate, slim body with shy smiles and a loving voice, entered the classroom. Beaming with smiles with her head slightly tipped on her right, she deposited the bouquet of flowers on my desk. "What is happening this morning, Grace?" I suddenly queried. "My father bought me a raffle ticket from England; that is the ticket that has won for me four hundred pounds sterling. Dad told me that he is going to put that money in a bank in England for me and in my name," Grace mused. I extended my hearty congratulations to my dear friend.

It was not always well and smooth in our sixth grade class. No doubt there were stormy days when we evidently lost our manners. In this case, as it is stated in the Epistle to the Hebrews 12, 5-7, 11-15:

"My son, do not regard the discipline of the Lord, nor lose courage when you are punished by him... for what son is there whom the father does not discipline... then you are illegitimate children and sons." In this light I felt empowered to discipline my students because I loved them all. Verbally they were chastised since indeed my instructors at college emphatically told us that the use of the rod in the classroom did not serve any useful purpose in the teaching and learning situation. As I saw it, nobody can accomplish anything for himself if when he or she has no effective control over himself. Discipline is that which instills or imbues in you how to subdue yourself in all circumstances. My line of communication was unimpededly flowing and the line separating the teacher from the students was always demarcated. I often reminded them, "Stay on your coffee farm while I remain on my cocoa farm." Or better still, "Stay in your orbit while you rotate." From time to time everybody acquiescently obeyed the rule of nature. In short, discipline dictated the becoming behavior on both sides of the coin in motion!

With my friend and colleague, Harry Tilly Nayou, I was on my own, living and surviving barely on thirty-five dry dollars a month. But the friendship of the two rural young men reinforced us. We shared with each other unreservedly. Since the two of us were the youngest in our class in college and fresh from school we felt that we were elite. About three-fourths of the class were people of the group gradually losing their vitality and vigor. they were middle-aged. We the very small minority was often driven into yielding to the blunt and cruel will of the majority.

Our professional courses, child psychology, educational psychology, philosophy of education, etc., were very stimulating and led to lengthy discussions regarding the teaching and learning situation. Our older classmates added their life experiences during the discussions, making them immensely rich and enlightened. But all was not always well in that class of seemingly responsible people. In our world history class, we thought the instructor, Reverend Father Owen O'Sullivan, SMA, was being childish in his presentation of the subject matter to us. For example, he wanted us to identify proper adjectives. With all due reverence to the instructor, I retorted, "I don't think we are here to do elementary grammar. For me, I learned that thoroughly in the sixth grade under my erudite elementary school teacher. In college it is my ardent desire to build firmly and continuously on my high school knowledge rather than do elementary things after advancing far beyond that." Partly the priest-instructor changed his childish presentation. But he came around in another guise through a course which he said was Music. Music appreciation, to be exact. On a gramophone he would spin records with his classical music. The class was then told to note the mood of the music. For me there was nonsense in the music as it thrilled the air and everyone in the class but me. The students were directed to jot down what each thought the mood of the music conveyed. I saw my classmates scribbling in their notebooks. Personally I could not figure out any mood from the shrill music or say what it was all about. I wrote nothing! On seeing that I wrote nothing, the instructor, seemingly cross, vented out, "Why don't you write?" "Father, you said you call this music classical music. I don't even understand simple music or ordinary music, let alone classical music. I don't want to deceive myself when I gathered nothing from the shrill sounds. I am very sorry for gross ignorance," I soothed him. As he beamed with smiles he inspected each student's work, nodding his head in approval at the students' work. I sat unconcerned. The class was enlivened by its discussion of what they thought the mood of the music was. While the gramophone record was barking, the great alarm horn was announcing some event in Hoffman station, a suburb of Harper City. In short, the horn was summoning all able-bodied men to rush on the scene of the happening. At once upon my Grebo blood sensing the magnitude of the happening I gathered my man form and moved aggressively about the classroom. The priest wanted to know why I appeared upset. "Do you hear and understand the horn, the sound of which is echoing around here?" I asked the concerned instructor. "Now..." he replied. "Oh, you don't understand what the horn is saying? The same way your classical music baffles me." I egressed. Outside I moved very fast towards Hoffman Station, wanting the class and the instructor to believe that I was really going to the place where all able men were being summoned. I disappeared behind the towering trees, and home I went. Later in the week, I heard the bishop saying that Father O'Sullivan would take his furlough. This meant that the clergyman would not teach for the rest of the year. My hope became a stark reality. Father Landry, replacing Father O'Sullivan, ably handled our world history course. I was highly pleased that Father O'Sullivan had taken away his nonsensical classical music and proper adjective nightmare. I was again home with my history course as Father Landry was so versed in history.

Slowly but steadily the years marched past. As the years went by, I grew in experience in my profession of teaching. At first I found it hard to understand why human beings are so different in their endowments. As human beings, I thought students should have the same abilities and capabilities... Sadly it is not... Having realized this through my years of experience, I grew sympathetic and addressed each case accordingly. Since I had been a good student through elementary and high schools I could not believe that some students, after listening during recitation period, could hardly remember what was taught. Truly there are individual differences as psychologists claim. Knowing these differences here and there helped me to adopt a Christ like attitude in dealing with the needy and slow students. As I saw it, a teacher had problems on two challenging fronts: the slow learners and the fast learners. Bringing up the slow learners was more time consuming as it required the patience of Job and the love of Jesus Christ. The fast learners just needed harnessing and supervision. Of course, there is another category that consists of the average learners; this group is more independent than the other groups. The challenges were keen. Guided by my studying of my professional courses, I was resolutely determined to solve my problems emanating from the teaching-learning situation. Gradually my fond hope and earnest prayer found me a way around.

Chapter XVIV "A Road Not Always Smooth"

As the succeeding years brought me a wealth of understanding and love, teaching was crowning me with colorful success. My garrulous female and sedate male students formed a combination of the well seasoned Grebo palatable palm butter dish. The teacher-student relationship could unbiasedly be termed as a relationship between a young father and his growing children.

The insatiable quest for knowledge rendered the class challenging? Certainly the onerous daily teaching task lost its weight as the class responded positively at recitation. Teaching roused me and greatly immersed me into the profession that would be my lifelong occupation.

We were strongly united members of the sixth grade family. In our household, sharing and caring embodied us. Working together and giving a helping hand to those who needed it was our watchword.

One morning, during the first period, when the class was busily engaged doing arithmetic problems, a clumsy, whimsical fellow did not work according to the page and numbers listed on the blackboard. When I discovered that he was doing the wrong thing, I spanked him on his shoulder. At once he sprang to his feet to fight me. It would appear that the female students were watching him. All of them shouted together, "What do you want to do?" In no time the vigilant girls repelled the rebels. This incident rocked the enviable record of a class that was said to be the most disciplined class in the elementary division of Our Lady of Fatima.

Christian doctrine, which was a thirty-five minute period following recess at ten o'clock in the morning, trickled into a heated discussion on SEVEN SACRAMENTS. The one in focus was the Holy Matrimony. I went into explaining the intricacies that God ordained to which God Himself is a witness to the covenant between a man and a woman as the celebrated American Catholic Bishop Fulton Sheen puts it in his book entitled, *It Takes Three to Make Love*. The third party in the suit of love is God Almighty. Before him and with him this lifelong covenant is entered into. Once that is done, God Almighty asserts, "What I put together, let no man put asunder." It would appear that Albertha Shannon, a member of the class, greeted my explanation with admiration for the young teacher.

Admirably she observed, "This man will make a good and loving husband since he already knows about marriage. I would like to marry him, but he is a native boy. When his rustics come to visit him, they will spit in the corner of our home." Her pertinent observation scored a perfect one hundred percent. But the remarks were pungent and degrading. Truth hurts. I was hurt but I said nothing! I simply looked straight in her face. I did nothing wrong to God that would Albertha's sarcastic remarks authenticated. That sunny afternoon my father arrived from the country, after riding over a fifty mile potholed road to visit with a son in the city.

That night, I gave him my small bed as I would spend the night with my friend Harry Nayou. The next morning, when I came back to my little abode I found my twelve by ten feet room all smeared with sputum. I was not shocked, but the pain Albertha inflicted the day before was acutely reawakened. Hurt, I found my way to school. I was sharply dressed that morning. Some of the sixth graders were in the classroom. When I entered, Albertha greeted me very warmly and stroked my waving necktie as the campus was breezy. "Albertha, keep your distance from me. I was brutally insulted by you yesterday. I don't want to see you hereafter, " I declared. The whole class became concerned. In unison the class cried, "What happened between you and Albertha yesterday?" "Don't panic, I'll tell you later. It is a personal thing that should not take our time for the recitation periods. I just made Albertha to feel rejected by her friend and big brother."

A few minutes to closing time, I drew the attention of the class for the story I had promised to tell. "Albertha seemingly expressed her admiration of what appeared to her to be my sound knowledge about Christian marriage. Causally, she remarked sarcastically that she would like to marry me since I had a wealth of knowledge about marriage but sharply rejected the idea on the grounds that I am a native boy and when we are married my country people would come into our home and spit all on the walls. By the way, my dear father came all the way from the Gedebo country to visit his son seeking education on the Cape of Palms. Since I have a very narrow bed I let my father use it alone. Mr. Nayou and I shared his bed last night. This morning when I went back to my room it was sad to see that my room was inundated with spit. This brought back vividly what I call Albertha's causal sarcastic remarks when the class was discussing Christian marriage yesterday. It was a bitter affront to me. Was she paving the way to continue for me to be an outcast as my people are, having laboriously and earnestly worked to earn my own place in the sun? Although a native, or a heathen as we are styled in Maryland, especially in Harper City, comparatively I had acquired more education than many of the average Americo-Liberians, who are not natives or heathens. The glaring and concrete evidence speaks eloquently by my presence as a teacher in the classroom where I daily nurture the Americo-Liberian sons and daughters to get the share of my knowledge through my well organized instruction. What is more rewarding and breathing welcome air of satisfaction is the fact that nearly all the leading politicians and civic leaders of this highly conservative Americo-Liberian enclave send their daughters and sons to a school, particularly the sixth grade, where a heathen or native instructs. I was just joking. I have nothing against my friend and baby sister Albertha for telling me exactly what is very true about my people. I guess Albertha did not know how her keen observation tainted me. Not only did it paint me black, but it would appear now to block my way of getting one of you beautiful young women to be my future life partner. I hope the slander will bear no fruit. I want to advise all of you to be careful how you make such degrading remarks. Please know that my education has made the difference between my people and me," I narrated.

Just before recess, I was trying to straighten my socks on my feet when, out of the blue sky, Angeline Anderson said to the hearing of all, "Mr. Reeves, you have fine fat legs. But what gets you so slim when you should be fat like your legs? If I were much older I would ask my father to allow me to marry to you," Miss Anderson prospected. Was my hope that Albertha's slander should not yield any fruit being realized? From this I gathered that each girl in the class was thinking independently. I was heartened. Coyly I was eyeing one of those rascals by the time our first year ended in college, when three of our older classmates dropped out. One of them, Mr.

Robert Quire, suffered a stoke and never recovered from it. The reasons for the other two were not revealed. However, we missed those devoted and committed teachers who wanted to improve themselves so as to continue the generous work of transferring knowledge to the hungry knowledge seekers. For those of us fresh from high school, the lessons were moving on at a snail's pace. During recitation and discussion periods the older folks found it hard to grasp what the instructors were driving at. At interval, one of those older ones would say to the instructor, "It hasn't reached home yet." This meant that the instructor's explanation has not yet been understood. This was their daily routine. In most cases the class spent meaningless time on a particular topic, discussing one thing over and over, waiting for it to reach home, while some of us were being frustrated.

With those elders gone, our class put on a new shining face. The class was more or less homogeneous. The learning situation seriously challenged us. Awakened from the slumber brought about by those who were trying to discover and recover themselves to the active teaching and learning situation, the remaining college men and women moved steadily, aggressively, and progressively throughout the remaining years.

Socially, my life knew no change; it was stagnant. Most of the time, if it was not all of the time, my daily melodious song was, "Je n'ai pas l'argent." I was really seeing stars in the noonday. However, God was wholly and solely in control of my socially drowning life, as I was constantly kept on course in the glaring facts of my impoverished life. The Catholic Mission's stringent rules and regulations controlling the conduct of teachers and the inadequate salary inhibited all my would-be social movements. Not engaged in frivolous things, I deeply concentrated all my time to teaching and the unwavering pursuit of my college education. God being on my side, I was experiencing success in each of my endeavors. But the stringent rules could not keep me in a vacuum, could they? They never could. In my juvenile years I could not be successfully restrained. During my high school days at Fatima there was a Miss who and I were always close like two peas in a pod. We were warm affectionate friends, despite my lukewarm attitude because of my baffling social conditions that tended to exclude me from those things my age group was socially entitled to do. My instincts were uncompromisingly suppressed. But once in a while they were deflected as they found an outlet. One recess period, my friend of the high school division of Fatima met me. While we were in close conversation, Father Love came by on his way to the priests' house on the hill. "William," the priest called, "come with me." I climbed with him to the top of the hill. Inside Father Love said to me, "I think that girl is deeply in love with you and you clearly seem to be truly in love with her, don't you? I would like for you to marry her. She comes from a good and rich family with a strong political standing. Her people will help you grow socially, economically, and politically," the reverend gentleman urged. "Father, I am not ready for such an onerous and responsible undertaking. I have no money and no education adequate to maintain a family now. Let me get my college education; then I shall later settle down with a wife. It is true that I love Lue, and no doubt, she sincerely loves me. But both of us are not ready. Bishop Fulton Sheen, that American television and radio star prelate, says, and I say with him, 'There is readiness for everything.' Father, readiness is not found in age, big salary, bushy mustache, or college education. It is found in maturity," I waxed the priest with rhetoric and stole away from him. On our way home after school, I told Harry the observation and advice of Father Love. "Do you have milk and eggs to feed that kwi girl?" scornfully Harry questioned me. "No," I replied positively. In the back of my head I was fully aware that with a meager thirty-five dollars monthly salary, the only source of income of mine, I could not adequately cater to my wife, who was used to eating kwi food.

Lue was my true love. With her I was not flirting. But my seriousness with her was always unbelievably restrained. I went along so far and no farther. Beyond that would get me into the web of unready marriage. Nearly every Saturday afternoon she brought pone of bread pasted with kwibutter. Saturday afternoons were spent in reading over my notes and doing home assignments. I had but a chair in my all-purpose room. When Lue came in she comfortably rested in my very small bed while I sat in my only chair. With her glamorous slender body and contagious smiles she would deliver her gift, which was reported with her ardent and fervent message of love for her former schoolmate and now teacher. Our hearts were closely knitted into a tight knot, but our physical bodies were as far from each other as east is from the west. Maybe there was an assault, but categorically there was never battery.

Since my name was sung in every nook and corner of this peninsula city perched on the Cape of Palms by my vivacious students, the name William Reeves was like a household word. One day I decided to visit Lue at her South Baltimore home nestled on the Cape of Palms. When I arrived at the house and knocked at the door, I was greeted by an elderly woman's shrilling voice. "Come in," the gentle woman called. Entering, I introduced myself as Lue's friend, who came to visit her in her home, where I hoped to meet her uncle with whom she lived. Lue had lost her father in her tender age, and was then in the keeping of her father's brother, whose loving wife was Lue's aunt-in-law and mother. "Is this that teacher Reeves the students of Fatima sing about," Mrs. Florence Cooper, having seen and heard my name, said. She then offered me a seat in her beautifully furnished parlor. Seated in soft cushioned chair, I told Mrs. Cooper that Lue, her daughter, was my personal friend and so I came to let her know about it. She welcomed me into her home and requested me to visit them anytime I was free to do so. She wished that the friendship that existed between Lue and me would grow into a lifetime partnership. After the first visit, infrequent visits followed intermittently while Lue's visits were frequent. Unluckily, Lue was knocked off course by somebody else.

Slowly again I became interwoven with another city lass. This one was very aggressive and congenial. This was alluring and was heading me for the burden I was trying to shun. With the help of God, that blazing temptation did not seize me. In general the social life of Harper was as enticing as it was corrupting, but the city strictly adhered to the Christian way of life. Guided by this, everybody, young as well as the old, moved circumspectly.

All the things that make life worth living must go on simultaneously. And so it was in my case. I did not wish any exception.

At my primary task, college study, I became totally involved after Father O'Sullivan's nonsensical history teaching. Reverend Father George Landry took the helm of the college and became the professor of history. Father Landry taught my senior high school world history and Christian Doctrine classes. His thorough preparation and effective delivery of respective subject matters endeared him to my heart. His presentation of the subject fired me again towards what appeared my dormant ambition about my becoming a medical doctor or a lawyer. He was at it again, of course at a higher level. Now I was challenged.

The philosophy of education and educational psychology broadened my horizon in teaching. Gradually my feet were being grounded solidly in my newfound profession in which, I confessed, I was a striving novice. The succeeding years found me on top of things as I was jaggedly determined to do that four year course in no more time than the time required. I had no time to lose. Forward march was my watchword, my trust being in God Almighty always. As I grew taller in college, I had a tighter grip on my young profession, in which I was getting indelibly imbued. The cooperation from my sixth graders flowed unabatedly. But it was not always smooth. I mentioned that earlier.

Eight o'clock every morning began our first period of recitation in arithmetic. This time I would list the page or pages and numbers on the blackboard to be worked by the members of the class. With the pages and numbers listed, the arithmetic textbooks were distributed among the students. A time limit to do the problems according to the pages and numbers was set. In the meantime, I went around, looking at each student's work to see whether each was on the correct course. Soon or late I discovered that student Yancy was doing the unlisted pages and numbers. On seeing his wrong work, I spanked Yancy on the back. He sprang to his feet and squared back to box me. To my great amazement, before he could lever his blow at me the internee young missies in the class seized and knocked him down flat on the floor. These furious girls wanted to tear him apart. Immediately I rushed to rescue insolent Yancy from the hands of the irritated females students who were angrily avenging for their teacher.

I delivered him from the claws of the vengeful students. I sympathized with the poor victim and strongly warned him never to assault any teacher or an elder. "Here in our Christian Doctrine class we are told to honor and obey our parents, including older people and those in authority," I reminded the arrogant student. But as it is often said that a monkey cannot hide its black hands, so Yancy remained an obstinate and disobliging teenager. His behavior isolated him from the other students of that dynamic group of young sisters in that sixth grade class.

In my junior year at college I was besieged by many vexing problems. For almost three years the room I lived in became a life hazard. It was dilapidated and I urged my landlord to repair it but to no avail. I decided to move to another house, where, of course, the rental fee per month would be twenty percent more than before. With a stagnant salary, where would I obtain this extra cost? I had no choice as I needed some safe and decent place to live. Without any source of extra money for help, I moved to a larger room in a house that breathed a more sanitary atmosphere and had relatively more personable neighbors. As soon as that one was undertaken, I received a sad message from my father saying that his wife had given birth to a baby girl, but that he was obliged to send the baby to a foreign missionary of Church of

110

God in Christ, Tugbake, Pleebo District, Maryland County. His reason was that this wife of his had given births to more than seven babies and only one lived. Engulfed in this perennial fear, my father rushed his sweet baby away from their home, hoping to save her innocent life.

The missionary was willing to help but not free care. The woman of God required my father to give her one heifer and four or more large tins of Lactogen milk to nurse. The penniless old man turned to his son who seemed to be in a better financial standing. The message gladdened and saddened me. I was happy that a girl child was born unto my father, who would probably be the only sister of mine.

What help could I give to the anxious village dweller? Sending the milk on a regular basis was completely out of question because I could not afford it. On the question of the heifer I advised him to get the animal from somebody and request the owner to give us a grace period of two short years to pay for the cow. According to my father the owner of the cow was asking for a cash payment of forty dollars. The humanitarian owner accepted my father's pleading terms. For the milk, the village elder was left alone to solve his own nagging problem. Helping him from my little income would spell suicide for me. There was no way at all. The little monthly salary was overburdened! In this impecunious predicament I studied and taught throughout 1958, my junior year in college. But because where there is a will, there is a way, my determination to keep fully abreast with my studies and practice my profession found lofty heights every day. Nobody can sow rice and reap cassava. Earnest labor, no doubt, pays meritoriously. At my studies, the year added another star to my academic crown. My sixth graders' annual records showed that the vast majority of the class earned meritorious promotions. This was another star planted to my teaching crown. This year my annual vacation would be honored in Kablake, my home village, where my parents, especially my mother, who had not seen me since my last visit with them following my graduation from high school, would set eye on me. No doubt, a jolly good time was awaiting the village boy turning kwi as the villagers, relatives, and friends would experience another happy reunion. For three long years I was absent from their festive celebration of the Yuletide. But just before I took the hard ride to the Gedebo Country, surprisingly I received an official letter from the Department of Education, now Ministry of Education, Republic of Liberia, to serve as an instructor of Language Arts at the Webbo Center, Teacher Vacation School, in January of 1959.

The letter explicitly stated that a compensation of one hundred dollars would be my remuneration at the end of a six week period of instruction. About three dollars per diem was added too. Gladly I accepted the lucrative recreation period job, which would afford me the golden opportunity of teaching in-service and prospective teachers. The idea of teaching older people, probably some of my former teachers, excited me. Since the upgrading course was scheduled for early January of 1959, I seized the opportunity to go to Gedebo to spend the whole of December in my village.

In mid-December I arrived in Kablake bustling with activities in preparation for the celebration of the 1958 Christmas. During my two week stay in that village entirely surrounded by high evergreen trees, I busied myself doing many little things close to my heart; one being gun hunting, my profitable hobby. Early one morning I went on a hunting trip deep into the dense forest, far from human habitation, hoping to knock down some monkeys, bush goats, gazelles, or antelopes. In the forest I heard a drove of chattering monkeys among the high trees. I crept slowly toward them. Each step I made toward them was dashed as they huddled together to be more watchful for an unforeseen approaching enemy. I continued this hide and seek ordeal for hours.

Little did I know that I was gradually losing my way around. Finally the chattering of the monkeys died away as they appeared to vanish into the wilds. Not hearing them again and knowing not where they disappeared, I resolved to find my way back to town as the sun was fast sinking beyond the horizon. Alarmingly I found that I had lost my way. "What shall I do?" I whispered to myself. I went right and left, trying to find my way home. Every earnest attempt proved futile. Wearied, I sat down to think about what to do next. Meditatively I began to wonder whether I would ever find my way out of the forest. "If my way is not found, the whole village, in fact the entire people, would be in an upheaval, hunting, trying to trace me all night, as the distance that separated me from the village must be straggling and long. I guess the treetops will be my roof and the leaves underneath will serve as my mattress and pillow tonight. My God, please help me to find my way," I prayed. Something suggested to me, "Why not try to say the decade of the Hail Mary?"

At once I fell on my knees and began to recite the Holy Rosary audibly, counting my fingers, substituting for the beads in the decade. Having finished reciting that decade of the Holy Rosary, I sprang to my feet and turned right. Before me was a broad path, obviously an old trail used by the people who roamed the forest, mostly hunters. Briskly I stepped forward onto the path and found my way home. Before, I said the Rosary with my fellow students with no meaning attached to it by me. I was not a Catholic. For me, it was just obeying the rule to save me my place in the mission and the school, as I used to call the school the Hail Mary school.

Today I miraculously discovered that the Hail Mary prayer is the most powerful to the most blessed woman of all generations. My sincere prayer to our Lord's mother and my mother was immediately answered and I was rescued. I, an African Methodist Episcopal Church member baptized by Reverend William Taylor White, presiding elder of the Cape Palmas District, was now converted to Catholicism. Secretly, without the Rosary I recited the prayer nearly every day afterwards.

My vacation ended in Kablake and I proceeded to Nyaake to take up my assignment with the Teacher Vacation School, Webbo Center, Township of Nyaake.

Just as I expected, my assignment as an instructor at the Teacher Vacation School, Webbo Center, would place me in an embarrassing and ugly situation. The teachers I was going to help in language arts no doubt, were men and women, many of whom were my teachers when I was in the elementary school in Nyaake, about eight short years since. This made me anxious as much as I was willing to share the little knowledge I was acquiring while I was still greedily and assiduously searching for more. On the day and date designated, the in-service and the prospective teachers assembled themselves in the famous Webbo District Council Hall, where the formal opening program was held and the training (teaching) conducted. My language arts teaching scheduled me for two periods a day. Two classes were to benefit from me, a pleasing trouble. Language arts ninth and tenth grades were mine. Each period lasted one hour and forty-five minutes. In the morning I had the tenth graders. The afternoon period took care of the ninth graders. In the tenth grade all the teachers were in service personnel and were, mostly, older men and women, about my father's age. The ninth graders were younger men and women, many of whom were prospective teachers. Comparatively, the ninth grade was unique. The class was more or less homogeneous.

Recitation began on a good note as everybody seemed excited for the brand new instructors the center was blessed with this term. On my part, the appearance of older people to be taught by a younger man like me filled me with anxiety. However, the request which I was about to honor was a national clarion summoning me, a young patriot, to national duty and when duty calls a patriot promptly obeys. The challenge was in my court. This appeared again like a crisis. Must I face it squarely or evade? The question pricked me! I could run away, but where? I took courage and got prepared in order to know exactly where were these educated people standing academically in general and in the language arts in particular, since the majority of the students in the tenth grade were men of the old school of several generations before me. I decided to give a brief but comprehensive diagnostic test in language arts to both classes. The test was administered accordingly and the results told me a disheartening story: each class was far below what was expected of each level. So as not to teach above their level, it was an uphill struggle to impart a new version of the changing English language, not even realizing that the educational materials, including textbooks, used in Liberian schools were now American, not English as before.

The new orientation baffled them as they felt that they were being dispossessed of their old form of the language that made them lords. The grammarians were deeply confused both physically and psychologically. "Everything is not wrong, only little changes here and there in those people's language, which is our second language. As we go on, you will readily notice the former usage and the present. As you will see, you are still home with the language," I assured. I was determined to do my best for my people and my country. My lesson plan for each class was prepared on a daily basis. The response from the tenth grade was encouraging and we made steady progress as the older members of the class cooperated immensely and heartily.

This made me happy as my daily instruction in that foreign language was taking roots in my elders. But one of the older teachers was so arrogant, conservative, and disobliging that she placed a hedge between the class and me as she deliberately, adamantly, and obstinately refused to do class or homework. Each time I requested for homework, Teacher Gibson would sit sulkily and noncompliantly. As I saw it, her belittling attitude was creating negative behavior, which I thought would erode my earnest endeavor. Would the class be prone to copy her uncooperative attitude? I reported this unwholesome attitude of Teacher Esther Gibson to Dr. Merle Akeson, USAID representative for the program (the agency was financing the Upgrading Training of teachers of the Liberian educational system). He advised that every morning, instead of my collecting the homework from each student, each must be required to deliver his or her homework at your desk. Those who remain sitting after requesting for the homework, call them by name and say to them that you are waiting for their homework. The next day I did exactly according to Dr. Akeson's advice. Mrs. Gibson totally refused to bring her work to my desk.

"Teacher Gibson, I am waiting for your homework," I reminded the elderly teacher. "I am fifty years of age, what do you expect me to do at night? Sit up, to do homework, to please whom? Do you mean you shirttail boy will compel me to do homework at night?" Teacher Gibson scornfully questioned. The peppery woman, an old termagant, was trying to ridicule me, failing to realize that I was an instructor sent to help her upgrade herself. "Mrs. Gibson, there is no doubt that you saw me wearing shirttail. Yours and my government requested me to give you some academic brushing up so that you would be better off to teach effectively and professionally instead of murdering the children as ignorant teachers ruin a community of nations. But don't forget that the age of Methuselah has nothing to do with the Wisdom of Solomon," I pointed out to the woman who appeared to be begrudging me for my marked advance in education, comparatively. With these exchanges Mrs. Gibson excused herself from the school and the class. Year in and year out I served as an instructor at that center. Mrs. Gibson did not find her way there again after her untimely departure. Never was she in attendance at any vacation school thereafter but she continued to teach every year until in the late seventies when she was retired. My afternoon section with ninth grade saw me at my best as the class cooperated fully. The class became very challenging.

In January the sun in Nyaake scorches. But as a rule, the poor teachers were compelled to strictly adhere to their dress code prescribed by the Department of Education, represented at the center by the supervisor of schools, Eastern Province.

The supervisor, Professor Henry Nyema Proud, was a former principal of Cape Palmas High School, where students were coercively obligated to wear coat suits every school day. The vast majority of these impoverished teachers in attendance were engaged by indigenous groups, who pay their teachers little or no salary, while a negligible number of the teachers served some foreign missionary organization. The rest of them were the scantily and irregularly paid government teachers.

People who appeared deprived of the necessities of life were obliged to measure arms with those who enjoyed high social status. It was no question that they did not want to be active partakers in the order in which they were and were living. They were only victims of their own society which, seemingly, ostracized them. They wore worn-out business suits everyday. Most of their coats were old fashioned ones, probably their sires brought them from Fernando Po and or the Gold Coast. For the female teachers, they were always regal in their attire as their loving partners took good care of them. Determined to better academically empower themselves, the teachers constantly cooperated. It was the source of my challenge to give them the best of my time so as to nurture them adequately.

In our language arts class, we had jolly times writing sentences talking about the things around us in our class setting. One of our many sentences was, "Black coats conduct heat."

Just before the vacation school was about to close, Father Love, on his pastoral visit to Nyaake, requested Harry and me to teach ninth grade in the high school division at Fatima, Harry to teach Latin and I to teach social studies. But Harry accepted the offer in reverse. "I don't think I can handle that efficiently, but William can, and so let me teach the social studies," Harry proposed.

The Teacher Vacation School came to a close with a colorful ceremony. The teacher speaking on behalf of the student-teachers said among other things, "We enjoy more out of this session than any other since the Webbo Center was established. We were blessed and honored that our own young brothers came at this time to help upgrade us academically and professionally."

With preparations for the 1959 school year underway, I got prepared to plunge into my heavy ninth grade Latin and sixth grade teaching load, gratefully determined to go the extra mile for my benefactor and principal, Very Reverend Dr. Joseph Alfred Love. At the same time, my academic program at the college was paramount in this, my last year, hopefully, time to strike harder and hit the nail on the head. Or as footballers put it, during the last rush, "Spare the ball, not the man." In my case, it was, "Spare no time, for this is your last year in college."

I worked overtime each day, depriving myself of any social activity while burying all my thoughts, words, and deeds into my studies, teaching the Latin course and sixth grade subjects. Although rough from the beginning, as time wore on and I became more immersed the double task became pleasing and no longer a burden. It was during this period I experienced a personal relationship with my heavenly father, a physical and spiritual conversion to Catholicism. It had occurred during my hunting trip in Kablake in December last. One day on our way home from school, I told my friend and brother, Harry Nayou, of my self-acclaimed conversion to the Catholic faith. Happily he had experienced a similar spiritual happening and was waiting to tell me about it. There and then we resolved to make our experiences known to the mission to become baptized.

We were received by a priest, Reverend Father Owen O'Sullivan, and we were baptized together that Easter, during the Holy Week.

Meanwhile, I received my compensation of one hundred dollars for the six week vacation job, the largest sum of money I had ever handled at one time.

The academic year again put my last gift in my fishing basket. I was told that I had successfully completed my course of study at the college and my labor would be rewarded accordingly at a convocation in December ensuing. Thus, I was crowned with success in both teaching and studying. In preparation for my graduation, I put my finishing touches to my teaching job. I was gratified, also, that my ninth grade Latin class was doing fine.

One day, as we prepared for our college graduation, Harry said to me, "William, would you like to go with me to Tchien to teach?" Surprised, I turned to him and delivered to him a torrent of words that were flooding my mind. "Are you stupid, Harry? How could you suggest such a thing to me? We come from different parents, don't we? Let me remind you. While we were working under a scorching sun, my father said, "My son, go to the spring and fetch me some fresh, cold water." In search of it I came here and after many hard but rewarding years, I have filled my pail and I am ready to deliver that fresh, cold water to my thirsty parents, brothers, and sisters, and the villagers of the Gedebo country. "Perhaps you weren't on the same mission, Harry," I continued. "How in the name of Bacchus can you ask me to abrogate my bounded duty to my people? Your suggestion is calculated to keep our growing friendship intact. But it is unacceptable. I cannot deprive my people," I castigated him. "Don't you remember, Harry, that at our baptism, you took the name "Faber," meaning "workman" and I took "Felix," meaning "happy." When combined, the names are knitted as follows: Faber est felix, the Workman is happy We were workmen in the vineyard of education and we have been wonderfully paid. It is about time we return to our respective parents and villagers to share our blessings with them. Harry Tilly Faber Nayou, we are friends and brothers for life but I cannot go with you to Tchien," I concluded. Was this a tirade?

Harry, calm and friendly as ever, only grinned and nodded his head. From this day, our friendship was firmly glued. But, of course, Harry knew deep down in his loving heart that he would win me over to work with him in Tchien.

The convocation program was conducted in the cool, spacious auditorium of Our Lady of Fatima High School, over packed with parents, relatives, friends, and well-wishers. The items on the elaborate program included the commencement address by Maryland County Superintendent, Honorable W. Fred Gibson, an eloquent orator, who told us that the pendulum of education had struck another hour as a new brand of teachers was prepared to serve mankind. The most thrilling moment for me came when each candidate received a Bachelor's Degree in Education.

Graduated was I, but what was next? My extra mile with the mission ended at this juncture. Would the Catholic Mission still need my service?

A day or two following graduation, Harry and I were asked to meet Father Love in his mission office. The likeable Irish priest highly complimented us on our steadfastness and courage in pursuit of high school and college education. "No doubt, you are academically and professionally prepared to serve your people and country. I want to sincerely thank you on behalf of Monsignor Carroll and the mission for your sacrificial services you rendered the mission," he blessed us. On behalf of Harry and myself, I replied, "We can never repay the mission in general and you in particular, Father. You have been a true sunshine in our lives as you afforded us the glorious opportunity of obtaining high school and college education. Rather than giving us fish to eat for a day, you taught us how to fish so that we will eat as long as we live. Thanks to God, fishermen we are. Physically, we will be away from you, but we shall always be with you in spirit." Thus marked the end of our time with the Catholic Mission.

Chapter XIX "Assignment to Nyaake"

In December I received a letter from the Department of Education, Liberia, asking me to serve again as vacation school instructor of language arts at the Webbo Center in Nyaake. With time in my favor for my vacation and the time for the vacation school, I stole out of Harper City and went to Kablake to be with my parents and to tell the many stories, both sad and pleasing, of my years as a student and teacher. The villagers gave me a red carpet welcome. Their son and brother had done it again! My reward, once more, was the well seasoned Grebo palm butter dish.

After closing the vacation school for the year, I returned to Kablake and its peaceful, unhurried village life in search of some needed rest from teaching people who resisted change in traditional subject matter. My energy and disposition were soon restored.

Webbo Junior High School, perched on one of the scenic hills of Nyaake, was the only junior high school in Eastern Province. The junior high school was housed in the unpartitioned Webbo District Council Hall. Each grade had its exclusive corner where students sat on two crude wooden benches and the teachers were without tables or desks. Three blackboards were rotated from class to class. Chalk was scarce; textbooks were in short supply. However, my new economic status gladdened me and so I sang God's praises as He had answered my prayers.

Coming from a school where school supplies were plentiful, I was frustrated and greatly disappointed in the government-owned school. I had come to share what I gathered over the eight-year period of my absence from the township and the district, but as I saw it, the task was being made difficult by the unpleasant conditions lamentably unconducive to the teaching-learning situation. Teaching in that crowded, shutter less hall was like being in a busy beehive, or in heavy traffic, or even the market place where sellers and buyers bargain loudly and endlessly. Even more frustrating to me were the students, older than those I taught in the sixth and ninth grades at Fatima. What a misleading thinking that since they were older, they would be more interesting in learning. As it turned out, the good and interesting things I taught my sixth graders seemed to give them no pleasure.

I was somehow encouraged, however, by the ninth graders' response to my English lesson. Of course, it took all my professional know–how and considerable sugar coating to make the subject palatable for the lazy students. "Do you know that this foreign language, English, which unfortunately is our second language, is the official medium of communication in Liberia? If you fail to acquire the necessary skills in this subject, how will you be able to extricate yourselves from some trouble or persuade someone to give you something you need? Let's get serious and settle down to our lessons in general and English in particular. Apply yourselves fully to your school work. The future belongs to those who prepare for it," I admonished.

After months of hammering home the importance of education to these rural students, encouraging signs signaled in hope and so I continued pleading with the students. My former teachers, now my colleagues, although age was telling on them, were still blessed with life and vigor. Mr. Peter W. Kun, my arithmetic teacher in the elementary school, was still at home with figures and the snuff shell he used to work miracles with numbers.

Although much had changed in the eight years, much remained intact. The school was still managed by Reverend Joseph Wodo Andrews, popularly called "Waka to." The school committee was still chaired by Mr. G. C. H. Gadegbeku, the prolific storyteller, still looking handsome and able. God continued to shower his manifold blessing on the only township in Eastern Province. In that eight years' period, the Liberian government had established elementary schools and salaried the teachers throughout the vast Webbo District. Although the salaries were meager, it was a good beginning. In spite of a shortage of basic school materials, archaic facilities, scanty salaries, and the lack, in most cases, of basic teacher training, these men and women were, in some way, professional and effective. They sowed what they had with care and love and the harvest was copious.

In 1963, Webbo Junior High School was blessed with two U.S. Peace Corps volunteers, a young married couple, John and Elizabeth Bachart, who helped us greatly in our task of educating the young. They and I became good friends.

John and Elizabeth rented a house from a local landlord, Albert K. Dzidzienyo, who, in addition to collecting rent from them each month, became a social pest, often begging them for cigarettes, and once, when John accidentally set fire to their outdoor toilet, a rickety wooden structure about four feet by six feet and about five feet high, not worth more than forty dollars, the landlord demanded four hundred dollars to rebuild the tiny hut. His claim was reduced to twenty-five dollars by U. S. Peace Corps, Liberia, which amount he received under protest. Because of their landlord's constant harassment, the couple asked for a transfer to another school in a different community. The transfer was granted and Webbo Junior High School was the loser, robbed of its hard working volunteer force.

Luckily for the school and the community, the Bacharts were soon replaced by two lovely young ladies, Marilyn Koepp and Linda Sayre, with whom I had much in common. We were young, teachers, and we had similar educational backgrounds. We became very good friends, especially Linda and I, as both of us liked to bend our elbows over glasses of Daniel Crawford's whiskey or a bottle of Beck's Beer after school. Again, it was Mr. Dzidzienyo who leased his two-bedroom house to the volunteers, who told him in no uncertain terms that he was not allowed to visit the house unless he was asked to do so.

These two young, dedicated American Peace Corps volunteers, a great asset to the school, reinforced Principal Andrews and his staff and contributed much for the enrichment of the students. They taught full time, and in addition, encouraged the weak students to visit their home to receive extra help.

Meanwhile, across the water, incumbent U. S. President Lyndon B. Johnson, a democrat, was being vehemently opposed by a Republican contestant, Barry Goldwater, vying for the U.S. presidency, the highest public office of their powerful land, which, when captured, makes the occupant the most powerful man in the world. As an honorary American and a democrat, I was the democratic campaign leader against the Liberian-based Republican Linda Sayre and Marilyn Koepp. It was no small political battle each day between us. The debate grew steadily heated each day as the parties unearthed the political weakness of each candidate, sarcastically pointing out where the candidate fell short of the quality, ability, and capability a president of an all-powerful nation of the world should have. In the meantime, Time Magazine carried a news items from a German newspaper saying that it did not know why Americans should campaign for an inconsistent, unduly conservative man like Barry Goldwater to seek the U.S. presidency, which, when won, would dangerously place him at the helm of power of a country that had the highest nuclear capacity and capability in the entire world. His incumbency, no doubt, with his inconsistency and conservatism with such a sophisticated nuclear power, would unthinkably plunge the whole world into mass destruction. Unabatingly the debate went on and on until it culminated into the November elections, which brought the incumbent President, Lyndon B. Johnson, a landslide victory, giving him a four year term mandate, having served the unexpired term of assassinated President John Kennedy of sainted memory.

As the records clearly showed, when the haranguing and the cheering stopped, the democrats were crowned with sweeping, overwhelming, and decisive victory, earning us both the White House and the Congress. Of course, as you know, in the American political tradition, Linda and Marilyn, the mercilessly vanquished Liberian-based Republicans, congratulated me, a Liberian-American democrat, for my party's victory at the polls. It was truly an intellectual exercise. During that campaign I voraciously devoured everything I could find in the world of literature.

Those many salient points of argument I raised during the energy consuming campaign led Linda to observe, "I don't want to believe that you are from a home of illiterate parents. I hold it very strongly that your parents are well educated from your large, rich, and flowery vocabulary." "Linda, I have nothing to hide about my parents. They live and are in good health. After a bus ride, it takes about an hour's walk on the trail to my village, where my parents reside. If we can catch a ride from here, the car will put us down at a point from where we will begin our one hour foot journey to Kablake, where you will meet the pots in which this well seasoned Grebo palm butter was cooked. Without a car, it will take us three hours to get there. Can you take a nine mile journey on foot? If your answer is in the affirmative, then let us decide on the time to go there," I urged. "Would this Sunday be alright?" my volunteer friends asked. "Certainly, that is the most appropriate time as the villagers stay home on Sunday," I assured them.

I made the necessary arrangement with a pickup owner, Mr. Bonifacius Itoka, to drive us to Worteke from where we would go on our hike. As we planned, we left Nyaake that sunny Sunday morning for the visit with my parents living in London, Gedebo. Our snaky trail led us through three closely connected villages before Kablake.

Upon arrival in the first village, Worteke, the capital of the Gedebo and the seat of the High Priest, Bodior, in the Gedeboland, we were given a rousing welcome as the youngsters shouted, "Kamma ja le nyanplee nyanu," Kamma brings white women. Elder Musu invited us to his house. According to the Gedebo tradition, he welcomed us by offering kola nuts with hot pepper and cold water. This also implied a question: What is your mission here? We accepted the kola, ate and drank, and thanked elder Musu. "These young ladies would like to see my village and parents and so we are on our way there," I informed the elder of our mission. My guests and I continued our journey.

Our next stop was Jolotoke, a large village. The usual pleasantries were exchanged and kola nuts were served again The next village, Baweake, my mother's home village, is a member of the Trio Villages. The inhabitants had gone to Tenzonke, where all the members of the Trio Villages would welcome my/their distinguished visitors. In Kablake, we met my parents and uncle, who gave the American ladies the typical Liberian handshake. My father gave us the traditional welcome and I told him that these young ladies had come to Kablake just to see and know you and my mother. They had wished to know you both personally. Briefly, my uncle took them on a guided tour of the small village. Linda wanted me to interpret my uncle's English for them. "If I do, you will not enjoy the fun of your visit. Try to figure out what he is trying to say and the fun will be yours from his kind of English language."

Later on, Linda and Marilyn had their audience with my parents. As you would expect, the village elder spoke his broken Gold Coast English and my mother said nothing, broadly smiling. After that we proceeded to Tenzonke where all had gathered to honor our special guests. In that village, Old Man Moses, the grand old African Methodist Episcopal Church local pastor, the vehicle on which Christianity and education had brightened and enlightened our villages and its people, welcomed and warmly greeted their white guests. "Are you married?" Pastor Moses suddenly asked Linda. "No, I am not married," Linda replied with a blush. "How old are you?" the pastor pressed his charming visitor. "I am twenty-four years old," Linda revealed. "Why is it that you are not married at this age?" Pointing to a lady, the pastor informed Linda that that lady was of her age and she was married and had a child. "Well, before I get married I will make sure the guy who wants to marry me has a good bank account and a lucrative permanent employment," the Western woman emphasized. "If that is the case, then you have this day found the man you wish to marry. I own everything here and around. These huts you see are all filled with rice, constituting my abundant wealth. Marry me and have a happy life with me," the old Kuotapi openly solicited. "Maybe you have all those riches. It would be a blessing for me to marry you only if you will promise me that I won't carry loads on my head because my hair is slippery. If that is guaranteed, I am ready to cut the cake with you now," Linda declared. (The old man's fortune was not large enough, and he did not guarantee that she would not have to carry loads, so she did not marry him.)

Following this heart-to-heart exchange between Linda and Pastor Moses, the village was set ablaze with accordion music and all the people present took their tread in the center of the village. During the brief entertainment, my friend Joseph K. Towaye, in charge of the whole arrangement, served the young charming white American ladies with nutritious Gedebo rice with cold water fish cravy. Marilyn and Linda ate heartily and took sips of the freshly brewed Gedebo palm wine.

On our way back to Nyaake, I inquired from Linda and Marilyn whether their question about my parents being literate or illiterate was answered. They replied in unison, "We are convinced and satisfied that your parents are illiterate. We must congratulate you for helping yourself so well in the use of our language, English, which is your second language," the US Peace Corps volunteers boosted me. "Let me thank you too for honoring my parents, Pastor Moses, and the villagers. As of today my parents will consider you their daughters as you are their son's personal friends. Your visit was a singular honor conferred upon me, too. Also, I want to thank you for your compliment that I have a large, rich, flowery vocabulary. I highly appreciate it. I promise you that I shall continue to richly replenish it from time to time," I sincerely promised.

By the end of the year, Linda became sick and was airlifted to the United States of America. On the whole, the school year ended successfully. Marilyn left immediately for the US when we closed for the year. Left alone I was!

1965 was a bitter year for me. Deserted, as it were, my fellow intelligentsia left Liberia for good, having served their two year tenure in two different communities in Liberia. I was haunted by a series of illnesses from the beginning of the year. Time and again, I visited the clinics in Lower Grand Gedeh County and hospitals in Maryland County, respectively, but to no avail. Continuously I battled with the poor health condition almost to the end of July.

In May, while I was seeking medical help in Pleebo, a close relative of mine in my home village mistakenly shot and killed his first cousin. According to the Gedebo tradition, when human blood is brutally spilled in that way, a cow is demanded plus a demijohn of cane juice and other things. Shedding of human blood on the Gedebo land is an abominable offense against the, as it is strongly held that spilled blood curses their soil, which will cause non-productiveness. And until a cow was slaughtered the land remained cursed.

Since I was very sick in Pleebo, I could not go home for that tragic death. But knowing clearly what it entailed, I directed my cousin in Pleebo to tell my father and others in our family (clan) to give one of my cows to the Gedebo people for the sacrifice and I extended my condolences to the bereaved family headed by my father.

Partly relieved, my family dispatched my younger brother to thank me and request me to give them the money to buy the demijohn of cane juice. Our family was in deep trouble. We had to be our own brothers' keepers. Should I hoard my money while my father was being harassed and ridiculed as the indigenous people spat in his face and demanded the other things for the cleansing of their land? Giving the cow and the other requirements were no tangible reason to be charged around while we were deeply grieving for such a tragic death of a promising young man, Toequie. A demijohn containing five gallons of cane rum was required. Seven dollars was the cost for the spirit. I honored the family request and handed the seven dollars to my brother for the cane juice.

Following this tragic death in my village was the passing into the great beyond of the octogenarian Paramount Chief Koffee Musu of Gedebo Chiefdom, of protracted illness. This venerable statesman, staunch politician, traditionalist, and reformer of the first order was a descendant of my family based in Kablake. The family was paralyzed by the home going of this illustrious son of theirs. At the time of the death of the paramount chief, I was recovering slowly but steadily and so I went home for the state funeral, which was attended by multitudes of people from all walks of life.

In July of that year, my poor health condition alarmingly deteriorated and I

121

was compelled to rush myself to Monrovia for an immediate medical help. In Monrovia I sought help in many clinics and hospitals in search of relief or cure. At first it appeared that there was no remedy in sight. However, I went everyday, knowing and trusting that the miraculous healing power of God Almighty would know my face one of these days. As the signs of recuperation beamed about me, in early September I received a radiogram through Senator Harry H. K. Carngbe of the newly created County of Grand Gedeh. When I visited him that sunny morning at his Clay Street home in Monrovia, the senator told me that he had a radiogram for me. "For me?" anxiously I asked. "Yes," the senator replied. He handed me the radiogram. But I could not open it because my whole being began to tremble, fearing that some sad news was contained in it. "Please open and read it for me," I implored the honorable gentleman. Beaming with smiles after reading the radiogram, the senator cleared the air, "Don't worry, it contains no death news and it is not from your wife or family, but rather it comes from Mr. Cyrus S. Cooper, assistant supervisor of schools, Grand Gedeh County. He is requesting you to replace Principal Harry Nayou, who is granted leave of absence to study for a year in the United States of America. As acting principal, you will be in charge of Tubman-Wilson Institute for the same length of time Mr. Nayou will be away. The school is located in Zwedru, Tchien."

Hesitantly I asked, "Au..au..dor..what do you say about the request?" "Well, the request was made to you through me. I consented, thinking that it might yield some personal benefit for you in no distant future," the senator assured me. "Since you think that there is something in the bargaining for me, I accept it in principle," I announced.

Having recovered considerably, I made myself ready for my back-home journey to Nyaake in preparation to take up my new assignment in Zwedru. In mid-September I flew from Monrovia to Harper in Maryland County, from where I rode in a passenger pickup to Webbo.

My wife was briefed about my new assignment. The next day I journeyed to Kablake to inform my parents, who, for a long heartbreaking period, wondered about my whereabouts, that my government was requesting me to take up an acting principalship of a school called Tubman-Wilson Institute in Zwedru, Krahn country. Upon arrival I found that the former village chief was out doing his perpetual job clearing bush from his cocoa patch in old Kablake. In the meantime, I briefed my mother, whose reaction greatly surprised and amused me. "If I had known that once you were educated, you would be taken away from me without my express consent, I would never have sent you to school," my mother grieved. In reply, I told my mother that my heart was aching to know that one of the worthiest things she did for mankind was now being regretted by her. "Ayee, I am sorry, it is too late. You cannot recant or undo this fine gift you ably nurtured for Liberia and the world. Don't worry, the distance that might separate me from you physically will be no barrier for fulfilling my filial duty and obligation," I consoled the village housewife.

I proceeded to the place where the old militiaman had gone to clean among his cocoa patch on an uninhabited village. When I met him, I pulled the radiogram out of my pocket and handed it to him while we were exchanging the usual pleasantries. "What is this?" looking curiously at the fancy envelope in which the radiogram was enclosed, the farmer suddenly queried. "That is what you call Tenglapo," I explained. "What does it say?" my father asked. Briefly I conveyed the message to him. "What! You are not going there, Kpe! This is what I say," the papi emphasized. "But why do you say that? It is our country that summons me to duty. Must I disobey and forsake the people in need?" I pleaded and appealed to his patriotism. "I don't want you to go there because Krahn people like to take people to court," my concerned father averred. "Do you know their reason?" I pressed him further. Angrily he snorted, "When you followed their women." "Have I ever brought such a trouble on you?" patiently I inquired. "No, not what I know about you," the polygamist mused. Then I vehemently assured him that he would never hear such an immoral thing about me in the Krahn country. With this, my father sanctioned my going to Zwedru.

As time was running out for the school year, I could not spend the night with my parents. By late afternoon, I was off to Nyaake to spend the night with my eight-month-old son, four-year-old daughter, and my wife, in our newly built home on Tendeh Hill, Township of Nyaake, Webbo.

On the 20th of September, 1965, I embarked, trekking on the winding trails through Webbo, Tuobo, Nyantienbo, Sarbo, Pallipo to Kanweake, Gbeapo, from where I would meet the highway that linked Kanweake in Lower Grand Gedeh and Zwedru in Upper Grand Gedeh. It took me four weary days to reach Kanweake.

Wearing a pair of mermuda, sneakers, a white helmet, a cutlass in sheath worn across my chest, and .22 rifle braced on my left shoulder, I marched into Kanweake, a large Grebo town surrounded by scenic towering hills covered with evergreen trees. Slowly I ascended the compound where the highups of the Gbeapo District lived, including the leading teachers of the place rapidly growing into a big commercial center in the countryside. My overnight landlord was a veteran old teacher, Professor Samson Chea. Just before I went to wash off the sweat from my weary body, an old man dressed in uniform entered and said to Mr. Chea, "The commissioner says he would like for the man who has just arrived to go to him." I rushed out to the quarters of the commissioner on the large compound. I forgot that Honorable Charles B. Cummings was commissioner of the district. I was warmly greeted by the highest administrative officer of the district. "I recognized you as soon as you came into view, but your outfit baffled me. And so I let you pass. I wanted to make sure it was you. You are officially welcome to Gbeapo District. Be at home, away from home," the honorable man noted. He then handed me a huge rooster for my supper that night. Grinning, the conservative Maryland County Americo-Liberian remarked, "Yes, it is very true that you can get a man out of the bush but you cannot get the bush out of him. I did not know that an educated man like you would recourse to his father's way of wearing cutlass across his chest." We bade each other good night and I excused myself. I had a restful night.

Refreshed from a restful night, September 25th found me on board a worn-out Renault bus bound for Zwedru in the Krahn country. Between seven-thirty and eight that night I arrived in Zwedru, a beautiful growing town nestled in the heart of the evergreen forest of Liberia. The bus brought me straight to the door of Mr.

Nayou's home. When I descended the duazet I was warmly greeted by Nayou's short, white-sparkling-teeth, contagiously smiling je bor dor. With her was a slim, dark-skinned young lady with a ready smile, who would later be my special and congenial friend in my Zwedru social life.

On the 26th of September, a Sunday, a day set aside to say "Thank you'" to God, I attended mass, celebrated by Reverend Father John Feeney, SMA, at Christ The King Catholic Church of Zwedru. After mass the priest treated me to breakfast. When I returned from mass, Mr. Cyrus Cooper came over to invite me for lunch. That bright sunny Sunday gave me clearly a bird's eye view of this sprawling Tchien town with its many and varied promises.

On September 27th, escorted by the assistant supervisor of schools, Mr. Cyrus Cooper, I walked on the campus of Tubman-Wilson Institute, about three hundred feet away from Mr. Nayou's home where I lodged and where I spent my one-year temporary assignment with the school. In his usual eloquent talk, Mr. Cooper introduced me to the school and officially turned the school over to me as acting principal, whereupon, I delivered my maiden speech: "I am happy to be here in answer to your call for help from any person willing to manage the affairs of your school while your learned principal seeks greater educational heights. In order to be successful, I need cooperation from all of you. One man cannot do it all by himself. So please regard me as an acting Liberian principal, not a Krahn, Grebo, or Kpelle, but an acting principal for all these heterogeneous groups. I would be highly appreciative and thankful for your support and cooperation in the smooth running of this school, which you know better than I do. Esprit de corps must be our watchword. Together we have the important task of imparting useful knowledge to these youngsters entrusted to our care and love," I asserted.

And so I was now the acting principal of the only high school in the newly created county of Grand Gedeh, bare as a deserted village, alarmingly understaffed and provided with many unqualified teachers, with the exception of a UNESCO teacher from India and a United States Peace Corps volunteer, Martin Alpert, who proficiently taught science. With a sparse student population, Tubman-Wilson Institute was rich with studious, diligent, and obedient rural students. Built in an L-shape, TWI was initially an elementary school, grades one through six. According to its history, the school grew steadily to its present status. The classrooms were sealed off from each other by hard boards.

In my get-acquainted meeting with the students and faculty, I found that this school was one of the good-for-nothing schools of the government of Liberia. It was totally unbelievable that this vast province, now a county, from which the government amassed huge revenue from its vast forest, which immensely enriched the coffers of the country was unattended. The students grievously informed me that they had not seen the results of their period tests taken since the school year (1965) began, and of other pertinent issues, which needed my immediate and speedy attention.

Sadly I was convinced that the students and their parents/guardians had the legitimate right to see and know the results of their schoolwork from time to time. That this had not been done breached the trust implicitly reposed in the institution by the public. What could I do?

Following the meeting, I at once contacted the office of the assistant supervisor of schools to find out whether student report cards as supplied by the Department of Education were available. Disappointedly, I was told by the local education boss that he had none in his office. There was an apparent "don't care" attitude on the part of the supervisory and the administration of TWI, negligence beyond measure. However, I decided to go to Monrovia to collect some report cards from the department. Seeing my deep concern about the students not getting their report cards, Mr. Alpert, the US Peace Corps volunteer in the school, made available a US Peace Corps/Liberia jeep that took both of us to Monrovia. Upon inquiring about report cards at the department, I was slapped in the face with this blaming question, "Mr. Reeves, this is no time to request for student report cards. What has your school been doing with the students' test results?" the department bluntly queried. No answer was relevant to the department question as I saw it. I hushed up and stealthily made my exit.

When we returned to Zwedru we decided to improvise. On ditto stencil, Martin designed a report card and hundreds of copies were dittoed off according to the enrollment of the school and some were reserved. On a school week day, Thursday, to be exact, Martin and I took our improvised report cards to Supervisor Cooper. As usual, many of the teachers of the Zwedru School System had gathered in the supervisory to present articles and to work on a weekly newspaper called the *Tchien Post*. I laid the cards before Mr. Cooper for his comment, if he had any, but to my heartbreaking surprise, an afternoon elementary school principal, David Swengbe, shouted at me, saying, to the hearing of the gathering of teachers, "You have no right to make your own report cards." Mr. Cooper perused the handy improvised cards without comment, but simply nodded his head, I guessed in approval. I did not rejoin as it made no sense to battle words with a non-professional teacher. One thing I was sure of was that the grades would be recorded on their respective cards and be given to the students the following school week. Distributed were the cards the following week. In early December, 1965, the school closed its doors, marking the end of a successful school year.

Away from home for several months, I was homesick. Relieved from the year's school work, I rushed back to Nyaake to spend the Christmas with my wife and children. The reunion and the Yuletide spelled jolly time in our new home.

The first week in January, 1966, the year President Kwame Nkrumah was ousted from power, found me tramping on the snaky trails to Gbeapo from where I would catch a ride in some worn-out Renault bus. Following my arrival in Zwedru, the Zwedru Teacher Vacation School was open for the transaction of business. This time I was serving as a coordinator of the center. The Zwedru Center was not like the Webbo Center in many ways. However, they were all geared toward improving the academic standard of each teacher and his or her professional performance.

During the vacation school, the Under Secretary of Education for Instruction and the Directress of Elementary Education in the Department of Education, Republic of Liberia, graced our center with their official presence. Sometime in mid-January, 1966, the UNESCO Indian instructor at TWI took away, without permission, a dirt block mold from the school premises. I ordered the mold back to the school. I demanded it from the person with whom I met it. This action within the scope of my authority angered the Indian instructor. When the Department of Education officials arrived, the Indian instructor made it his point to report me to the under secretary just before I had the time to meet the honorable gentleman. Later on, Supervisor Cooper and I together with the Indian instructor met our distinguished guests in the Grand Gedeh County Superintendent's official residence where I was questioned about why I took the school mold from the Indian teacher who had lent it to an outsider. "The mold was taken away from the storeroom of the school and that it was taken away without my consent is a complete and flagrant disregard of the constituted authority I represent," I angrily retorted. Quickly the directress broke in and observed, "I don't think it is fair, proper, or legal to disregard the principal in this case. At least, let the principal exercise his authority, although we do not pay him the same salary according to qualification and tenure of service. He and the so-called UNESCO professor have the same qualifications, yet the Indian teacher gets a bigger salary and huge other benefits. Why must he usurp the principal's authority, who is the sole custodian of everything and anything belonging to the school?" The victory fell on and swelled me.

In welcoming the distinguished visitors the next day at the Zwedru Teacher Vacation School, I said, among things, "On behalf of the instructors and our ambitious teachers assembled here to upgrade themselves academically and professionally, and in my own name, I welcome you to this center where your teachers are busily engaged upgrading themselves. Indeed, we are singularly honored that you laid aside your daily busy schedules and risked your precious lives on these pothole-ridden roads to officially grace our center with your presence. But Honorable Under Secretary of Education for Instruction, let me remind you what William Shakespeare, that prolific 16th century English writer, says and I say with him, "He is well paid that is well satisfied and I delivering you I am satisfied and considered myself well paid." For the poet, this was his philosophy of life. But we the teachers, as much as we are imparting knowledge to our young people for a better tomorrow, are satisfied but we are not well paid. In short, Mr. Under Secretary, please give us a better salary consideration in this sacrificial but noble profession. We are being socially degraded because of our scanty, stagnant salaries. In short, we are underpaid.

Just before the 1966 school year started, Mr. David Y. Swengbe, father of one of our senior students of the year, the first 12th graders in the history of the school, came to my window early one morning requesting for his son's transfer. Why did he want Joseph's transfer at this time? I had nothing against that. "No transfer forms are available now. The supervisor is in Monrovia. Perhaps he might bring some copies," I discretely informed Mr.Swengbe. "Can you prepare one on your typewriter?" Mr. Swengbe pleaded. "A teacher is not allowed in these parts to improvise. Is it permissible now because you want your son transferred?" I demanded. "And so you want to sabotage my son's interest and education? I am going to report you to the Secretary of Education, Republic of Liberia," Mr. Swengbe threatened. With this he rushed away from my window. "Wait a minute, Mr. Swengbe. Remember that the Department of Education would rather get rid of you than William K. Reeves," I asserted. Obviously provoked, in a confused mood, Mr. Swengbe hysterically and loudly asked, "Why do you think so?" And so I told him because I am more qualified in the teaching profession than you. Simple as that! My reply choked him and he moved slowly away from my window.

Just as Mr. Swengbe threatened, he reported me to the Department of Education but got a blinding slap in his face, a slap that reflected what I told him. The 1966 school year brought the full grip of the administration onto this teething rural high school with little or no facilities. The problems here alarmingly found no parallel anywhere in our system of education. Fact and ingenuity were needed to characterize every step the administrator would take. Irregularity, tardiness, and uncouth appearances on part of the students and teachers alike spelled obnoxious. In and around the school feceswere smeared here and there every morning. A very strange environment this growing school was placed in! The unhygienic conditions were sickening.

In order to alleviate the unsanitary conditions I needed the collective efforts of the constant cooperation of the Tubman-Wilson Institute family and the civil community. Headlong I launched the campaign in an all out drive. The police of the county were a great asset to my endeavor as they diligently patrolled the campus area every night.

The superintendent of the county made some strong public pronouncements regarding those who nuisance abused the classrooms and campus of the only high school in Zwedru and the county. Irregularity, tardiness, and untidiness were my personal administrative matters, I assumed. With the cooperation of those directly concerned, in a month or so, irregularity, tardiness, and untidiness completely became isolated happenings at Tubman-Wilson Institute. The rules controlling irregularity, tardiness, and untidiness were rigorously enforced to the letter and those who fell victim to them were penalized according to the rules made and provided in each case. In the succeeding months of the school year the reforms were gaining glaring evidence in and around the school. A parent who came to make some query about how her child was coping with the stringent reforms remarked, glancing here and there, "Mr. Reeves, you are an accomplished reformist." Another called me Keyan pepper. At the end of the first semester our seniors, four in all, Thomas Zulu, Joseph Swengbe, Philip Davies, and Railey Sole, were unquestionably qualified to register as candidates for the National Examinations, which were due to be administered in October that year.

At the beginning of recitation period one morning, a student entering seventh grade classroom was driven back by his math teacher. "You are drunk, get out," Teacher Wilson Weeks shouted at student Barford Jolo. "You are drunk too," retorted the student. Foaming at his mouth, Mr. Weeks rushed to where I was standing. (By the way, anywhere the principal stood on the campus was his office since indeed there was no office space for him in the school) "Mr. Principal, suspend student Barford Jolo. He called me a drunkard in the presence of the entire class. Suspend him now," the furious and overwhelmed with emotion Teacher Weeks ordered his principal. I said to myself, "The old teacher is rapturous. The disturbed old teacher told the student that the student was drunk whom he allegedly insulted him by calling him a drunk. "Look, my friend, come here at once," I beckoned to the student. "So you called my teacher a drunk?" I patiently inquired. "He told me that I was drunk and so in turn I said he was drunk too," he student explained. "And so it is true that you called him a drunk? Go home now and report here tomorrow morning for further investigation. Leave now," I pretentiously commanded. The poor fellow left the school at once. I then invited the teacher in my office without space, chair, or desk. "You are an elderly man and experienced teacher. As such you must control your emotion. You don't throw stones at somebody else's glass windows when you know that your house has glass windows too. Why did you call the student a drunk when you are as guilty as the student might have been. Up to this time you cannot balance yourself on your legs. From where I stand, a distance about ten feet away from you, the strong sour odor of palm wine is almost getting me intoxicated. Bathed in palm wine, as it were, can you call your Bacchus friend a drunk? As you staggered toward me in order to complain about the student who allegedly insulted you, you were cutting 'exes' displaying demonstrably the embarrassing attitude of a man overpowered by King Alcohol. Anybody seeing you now will readily testify that you are indeed drunk. No doubt then, the overpowering alcohol in you arrogantly propelled you to demand the principal to suspend a student without knowing what the student did. Please behave according to your age and position and the sacred trust reposed in you by the taxpayers," I strongly warned the "wizard," as he was popularly known by the students.

As the National Flag Day celebration was drawing nearer, the teachers of the Zwedru School System met in a joint faculty meeting under the chairmanship of the principal of Tubman-Wilson Institute. Among other things the meeting was to organize a suitable program for the celebration of the natal day of our national ensign on August 24th. During the meeting I interposed a pertinent question: "On the day of school's parade, such as the one we are planning, how do the schools line up?" Forthwith the answer came from Mr. David Y. Swengbe, Principal, Antoinette Tubman Elementary Day School. In a dramatic mood, Mr. Swengbe declared, "Schools line up in a parade according to their chronological respective ages, that is, the time each was founded." He added, "Since TWI is a high school, she is an exception. She leads the parade followed by God Assembly Elementary School, St. Philomena Elementary and Junior High School, Baptist Elementary School, etc." "Well, as I know it, schools march in parade according to grade level and not a time a school was established. In the ensuing parade for the celebration of the Liberian National Flag Day, the formation I am strongly proposing is that the former formation be changed so as to paint the academic reality on the ground. In this light, the new formation will be as follows: TWI followed by the junior high school and the elementary schools." This sparked a stormy objection from Mr. Swengbe and all who believed in the age of schools rather than their grade levels. Blatantly they told me and the majority of the teachers present that I was/am a Catholic and because of that I was trying to promote St. Philomena Elementary and Junior High School. The majority wholeheartedly accepted what they called my timely and inspirational proposal. "We are not going to march according to your biased proposal," those unreasoning teachers shouted in unison at me, the chairman and acting assistant supervisor of schools at the time.

On the day of the program A/G ATD and others boycotted the parade and the proposed formation, except TWI and St. Philomena marched according to the new formation. Instead, gross obstinacy took Mr. Swengbe and his disobliging followers to go to escort the Honorable Superintendent, Moses P. Harris, and his official councilmen to the national celebration. When these breakaway schools arrived on the superintendent's compound, from where the superintendent would be escorted under the grand parade of the students and teachers of the Zwedru School System to Tubman-Wilson Institute's campus, the venue of the national occasion, they were driven back fast by Deputy Inspector Major David Gaye, saying, "You are not the schools to escort the superintendent to the program, not afternoon schools. Get back, you afterwards people. By the way, where is TWI? Where is Mr. Reeves, who as chairman extended the invitation officially to the superintendent of the Joint Faculty of the Zwedru School System? How do you now unilaterally come to escort us to the program without TWI and its principal and teachers?" Major Gaye relevantly questioned. Mr. Swengbe could not answer the burning question but shamefully bowed and crept away. In the meantime, TWI, St. Philomena, Baptist, my teachers and I arrived at the superintendent's residence. At once I apologized to the superintendent and his officials for being so late and then explained briefly the reason for my lateness. Without a word about the lateness, the superintendent simply said, "Let's go to the program," and off we briskly marched to the site of the program. Honorable Silas Hue, Grand Gedeh County member of the Liberian National Legislature, delivered the National Flag Day oration. He was eloquent and gave us food for thought. In his remarks Honorable Harris said that God intended for one man to lead at a time and so he gave man one head and not two heads. "There was nothing wrong about the formation of the lineup of schools in a parade, this is what is done all over Liberia. Schools are formed in a parade according to grade levels. Flagrantly you teachers exhibited gross disobedience to constituted authority, a perfect defiance and example for your students to exactly copy," Mr. Harris strongly observed and warned.

In early November, Mr. Harry T. F. Nayou, Principal of TWI, returned from the United States of America, having earned his Master's degree in school administration. As he increased, I was to decrease in another way. Our first graduation at Tubman-Wilson Institute was pageantry. Promotions were awarded accordingly. Decreasing I found my way back to Nyaake in mid-December, 1966. In Webbo, I enjoyed my timely reunion and Christmas with my wife and children first and then I made an unceremonious disappearance against their consent. I had some inner satisfaction about my brief stay as acting principal of Tubman-Wilson Institute. As I meditatively reflected I realized that my work at that teething rural high school was almost a total success story. With tremendous constant cooperation of both students and teachers, the school over less than two years was physically and academically changed. Was this my personal feeling or was it really what happened at the school?

When I happily returned to Nyaake to resume my teaching assignment with the Webbo Junior High School, as usual, I went about the hilly township, visiting with elders, relatives, and friends of this rural conservative town perched on the west bank of the longest and largest of all the multiplicity of rivers that drain Liberia. I mean the

Cavalla River, which forms the natural boundary line between Liberia and her eastern neighbor, the Republic of the Ivory Coast (La Cote d'Ivorie). My first call was at the home of Mr. and Mrs. G.C.H. Gadegbeku. Mr. Gadegbeku was chairman of the Webbo District School Committee, from where I obtained my education. It was always rewarding to visit the prolific and didactic storyteller. I first met his charming middle age wife always with a ready smile. "Howdo-o, Ma, and where is Foofee (as his nephews and nieces affectionately called the old man), your husband?" She exchanged the usual pleasantries with me and welcomed me back home and then pointed in the direction in which her better half was relaxing. I moved slowly over to the ever-thinking man!

In a room breathing the air of a sanctuary with a candle glowing on a shelf, appearing senile, Foofee pointed to a chair right opposite him. Leisurely I rested myself in the soft cushion chair. "Rees, welcome to Nyaake, your home. What do you drink?" New Idea suddenly asked. I was completely confused and greatly taken aback by what I called an abrupt question. I had known the old man over a long span of years. I never saw him drinking a bottle or a glass of beer. Without thinking I absentmindedly rejoined, "Anything you drink." With this, he drew a bottle of well brewed wine from his shelf and two glasses to bend elbow with his son. He poured the reddish wine into one of the glasses and emptied it into the other glass and handed me the one he emptied out.

"Charge your glass and let us drink to your health and success at Tubman-Wilson Institute," the old man pleasurably toasted. What was he talking about? I wondered and wandered. After we drank, may I say lustily, perhaps soberly the old storyteller toned in, "In my home (meaning his native home Togoland), our children do not eat with us. When a parent asks his son or daughter to eat with him it means that his son or daughter did something very pleasing to him. Reeves, I am very happy and proud to know how well they say you administered the affairs of the school during the one year period, and because of this I requested you to drink with me," observed the sage.

Far in Lower Grand Gedeh County the news of my one year good work at the school spread like wildfire. It was God Almighty who led it all for the school and the Zwedru community to have cooperated most heartily. I went to Kablake with my head and heart heavily pregnant with thought of improving and extending my little rubber farm I started since 1962 and also to increase my livestock, which was multiplying gradually. I had thought seriously and was planning accordingly that the year I would turn forty-five I would definitely retire from teaching and wholly and solely devote my retired life to farming. Unfortunately I was unequally yoked. While I was in Zwedru nobody, including my young wife and my father with his children, took interest in my farm. The young rubber trees were covered with towering grass and trees while guinea pigs (ground hogs) had their toll on the budding trees. My father, the village patriarch, and his children (men) unceremoniously snatched some of my cows and goats away. How long was I away that my little livestock and rubber farm I was trying to develop could be so destroyed? A year's absence had almost destroyed me beyond repair. My life plans had fallen apart! But I was determined to do my best and improve my lot.

Chapter XX – "My Lonely Life in Zwedru"

What happened to me during the one year transfer from 1965 to 1966 and after I was permanently transferred and assigned to Zwedru shortly before my wife and children joined me? Did I keep my solemn promise to the former village chief? Was I really and truly chaste?

"I am summoned to Zwedru to take over the acting principalship of Tubman - Wilson Institute," I patriotically informed my father. "You are not going to that Palm Country," my father categorically barked when I revealed my new mission to "Amos," as my father was popularly called by his contemporaries. "Baa, when duty calls all patriotic citizens, without reservation or hesitation, they must briskly march to the call of duty. I must not be an exception to that clarion summon." I pressed him further, "I understand that illiteracy is ravaging the countryside, especially as the principal of that institution is on a study tour in the United States of America. Desperately my country needs me to fill in the vacancy so as not to give illiteracy a breathing time. The fierce battle is on and I must not lose any time in girding my armor on to take my place in the vanguard. Ignorance like cancer is eating away our inalienable rights and civil liberties. Your fear that the Krahn people might take me to court when I intrude in marital union will form no part of my all-out war against IGNORANCE, which I strongly believe is the devastating source of the dehumanizing poverty that engulfs our beautiful and serene countryside." I added, " Pleasure with other people's wives has not and will not be part of my heroic battle cry. My dear father, be resolutely assured, " I solemnly promised the concerned Gedebo elder. Moved patriotically, but feeling very deprived and anxious of his "book son," my father breathed his paternal blessing on me. Clothed with that wholesome blessing and my personal vision and courage I determinedly went to Zwedru to battle headlong against ignorance. But in passing let me not pretend that I am not in the flesh. We are all aware of human weaknesses. Knowing what human nature is, the Book of books says, "To err is human and to forgive is divine." On the other hand, William Shakespeare bluntly puts it this way: "Frailty thy name is woman." To me the ancient writer was anti - woman. The way I see it, it should be: "Frailty thy name is human being, man as well as woman." We all have our pitfalls or shortcomings. In spite of the resolute promise I made to Mennua (a Twi word for brother, as the social clique who worked in the Gold Coast, now the Republic of Ghana, styled each other), something happened. The long straggling distance that separated me physically from my spouse caused me to reluctantly breath the covenant; temporarily I went the wrong way. But completely I felt short of putting asunder what God had put together. In short, I had no sinister dealing with such people so blessed.

With my long-standing track record of not having sex with people's wives, I was absolutely determined to keep my posture vertically and virtuously moving so as to do my father the honor and myself the prestige. In this light I became cognizant of what Harry Kine of Zwedru once said, "There is a difference between people and person." If that holds true, then there are women who are women people and women persons. In this case it is said that women who are not married are the women persons. Women who are not married are likened, therefore, to a Grebo palm butter dish without cover and so Mr. House Fly observes, "Any food that is not covered is open to the public."

Fearing being taken to court, I discreetly seized the opportunity of associating with the women persons. To get indulged into the exciting, tantalizing, enticing, and sometimes openly inviting social life of Zwedru, I needed a passport and a key to enter and unlock the social arena. As my passport was handy, myself being the passport, coupled with my way of life in the bustling Zwedru community, a countryside town rapidly budding into a city, a social terminology of the social group in focus to do your fishing or present your case, without wavering I plunged bodily into the social struggle. Wishing to be actively involved in the enticing social life of the fastest-growing city in the making, I moved aggressively to equip myself with comprehensive technical words to make a persuasive drive to get a temporary company, as my dear consort was in Nyaake, from where I was transferred. After a brief stay in that vast rural town I carefully gathered some salient and pertinent social vocabulary such as the following:

1.   Asn - Kon - de da - a?   (Do you have husband?)
2. .   Aan bon - un - wen.   (I want you.)
3.   Aa bon - un - wen Ka -a?   (Do you want me too?)
4.   Za - o + kpa.   (Open the door.)

Having equipped myself with the necessary words or expressions, I perambulated consciously and sedately the beautiful town nestled in the very heart of the evergreen forests of Liberia. Here I fished for my je bor dor.

After I credibly served the one-year term transfer, I returned to Nyaake, a township in the Webbo District, Lower Grand Gedeh County. But as you have read already in this story, I was permanently transferred and assigned to Tubman-Wilson Institute, a public high school, popularly know as TWI, where I served as vice principal and later as a full-fledged principal until the end of 1977. Of course during this long period of time my wife and children joined me. Humanly my marital vows became my guiding principle, but I was still a Liberian and of course an African.

Chapter XXI "Struggles in an Uncertain Time"

The 1967 school year began promptly at the Webbo Junior High School. It was a rousing welcome from the students who said that they had missed me from school and them. Although a junior high school, it was better in many ways: It was situated in Nyaake, with a sparse, highly literate population, which was about seventy-five to eighty-five percent civilized and Christian. Defecating in and around the township, let alone, on the campuses of its schools, was severely punishable according to the ordinances the township made and provided in that case. Regularity, tidiness, punctuality, and studiousness all were the outstanding sterling qualities that characterized the Webbo Junior High School. Being back in such a wholesome surrounding was rejuvenating as much as exciting!

As a young committed teacher I needed to prove myself by concrete examples of what I thought I represented. I did it in every way human. In Liberia it is widely held that teachers should not partake in power politics. For me, this is purely nonsensical and has not an iota of truth in any premise in logic. Politics, as Webster defines it, is the art or science of government; the art or science of guiding or influencing government's policy; the art or science of winning governmental policy. Politics, as you read above, teaches the art of science about government. If these definitions hold true, then who teaches or whom does this teach? Are teachers not part and parcel of the Liberian body politic? By the way, how do the people in politics get educated? If your answer calls them teachers, then why teachers should be unwarrantedly excluded? If the teaching position does not clothe the teacher as a politician, then he or she is not in politics, but definitely politics is in him. No doubt, because politics is in him, he makes a progressive transfer of this nutritive science of government to his students, who in later years become erudite politicians. On July 27, 1964, then Eastern Province, Grand Gedeh County became one of the three newly created counties of Liberia. Their respective county governments were instituted. After more than two long years in office as the highest administrative officer and vicegerent of the President of the Republic of Liberia in the county, Grand Gedeh County Superintendent, Honorable Moses P. Harris, had yet to visit the township of Nyaake, the cradle of civilization, education, etc., and the only township in then Eastern Province and the section of Grand Gedeh County from where the Superintendent hails.

The Nyaake Township, on hearing about the pending official visit of the county superintendent, went wild. Accordingly, the township commissioner, Honorable Benedictus A. d'Almeida, conveyed general citizens' meetings every day to organize an elaborate program for our distinguished visitor.

Since it was chartered on May 4, 1947, the Nyaake Township government had worked transparently under Commissioners Henry P. Collins and William D. Farr, respectively. Discrepancy, corruption, mismanagement, and sometimes incompetence characterized the township administration under commissioner d' Almeida.

When I took up my teaching assignment in early 1960 in the township, the corruption had mounted to an alarming proportion and unparalleled height. There

133

were already some political activists who wanted the grab-and-go syndrome radically reduced. I joined them.

In anticipation of the superintendent's visit, the political activists gathered and prepared our complaint against the township administration to be presented to the superintendent during his official visit with us. Knowing this, the township commissioner and his cohorts tried to manipulate and discourage the citizenry not to prepare any elaborate welcoming program that would be worthy of the distinguished visitor and his host. At our last planning meeting for organizing the official reception program to honor the superintendent and his entourage, openly the commissioner declared that such an honoring program was not necessary for a man who for two long years administered the affairs of the county without visiting his home area in the county. "That the superintendent had not visited his own people is not an official issue. As the administrator of this vast county, he has been felt in every corner and nook of Grand Gedeh. The man needed adjustment in his new busy position. We must, as a well organized political entity, elaborately welcome and entertain the county superintendent, our own dear son, and his entourage. It is not our right to question the honorable gentleman as to why he did not visit us before this time. Nyaake is very liberal in welcoming distinguished visitors into the township, the only township in the county. I am quite sure that every citizen here, including former provincial commissioner Joseph Itoka and County Inspector Edmund B. Gibson, is quite in agreement with me as we have been planning it," and I so moved. The motion was seconded and cast by the township commissioner, who was presiding over the crucial general citizens' meeting. He had no choice but to rehearse the motion as made and seconded. "You have heard the motion saying that the Township of Nyaake, Webbo, must give the superintendent and his party the kind of reception the township is famous for and remembered all over our one Liberia," the commissioner pushed against the wall narrated. The hand count showed an overwhelming majority in favor of the motion as stated. The commissioner and his cohorts had no other alternative but to shamefully bow to the sweeping will of the very vast majority.

As soon as the motion was carried, Inspector Gibson offered a motion for voluntary contribution for the reception program. It was seconded and unanimously carried. There and then we raised three-hundred fifty dollars for entertainment and other items for the reception. Revenue Agent Johnny Jackson, Sanitation Inspector Thomas W. Toogbaboo, and Teacher William K. Reeves were named the Ways and Means Committee, chaired by Mr. Johnny Jackson.

The bitter political battles were grievously lost by many who thought that they were the right people to be elected to such positions as senator or representative for the newly created county of Grand Gedeh. Mr. Joseph Itoka was one of the bitterly aggrieved losers. The aftermath of the political battles unusually shattered the township's onetime solid esprite de corps and placed the Nyaake community in different political association camps. I was on the camp of Harry Carngbe, who won the senatorial seat sought by self-assured would-be winner, Honorable Joseph Itoka with two other losers. Those of us who sided with the winner were openly begrudged and were the targets of venomous hatred of Mr. Itoka and his followers. They personally ridiculed me while the grand old politician and his young wife literally kept their speech from me since the caucus of 1964 where General Carngbe was chosen by the hierarchy of the True Whig Party then. But after that crucial township meeting convened to plan for the official visit of our county superintendent to the township, Mr. Itoka was slowly and meditatively descending the stairway of the Webbo District Council Hall when I caught up with him. As usual I warmly greeted the old politician with no hope of any reply. To my utter surprise the German-trained Togolese accountant/bookkeeper, but a naturalized Liberian, all of a sudden said, "Reeves, you saved the situation today. I don't know what Commissioner d'Almeida was trying to play with us, the erudite politically seasoned citizens of the Nyaake Township, but I was very happy you undid his trick and threw him into a booby trap. Let bygone be bygone, my son," Old Man Itoka reconciled. This was another reconciliation between me and two elderly Catholics. Mr. Gabriel Gadegbeku, who and I had some altercation sometime in 1965 shortly before I went to hospital in Monrovia, had reconciled with me when he spontaneously and willingly offered me a glass of wine and he and I exchanged cheers and drank lustily to each other's good health and prosperity and long life. Now it was Colonel Itoka's turn. "Goodness, we Catholics were being Christ like in dealing with each other," I exclaimed.

To honor my heroism in that politically sensitive citizens' meeting I was unanimously selected to officially welcome our distinguished visitor, Grand Gedeh County Superintendent Moses P. Harris into the Township of Nyaake, Webbo.

His ill will having been vanquished, Honorable Benedictus A. d'Almeida, Nyaake Township Commissioner, fell in line with the erudite politicians and the hospitable people of the township and the district to welcome the county superintendent and his entourage in the grandest style, befitting the distinguished guest and the host. Accordingly, the superintendent and his high ranking county officials were lavishly welcomed and entertained.

In my welcome statement I noted, "It is indeed a singular honor for me, a classroom teacher, to welcome on behalf of the people of the Township of Nyaake, Webbo, and the entire people of the former Webbo District, now known as Lower Grand Gedeh Country, Grand Gedeh County Superintendent Moses P. Harris." Once that was done, I went my own way to compare and contrast the two ethnic groups, the conservative Grebos and the sophisticated Krahns who predominantly inhabit the county. In Lower Grand Gedeh County, the home of the conservative Grebo, government officials, especially the commissioners, unceremoniously take away the household things placed in their respective headquarters by the impoverished taxpayers, whereas no government official, including commissioners, can dare to take away the property of the Krahn district without meeting the justifiable obstruction of the taxpayers. In the Grebo section of the county the taxpayers sit supinely while the commissioners, who get handsome salaries from the taxpayers' sweat, make double gains by taking away public property. This was the reason the Krahn section of the county was able to win the county seat, because they maintained and sustained a well furnished district headquarters. In their claim for the county, Lower Grand Gedeans said that they inhabit the oldest district in the then Eastern Province. I questioned, "What has age to do with where a government seat should be located? We are looking for a place that is more physically developed in the former province. Your one zinc-

135

roof building without furniture and other necessary household things for the superintendent would be the glaring sign that the people of Eastern Province are not ready for a county government, I would think, and hence the denial.

We in the Grebo section of the county often said that the Krahns were spoiled, cantankerous people who believe in discrediting and making trouble for every government official who served in that district. According to the old Grebo mentality, people in authority should never be questioned, and so they allow their government officials to bullwreck them. And so for every incoming commissioner, the impecunious taxpayers must refurnish the official residence of the commissioner."

After I painted clearly and factually the wrongs the Grebo had done themselves, I resigned the floor amidst the loudest and the longest ovation I ever received after making a public statement. The superintendent of Maryland County, Hilary Brewer, our special invited guest, was the first to embrace me, then came the hundreds of people of the township and the district who hugged my puny self almost to death. Obviously, the masses well received my message and completely shared my views. On the other hand, the officials of government and politicians felt very much discredited. It seemed that I had now become their enemy because I told them the living truth.

The day following the reception program, Honorable Dogboyou Toe, a member of the Liberian Legislature from the district, came to me to request a copy of my speech, after singing praises of commendation for the speech which he considered a masterpiece. "Honorable Toe, I cannot give you a copy now because I have only a copy. Many persons would like for me to give them copies of the speech too. Tomorrow I will make more copies and then I will serve you with one copy," I politely turned the honorable gentleman down.

As soon as he left, I asked myself, "For heaven's sake, what does he want with a copy of my speech when he does not know how to read or write?" I strongly felt that some sinister plan against this schoolteacher was taking place among the politicians of the district and township. Instead of running more copies on the memo machine, I went straight to Mr. William D. Farr to tell him of my fear about the illiterate honorable man requesting for a copy of my address. "I saw those sons of bitches hanging together after you made that factual speech last night. They are out for their deviltry. Don't give them a line of any of the speech you delivered last night," Mr. Farr, a former commissioner of the Township of Nyaake, Webbo, strongly advised.

In sheep's clothing, Honorable Toe came the next day to collect the copy of my speech as promised. "I can only give you a copy of my speech if you will pay forty dollars for it," I told the unlettered lawmaker. "Why should I pay for a public speech delivered by a public school teacher?" Honorable Toe questioned. "Honorable Toe, the public did not pay for my education. I struggled alone for it. This is the reason why you must pay for a copy, if you need it," I emphasized uncompromisingly.

Later, I gathered from a source close to the politicians that I had grossly insulted and discredited them, and so they were planning to imprison me for their alleged insult and discredit. The diabolical plan did not bear any fruit.

Back with my old family members of the Webbo District School, now called

Webbo Junior High School, and my own growing family, now made of a girl and a boy and their mother, my young wife Caroline, I began to reorganize my life. I made frequent visits to Kablake to get my farm going again. 1967 brought me reassurance that once I was on the spot, my farm would be expanded and none of my livestock would be stolen. With that high hope buttressed by my personal tenacity, with God in control, I would achieve my goal. But as I was planning, Supervisor Wilson had his own plans for this his public school teacher.

In early April, 1969, Supervisor Wilson came to my house, newly built on Tendeke Hill, New Road, Nyaake Township, Webbo, to request me to accept a transfer for a permanent assignment to Tubman-Wilson Institute in Zwedru, Grand Gedeh County, Liberia. "Why me again?" I surprisingly asked. "Based on your successful one-year service rendered the only high school in our newly created county, Assistant Supervisor Cooper and I are quite convinced that with you back there the school will run better. Presently, it is disintegrating very fast, and before it gets too late, I would like for you to take up the assignment as early as next month (May)," Professor Wilson pleaded. "I served as acting principal of the school. This meant that I was in charge of running the school and therefore I made all the decisions. But now the principal is there and you are saying that I must go back there because I succeeded well during my acting principalship. What will be my role in the administration of the school?" I questioned. "We know that Mr. Nayou, the principal, is your former high school classmate and college classmate and an intimate friend of yours too. Because of these close tight links that hold the both of you together indivisibly, we hold it very highly that your presence in the school will bring some influence in the smooth running of the school," Mr. Wilson asserted. I was sincerely convinced that I was most needed at Tubman-Wilson Institute, and so I accepted the permanent transfer. In mid-May I departed Nyaake for Zwedru.

Round about the 20th of May I arrived in Zwedru, the county's capital, and the next day, in a school ceremony, the assistant supervisor of schools, Professor Cyrus S. Cooper, inducted me as vice principal on the staff of Tubman-Wilson Institute. The principal of the school, Professor Harry T. F. Nayou, a personal friend of mine, with his teachers and students, said," With an open heart I receive my friend and colleague into the walls of TWI, a school he knows so well. Today the school is blessed with a man whose concern is to improve the lot of his students." There was nothing in the school to show that there were some slight improvements in the overall problems that plague the school.

Clothed with a lesser title at TWI did not weaken me in carrying out my duty and obligation as teacher and vice principal, rather that conferred upon me double trust and so I got totally immerged in my assigned task. But unfortunately, the month following (June) I became very sick and so I requested the supervisor to take me back home to Nyaake, where I would get my immediate family attention and care. Home again I was.

In early July of that year I received a note from Mr. Cooper requesting me to proceed to Monrovia at once. The note read, "The Department of Education, Liberia, would like you to participate in the International Teacher Development Program sponsored by the United States Office of Education. The Liberian participants will leave Liberia for the US in late August this year."

My health had improved very much before I received the note. But I thought I needed to consult and get the advice of a medical doctor before undertaking so long a journey in and out of Liberia. With this in mind, I went to J. J. Dossen Memorial Hospital in Harper, Maryland County, where I consulted a Haitian doctor, who, after a series of medical tests, pronounced me well and fit to make the journey after a series of medical tests.

"For about six long months or a year, you and our children might not see me around. The doctor pronounced me well and fit to travel wherever my government wants me to go. Tomorrow, I shall begin the long, uncertain journey from here. Take good care of the children while I go to attend my country's business," I told my contagiously smiling young wife.

About July 20, 1969, early that morning I boarded a bus heading for the provincial capital, Zwedru, Grand Gedeh County. When I arrived that late afternoon in the budding rural city in the making, I was quivering with high fever. "What is happening now?" inaudibly, I questioned myself. For a while I rested in bed. In that time Teacher James Keh came in and I told him how sick I was feeling. "Send for a bottle of schnapps while I get some lime," Teacher Keh, Grand Gedeh Poet Laureate directed. The schnapps was brought and Mr. Keh squeezed the lime and mixed it with the schnapps in a glass. "Drink all of this and get in bed and let me cover you up with this blanket. After some time, you will perspire. The fever will disappear and you will be fit to continue your journey to Monrovia," Teacher Keh predicted.

Feeling well and strong, I began the three-hundred-odd-miles journey to Monrovia the next day. By four-thirty that sunny afternoon I arrived in Monrovia. At once I plunged into searching for Supervisor Cooper upon whose summons I came. Upon meeting him, I was briefed about the grant the US Office of Education was offering a group of select Liberian teachers, including me. "The Department of Education will explain in detail about the grant," Mr. Cooper revealed. For about a month, the Department of Education, Liberia, and the United States Education and Cultural Foundation, Liberia, had us the ten Liberian teachers making all the necessary arrangements to meet our counterparts of the International Teacher Development Program Participants in Washington, D.C.

With everything set, the big ten departed Liberia on the 31st of August, 1969, and we arrived at the Kennedy International Airport, New York, USA, September 1, 1969. While in the United States, the following pages tell of my activities. *SEE APPENDIX*

At about eleven that morning, seven of the ten Liberian participants in the International Teacher Development program arrived in sunny Liberia at Roberts International Airport. For the first time in six months I was sweating on disembarking from the PANAM aircraft. After the long entry procedure I was driven away to the Liberian capital. My first time on the Monrovia-Roberts Airfield Highway enroute to the United States of America, I thought, comparatively, it was the best feat of the Liberia ingenuity in road construction. So far I knew Monrovia was the most beautiful city in the world. But after my American experience, my contrary view about my home capital was a disheartening one. The Monrovia-Roberts Airfield Highway was like a path leading through a sugar cane farm. All the tall buildings in Monrovia were now looking like they were being seen from the air as they appeared dwarfed to the ground. Not only that, but they looked deserted and dirty.

Was this really my nation's capital that I had cherished over the years? It was the same Monrovia, but only my sense of beauty was enlightened and broadened. In Monrovia the returnee participants in the International Teacher Development Program met with their local sponsor, The United States Educational and Cultural Foundation director, Blay Robinson. We were well received and heartily congratulated on our successful tour of the United States' abundant educational facilities and their question boxes, the students, whose insatiable quest for knowledge is an example unimaginable? After a brief discussion of the highlights of our visit, Mr. Robinson told us that the next day we would meet with the US ambassador near Monrovia. The time was nine in the morning. Imbued with the American punctuality, seemingly, the Fulbright grantees were at the US embassy by eight-forty-five that sunny morning. At nine sharp we were ushered into the office of the ambassador. After a brief chat with the US envoy we were honored by taking photos with the ambassador, Mr. Chesterfield. The next day a newspaper, The Liberian Star, carried our distinguished photo with the ambassador that made front page headlines. At eleven that same morning of our visit to the US embassy, we were requested to call at the Liberian Department of Education, where the Under Secretary of Education for Instruction would talk to his teachers. When we arrived at the department, the under secretary's receptionist told us that the honorable man would not be in his office until about two in the afternoon that day. "Come back then," the receptionist urged. At two we were back to find again that Honorable Sanford Dennis was not available. We hovered around and melted away. We had yet to meet with the undersecretary of education for instruction under whom the administration of all the teachers of the Republic of Liberia rests.

A week later in Monrovia, I journeyed to Zwedru, Grand Gedeh County, where I had unwillingly lost one semester's work in language arts and literature classes. In the next few weeks I had myself organized to pounce on teaching, as it were, as I was very happy for the reunion with my students and the community. In the meantime, unknown to me, principal Nayou, staff, and students were organizing an elaborate program to honor me at a reception. A week following my arrival in Zwedru, the fastest growing city in Southeastern Liberia, Tubman-Wilson Institute, at a sumptuous reception they honored their vice principal on the ground floor of Tubman palace, an elegant building, the county's pride. Speaking on behalf of the student body, Senior Dementry Sobou said among other things, "We the students of Tubman-Wilson Institute wholeheartedly welcome you back from the United States of America, where, no doubt, you drank deeply in their system of education and you have brought us the knowledge, which I believe you are going to generously share with us. As you know, your absence from the school created a deep seeping frustration during the second semester of last year. However, we are glad you are here at last. Your love for the students and the school will again propel us students to action and commitment to our studies. It is therefore my greatest pleasure on behalf of the principal, teachers, and the entire student body to once more welcome you, our father, teacher, vice principal, and friend indeed.

Early March of 1970 found me immersed in the full activity of the school, including my heavy teaching load. Early morning at seven-thirty, to be exact, I would slowly walk to school, just a stone's throw from my living quarters. At seven-forty-five the teachers and students began the daily routine of hoisting the national ensign, and devotion followed by announcement by the administration. Eight sharp lessons, that is, recitations swung into gear in every grade with a class period lasting forty-five busy minutes. Busily I was occupied by four periods of the six-period school day.

Refreshed by my wholesome and didactic educational tour of the United States of America with its altruistic, affluent, and affable people, I was more challenged in teaching than ever before. Enriched with new marketable ideas in both life and education, I became totally interwoven in my lifelong profession.

One morning I was introducing some words considered surprises and inconsistencies in the English language, my second language. "As I saw it, BRING and SING have ING in common. Surprisingly the past tense of BRING is BROUGHT, while that of SING is SANG. Why? Why is BRING not BRANG? Where does OUGHT come from? Why don't they keep the same form? These surprises and inconsistencies perplexed us who were learning English as a second language. The English language is the official language of the Liberian Government. In other words, it is the language in which all government transactions are conducted. In order to take part in this process and be effective, one must of necessity study the language very seriously. Intensive study of the language, for me, is a must. Study your words well by making the dictionary, a good dictionary, your partner in process and progress. Exceptions in rules in grammar abound in this language largely spoken in many parts of the world." Before I could come to the end of this long explanation I heard a strange sound from outside: "Is that William K. Reeves? I cannot believe it," the voice excitedly said. It was one of the 1950s peaceful invaders of the conservative Southeastern City of Harper in Maryland County. A country boy, a heathen or native, Daniel T. Goe was one of those young men who penetrated the Americo-Liberian enclave to pursue high school education. In the city Daniel and I were casual friends while he was attending the Cape Palmas High School. During that time I was doing my Maryland College of Our Lady of Fatima in the same city but closely we identified ourselves as native boys in the Americo-Liberian town. At the end of 1959 Daniel graduated from high school while I earned my Bachelor's degree in Education. Both of us departed the city that year.

In the early 1960s I took up teaching assignment in the Township of Nyaake, Webbo, Eastern Province. I guess Daniel went wild meticulously looking for a fountain of higher education from where he would drink lustily. For years, although I had still thought of the Barrobo young man, I had not seen him physically and did not know his whereabouts. Both of us were so excited about our encounter after so many years of undesired separation. After exchanging the usual pleasantries in both English and our mother tongue, Toe told me that he was working for US Peace Corps/Liberia as assistant director/education. "I am on my way to Greenville, Sinoe County, to visit the volunteers there. Definitely I am postponing my going today to tomorrow so that we will spend the night together so as to celebrate our overdue reunion," gladly Daniel asserted.

Daniel spent the whole night with me in one bed. During the seemingly fleeting night we tried to recall all our sweet and bitter memories about that beautiful southeastern city and its rich conservative but hospitable people. As dawn was peeping through the window cracks Daniel whispered to me, "Bill, I would like for you to go with me to Greenville so that we will continue the celebration of our happy reunion." I had no excuse disobliging such a friendly and timely request, especially as Saturday was not a school day. Heartily I accepted the spontaneous offer. On our way to Greenville, smiling broadly Daniel revealed in our vernacular that he would like for me to take part in the Peace Corps/Liberia Training Program. "Presently a meeting is being organized to invite the would-be trainers and site administrators," Daniel hinted. He added, "Peace Corps pays handsomely." There was no reason to tell him that my teeth were rotten when he was offering me a fat bone. "Yes, Daniel, I would love to get something extra," I promised. The two hour long drive journey by a land rover took us about four short hours as Daniel drove slowly to accommodate us conversing. We returned late that day. Again we had the night together. Before Daniel left for Gbarnga, the next day, he assured me that Peace Corps/Liberia in no distant future would send me an invitation to attend their planning meeting. About a week following Daniel's departure for Gbarnga, where he was based, I received a letter of invitation from Peace Corps/Liberia's Director's office. According to the stipulated time, I rode to Gbarnga for the meeting. Actively I participated and at the close of the meeting I was appointed Site Administrator for Zwedru.

Later in the years Daniel was promoted as deputy director of Peace Corps/Liberia and Mrs. Dorothy Musieng Cooper succeed him. Under Mrs. Cooper I worked assiduously, and accordingly, I was handsomely paid.

Being a Peace Corps/Liberia executive helped my school Tubman-Wilson Institute, immensely. I had direct contact with the organization, whose volunteer service was at the disposal of any school in the country which requested it. With this, every two years the school got two or more volunteers in different subject areas for teaching. Before that time TWI was academically deficient and desperately was trading in every annual result of the National Examinations. Every year the school's National Examinations average was D. This was disgraceful and humiliating for the school and the county. The school was the only senior high school in the newly created county of Grand Gedeh. The reason was alarming but simple: Tubman-Wilson Institute was miserably understaffed and the majority of the teachers were not high school-oriented instructors. On the whole, there was nothing in the school to be desired. This was a very serious problem which needed to be immediately addressed sincerely, earnestly, and promptly.

The Peace Corps volunteers at the school constantly complained that the principal did not seem to know that they were part and parcel of the teaching staff. When I took up permanent assignment in the school in May of 1969, in less than three months I was snatched away to enjoy academic refreshment from the Fulbright grant to tour some educational facilities and the way of life of the people of the United States. During my six month absence I could not help my fellow teachers in the school, and then when I came back home I found that the volunteers' constant heartbreaking and frustrating complaint was at a dangerous breaking point. "Mr. Reeves, we are glad you are back. Since you left we have been planning to leave the school to get a fresh assignment to another school anywhere in Liberia. We are planning to quit unless the administration of the school gives the attention and care we deserve and desire. Can you help us, Mr. Reeves?" the volunteers asked. "In the school where I am vice principal and Peace Corps/Liberia representative in this county, be assured that you are here in double trust. This embarrassment is known now. I shall in no time alleviate it," I sincerely promised my colleagues.

Shortly following my first Peace Corps/Liberia meeting I received another invitation to go to Gbarnga where the Peace Corps would interview me for their possible choice for me to go to the Virgin Islands for training or some orientation before coming to Liberia. With this I went to Gbarnga but when I got there I changed my mind. I decided against going in for the interview but rather to meet the director in person to urge him to erase the impression the TWI volunteers gave him that the principal did not care or did not appreciate their presence and help in the school. When the time for the interview finally arrived, I slipped into the office of the director. In the office I discussed at length about this ugly situation that our volunteers complained about. "Yes, Bill, it is our plan to withdraw our volunteers from the Zwedru High School sometime at the end of the first semester this year. However, since you have ably intervened and you are an integral part of the administration of the school in question, I shall tell you our final decision in the case before we close the meeting," the director promised.

At the close of the meeting the director invited me to his office to tell me his final decision. My anxious heart palpitated! "Well, it was encouraging when you vehemently assured Peace Corps/Liberia the other day that you would seek daily the welfare of the US Peace Corps volunteers at your school, our plan to withdraw them is hereby cancelled. You will have them as long as you continue to treat them well," the director declared.

For me the interview to ascertain whether I was prepared or qualified to go to the Virgin Islands for the training of US volunteers was intentionally boycotted by me because I had decided against leaving the country so early after having left the taxpayers' children almost without suitable attention in my area of instruction for six unbroken months. But we had strong, qualified teachers in the persons of the young US Peace Corps volunteers, resolutely determined in collaboration with the seemingly don't care administration to move the school forward academically. The idea that our volunteers would not be withdrawn filled me with burning enthusiasm.

I returned to Zwedru with all the surging hope that Tubman-Wilson Institute was now placed in the proper gear for positive action. Briefly I told the principal what had transpired between the US Peace Corps/Liberia director. In no veiled terms I told him that he should change his negative attitude toward the volunteers and the rest of the teachers and other staff. I was dutifully obliged to say and do, remembering the reason why the supervisor, Mr. George Wilson, had requested me to take up permanent assignment with the school and principal, my former classmate and friend. Making him to be aware that his negative attitude which undoubtedly created unwholesome non-communication between the administration and the teachers was a cancer eating up the very fabrics of the school. Would the scholarly principal change for a better administration? I leave the question to the reader. There was a positive change in the administration. I suggested and urged the principal to have faculty meetings forthnightly. I thought this would breach the communication gap between the administration and the teachers. My timely suggestion fell on fertile ground. Forthnightly meetings were conducted regularly. Soon or late the school was running smoothly and progressively and the academic upheaval gradually accelerated to an appreciable height.

Adjusted in all aspects in what it takes for the comprehensive and smooth running of school, Tubman-Wilson Institute was then on course. Curricular and extracurricular activities gripped the school. Happiness and commitment to study engulfed the students; the teachers were no exception. Progressively the school forged ahead over the succeeding years.

With all the positive changes which were sweeping in and around Tubman-Wilson Institute, the students' academic achievements were minimal. The fact of the case was that most of the students who enrolled at the school came from very poorly run schools in the countryside. Their teachers were in most cases, if not in all cases, academically and professionally deficient. According to the schools last attended, the students claimed grade levels in which they were not adequately prepared for the respect and honor of colleague students. The grades they claimed on their face value. These village schools, meagerly supported by peasant rural village dwellers, employed Tom and Dick who said they were educated. The teachers, as you can see, were employed on face value too. This practice was prevalent in the then Eastern Province. There was no other alternative. If you wanted school, you just had to employ someone who said he knew book. It was so when the province obtained a bigger political status, Grand Gedeh Country, one of the three newly created counties in 1964, the practice took a corrupt form. In the new county all the so-called public school teachers were given each some kind of a salary. The whole of the Grand Gedeh public school system was inundated with academically and professionally unqualified teachers who came to the system through the back door. A cow and a huge billy goat were given to the supervisor of schools to duly qualify a prospective teacher to get employed in that noble profession, the only source from which other professions come into being. During the first year of his employment, the teacher who bribed his way into the system forfeited six months or a year's salary to the opulent supervisor as what the people in high positions in the Liberian Government called CLP, Common Law Practice, a normal token of appreciation for one's employment. But said a token. Six month's salary taken from an employed is criminal and inhuman. But this was what destroyed the taxpayers' children academically.

While the taxpayers obtained no academic benefit from those substandard teachers, the supervisors were lavishingly enriching themselves. Another was whether a teacher was dismissed from service or dead his/her name remained perpetually on the payroll. This was another lucrative source that abundantly accrued money to the supervisors' coffers while the living or working teachers knew no increment in salary over the donkey's years of their drudgery.

In the early history of the public school system in the Eastern Province the

143

succeeding supervisors were men of high moral standing, whom the spoils of office could not buy.

Once a young man seeking for a teaching job in the province came to the office of supervisor Henry Nyema Prowd in Nyaake. With reverence the prospective implored, "Sir, I would like to get a teaching job here. I attended school and stopped in the fourth grade." "What can you teach?" Professor Prowd patiently inquired. "I can teach from kindergarten through third grade," the eager job seeker asserted. "Do you really want to teach with the level of education you have?" the veteran educator honestly asked. "Oh, yeah, certainly I can teach satisfactorily in that area," the self-confident prospective teacher emphatically assured his would-be employer. "Young man, what you are really saying is not to teach but rather to CREATE," the supervisor retorted. He continued, "I would rather have no teacher than to have somebody like you to murder the children." In conclusion, professor pierced his prospective teacher's heart. "I am sorry to say that this supervisory cannot knowingly employ people who have not what we term basic education. Go back to school and prepare yourself better if you desire a place in this noble profession."

At another time, a young man hunting for a teaching position brought his letter of application to the eastern province supervisory. He hand delivered the application to Professor Prowd just about the time Honorable Prowd was leaving on a journey to his family in Harper, Maryland County. Prowd schemed the letter and after reading, said, "Well, while I eat let's chat. In the meantime I would like to administer a test to you to satisfy me whether you are qualified or not. Since I cannot do it now, maybe from our casual talk I will be able to give some kind of a reply to your request," the learned supervisor advised. With this they started rolling the ball, which unfortunately rolled into the water. In a happy mood, the young job seeker went deep into his grammar, "You is the right man, in this position, Mr. Prowd. Ain't good to put people in position who does not know nothing. I loves you. You really knows book. When I teaches, I telling the students that this book business be good. If I get the job you will saw how I will does the work. Try me and you will see for very true who I is," the prospective teacher pleaded. "My young man, this supervisory cannot employ you as a teacher in this province. It would not be in the interest of the taxpayers to employ you so-called students. Go back to put your English language together better," the supervisor bluntly advised.

In the 1940s and 1950s this was the regular order of things as regarding the employment of teachers in the province. I note here with pride to say that from this careful screening of prospective teachers by the scrupulous supervisors of those two decades in the province earned the grade schools in the province a distinguished, enviable place in the community of grade schools in Southeastern Liberia. Students who were privileged to attend high school in the county, in most cases, were honor roll students throughout high school. This laudable achievement was criminally eroded by the corrupt supervisors who took over the administration of the public school system of Eastern province from the late 1950s to now.

Locally and nationally, this little West African country called Liberia was/is plagued with many and varied cancerous ills, corruptions in all kinds of shapes and shades. In Eastern Province, the supervisors of schools and the district commissioners clandestinely staged what I call their "highway robbery" on the underpaid teachers' salaries. Under this vicious plan, the supervisors of schools employed unqualified teachers, whose gifts of billy goats and cows automatically ushered them into a system that required long years of academic and professional training, without the least preparation to equip them for the teaching profession but cows and billy goats presented. As these billy goat and cow-prepared teachers knew that they were in the wrong place, they chose to be stooges in their own country, with no ground or right to fight for. For six or more months the billy goat-employed teacher would forfeit his salary. In addition to this heinous practice by the supervisors of schools, the district commissioners and the supervisors of schools unbelievably piled the teachers' payroll with ghosts and dead teachers' names. From the monthly salaries of the nonexistent teachers the province officials exploitatively accrued huge sums of money and lived luxuriously while the working living teachers remained literally stagnant with their meager salaries for untold times. The few of us who had the requisite qualifications for teaching, no salary increase was considered after employment for a period of twelve long unbroken years of creditable, diligent, professional service. It was, therefore, held to be true that the just would suffer with the unjust; the trained and qualified would suffer with the untrained and unqualified.

In the twenty-seven years of the unprecedented life of a government in our national history, in the William V. S. Tubman regime, there was a plan called. This "no money" plan forbade the raising of salaries in any category of the national workforce.

The masses in the country were economically halted and stagnant became the order of the day while the elite sumptuously enjoyed life in their luxurious cars and magnificent mansions. On the other hand, every government employee in the ruling True Whig Party government was deprived of fifty percent of his May pay each year. Such a deadly squeeze and unthoughtful grab of a scanty income was gloriously considered and styled as a patriotic voluntary contribution for Old True Whig Party. Being employed by the True Whig Party government made you a bonafide member of the party. Were you? The masses had the sugar cane on their shoulders while the privileged few sucked the tasty juice away. Of course, we the inhabitants of the provinces were second class citizens in our one Liberia. The divide was the law that governed each: the counties (five then) were governed by a code of laws, and the provinces (three) were ruled by Interior Regulations. As one could readily see the rural inhabitants, those living in the provinces, the indigenous Africans, had plenty to argue for but there was no law to support the would-be claim with the authority of the Americo-Liberian counties. Impoverished, we tarried in poverty, disease, and ignorance from 1847 to 1964, when we were finally brought into the limelight as integral parts of the Liberian nation.

In early 1970, the president of Liberia, William V.S. Tubman, the eighteenth Liberian president, granted Mr. Harry T. P. Nayou a scholarship to pursue a postgraduate course in dramatics after Mr. Nayou had authored a drama entitled: "The Great Man," a drama depicting the legal and political life of the former Maryland county senator and former associate justice of the Liberian Supreme Court and president of Liberia. The drama was first staged about March that year when the president paid an official visit to the county of Grand Gedeh. The drama scored sweeping success on its debut. The then vice president of Liberia, William R. Tolbert, Jr., advised Dramatist Nayou to polish and amend his script to more substance in preparation for staging it in Harper, where the Liberian nation would be celebrating the diamond jubilee of the birth anniversary of President William V.S. Tubman in November ensuing. Again the drama scored a huge success.

As soon as the stage was set for Nayou to enjoy his tour of study in the United States of America, it would appear that his supervisor of schools, Professor Cyrus S. Cooper, with his behind-the-scene politicians, began to search for Professor Nayou's replacement. In company with me one day, Professor Cyrus S. Cooper, supervisor of schools for Grand Gedeh County, said to me, "You know, we have to keep up the prestige of Tubman-Wilson Institute." He continued, "By this I mean that Mr. Nayou, the current principal, holds a Master's degree in Education Administration and so in my opinion his successor must be so qualified." Without a word, I began to wonder what did his declaration imply. Well, I guess his assertion implied, in my strong opinion, that although I am the vice principal of the school, the order of succession cannot be adhered to because I don't have the requisite qualifications," I concluded. This was no regret of mine. There was one glowing satisfaction in my heart—that I efficiently and professionally managed the affairs of this school for one academic year as acting principal. After about two years, I was called again and humbly requested to take up permanent assignment in the school because things were radically disintegrating under the principalship of a Master's degree holding principal. But now because of the so-called prestige, not having a Master's degree disqualified me. In my candid view, the supervisor's reasoning, if he reasoned at all, was faulty and not logical. From all indications, William K. Reeves, the warrior hired from the Grebo country, who relentlessly waged war on ignorance in Grand Gedeh county, especially in Upper Gedeh, the home of the sophisticated Krahns, was the most eligible for the principalship of Tubman-Wilson Institute. Anything outside of this would be dangerously erroneous and detrimental for the smooth operation of the school because in no time the school be radically disintegrated. I made no fuss about it. I kept my peace. Time would tell. I knew Mr. Cooper was a political stooge of the political establishment of Grand Gedeh county and he was prepared to satisfy the diabolical whims of the misguided so-called politicians for the apparent destruction of Tubman-Wilson Institute.

Time went by slowly but steadily as the question of who to succeed Professor Nayou lingered on. Finally, the politicians, the powers that be, nominated and appointed a Master's degree holder in world history, Professor Tebli Dweh, a son of Lower Gedeh. Perhaps it does my writing honor and justice by calling him a Master's degree holder. It would appear that the professor, in reality, did not honestly earn the honor ascribed to him. Of course, this was the old tradition of the supervisors of schools of the former Eastern Province, now Grand Gedeh County, to accept and employ people in the field of education on face value.

Up to the time of the wrangling and naggling about who to succeed Mr. Nayou, my family and I were living in a government lease house. Before Mr. Dweh arrived to take up his principalship of Tubman-Wilson Institute, Mr. Cooper

146

summoned me to his house to tell me in the presence of Mr. Amos Kamara, Regional Forester for Southeastern Region, that I should vacate the government lease house to give way to Mr. Dweh, the principal designate. In a very surprised mood and seemingly angry about Cooper's unthinkable and mean statement, Mr. Kamara intrusively inquired, "For a long time Mr. Reeves has been serving well this community and the school. We all know well his ability and capability. Why must you push him aside to usher in somebody who is strange and unknown to you, the school, and the community? Remember you begged Mr. Reeves to take up permanent assignment with TWI because of the excellent job he did for the school when he acted as principal in Nayou's stead while the latter studied for his Master's degree in the United States of America. Do you mean you have such a short, ungrateful memory? Be grateful Mr. Cooper to Mr. Reeves for bringing up the only high school in the county."

There was nothing Kamara could do to change their inner-circle plan to humiliate William Reeves, the tested school administrator. When Professor Dweh finally arrived in Zwedru that afternoon, I received an official note from Superintendent White directing me to give the largest room plus one in the house to Mr. Dweh and his family. This meant that my family and I would be left with one room. I was degradingly embarrassed and I felt discouragingly deserted by those who pleaded with me to take up permanent residence in Zwedru. I could not fight them all. They were political giants of the county. Obviously one man cannot fight a dozen odd by himself, let alone, ignorant political giants. Definitely my family and I would never succumb to such a devastating humiliation. Did I have a way out? With God, my answer was in a vibrant affirmative. Truly, as I hoped, the next day, Honorable Samuel G. Davis, a Debt Court Judge, marched into the house and ordered me out. "Pack your things. I am going to get a truck to bring your things to my house I use as a shop where my wife and I want you and your family to stay until your house under construction is ready for habitation. Your sister, my wife, and I have resolved to take care of you and your family," Mr. Davis directed. Accordingly we packed our belongings and gave the government house up. Slowly but gradually the Reeves-Cooper's water was rolling. In order to keep up the prestige of the school, a Master's degree holder took charge as principal of Tubman-Wilson Institute. William Reeves, who holds a well seasoned Bachelor's degree in education and ten or more years of rich and creditable and effective teaching experience, was blindly and selfishly shoveled aside to honor an absent glory, the prestige of the school. As I know, no one can take away what is mine. There is nothing in the tongue of man to alter God's plan for me. Always what is required is patience waiting obediently for God's time, which, over the years, is known and wholeheartedly accepted to be the best. However, my second place was still mine, while Professor Dweh was the boss.

I was a teaching vice principal. I carried five teaching periods every day of the school week. This was burdensome. But because the school was markedly short of trained and qualified man-power, especially in my area, language arts and literature, there was no way out. The 1973 seniors of the school were hard at their studies, earnestly preparing for the ensuing National Examination to be written at the end of the year. The principal was their history instructor. I would appear that he was confusingly busy adjusting himself to his daily administrative routine. Caught between administration and teaching, Mr. Dweh paid more attention to his administration than his daily history period. The five-period-a-week class was once attended a week at the most. The senior class, twelfth grade, before long, alarmingly realized that they were being neglected in one of the major subjects of the Ministry of Education and the National Examinations curriculum. Concerned about being placed at a losing end, the seniors sent a strong one-man delegation to me, begging me to take over the teaching of their history. Senior Fred D. Cherue ably delivered their appeal in person to me. "My class and I strongly feel that we are being neglected by our history instructor because of his administrative work. Realizing that we tend to lose at the pending National Examination, we decided to appeal to you to substitute our history instructor. Please help us by accepting to save us from losing at the examinations," Fred honestly and ardently appealed. Fred prayed on, "Since you taught us the course before, we have no doubt whatsoever that you are a suitable, proficient, and timely substitute. Since our journey in high school, you have been our history, language arts, and literature instructor until Mr. Dweh came in." "Fred, sincerely I sympathize with you and your class. But for me to accept to teach a subject already assigned to a teacher without his expressed consent would be unethical. Besides, I have more than enough of a teaching load, five periods a day.

This is an arduous task, which is evidently having its toll on my frail and sickly body. But I would rather die for a worthy cause, giving up my life to get you young people prepared for your shining future filled with high hope. But Fred, let us do it this way: ask the principal to call a faculty meeting because you the seniors would like to make a humble request through the faculty. At this faculty call meeting you will present your petition. In the presence of the teachers, the reaction to your request will be made by Mr. Dweh," I advised Senior Cherue.

The next day Fred requested the principal for the meeting. All the instructors were present at the meeting. Through the teachers, student Cherue appealed on behalf of his classmates to senior history instructor Dweh to relinquish his history class to Mr. Reeves because Instructor Dweh was trying hard to adjust himself to his onerous work of the administration of the school. "The palaver reached you, Mr. Reeves," Dweh retorted. "No, the palaver is not mine but it is definitely yours," I averred. "You, Mr. Dweh, are to say to us whether you are willing or see reason enough to relinquish the subject as per request of the senior class. It is not for us or Mr. Reeves to accept the request of the seniors," Jim Bernard, a US Peace Corp Volunteer science instructor, interposed. "Well, as it has been rightly said, I am very busy trying to condition myself with the daily routine of the administration. In this pressing situation, I have no choice but to appeal to Mr. Reeves to kindly take over completely my senior history class and I place this request throughout the faculty. Please treat me with brotherly understanding," Professor Dweh asserted. "I am happy that I can still be of more service to my students whose academic welfare is the center of my interest in them. With the help of God Almighty, I shall try," I solemnly promised.

"We too want Mr. Reeves to teach our history class," student Richard Nyenuh of the tenth grade, interrupted. "It is not possible, my son. Six teaching periods a day and seemingly an effective job is not done. That would really tire me

148

and being tired is not laziness, is it?" politely I turned the request down. But to pacify the situation I added, "Since Mr. Dweh is relieved of one instruction period, I guess he is going to have ample time for his history class with you the tenth graders." "No, it is not that Mr. Dweh does not have time to teach our history class, but the problem is that he does not know the subject matter," Nyenuh bluntly split open the stinking poopoo. All of us teachers were shocked, insulted, and brutally humiliated. But what could we do? Could punishment meted out to the student erase the hard fact as defiantly stated by student Richard Nyenuh? The young man had said without reservation. The protruding and striking question was, would the pungent and degrading allegation against Mr. Dweh strengthen or weaken him to continue teaching his tenth grade history class?

In passing, let me say briefly who this Fred D. Cherue is at whose urging I succumbed and overloaded myself with an unusual teaching load. I guess it was in mid-December, 1970, at an annual school closing program of the Assembly of God Elementary and Junior High School in Zwedru, Grand Gedeh County. Fred was one of the ninth grade school leavers on that unique occasion. As a member of the Zwedru school community, I was invited with other leading personalities. At the program with me in the same seat was Reverend Father John Feeney, SMA, of Christ The King Catholic Church of Zwedru. Particulary and attentively we listened as each item of the program was being rendered. Soon or late, the time came for one of the program's main items – the farewell statement by the student who led the class of 1970, Fred Doe Cherue. Short, dark, slightly stuttering, appearing unassuming with sparkling white teeth, well built, Mr. Cherue eloquently delivered his well written statement. After listening admiringly, I said to myself, "The young man had something to say and he has positively said it."

As I gathered, I thought Fred was a ready tool for senior high school. But would he like to continue? If so, could he be financially able? If not, could I personally assist him one way or another? But one hard fact was questioning me, "With your meager income and sickly condition, which requires regular medical attention, can you make any small or big financial commitment? Don't embarrass yourself by making some big commitment to the young man, who, no doubt, is in urgent need of pecuniary help. Do you mean, my Lord, I cannot try my small self?" I inaudibly pleaded with myself. "Let me do the widow's mite for the promising young man, O Lord!" I urged myself. By dawn I was told to do my best. Therefore I resolved to pay Fred's registration and school fee the year of 1971. All was how much, one would like to know? For everything for the whole school year, the senior high school student was required to pay ten (10) dollars. Ten dollars? Yes, ten dry dollars!

The next morning I found Fred strolling past my dwelling place. I recognized him and hailed him. Although I had met Fred before, from the first encounter he had been indelibly fixed in my photographic mind. Seemingly meditating on some child problem, Fred hastened toward me. "Are you the young man who made the eloquent farewell statement on behalf of your class the other night at the Assembly of God School?" I queried. Not knowing what I was about, Beta Doe hesitantly answered, "Y-es!" "Do you want to continue on to senior high school next year and where?" I pried him. "I would like to attend Tubman-Wilson Institute, if I

149

can find the means," with an uncertain tone Fred revealed. "If that is your desire I shall pay your tuition fee for the year. I will personally pay to the register and hand you the receipt. Would that be alright with you?" I solicited. "Yes sir, I shall highly appreciate it and please accept my grateful thanks in advance for your fatherly assistance," Fred acknowledged. It was from this point that I got to know Fred intimately and he became an active part of my life, both as my son and student.

The Tubman Wilson Institute, under no direction of the administration of Professor Tebli Dweh, encountered many vexing problems. However, the 1973 school year brought an overwhelming victory to our seniors and the school.

All the members of the senior class passed the National Examination with high grades in each subject. My onerous task of the year paid off well. I was truly thankful to God the giver of all good gifts for the wonderful strength and guidance he gave me to have successfully carried such a cumbersome and unusual teaching load.

With Professor Dweh as principal, TWI opened her doors for the 1974 school year. One way or the other, the school had regular recitation periods. This year I accepted and carried four teaching periods a day. Being not principal did not bother me. In all respect, I was still the vice principal and an instructor of language arts and literature. I had nothing to worry about, strongly believing in waiting for God's precious time. After about the second period test, all of the students of each of the history classes under Instructor Dweh surprisingly and miraculously scored one hundred percent each on the history test. To them this was ridiculous, negligent, and unrealistic as it dressed them in borrowed sparkling golden robes that please only the eyes but have no tangible value. The appalling news leaked out to the school supervisory in Zwedru which instituted investigation at once. Principal Dweh was immediately summoned and accordingly interrogated. The evidence against him was preponderant. The professor's act was unprofessional and it tended to degrade the school. The supervisor of schools would not tolerate this unprofessional behavior of the professor. For this unprofessional act on the part of Principal Dweh the supervisory absolutely felt that it was clothed with no other alternative but to suspend their Master's degree holder for time indefinite, replacing him with a Bachelor's degree earner, the veteran teacher, TWI kanyan pepper, and a man whose earnest labor and dedication to his profession markedly and indelibly brought TWI from nowhere to somewhere, William Kamma Reeves, who begged from the hilly Township of Nyaake, Webbo, built on seven scenic hilly hills. At TWI I always felt that the best administration of the school at the time could be well done by no other than the vice principal, the old broom that knew all the nooks and corners of this rural high school, and the most neglected. The so-called school authority realized that it was absolutely necessary to pass the mantle to the professional who merited it. I had a strong feeling that the supervisory was terribly embarrassed to appoint me, having unscrupulously pushed me aside. I was glad they came back soon to make good their grievous error. With goodwill I courageously accepted the temporary assignment.

In the second semester of 1974, about early August, I received a radiogram from US Peace Corps/Liberia to proceed to Monrovia for a workshop. In that time the women of the Grace Baptist Church of Zwedru requested me to speak for them and to them on some big church occasion. But because of this important call from

Monrovia, I was unwillingly compelled to turn the request of my friends down. While I was waiting for the time of my departure for Monrovia, one midday, Mrs. Kathryn White sent her driver to the school to inform me that she would like to see me while on my time home from school. I could not wait for that time as I had nothing to do then, and so I took a free ride to the call of a friend, Mrs. White. "You told us the other that you were about to attend Peace Corps meeting in Monrovia. Between you and me, recently my husband received a radiogram from the Minister of Education saying that he and his deputy for instruction will arrive in Zwedru the 24th of August, 1974. With this information, it is my strong and perhaps timely advice that you don't stir our of here. Be on your job site. No doubt, the minister will set up the new administration of TWI. If you are not here, who would you expect to talk on your behalf? Inform Peace Corps that your overall boss is due here as such, and that it is not physically possible to attend the scheduled meeting," Mrs. White strongly advised. The expression, "Who would speak on your behalf," as strongly expressed by Mrs. White, kept ringing in my ears as I left for home under the blue sunny sky. At home, my lunch did not matter to me. The urge of getting my excuse to the Peace Corps was the only burning issue at bar. At once why not use different words to the typewriter for subsequent submission to the Peace Corps in Monrovia? The message read in part, "Minister of Education due here very soon, not permitted to leave post stop." The message was dispatched to Monrovia. That afternoon of August 24th, Minister Jackson Doe and his Deputy Minister for Instruction, Dr. Joseph Morris, arrived by air in sunny Zwedru bustling with the Liberian National Flag Day celebration.

Upon their arrival, all the teachers of Tubman-Wilson Institute were cited to a meeting with the Education Ministry officials. "Well, we are happy to be here for the very first time since we became ministers of education of the Republic of Liberia. We come for no reason other than to see you in person and perhaps you have a problem or problems you would like to relate to us," Minister Doe broke word on the reason for the visit. Having heard, this Mr. Dweh jumped on his feet to complain Supervisor Cooper and former principal Nayou. According to information, his complaint was a long-standing misunderstanding between him and Cooper. Reliable sources had it that Superintendent White had investigated and settled the matter. It would appear that Dweh did not like the way it went. His next complaint was against me. In brief, Mr. Dweh stated that I had taken his twelfth grade history class from him because I had a girlfriend in that class. After Dweh alleged falsely and ridiculously in that statement clothed with malice and character-assassination, bearing no iota of truth in it and which grossly exposed his wildly and widely spreading ignorance, Minister Doe suddenly and derisively asked, "Can you and I throw the first stone?" All of us burst into wild laughter.

In my rebuttal I explained how the senior class of TWI requested him (Dweh) in the presence of the entire membership of TWI faculty to give up his twelfth grade history class to me because according to the class it was hard on him to get adjusted to his daily administration routine. He acquiesced and was relieved by me. "Mr. Minister, these teachers are my living and eye witnesses. In your own judgment, could a teacher take away another teacher's teaching load, let alone, the principal of the school, without his express permission?" I questioned. My strong wordy explanation was greeted with big laughter. The minister, without posing any question to me or Professor Dweh, said, "The teachers shall continue the meeting with us, except Messrs. Nayou, Dweh, and Reeves will excuse us now." At once we stole away.

The morning of August 25th found me at my desk in the school. At about eight o'clock that busy morning I received a note from Mr. Cooper citing me to a meeting with the minister in the county superintendent's office. I knew in my anxious heart that the minister was going to hand down some kind of decision regarding the leadership of Tubman-Wilson Institute. I was dressed in a well tailored business suit, thinking that if I was denied the principalship of the school, my students would have the memory of how I was handsomely dressed on the morning I quitted my teaching job. I had resolutely and solemnly resolved to quit once I was deprived of the principalship of a school I spent my youthful days to bring from nowhere to somewhere. Hurriedly I went to the administration building where the meeting would take place. For the first time in my public life I was late this day—ten minutes behind! The honorable gentlemen, including the superintendent, were seemingly waiting for me. "Here, sit with us; you don't finish space, Reeves," (he was referring to my size) the minister joked. The minister and the superintendent were sitting side by side in a settee. I joined them with each of them finding the principal in hope. "We want to settle the principal business and other matters here. First, the ministry wants to establish a mobile team that will help the elementary school teachers with their lesson planning in the county. This team would like to be headed by Mr. Dweh. To this Mr. White vehemently objected, saying that Dweh was not good and would serve no useful purpose being the head of such a team intended to help others. "Mr. Dweh had some quarrel with Supervisor Cooper and Mr. Nayou. I called them in my office. The matter was probed into and settle amicably. They shook hands and presumably the matters ended there and then. I was shocked when I learned that that same matter was brought before you yesterday by Mr. Dweh.

Dweh cannot be the team leader while I am the vicegerent of the president of the Republic of Liberia in these parts," the superintendent concluded. This official pronouncement of Mr. White chilled Mr. Dweh. He trembled from hand to toes. "Please, please, Mr. Superintendent, please forgive me. I promise to change for better," Dweh lamented. After the emotion of the superintendent seeped away and the minister explained his reason for choosing Mr. Dweh as a team leader, the big people amicably came to one understanding and Mr. Dweh was appointed.

"The principalship of Tubman-Wilson Institute is definitely yours, Mr. Reeves, provided the political obstinate in your way is resolved now. According to the county administration, you fail to cooperate all the time. Perhaps you can exonerate yourself now, can you not?" the minister queried. "Thank you, Mr. Minister," I began. "I am an individual and I strongly believe in and cherish my individuality. In this turbulent world I will never permit anybody, high or low, to take that away from me and so it is with my freedom of movement and expression. Nobody under the burning sun should attempt to restrain them. I am not against the Albert White county administration, but father, I am its most staunch supporter. Mr. and Mrs. Albert T. White, Mr. and Mrs. John F. Collins, and I are the big five in Zwedru. Out of our elite number Grand Gedeh County chose its superintendent. This is a singular honor for me and our group, the Big Five, and Mr. White knows this very well." The question of my uncooperative general political meeting where a motion taxing all school-going children the sum of one dollar each was made. I was not ready to vote for the motion. Subsequently I was asked to state my unreadiness. "The school children are no salary earners. If the county wants to tax people again for development purposes, I would humbly suggest that the salary earners carry that burden alone. The reason is very simple: All of you remember well perhaps that each salary earner in the county paid fifty percent of his or her monthly salary this very year and at the same time each student paid one dollar. This was strenuous on the parents who have many children in school. Let me be very specific because I want to drive my point into your souls so as to tighten your thinking caps. Mr. Peter Sherleaf earns a net monthly salary of $80. Fifty percent—forty dollars—was taken away from him. From the balance of $40 he paid one dollar for each of his nineteen children in school, leaving him vulnerable to hunger and disease. Take another case. Mr. Peter C. Nayou of Kanweake, Gbeapo, earns a net monthly salary of $150. The county took half of that from him that month. He too had to pay one dollar for each of his thirty children in school. How did he and his large family survive on $45 is the puzzle for all of us. With the foregoing explanation, it is my suggestion therefore that whatever amount of money we need for further development, let us tax only those who earn money. The other problem is that about seventy-five percent of our students in this county support themselves for everything in life. Why should we tax them all the time? Is it another way of turning them off from seeking education?" I asked.

I added, "To save my brothers and students from this constraint I would certainly vote for the motion carrying an amendment taxing only salary earners." As soon as I stated my unreadiness Mr. White assailed me literally with ugly abuses. Publicly insulted, I shamefully left the meeting. "Mr. Minister, is this being against Mr. White's government as alleged by the Honorable Superintendent?" I questioned. This well worded elucidation which placed Mr. White on the front page laid him bare in front of the Honorable Minister. Seemingly my statement pierced his conscience once making him realize that his emotional actions were often misdirected. "Mr. Minister, appoint this principal; I have nothing against him." With the political barrier knocked out of the way, the Honorable Minister handed the envelope containing the letter of appointment to the Deputy Minister for Instruction, Dr. Joseph Morris, and Dr. Morris passed it on to Supervisor Cooper, who finally handed me the document.

William K. Reeves was now principal of a school he worked for hard and long. I was an old broom in the school and so I did not need to be shown around. I began to put things in order for the smooth operation of my TWI. I wholeheartedly seized the helm of the administration which I had managed practically for the past six long years.

Up to the time of my full principalship of the school, there was nothing much in the school to be desired. The basic instruction materials were surprisingly and frustratingly absent from the only government high school in the ten-year-old county. The education authority was avariciously interested in adding more ghost names to the teacher's payroll while the education of the taxpayers' children was being compromised. But what could I do? My first teaching experience was with a school that was materially rich. Instructional materials were in abundance. Teaching in a school where even the basic instructional materials were nonexistent frustrated me. The challenge was aggressively defiant. In short, the school was problematic: no instructional materials, lack of adequate seating, no office for the administration, no faculty lounge, etc. All of these constituted the plight of the young rural high school housed in a building purposely designed for an elementary school (grades 1 through 6). As I saw it, Tubman-Wilson Institute was bitterly yearning complete, immediate restructuring. It was a must if the new administration hoped to bring about the overdue improvement in every aspect of the sick institution. As a teacher and vice principal of the school I lived with those vexing and demanding problems. Since I was wearing the crown, my head became uneasy.

At the end of the 1974 school year I called an extraordinary faculty meeting before which I placed the short term plans for the reorganization of the school. One of the things needed was a space where the teachers would sit to plan. This would require a structure providing office rooms, library, storage, etc. Another proposal was the rigid screening of the incoming students at the beginning of each academic year. My proposal to the young faculty members, including two US Peace Corps Volunteers, was overwhelmingly accepted and endorsed.

As regarding the construction of a new structure on the basis of self-help, I strongly suggested the principal and teachers of the Antoinette Tubman Day School be invited since she too conducted classes in the same building in the afternoon. In the joint faculty meeting it was unanimously agreed that we would build a structure on a self-help basis. Students, for the construction of the proposed building, would be taxed ten dollars each, payable during the first semester registration of the 1975 school year. The teacher would contribute meaningfully too. A campaign to raise funds was organized. Letters to our friends, parents or guardians, and government officials as well as logging company executives were circulated. US Peace Corps volunteer Bill Kogut was to draw up the blueprints of our big dream. In the meantime, both student bodies of ATD and TWI had their deliberation on the proposed self-help building project. Overwhelmingly they voted to do everything in their power to help physically and financially with the construction of the project. A series of meetings followed during which definite and concise plans were drawn up about when actual construction would commence.

At registration during the beginning of the 1975 school year, each student paid her/his taxation of ten dollars for the self-help building project. Our letters soliciting material and financial help were sent to our respective would-be donors. With our hope highly raised, we decided to build with sun dry blocks for the construction of a building consisting of a large space for library, two office rooms for the principals of the schools, and an office space for the registrar for TWI plus spaces for storerooms for both schools.

One of the prominent men we sent our begging letters to told me that we would never accomplish our objective if we used mud blocks. "As I know it from personal experience, self-help project undertakers never have the money needed to carry on the project steadily and rapidly. If you are lucky, the materials and money will come in bits and pieces. The mud blocks, cheap as they are, might land you spending more than you previously planned because when the rains come they will undo the construction in no time, washing away your time, materials, money, and labor. Again you must start from nothing. I would therefore suggest that you build your self-help project with cement blocks to avoid the erosion of your strength. Build with cement blocks to move according to how your prospective donors will respond to your appeal," Mr. Philip N. Collins, Zwedru Liberian National Bank Executive and self-help patron in Grand Gedeh, averred. I conveyed this timely message to the joint faculty meeting. The idea was tossed about and finally we reached a consensus and then resolved to build with cement blocks. To concretize his wholesome suggestion, Mr. Collins donated forty six-inch cement blocks. Everybody was busy hunting for sources to finance our project. Bill Kogut, popularly called Zanbedo, Rooster, in TWI circles and around Zwedru, was no exception; Bill found a source and reliably informed us that there was a program called Peace Corps/Liberia partnership program. This meant that for such a project we were undertaking, if we appealed to Peace Corps/Liberia, they would help to sell our idea to some goodwill people in the United States. In other words, we had to state precisely the need for wanting to build and where the project was being constructed. All must be in writing. This is what Peace Corps/Liberia would send to the Peace Corps/Washington D.C. office, I guess to disseminate.

Not knowing exactly what to write, as I had not done such a writing before, uncertainly I put some ideas together and wrote something, which I personally and realistically felt would reveal and convey why we were undertaking such a project. I called my writing an Open Letter entitled: "Tubman-Wilson Institute Wages War on Ignorance." Then bla..bla... We made several copies on an old memo machine and dispatched them to the Peace Corps office in Monrovia. About three weeks following the dispatch I received a personal letter from a seventy-five-year-old retired teacher, Marilyn Myers in the United States of America. "Mr. Reeves, the heading of your letter rallied me to action. I will raise one thousand five-hundred dollars for your project, which I will send through Peace Corps/Liberia to be delivered to you in the course," Ms. Myers concernedly penned. My fellow principals in some high schools in America did not want to be left out. "We are here with you in your self-help project. Here, through Peace Corps/Liberia, is four hundred fifty dollars to help you with your project," a high school near Washington D.C. declared.
Another US high school rallied for us and sent through Peace Corps four hundred fifty dollars. As it was readily seen, our project gathered from our concerned colleagues in that affluent country with its concerned people two thousand four hundred dollars. What a timely boost it was!

Our letters of appeal were hand delivered to all the logging companies operating in richly marketable wood in the evergreen forest of Grand Gedeh County. Seventeen big logging companies engaged in lucrative business from our national resources and treated us like nobody. We wanted timber and planks from them, but like many other foreign investors who exploit our rich national resources, they abundantly accrue hundreds of millions of dollars enriching themselves and their various nationalities of their respective countries of local need. They treat us like the

Grebo parents. When a man and his wife are made grandparents by a birth given by their daughter, the daughter and baby are invited in order for the baby to be given a treat. A huge rooster is slaughtered for a month or two old baby's consumption. A month or two old baby to eat chicken? A well seasoned Grebo palm butter of the rooster is prepared for the guest of honor, the baby. When the food is served tiny pieces of the meat and palm butter are placed on fingertips and rubbed on the lips of the baby with the elder saying, "This is what we are eating." My question now is, who are those eating? This is what our investors do to us but this time they do not even place a speck on our lips. Eagerly we waited for a positive reply, but to no avail.

When I showed our blueprint to Supervisor Cooper he tried to discourage us from implementing the project as he thought the response from our appeal would be very negative. Absolutely I shared the extreme opposite and determinedly insisted that with my students, teachers, and the other school working hand in hand with us as a community united for common good, surely our worthy objective would be accomplished. I suggested that he and I take the blueprint to Mr. White, the county superintendent, to see what he would think about it too. In the superintendent's office I presented the blueprint of our big daydream. Carefully Mr. White scrutinized the amateur drawing and then suddenly asked, "Do you think that you can build this structure to finish?" My answer was a clear-cut "yes," adding, "with your financial, moral, and material support." Mr. White declared, "I think the project is worth supporting. I shall direct that all business entities in Zwedru donate each a bundle of high grade zinc for the roof of the building. I am included as a businessman. That was another boost and big promise from a man of high principal as I knew him. Many people in and around the country poured in gifts in cash or in kind. Beside the building self-help project, which was an extra-curricular activity, classes ran smoothly and regularly. 1975 was a different academic year at Tubman-Wilson Institute. At the end of each marking period test, all students failing in two or more of the principal subjects, science, math, language arts, and social studies, were told to take the next grade below or leave the school. This exercise generated seriousness and awarded the students academic excellence. Our seniors and the ninth graders' performance on the national examinations proved in no veiled words that there was truly academic reawakening. The National Examination scoring records plainly showed that our seniors were graded B-plus. Before, the TWI average was always D. That put the school in the substandard category. We held our heads high, hoping to continue improving in the succeeding years. In preparation for the National Examinations, TWI science and math teachers were requested by the Ministry of Education to prepare questions in both subjects for submission to the ministry, which, according to them, would form part of the questions for that year's National Examinations. I was highly elated that my able lieutenants and I working harmoniously together were diligent in bringing about the much desired academic change in the right direction.

Mr. Cyrus Cooper was one of the officials of the county from whom we were expecting generous contribution. Instead of that he surprisingly sent us ten dry dollars. For us it was shameful, but what could we do? We needed every cent that we could lay our begging hand on. We accepted his stingy gift. But what was more

156

surprising was that after giving so miserly, Mr. Cooper one misty morning sent me a note saying that from the school money (meaning money for the project) I should loan him four hundred dollars to be paid in due course. His request was scribbled on a scrap of paper not larger than my small palm. On a scrap of paper and in due course? What does due course mean? This upset me and I became bitterly furious. The chief administrator of the schools of Grand Gedeh County continued to roll the water of harmony between him and Reeves to brighten his corners. "In the name of Bacchus and the devil, why should I loan him money being raised for the construction of a building that will bring credit to his idle administration and enhance the work of the administration of Tubman-Wilson Institute, where there was never an office, a chair, or desk for the principal. Instead of Cooper supporting this laudable venture, he was devising his usual money tactics to defeat our selfless efforts. "Beware of Cooper; he is a snake in the grass," Harry Nayou warned me once.

Angry and frustrated, I directed my registrar, Mr. Alfred S. Barbley, to write and inform Mr. Cooper that TWI was not a money loaning institution. Mr. Barbley hand delivered the letter to Cooper, who was geared up to undermine us. This heightened his growing begrudging of me. Over the years, Mr. Cooper irritably noticed that the officials from the Ministry of Education visiting the county would rather talk with me about the education in the county than Mr. Cooper, the supervisor. Their reason I don't know. I guess erecting such a building would convincingly depict my ability that I could better serve in Cooper's position. That phobia was unfounded. I had no ambition of becoming supervisor of schools in his stead. For me, that was not an active position. I always wanted to be where the action was and that is in the classroom. The students directly needed me most. My God knew my plans.

In 1976 the work on our cherished building project moved steadily and progressively. The masonry had reached roof level. The carpenters loitered around to put the roof on, but the logging companies were still not responsive to our appeal until Hon. A. Benedict Tolbert, a member of the House of Representatives from Montserrado County, served as our commencement speaker at the end of the year. When the honorable gentlemen, A. B. Tolbert, the son of Liberia's nineteenth president, arrived in Zwedru upon the invitation of Tubman-Wilson Institute, I apprised him of our pressing need of our self-help project under construction.

At the graduation, without a scrap of paper in hand, Mr. Tolbert had his eager and attentively listening audience spellbound for two short hours. It was a romantic occasion as our guest speaker styled the annual festive occasion without electric light, but candle lights beamed from window sills. As usual, the Liberian Electricity Corporation could not supply the city with light, let alone the City Hall where the elaborate graduation program was celebrated. Honorable Tolbert made a generous gift of four hundred fifty dollars for the school's agricultural program.

As regarding our self help project A.B. promised that he would urge all the logging companies in the county to supply us with all the wood we needed. About a week following the Mr. Tolbert's departure from Zwedru, nearly every morning a logging company executive would call on our campus inquiring about the principal. This was in response to our appeal for timber and planks. No doubt, Mr. Tolbert had placed a blazing fire on their stubborn backs and they were responding fast.

In no time we had enough wood delivered and the carpenters moved in to place the roof on. Mr. White and his businessmen delivered about twelve bundles of zinc for the roof. There was nothing in the way of the construction of our big dream. With everything in place, that is, hoping then that the project would be completed, I began to wonder from where could I find books to put in that large space I called library. The school had no means to purchase even a book for the space called library. Would the large open space only and simply bear the good sounding name? "My dear God, father of the needy, let some people come to my help," I cried inaudibly. In a low but clear whispering voice somebody said, "Why not write and request your former Peace Corps friends, Nancy Simmons and Carolyn Ross?" Those beautiful young American ladies as my colleagues in the teaching field rendered my country and me valuable service. Losing no time, I searched around my house for their respective home addresses; Carolyn Ross, a black American, was living in Miami, Florida, and Nancy Simmons was living near the Washington D.C. area. I penned each of them a begging letter, appealing for some used books for the library of the school. In the meantime, the floors and the walls were being plastered with cement while the carpenters were busily engaged with their callous palms building the shelves of the to-be-library and other wood of the building. As everything appeared to be on course, my hope that the building would surely be completed was on solid ground, not flinching at all!

In about a month's time after I posted the letters to my warm American friends, I received their respective replies in the Liberian mail. "Sure case, I am willing and obliged to help you and your school. As soon as I received your letter I took it to some Christian organization. Having read your touching letter, the members unanimously consented to collect some used but useful books for your reading room. Herein I enclosed the pictures of the young concerned people gathering the books for the proposed library," Ms. Ross assured me. In her reply Nancy noted that a high school, her alma mater, would obligingly honor her request. "My high school will send you a big collection of useful used books. The consignment is due in the shortest possible time," Ms. Simmons promised. "Bravo! Bravo!! we are doing it!" I shouted.

At the end of 1976, the large bags and cartons of books from my dear American friends crowded the post office of the county. Without any specific reason, at my leisure time after school I strolled to the administration building, an imposing government building where most of the county government offices were located, included the post office. The post master was an elderly Grebo man whom I teasingly called "young man," and he in turn called me "old man." Seeing me through the main exit door, Mr. Wah Harris, the post master, shouted, "Old Man Reeves, will you please come now to clear these rubbishes of yours from my office." I had not the slightest notion of what the young old man was talking about and so I entered to discover a huge consignment of books consigned to Principal Reeves and his school. What a relieving and happy sight it was! In a clear and concrete Manifestation, Nancy and Carolyn had done it for their former site administration, Zwedru Peace Corps/Liberia training program that prepared the US volunteers to get integrated into the Liberian school system. With the help of some of my students and a pickup, the consignment was readily delivered at the school. As many of the shelves were already in place, the next day we began to stock them.

Early 1977 brought us what we had longed for: our seemingly wild daydream, constructing a building that would enhance the administration of the neglected Tubman-Wilson Institute and other related activities of the school. Proudly I moved into my new office. Dedication of the building would take place during the annual commencement season when the Assistant Director of Education for Peace Corps/Liberia would be invited to the program, which was going to be elaborate with pageantry. Breathing the air of grateful satisfaction in my spacious office, I saw an elegantly dressed man in my doorway. "May I come in?" the uninvited visitor asked. "Certainly, yes! You are welcome. Have a seat," I offered. Mr. Yancy Peter Flah, principal designate for the Zwedru Multilateral High School, yet under construction, squared himself in one of my new wooden chairs, right opposite me sitting behind my well polished Grand Gedeh County redwood desk.

After exchanging the usual pleasantries, Mr. Flah had this to say: "Next year (1978) this school, meaning TWI, will be merged with Zwedru High School. With TWI gone, would you like to take up assignment in the administration of ZMHS or as a classroom teacher there?" Bluntly I replied, "Mr. Flah, I have no such intention at all. I don't want to work in the administration; neither do I want to teach there." Mr. Flah tried to urge me to accept a job there, but to no avail. His request left me wondering about Mr. Flah's invitation asking the principal of Tubman-Wilson Institute to accept a teaching position under a principal designate. For me this was a laughing affront to me, a seasoned and experienced teacher and administrator. In no uncertain way I was grossly insulted. Anyhow, I kept my peace. I had nothing to worry about. Sabey get no worry. Within myself I knew that I was a professionally trained teacher. I had shining track records in my profession. There was no gainsay about it. The whole situation was aggravated by the fact that my government, that is, the Ministry of Education, deliberately disregarded me. Since the working relationship was on a breaking point between Supervisor Cooper and me it went without saying that Cooper kept the pertinent information from me so that it would pay Cooper's way by which I would be sacked. Remember, Cooper was like a snake in the grass. That whole day I seriously meditated whether it was the planned intention of the Ministry of Education represented by Supervisor Cooper in the county to slyly kick me out.

Each time I thought of it I pacified myself, "Reeves, you are qualified. Losing the government job will not exclude you from teaching in Liberia. Why worry when you can pray?" I left everything in the hands of our Lord Jesus Christ. And so it went! As my good Lord would have it, while this information about TWI merging with ZMHS bothered me, I received a letter from the Most Reverend Boniface Nyema Dalieh, bishop of the Catholic Diocese of Cape Palmas, requesting me to have some talk with him in Harper, Maryland County. "I'll pay your way to and from. Come by plane or car," the bishop added in his letter.

"What does he want now?" I soliloquized. Miserly as the bishop is, how could he creditably tell me that he would pay my way to and from and add either by plane or car. It sounded so unbelievable that I did not want to make such a fruitless trip. However, I took the letter to my parish priest, Reverend Father George Landry,

SMA, and after reading it he told me that he would be willing to drive me to Greenville from where I would pick up the afternoon plane flight to Harper, and would wait for me there the next day from Harper. "I know what it is all about but I won't tell you," grinning, the priest said. "If it is all right with you, I would like to make the trip this weekend," I requested. We left that weekend by way of Greenville. At about two that hot afternoon, I boarded the plane for Harper.

When the plane alighted I met Reverend Father Benedict Dortu Sekey, then coordinator of the Cape Palmas Diocesan School System. He told me that he had come to the airfield to take me to the bishop's house in East Harper. Seemingly to greet his invited guest, the bishop was standing in his doorway. He warmly greeted me in the old conservative Grebo tradition and ushered me into his roomy mansion. When I was seated, he said to Father Sekey, "Tell him now what we called him for!" "No, you tell him. You are the bishop," Father Sekey resisted. "But you tell him because you are the coordinator," Bishop Dalieh insisted. At last Father Sekey broke word: "Mr. Reeves, we would like for you teach for us in Zwedru. We need you for the principalship of Bishop Juwle High School. In surprised response I asked, "Do you think I am capable for that high position?" "Yes, from our own observation and from what people upon inquiry tell us. They say unreservedly that you are professionally and morally qualified in all respects and because the mission gives complete credence to such convincing evidence we are offering you the principalship of our young high school in Grand Gedeh County," Father Sekey stressed. I wondered and asked, Am I being dressed in a borrowed robe? "Since you have that much confidence in me, please give me time to think about it. In the shortest space of time I shall inform you about my decision through Father Landry, I hope," I concluded.

As I though of the big offer I inductively concluded that the Catholic Mission was indirectly demanding their "thing." What would that be? one would ask. At times short memory can cause problems. My inner man whispered to me, "Do you forgot so soon, few years back the mission wholesomely nurtured you by giving you education without any cost to you?" "If your answer is in the affirmative then the thing the mission is demanding indirectly from you is your service in return for the education given. Is that clear?" my conscience queried. Inwardly I prayed, "This time around I am going to dictate the terms of the contract in no uncertain terms." Back in Zwedru I consulted my initiate friends, Mrs. Karthryn White and Mr. Amos Kamara. Both of them strongly advised that I should take the job. As they put it, "These Krahn people are gearing up against everybody. Get in that private corner, especially since it is your church that needs your services."

I knew deep in my heart what the mission was saying in essence. Implicitly the mission was saying, "Give us our thing," meaning the education through the help of the mission I obtained. There was no qualm about their claim. Calmly did I accept the timely offer. But I urged that my friends, especially Mrs. White, should treat it as a classified secret. This was in May, 1977. During the rest of the school year I worked tirelessly soliciting help from here and there to furnish our big pride, our self-help building project.

Our engagement in the self-help building project dawned a new day in the way of life at the Tubman-Wilson Institute. All the students were acting responsibly.

They became more studious and regular in attendance. Our morale was high. A month before graduation, the graduating seniors began to hunt for their commencement speaker, Mrs. D. Musleng Cooper, Peace Corps/Liberia Assistant Education Director needed the list of prospective commencement speakers. As you expect, Mrs. Cooper's Peace Corps/Liberia connection with TWI she was unanimously selected from among many qualified people. That was a happy coincidence. Already Mrs. Cooper would represent the Peace Corps at our pending dedication of Tubman-Wilson Institute's Multipurpose Self-Help Building. As my personal friend and boss, Musleng, no doubt, would unhesitantly honor our invitation and request. We were duly honored.

Commencement season was slated for the first week in December, 1977. Massive preparation for the graduation and reception went underway. According to the arrangements and the program of the season, a day before graduation, the multipurpose building project would be in an elaborate ceremony dedicated. All the books generously donated through my kind and solicitous friends' help were neatly and orderly stacked on Grand Gedeh redwood shelves, with the background of walls shining with white enamel paint and the librarian's seat well in place. The building was gayly decorated. Finally the day of the dedication arrived, and with pomp and pageantry the TWI family and their invitees assembled to give glory to God Almighty and ask Him to shower His unlimited blessings on our self-help building project, the first of its kind in the history of education in Grand Gedeh County.

In remarks, I sincerely thanked those who generously aided us in making our then seemingly wild dream come true, especially the county superintendent, Honorable Albert T. White, whose political influence and business ingenuity immensely helped us to score our desired goal.

Our partners, United States Peace Corps/Liberia, Mrs. Marilyn Myers, that septuagenarian American humanitarian, a concerned retired teacher, and my American colleagues, the two high school principals of that affluent country with its altruistic and affable people who shared their abundant wealth with my school and me were appropriately crowned with high honor and praised. My students and teachers were heartily congratulated for their steadfastness by their highly elated principal. I told the people of Zwedru, especially the students of the other schools in the Zwedru community, that the library was constructed for the use of all.

"Come and use freely this beautiful facility, a fountain of knowledge," I invited. At the graduation Mrs. Cooper delivered a challenging message. In her modulated voice, Mrs. Cooper challenged the graduating students, particularly the female students, to meet life headlong. "Life is a battle. You must gird your armor on," the seasoned educator emphasized. In my well thought remarks, I spilled the crocodile's poopoo out, my seven month top secret. Without a speck of emotion I stated, "From some source I learned with dismay that TWI will be merged next year with the Zwedru Multilateral High School, still under construction. Since the source is a reliable one, I would presume that there will be no TWI. As TWI will not be anymore, it goes without saying that Principal Reeves will be no more too. But I am glad that I am still useful and needed. I am qualified.

I am like a good hunter who gets ready his gun by putting his cartridge in the gun just as he leaves town. I placed my cartridge in the gun a long time ago by going to school and obtaining a satisfying degree of education. With my education, I think I am well prepared for any eventuality. It is very unfortunate that mine and your Ministry of Education, represented by Professor Cyrus S. Cooper, failed disobligingly to inform me. It would appear that this was one of Cooper's sinister devices to snatch away my daily bread. If it is what he contemplated, I would say to him that he missed his calling. In this public place let me tell you what has been happening behind the scene: the Catholic Mission is demanding its thing, William K. Reeves, blessed with rich Catholic education. Next year, God being in control, William K. Reeves will assume the principalship of Bishop Patrick Kla Juwle High School right here in Zwedru. Perhaps I am Cooper's poison, but now I am the Catholic Mission's meat since the mission itself cooked the meat. For the mission I guess the meat is very palatable since they seasoned it. Get educationally prepared to bravely and successfully battle with the consuming problems of this turbulent world with its host of miscreants." This was how my seventeen years in the government business of education ended in Grand Gedeh County. Twelve of those challenging years, rift with frustration and disappointments, were spent in Zwedru, a beautiful rural town nestled in the very heart of the evergreen forest of Liberia.

When the country of Liberia was founded, we the indigenous people of the country were completely left out of the body politic of our one country. We were totally segregated against. By the way, what kind of segregation was that? Racial? It could not have been on the ground of race because all of us are black. Perhaps it was superiority segregation because the western-oriented blacks had spent centuries in slavery in the United States of America and somewhere else in the west. With the incumbency of William V.S. Tubman as president of Liberia in 1944, about ninety-seven years after Liberia declared her independence, the indignity heaped on us the fathers of our God-given land was gradually melted away over the twenty-seven years of his long rule, of course leaving behind glittering vestiges of that inhumane treatment by our freed slave brothers. What is surprising and appalling now is that we, who had no political standing in our country then, having been liberated by Tubman during whose magistrate we were made part and parcel of this land of liberty the indigenous became not in segregating among themselves on ethnic line. The episode in the Cooper Reeves situation typified. It seems to be our tendency to pull our fellow Liberian down because he is not part of an ethnic group. Can we successfully build our country that way? Well, although my government did not inform me that TWI would shut down and be merged with ZMHS, I was still a professional and must always behave like one.

Bearing this in mind, I sent my letter of resignation to the Ministry of Education through the Deputy Ministry of Education for Instruction, Mrs. Christian Tolbert-Norman, a young woman who seemed to be very concerned about long serving, trained and experienced teachers. A copy of my letter of resignation was served the county supervisor, Mr. Cyrus S. Cooper. In my letter of resignation I told the ministry that I was sick and could not continue teaching and then requested for retirement benefit. When the deputy minister received my letter she sent for me at once. In Monrovia Mrs. Norman requested me to accept the principalship of the high school on president Tolbert's farm somewhere in Bong County. "I am told that you are a very good, experienced teacher and an administrator of no mean standing. I promise you, it will be well with you there," the deputy minister of education for instruction pleaded. "I am singularly what by your offer. But I guess you can see the strands of gray hair in my hair.

No doubt, this clearly suggests middle age, doesn't it? Since I started my teaching career, Zwedru is my third station of assignment in this sacrificial but noble profession. Madame, please, I cannot move to another new place at this age of mine. Let your government give me small thing just to sustain my ageing life," I humbly solicited. With this frank exchange I left my boss, breathing the breath of honor. I returned to Zwedru.

I took a two week vacation to Kablake, that home village of mine, to personally inform my parents about what I called "My New Old Job." I was deeply happy to enjoy the beautiful, peaceful village life with my aging parents, relatives, and friends. The two weeks were just like fleeting moments. I rushed back to Zwedru to get myself ready to take over my new administration of Bishop Juwle High School. I arrived in Zwedru about the tenth of January,1978. My service with the government of my country would be completely terminated on the thirty-first of January as stated in my letter of resignation. Upon arrival, I met Supervisor Cooper's letter requesting me to turn over the property of TWI to his office on the tenth of January, 1978, the day on which I arrived from Kablake, my home village in Maryland County. I found it impossible to turn over the school's property to the supervisor that day after reading his letter, as it was about four o'clock that sunny afternoon. I went to Mr. Cooper to appeal to him that I could not turn the school's property over that day as I had just arrived from Maryland County. He readily accepted my excuse and postponed the exercise to the next day.

The next day, Teachers Joseph S. Grear and Alfred S. Barbley and I were ready to turn over the property of the school to Mr. Cooper's two-man team and the exercise began. We delivered everything, including broken metal cabinets and other literally rotten items. The team then produced a long list of things the supervisor said were in possession of the school; such things as timber, planks, typewriters, teacups, teaspoons, saucers, etc., etc. This nonsensical and absurd list irritated Barbley and Grear. I intervened and said that there was nothing we should haggle over.

"The school is a place of records. Perhaps you and I were not here when the supervisory delivered those things here and the person acting in my stead received the items being demanded." I requested, "Please tell the supervisor that we don't have his listed things here. If those things were sent by him and the acting principal signed for them, I shall pay for each item. I don't have them and I don't know about them." With this the team left.

Having turned over the so-called property of TWI to the supervisor of schools for Grand Gedeh County, Liberia, I had willingly, conscientiously terminated my eighteen unbroken years of dedicated and professional service directly to my government. But my whole being belongs to my government and people of Liberia. Only this time around, I am going to serve in the private sector of my country. In no way should I continue serving generously with the talent God Almighty entrusted to my care. In the meantime, at the end of the month (January) my little thing (salary) would be given to me as the final mark of departure from active government service.

Early February, 1978, happily brought me back into the active service of the Catholic Mission, Cape Palmas Diocese, my benefactor. But this time I was here, as Shakespeare puts it, in triple trust: a personal friend of the Bishop of Cape Palmas, a teacher and administrator, and principal of Bishop Juwle High School. Seeing me in my position, a position that seemingly promised lucrative salary, comparatively, presuming on his part, Supervisor Cooper was enraged and his longstanding unwarrantedly envious campaign against my straightforwardness aggravated him.

I was not surprised when I received a letter from the country attorney, charging me of robbing TWI of things like chalk, teacups, saucers, and other items. In his letter to me, the county attorney, Honorable David Y. Swengbe, wrote, among other things, "Your taking away those things from the school is criminal, if it is true that you did it."

The contents of the letter of the prosecuting attorney elated me for two simple reasons: I had somebody to hear my side of the libelous information given the county official government prosecutor, and the second was that my illiterate parents had made a marked difference between their lives and my life; they gave the blessing of education; they sacrificially but willingly encouraged me to drink deeply and wholesomely at the ever-flowing fountain of education. I asked myself, "Did I go to school and did I acquire anything worthwhile?" Old Man Tallawford of sainted memory said it this way: "Did I buy anything worthy of note from the market of achievement?" I told my typewriter, "Get ready, I want to spread book from your keys." Briefly I wrote, " I am humbly requesting through your office a copy of those things I allegedly robbed of the school as stated in your letter. I shall repay all if I received them under my signature." No reply came from the county attorney. Mr. Cooper, laden with malice and jealousy, took another course. He wrote a long letter charging me of stealing Tubman-Wilson Institute's property and taking them over to Bishop Juwle High School & Catholic Mission. He served copies to all the top people of the Ministry of Education, Republic of Liberia, and superintendent of the county. I was honored with a copy too.

While I was talking with Reverend Father Sekey on administrative matters, then coordinator of the Cape Palmas Diocesan schools, Reverend Father Gessler, SMA, came in with Cooper's letter and handed it to Father Sekey, biting on his long pipe in his mouth. Father Sekey merely glanced at the letter and handed it back to Father Gessler. "What do you say about the letter?" Father Gessler asked. Father Sekey retorted, "Say what, or *do* what?" He added, "You and I did not employ Mr. Reeves. If Cooper wants him sacked he should write the bishop who employed Mr. Reeves." With this Father Gessler left. I had a copy of the letter served me by the Cooper supervisory but I said nothing about it to Father Sekey. That very day Father Gessler left for his furlough in the United States of America.

From Zlehtown Reverend Father John Feeney, SMA, came to take charge of the Zwedru parish following Father Gessler's absence form the parish the day before. In my office, Father Feeney said, "William, here is a letter from Mr. Cyrus Cooper saying that the mission must not employ you because you took away the property of TWI." "Father, if the mission acts on this nonsense Cooper wrote, I shall fare well

164

from the money I will get from the mission by taking it to court and having competent jurisdiction in that matter," I asserted. "What would be your advice to your priest?" the priest, looking very concerned, asked. "Father, tell Cooper that William Reeves is a Liberian. So far you know, you have nothing against him and as such you cannot sack him or cancel his employment with the mission. Leave us out of it, please," I would advise. I heard nothing further about Cooper's struggle against me.

Daily I was busy at my new desk. "The superintendent asked me to tell you that he would like to talk with you in his office now. Please come with me in the jeep," the superintendent's driver requested. Without hesitation I went with the driver to know that Mr. Cooper was clandestinely determined to physically and morally cut me down by all means. Cooper had alleged that when I turned the school's property over to his supervisory, I refused to give him the keys to the TWI building. This was a sabotage according to Cooper. "Mr. Reeves, is it true that since you turned the property of the school over to the supervisory you refused to give the keys to Mr. Cooper?" Superintendent Kudar Jarry inquired. I was profoundly shocked by that question. To answer I was completely out of words. But as my blessed Lord would have it, Mr. Alfred S. Barbley, one of the young men who helped me to turn the property of the school over, was sitting in the superintendent's office. Suddenly he spoke out, "Mr. Cooper, do you forget, Principal Flahn wrote you to let us use the TWI building to administer the Zwedru Multilateral High School entrance and placement test? I personally delivered the letter to you." Mr. Cooper had nothing to say. Before I thanked Mr. Jarry, I said to Cooper, "If you had said that to me outside of this office I was going to kick you in your posterior." There was a big uproar among the Krahns in the office because, according to them, I had insulted their professor. They had forgotten to realize all the evil motives Mr. Cooper harbored against me. In this meeting too, the county attorney revealed to the superintendent that Cooper wrote him, charging ex-Principal William K. Reeves of robbing TWI; "I inquired from him whether he had documentary evidence to produce against Mr. Reeves? If no, we cannot take him to court. Without any such evidence when we enter a legal suit against him in court, he will ridicule and literally abuse us. You know him well as well as I do. I think we have no case against him. He was a good public relations principal, and as such, many people gave him gifts. The school is baseless and lacks legal ingredient. In face of this legal explanation, Supervisor Cooper bitterly rebuked me, saying that I failed to prosecute Mr. Reeves because he is a member of my ethnic group, the Grebo. Did Cooper forget the biblical verse that says, 'Touch not my anointed and do my prophet no harm'? I did not come to Zwedru in search of a job. My performance in my profession anointed me and made me a prophet. All Cooper's malicious attempts against this sincerely dedicated teacher did not prevail on me."

January, 1978, salary checks came in. I collected mine. Shortly before that, Deputy Minister Norman sent me a radiogram informing me that my request for retirement benefits was before the President of Liberia for his timely consideration. In the meantime, I would receive three months pay for sick leave.

When February salary checks arrived in the county I went to the pay office to collect my check, but the paymaster refused to release it to me. "You are no longer a teacher of the government, according to the list the supervisory certified to this office," the paymaster declared. Was this man trying to deprive me of what I thought would add more grease to my elbow? Without a word, I took out my radiogram from my pocket and handed it to the paymaster. After reading it, he said, "Well, go to the supervisor for your clearance." "Who is this Cooper? Is it not the Cooper who is my fellow employee of the Ministry of Education? He is what? Would you require him to get a clearance from me too? In short, I would strongly advise you to deliver my hard earned check to me or be prepared to get what might follow," I vehemently warned him. Gladly he did deliver my government-given check. All my sick leave three months pay came without hindrance.

The Catholic Mission had rightfully and justifiably claimed their mission-educated William K. Reeves. I was glad to be back home. The new atmosphere surrounding my new principalship was richly enlightening. My predecessor was my former social studies teacher at Our Lady of Fatima High School and history professor at college. It would appear that this new principalship was more highly placed and more challenging. Reverend Father George Landry, my predecessor, was of high academic standing with vast experience in school administration. Yet I was chosen to carry on from him. Since I willingly consented and accepted to be the choice of the mission, I began to think seriously with Dickerson as I whispered his lines, "Since I am chosen, I am the only one, of all who live, by whom this job can be done in the proper way." Would my assertion and presumption suffice, and for how long? Well, I was deep in the cold water and there would be nothing to alleviate the biting cold from me.

However, I took solace when I vividly recalled that late Sunny Sunday morning, immediately after Mass, when Sister Helen Reed, SSND, called me aside and in undertone, she said to me, "We think that you, the trained, qualified, and experienced Liberian teacher, can handle the Liberian school principalship better than any highly trained qualified expatriate. The sisters and I were thinking of requesting Bishop Boniface N. Dalieh to make you principal of Christ the King High School." The incumbent principal, Sister Helen Reed, was principal of Christ the King High School, as the school was formerly called. When Bishop Patrick Kla Juwle, the first Liberian Catholic priest and bishop, paid Zwedru his pastoral visit sometime in early 1972, Grand Gedeh County Superintendent Albert T. White, at a sumptuous party in honor of the Catholic prelate, officially requested the bishop to raise St. Philomena Elementary and Junior High School to high school stature. With his people's welfare always at the center of his heart, yearning to provide them with every possible available means to bring Christ and education to the people of Liberia, Bishop Juwle honored the superintendent's timely request. The following year St. Philomena was deprived of her junior high section and Christ the King High School was founded.

After honoring Zwedru and Grand Gedeh County with a high school (the second in the county), Bishop Juwle was ceased by the cold hands of death. Subsequently the President of Liberia, Dr. William R. Tolbert, officially visited Zwedru and Grand Gedeh County. Through the county superintendent, the Catholic Mission requested the president to break ground for the new high school. At the groundbreaking, President Tolbert benignly suggested that since the bishop who

166

openheartedly gave Zwedru and Grand Gedeh their second high school had gone to be with the Lord before his wholesome plan bore fruit, the new school should be named in his sainted memory. The Catholic Mission authority wholeheartedly accepted the suggestion of the Liberian President and accordingly named the school Bishop Juwle High School.

. What relieved me of my anxiety of the principalship of Bishop Juwle High School was that according to Sister Helen, the School Sisters of Notre Dame of Zwedru had discussed turning the school over to a Liberian teacher. As I held it to be the truth and nothing but the truth, I was being placed in the able, religious, and professional hands of the celebrated School Sisters of Notre Dame of Zwedru, Grand Gedeh County.

Before my coming to take over the administration of Juwle High School, as I would like to call their school, I knew the sisters individually but not intimately. However, though my casual conversations with them from time to time, I gathered that each of them had an implicit confidence lodged in their professional hearts for this skinny, talkative Grebo teacher. With this kind of blessed assurance I unhesitantly and proudly assumed the arduous and onerous task of the principalship of the five-year-old Bishop Juwle High School, perched near Feeney Avenue in Zwedru, Grand Gedeh County, a county sparsely inhabited, but vastly covered with evergreen forests rich in marketable wood coveted by logging executives from all over the world.

There was nothing hidden about my being back in the system of education in which I was partly educated and where I launched my life's career, teaching. Here, obligatorily, religiously, and patriotically, I was in triple trust, seasonably and richly Catholic educated, a Catholic and Liberian. For which of the reasons was I selected principal of this young, promising academic institution? God Almighty, no doubt, you directed and guided this appointment and assignment of mine. I want to believe that all the reasons are embedded in this trust, taking into account all what they say I am and so help me, my good God! Amen.

In February, 1978, registration, which preceded the entrance and placement test, began in earnest at Bishop Juwle High School. While the sisters were registering the students, I posted myself in the principal's office. "If you have any problem regarding transcripts of any of the new coming students, be free to call my attention," I requested. Sister Petronilla, SSND, was in charge. Shortly after, the sister referred a transcript to me. For her part, she found nothing faulty about the transcript but she just wanted the principal to have a look at it. The student bearing the transcript handed it to me. Within a split second of scrutiny I discovered that the transfer was not genuine. I walked into the faculty room where the registration was being conducted. I said, "Sister, there is something wrong with this." "What do you mean, Mr. Reeves," Sister Pet softly exclaimed, apparently in a surprised mood. "The trouble here is glaring and clearly simple. I'll show you in a twinkle. The official signature of this transfer is seemingly forged. As I can readily see, heaven knows that Mr. Jacob Slah, whose purportedly official signature is affixed on this transfer, cannot misspell his surname SLAH. Look here, Sister, the principal's surname is misspelled. I know the man personally and I am acquainted with his signature. He worked with me on the US Peace Corps/Liberia In-country Training Program here in Zwedru. I cannot

167

believe that Mr. Slah would misspell his own surname. And therefore this is my solid ground of rejection of the transfer," I explained. In that time, Reverend Witt, principal of Nike Tuleh Wilson High School, an Assembly of God institution in Zwedru, walked in. I showed the transfer to Principal Witt, a Canadian. "This young man cannot be in this grade he is claiming. He was a student at my school last year, and before the first semester ended, he left, leaving incomplete records behind, which he has yet to request for, and hence we have not certified them to any school," Reverend Witt asserted.

Many expatriates, if not all, believe that they possess full knowledge of Liberia and Liberians. Can you believe it? For me, certainly not. I was born in Liberia, I live in Liberia, and I hope to die in Liberia. It is completely misleading, erroneous, and dangerous for anybody to pretend having full knowledge of any country, Liberia being no exception. From this incident above, Sister Pet, who was my closest friend among the School Sisters of Notre Dame of Zwedru, was quite convinced that I knew more about my country than any expatriate, regardless of the length of time they had lived in Liberia. Unfortunately, Sister Pet took up a new assignment at Arthur Barclay Vocational Training School in Monrovia.

BJHS was blessed that year, 1978, with a young Catholic nun, Sister Loreen Spaulding, SSND. With inexhaustible energy and never-complaining, unassuming, and lovable, Sister Loreen was a caring religious and a dedicated teacher. Our twelve-year stay together at BJHS found us working harmoniously in reasonable accord. In short, Sister Loreen was my ablest lieutenant. A versatile teacher, Sister Loreen stimulated and vehemently propelled the eager and docile students to action in their academic quest for knowledge. Briefly, Sister Loreen was the very center of all the laudable happenings, events bringing the school into the limelight of academic excellence in the county and our one country, Liberia. Really she generated useful actions!

Sister Kathleen Wahl, SSND, who had been working with the school since its inception, was another ready helping hand in strong support for the smooth operation of the school. In fact I was wonderfully blessed with the willing and spontaneous cooperation of all my teachers, including the Liberian teachers and our African expatriate teachers, Ghanaian, to be exact. With this literally aggressive team working assiduously hand-in-hand with the administration, we diligently moved to nobler heights each academic year. It was real teamwork!

Up to my incumbency, BJHS had not been able to house the six classes (which constituted the school) on one campus. The seventh and eighth grades were still housed on the campus of the Mother school, St. Philomena. I told the bishop in no veiled terms that I did not think I would effectively manage the affairs of the school with the classes here and there. I strongly advised him, therefore, that the school needed another building to accommodate the two classes having no room on the BJHS campus.

Bishop Dalieh and I met with the nuns to discuss the possibility of erecting additional classrooms. After throwing the idea around, we unanimously agreed to build a structure that would contain two classrooms, a laboratory with a prep room, and storerooms for each of the classrooms having closets for storing text and supplementary books. The total cost of the building was estimated at twenty thousand dollars ($20,000) for the two-classroom structure with its accessories. The principal was named the construction manager while Sister Loreen was honored with the title of business manager. Bishop Dalieh made available fourteen thousand dollars ($14,000), and the sisters added a substantial sum of money to start the work at once.

The business manager, with a bustling energy like a fire brigade, moved into action at once. At the end of first semester, 1978, the new building was ready for dedication, earning me a high place in the first few months of my young administration in the school. After the colorful program of the dedication, the seventh and eighth graders, then enjoying uncurbed running around and truancy, soon found themselves in the full grips of the BJHS administration. The building had cost twenty-five thousand dollars ($25,000) by the time construction ended. Prices of building materials had rapidly risen with the succeeding months during our construction.

President William V.S. Tubman, who ruled Liberia for twenty-seven unbroken long years like a legacy from his ancestors, had passed from labor to rest. It was a little less than seven years when Catholic Mission crowned me with the distinguished honor of succeeding Reverend Father George Landry, my high school social studies instructor and my history professor at college.

Taking the mantle of the State of Liberia was the veteran politician, Dr. William Richard Tolbert, who devoutly promised Liberians to build a great country by bringing it to higher heights. Certainly he had shifted his ship of state into high gear and had begun to mount progressively to the heights he had envisaged. Under his participatory democratic leadership, for seven short years, Liberians and Liberia saw a glimmer of hope, positive changes in every sphere of our national life, from a flamboyant public lifestyle and promiscuous lasciviousness. While this political, social, economic, and moral renaissance was speedily gaining momentum and glowing radiantly in every nook and corner of our country, some grossly ignorant people read Pastor Tolbert's national blueprint upside down and clandestinely ate at our political and social fabrics and inhumanely burst our national sovereignty. April 12, 1979, galloped in the civil unrest that characterized our sparsely populated and grossly underdeveloped country. In the upheaval President Tolbert lost his life in a bloody coup d'etat staged by a handful of untrained, uneducated, and unscrupulous non-commissioned officers and enlisted men of the Armed Forces of Liberia on April 12, 1980. Without effective national direction we entered the decade of the eighties.

For six long years without a companion I tarried in the bustling rural City of Zwedru, so named because it is geographically located at the source of a stream or creek called Zwe lying parallel on the northeastern side of the city. My married life had been broken, shattered, and destroyed by my partner, whose unfaithfulness devastated our striving married life. Because of this sad, disheartening, frustrating, and disappointing and ugly event, which I termed, "Untimely devastation of this lifelong partnership," I had vowed never again to get indulged or entered into such a partnership. But when I accepted the principalship at the Catholic school, I received a very wholesome, timely filial advice from my daughter, my oldest child, Christiana, to rethink about my candid and resolute decision never to get married again. Christiana wrote, "Your social life will not be secure as a principal of an oriented religious institution when you are not domestically balanced." Although young and inexperienced, Christiana's advice came from an old head, seemingly. I was quite convinced and at once resolved to get going again. On July 22, 1978, I took another pleasing trouble.

Although the political, social, moral, and economic life of our nation was now in the hands of depraved leaders, BJHS appeared unaffected. The students, faculty, and administration rode cooperatively, productively, and harmoniously on the vessel of progress. To enhance our academic activities, many clubs came into being in the school as extracurricular activities to buttress the academic activities. Such clubs as dramatic, journalistic, team time quiz, to name a few, were the vehicle that propelled the versatile, docile students, insatiably seeking for knowledge, into action each day.

In a country overwhelmed with confusion and political unrest, anybody living in that hurly-burly could not deem himself an island. BJHS was no exception. Two days following the bloody coup that snatched away the life of a man who promised to build a great nation for the Liberian people, leading them to nobler heights, the students of ZMHS went on a rampage in the streets of Zwedru to oust their principal, Peter Yancy Flahn. "We don't want Flahn," the multitude of students exclaimed and shouted. As their hullabaloo continued, they came down White Avenue and into Feeney Street, lying parallel to the east of BJHS. Rampaging, screaming, and shouting, the rowdy crowd, passing within the earshot of the school with their earsplitting, boisterous noises, profoundly distracted the attention of Juwle's students, buried in their lessons at the time. However, they did not physically enter our campus.

Thinking that our students might follow suit, perhaps, Sister Marie Dooley, SSND, suggested to me that we should assemble the students to caution them about such lawlessness being displayed by ZMHS students. "I don't know what to tell them. As you desire, I must assemble them now. Perhaps, after saying what you have to say I might have gathered something to tell them in that regard," I explained as I gave in to her suggestion. With this, the students were assembled in the twelfth grade classroom. In her usual religious mood, she told the students not to act rashly but to think positively. In my remarks I said, among other things, "I have not witnessed a coup, but I read about the French Revolution, which history says was the most bloody known to the world. What I noted from reading was that that kind of revolution is like a cutlass you throw at a fish in a stream of water. Instead of hitting the fish as one desires, the cutlass boomerangs and cuts the thrower on his foot. To put it another way, this kind of revolution is like a narrow Kru canoe plying the angry waves. It capsizes most of the time. In this case the revolutionists go against one another's throats, creating more chaos in the country. Carefully, let us look on," I seriously warned. Our students did not take to the streets but found their own outlet.

About a week later I received a letter under the signatures of Kwame Ireland and others, all in the senior class (12th grade). In the letter, the learned students had eight point charges against me, the principal of BJHS, and demanded me to hold meeting with them immediately after school that day to answer to their charges, which included, (1) restraining their movement by not allowing them to play football games with ZMHS; (2) withholding their sports money, etc., etc. The letter was personally delivered by Kwame Ireland. As soon as I read the letter I immediately summoned the class to appear in my office without delay. Excited and seemingly anxious, and perhaps traumatized by the sickening fever from the SEVENTEEN MAN SAMUEL DOE REVOLUTION, the seniors of the year filed into my office. I began to poll them individually by asking, "Is this your signature?" and at the end of the exercise, that is, after every signature had been affirmed or confirmed, I squared myself in the principal's chair that clothed me with the authority of the school. "You have one thing to do now or you face one long month of suspension from school as of today. You must apologize to me. Do you have any iota of right to demand the principal of BJHS to hold meeting with you immediately after school today?" I angrily questioned. "This obstinate behavior of yours is a complete disregard of the constituted authority I represent. Individually, you must apologize to me or you must consider yourselves suspended for one long calendar month each. Do you understand me?" In unison they regrettably answered, "Yes, Mr. Reeves." Kwame led the way and one after the other they all apologized. In a fatherly mood, I accepted the apology and strongly warned them to always request for time from their superior whenever they want to meet him. "You know I like to talk with you about any problem in the school, as I believe it is the best way you will know what I think, and likewise what you want or need in the school, which is your school and not mine. Begin to do the right thing now while you are within the walls of this institution whose education is enriched with Catholic religious culture," I urged them. In the meantime, I would consult the faculty about when to meet with them in order to hear their complaint against the administration.

In a brief emergency faculty meeting that day I presented the letter charging me with eight counts. The faculty unanimously agreed to meet in conference with the complaining students the next day immediately after school. At the morning daily devotion I informed the complainers about the time of the meeting between them and us. At the meeting, presided over by a faculty member other than the principal, the accused, the letter of complaint was read. In response I said, "To begin with, BJHS is not a football academy. There is no reason why you the students should complain about not being allowed to play football with ZMHS. The administration thinks that this complaint is a frivolous one together with the fabricated ones. Having said this, let me quickly explain the reason why we have not permitted you and why my faculty and I have no mind to rescind the pertinent lifesaving decision, which we think is in our interest and safety. As you know, as well as I do, the students of ZMHS are not sportsmen. They adamantly refused to accept defeat each time one was inflicted on them. Hooliganism is their way of sportsmanship every time they are defeated. There are over seven hundred students in that school as compared with our number which is a little less than three hundred. Can you imagine what would happen to you the students if you defeated ZMHS at a football game and their hooliganism was sparked? They would drum on you like torrential rain. They would brutalize and suffocate you to death. Since you are entrusted to our care and keeping, acting in lieu of your parents or guardians here, unless ZMHS changes that unwholesome practice, my faculty and I shall never allow you to play football with the school, and so help me God," I decidedly asserted. I continued, "According to our budgetary allocations this year, three hundred sixty dollars was appropriated for sports for the school year. Each class in this school has a copy of this year's budget. Out of this amount, you have withdrawn fifteen ($15.00) dollars for the repair of your boots, twenty-five ($25.00) dollars for camping, and three hundred fifty ($350.00) dollars for new jerseys and boots recently bought and delivered to you by Father Landry. My simple arithmetic tells me that the sports department of the school is in deficit. As you can readily see, if you are at home with your little fundamentals of simple addition and subtraction, you realized that you have withdrawn three hundred ninety ($390.00) dollars, knowing that you had only three hundred sixty ($360.00) dollars allocated for the purpose. From where would I continue to give you money?" The other charges, such as the seniors must not be punished when they come to school late, were dismissed as rubbish by the faculty. The presiding officer brought the meeting to a close by demanding the student-accusers to apologize to the administration. The apology was extended and accepted.

At three different graduation ceremonies I pleaded for the building of an auditorium, where, among other things, our annual graduation exercise would be conducted instead of in the building booths every commencement season. The fever caught some of the students like Alphonso Nyenuh and members of his 1986 class in the mid-eighties. But how high was the fever and to what extent?

With all the classes housed on one campus, now the administration was quite at ease, but not complacent. By then BJHS was well furnished academically as our library and laboratory were well equipped and most of our teachers were highly professionally experienced and our students were duly challenged as they in turn challenged us. What a mutual, rich, and challenging experience that engulfed the Juwle family!

One day the student council came up with a viable suggestion: "Let's take our dramatic club to Harper City to stage one of our dramas and have football games with a number of schools in the city." That was an excellent idea but it needed some negotiation with the Catholic Mission in Harper and the schools we would like to friendlily challenge for the football games long before we decide to go. "First of all, let us send a strong delegation to make the necessary arrangements. Once the arrangements are made beforehand, we shall then go to that beautiful southeastern city to knock off the rust from our rural selves," I advised the council. There and then we agreed to send a strong one-man delegation to Harper to negotiate with the proper authorities for our proposed visit. Senior Kwame Ireland, the student council's so-called Foreign Minister, was dispatched to Harper. After spending about two days, there Mr. Ireland returned.

Back in school Kwame was asked by the administration about his mission to Harper. He retorted, "I shall tell you later." Patiently I waited for Kwame to brief me on the mission on which he was sent at the expense of the school. The school day slowly but steadily came to a close without a word from Foreign Minister Ireland. I did not bother to ask him either.

At about seven-thirty the next morning, upon arrival on campus, I saw students laden with haversacks. Inaudibly I asked, "What is happening here?" Soon or late the campus was crowded with students dressed in traveling attire. This was a school day and precisely the time for our morning devotion to begin the day's work. I rushed from my desk from where I had been watching the commotion on the campus and I rang the bell for the morning assembly, but to no avail. I then summoned Kwame and other senior students into my office and I questioned them, "What is going on?" "We are going to Harper to play some football games with the high schools there," our emissary revealed. In that time their chartered bus driver intruded into my office. "What time we can go now. Time passed plenty. Harper abe too far from here," the seemingly angry chauffeur cried. "What is this? Are these students trying to disregard the authority of the school?" I questioned myself. I sternly added, "They need my injunction now. I will not tolerate lawlessness here."

Before this, the students who were in conference with me abruptly rushed out of my office to talk with their driver. I took my usual place for morning prayers and rang the bell again for the students to assemble. Disgruntledly they moved away from the assembly line. In a clear, loud demanding voice I shouted, "My boys and girls, what is happening this morning that you are not in your respective classrooms?" Boisterously they shouted, "We are going to Harper." "No student or students leaves this school without an express excuse from the administration. Any student or students who violate this directive will be subjected to immediate expulsion from this institution, BJHS. If you doubt, try it," I dealt them the blow. The students knew at once that those words came from the mouth of no two-tongued man. William Reeves says exactly what he means.

The driver hastened toward me and said, "You go pay my fee since you say the children cannot go." "Get out of here. Did I make any arrangement with you? If you don't leave this campus now, I shall send for the police to eject you out of here," I warned him. The frustrated and displeased students ascended the hill, no doubt, to complain about my action to the parish priest, Reverend Father John Guiney, SMA. Father Guiney came to the school. Passing by my office, he simply said, "Good morning, William." He entered the faculty lounge and for a few minutes I overheard him saying that he was a member of the faculty of the school and as such he was unquestionably amenable to the authority of the principal. "What the principal told you is the official position of the school." Having said this, the father ascended the hill for his comfortable parish rectory. It would appear that the students burdens on their backs were much heavier now than they were when they were eagerly gathering for their so-called trip.

I was glad that I decisively forestalled what was going to be a crisis. But up to this date I cannot figure out why the students, seemingly under the direction of Kwame Ireland, could have so grossly and flagrantly ignored and completely disregarded the constituted authority of the school.

Before, Kwame was one of the most respectful and punctual students of the school. Anytime between seven-thirty in the morning, and when I arrived on campus, Kwame was always there leaning against the flagpole, telling his white pleasing lies to his buddies.

173

Kwame is the son of Mr. and Mrs. Albert A. L. Ireland of the Township of Nyaake, Webbo. Mrs. Alice Gadegbeku-Ireland is the daughter of Mr. Gabriel G. C. H. Gadegbeku, former chairman of the Webbo District School from where I obtained my eighth grade certificate as a graduate. Alice and I are of the same generation and former schoolmates in Nyaake, where I had sojourned in search of education. The Irelands and the Gadegbekus are descendants of their sojourner-parents who came from a West African neighboring country called Togoland and from an ethnic group known as Ewe.

Intimately I was interwoven with Kwame's relations. Colonel Ireland commanded the Ninth Infantry Regiment, a militia entity of the Armed Forces of Liberia. I served on his staff as a major, an intelligence officer of the staff. Besides, Kwame was one of my right hand students, students I greatly counted on to help keep the school orderly. That Kwame deliberately and arrogantly led an open defiance against me was my most disheartening and shocking incident during my twelve-long-years stay at BJHS. On the whole, Kwame is my son and student. He, therefore, was in double trust. But perhaps it was obviously true that familiarity breeds contempt, a contempt which would erode the authority of the school, if not checked. That my prompt injunction yielded immediate results sharply taught me a lasting lesson to be prompt and decisive in addressing problems that require urgent and drastic resolution. The Kwame trip was never undertaken. However, a year following this disturbing event, the school staged exciting dramatic exercises in the modern theater of the Harper City Hall, found on the east of the sparkling city, partly perched on the Cape of Palms.

Around the end of 1982, Father Guiney left for good for his home in the United States of America. An Indian Catholic priest, simply called Father Jacob, took charge of the Zwedru parish. The school's finances were left in his care as they were stored by the previous parish priest. After some time I went to Father Jacob to withdraw some money from the school administrative funds. "How much does your school have here?" the priest inquired. I replied, "I don't know for sure, but the book is here." "You have the brain of an eight-year-old in that a principal like you does not know how much you have in your account!" the priest snorted. I was unbelievably shocked! I felt chilly from such an expression from a strange priest. In that impulse I retorted, "I vehemently demand you to take back immediately your belittling expression on my long years of unquestioned integrity. If not, I shall tell you exactly what I think about you." Instead of pacifying the situation, the Indian Catholic priest held stubbornly to his ugly assertion. There was no way I could leave Father Jacob without his redressing me. Repeatedly I told him that I had respect for my priests and religious without exception. In return I want my priests and religious to have respect for me too. If not, I shall have no other alternative but to demand my respect from them in a way I deem it necessary. Father Jacob did not budge and so I heaped all the Sunday School terms at my command on him. He was glad to give me the money and I left.

The strange relationship continued for several months. But every weekend I was there to deposit money for the school. For his unpriestly behavior, the members of the parish kept their distance from him. He became concerned as he was gradually being isolated. He reported me to Bishop Dalieh. The bishop invited me to his headquarters for a routine consultation, as he put it.

Without the complainant I met a panel of priests, including Reverend Father Dasey, then parish priest of St. Theresa Parish in Harper, Cape Palmas, Maryland County. I was questioned about what had transpired between Father Jacob and me. I told them how the priest insulted me out of the clear blue sky. I pointed out, "As I speak to you the anger caused by the unprovoked insult I experienced surges in me. I feel strongly that I was humiliated for no reason or cause. The outrageous, degrading insult did not only affect me personally, but it affected my country and my principalship. The only thing that saved him from a heavy kick in his posterior was that Bishop Dalieh, a indigenous man of mine, is the spiritual head of this diocese. If not, the story was going to have many interesting scenes. For Bishop Dalieh's sake, God buttered Father Jacob's bread. As I see it, this kind of priest cannot help me see the face of God. As you can readily see, his unpriestly attitude is dragging me to hell, don't you agree? Agreeably, the priests trashed out the altercation that was eroding the relationship between a priest and his layperson. I told the panel of priests that I heartily regretted the episode that for a long time separated me physically, and perhaps spiritually too, from my parish priest. With that mended, I came back to Zwedru where Father Jacob and I would meet physically to reconcile with each other. In that mood I visited with the priest to tell him how sorry I was for the happening. When I entered the rectory, surprisingly, I was warmly greeted by Father Jacob. "Mr. Reeves, Dr. Gordon, the medical doctor at the Martha Tubman Memorial Hospital, and Mr. Jacob, the Indian instructor at the ZMHS, told me that you are one of the worthiest Liberians they have met. When I told them what transpired between you and me, they regretted that I was abusive to you. I promised them that as soon as you came back to Zwedru I would apologize to you. Would you please pardon me?" Father Jacob pleased. "I am very sorry for the happening too. You are my priest and I am your lay member," I implored. Bygone was now bygone. It would appear we were friends again.

At a parish council meeting, it was suggested that the two parish schools, St. Philomena and BJHS, help with some parish project. In response, I said that my school, Juwle, would be willing to help in our own weak way. "Why should you call the school your school?" Angrily, Father Jacob pounced on me. "But the school is my school, isn't it?" "Only I alone have the right as parish priest to call the school my school, and not you," pounding on the desk, Father Jacob snorted. "The school is legitimately mine. The law allows it and Catholic Mission thus awards me. As long as I am lawfully charged with responsibility for the administration of BJHS, the school is my legitimate possession. To deny it is to say that I am not the principal of that school. Only those without eyes, ears, and perhaps are not living, can deny this hard, protruding, glaring fact," I narrated. Foaming at the mouth, Father Jacob left the meeting unceremoniously. Unlike people of his vocation, as I saw it, Father Jacob was interested in worldly things. I resolved never more to banter word with Father Jacob.

On the whole, Father Jacob thought his brown skin was superior to black man. This landed him in a labor court in Zwedru. He literally abused his cook because the cook ate the crust of the rice he had cooked for him. Soon or late, the Catholic clergyman was a nuisance to himself. Gradually his Zwedru world was rapidly narrowed and he became isolated.

He sinisterly muddied the water of the Cape Palmas diocese. "Mr. Reeves, I understand you are a close friend of Bishop Dalieh. Please help me to explain to the bishop how I got mixed up with some money between the diocesan bursar and me. The bishop wants me to return a certain amount to the diocese before I will be given my exit back to India," Father Jacob lamented. "Father, that matter is within your circle, the priestly circle. I am not a member of that society. I don't think I should know what is happening between the two of you. Please, let me stay out of it," I evasively advised. Unceremoniously Father Jacob left Zwedru.

Before BJHS was founded, US Peace Corps volunteers had been serving in St. Philomena Elementary and Junior High School, the school from which BJHS sprang. The young school too was blessed with US volunteers. With me at TWI was a young, brilliant, unassuming and talented lady, Karen Price, a US volunteer. When I told her in late 1977 that 1978 would not find me at TWI, but rather at my new station, BJHS, "I'll go with you. I can't stay when you are not here. To do what here when you are gone," Karen cried. Truly with me she went to BJHS. Her versatile talents in the teaching profession highly boosted my new administration. That year also, a fresh new female US volunteer was assigned to the school, although I was not working for the US Peace Corps/Liberia-Country Training Program yet. I was still blessed and honored for my many years, I guessed, of invaluable service I rendered the program.

A male US volunteer, Russ Wilson, taught at BJHS before me. According to the nuns, he had arranged to pay the tuition fee of a student, a Zaar, throughout his school life at BJHS. In case Mr. Zaar decided to attend another school, he would automatically lose or forfeit the scholarship grant. This was intimated to me when the young man decided to leave Juwle. The sisters requested me to prevail on the young man not to leave the school. I invited the young man in my office for a talk. Patiently I asked him why did he want to leave the school he has known since he became a student, having admitted all the conditions attached to the grant. From his no-reason answer I advised him not to rashly lose his God-given blessing, longed for by many needy students all around here. Seemingly he expressed his thanks and appreciation to me for what he called "your fatherly advice."

A few days following our frank exchanges, Mr. Zaar furiously entered my office one morning. "Why should you restrain my desire and movement? I want to go to the school of my choice, but you blocked my way with your so-called advice so as to increase your income from tuition fees," Mr. Zaar derided me. Profoundly shocked, I retorted, "What will your absence or departure from here do to me physically, morally, socially, or financially? We have hundreds of students on our waiting list, students longing to get admission. Your departure from the school will be a blessing and a golden opportunity for a waiting student, who has been eyeing longingly for the school. Personally I have nothing against your leaving. Go in peace," I sincerely breathed my blessing on him.

It would appear that my words of blessing aggravated Mr. Zaar. He took his case to the superintendent of the county. At devotion time the next morning, Honorable Kudar Jarry, the superintendent, came in to inquire about what was happening between student Zaar and me. Behind closed doors in my office, Mr. Jarry probed the nonsensical, baseless issue. At the end of his probe in my office, Mr. Jarry declared in no veiled terms, "Mr. Reeves is not in your way. Do whatever pleases you. Please don't insult your principal." He ordered, "Tomorrow morning in front of the whole student body of this school you shall apologize to the principal, Mr. Reeves." For me the matter was closed, whether Zaar apologized or not. Since that day Mr. Zaar was never seen again in the school.

About a week later I received a note from Dr. Togba Nah-Tipoteh, an executive member of the Movement of Justice in Africa (MOJA). Among other things the note read, "Please come to see me at Dr. Veddy's home here in Zwedru, at three this afternoon. One student complained you." Having done nothing wrong to any student, I had no qualms about meeting Dr. Tipoteh to hear what he had to say. I met Dr. Tipoteh at the appointed time and place. I was there long before Mr. Zaar arrived. Before Zaar came in, Mr. Tipoteh asked what was the problem between student Zaar and me. I went over the story that brought the county superintendent to the school and the subsequent happening. I told him that I thought the young man had no respect for me as he deliberately showed me the other day. I met Zaar coming from the opposite direction. All of a sudden the young man rushed to me, almost knocking me down, and then walked away, grinning. When Zaar came in, Mr. Tipoteh and I were sharing seat in a settee. Mr. Zaar crossed his hand over me to shake Mr. Tipoteh's hand, but to me he said nothing. "Before you arrived, Mr. Reeves told me that you have no respect for him. Clearly and deliberately you willingly exhibited the gross disrespect to your elder and principal. I think you have some serious personal problem. It would appear that you are quite displeased with your own world. You have no case against Mr. Reeves. Leave him alone," Dr. Tipoteh advised.

The 1980 coup, which toppled the Tolbert government, a government that unequivocally and profoundly raised the hope for a better Liberia in no distant future, had pulled out of joint every aspect of our national life. According to the coup plotters, the Tolbert government was brutally ousted because of rampant corruption in high and low places in the government. Truly, the diagnosis correct as it was undoubtedly unquestionable. But having known what had gone wrong, could this untrained, uneducated, inexperienced, noncommissioned and enlisted seventeen-man junta redress the wrongs of the toppled government? Can somebody give what he does not have? Without any basic training in anything; the junta gambled with our national life, the mania of lasciviousness buttressed the policy of their anarchic government.

What could the traumatized public do? Before this People's Redemption Council Government, in the previous governments, as I saw it, Civilian Corruption was generally clad in black suits while in the PRC government Soldier Corruption was gaily dressed in sparkling white linen suits. In short, corruption was the daily cadence by which the highway marauders, the so-called soldiers, marched majestically. Rampant corruption, gross abuse of human rights, nepotism, etc. were

177

amalgamated into malignant cancer that devoured our national fabrics. In this uncertain national upheaval, things progressively disintegrated and landed us in whirlwind of bellowing chaos.

In the Krahn country, Upper Grand Gedeh, where I was teaching long before the coup that toppled the Tolbert government, life became aggressively meaningless, in Zwedru, for those of us who were not of the Krahn ethnic group. Once you were not of the Krahn ethnic group, I don't care whether you were a teacher or government official, you were regarded and treated like an outcast in your own native Liberia. William K. Reeves, the warrior hired by the Krahns from the Grebo country to wage war against illiteracy that was ravaging the Krahn countryside, former teacher and principal of TWI and now principal of BJHS, both of Zwedru, Grand Gedeh County, with his twenty-two long years of faithful service in the war against ignorance, was no exception to the degrading, inhumane, nepotistic marginalization.

General Thomas Quiwonkpa was one of the non-commissioned officers of the seventeen-man junta, who later ran through the ranks of the Armed Forces and became a general, commanding the entire Armed Forces of Liberia. It was said that among the many members of the ruling council, General Quiwonkpa was the only person with one eye, the one people could reason with and who was more understanding. The public revered the general as he was approachable and more understanding. Like in many a revolution, sharp disagreements generated and pulled the members of the ruling council apart. The head of state and chairman of the ruling council, CIC General Samuel K. Doe, became uneasy when he observed that the general was rapidly getting popular and beat up a case of subversion against him. Threatened and fearing apprehension, the general took it to his heels and fled the country. Doe's despotism grew unabatingly and devastatingly into the decade of the eighties.

In 1985, following the presidential and general elections, which were openly rigged by Doe and cohorts of the National Democratic Party of Liberia, General Quiwonkpa mustered an invasion from some country and invaded Liberia on October 12, 1985. This hardened the dictator as the invasion was failed.

On the morning of the failed invasion, just about six that morning, on my radio set, I tuned into ELWA, a private radio station based in Monrovia, Liberia. Surprisingly, the radio was playing solemn music: Marshall music, as it is called. "What happened again, my God?" I loudly questioned myself. For about ten breathtaking minutes I listened attentively to the music of the radio, thinking that some announcement would come forth. Without that, I kept the radio on while I readied myself for the day's job. Up to the time I left my home, about seven-fifteen, there was nothing on the radio to say what had happened. "I cannot wait for trouble or whatsoever it is; I must go to school now," I urged myself. And off to school I went. In school, after trekking there, I meditatively entered my office and took my seat behind my desk. For a few split seconds I sat but I became restless as I kept wondering about the solemn music. I rushed out and stood contemplatively on the threshold of my office door. In that time Sister Lourene arrived with a radio set under her arm. "Mr. Reeves, do you know what happened?" the science and mathematics instructor suddenly inquired. Wearily I replied, "No, sister." I then took the radio from her and made for the faculty lounge where I plugged the radio's electric cord into a socket, but the city's electricity was off as usual. "It has battery. Let me tune it," Sister Lourene requested. As soon as the radio was tuned, the devastating announcement, "General Thomas Quiwonkpa has seized power of the Liberian Government," rang resoundingly. On hearing this heartbreaking announcement, with hands hopelessly placed in my pockets, I moved slowly away from Sister Lourene to a window in the faculty lounge.

Away, I began to shed tears of deep sorrow over the fate of my country and its people. After a few minutes of tearful silence, I pulled myself together and came back to the sister. Almost at the brink of shedding tears I lamented, "Sister, this country has been driven backward one hundred or more years. Our hope for a better future for our posterity is brutally crushed. By then the campus was full of students ready for the day's school. But on hearing the sad announcement, the students went wild, yelling, shouting, and screaming. I hastened out of the lounge to calm them: "Please, let everybody get in his or her classroom at once. We are out for business," I directed. Acquiescently the students filed through their respective classroom doors. Sister Kathlyn joined Sister Lourene and me. For about thirty intermittent minutes we listened to the radio, hanging in a dashing cloud of suspense. Unceasingly the radio relayed the sad, paralyzing event to the bewildered people of hungry Liberia. No other teacher came.

The commotion in the streets was unbelievable, as people rushed here and there in search of wife, husband, son, daughter, or relative. Sister Kathlyn suggested that we send the students home so that they would be with their parents during this uncertain hour. I then went from classroom to classroom telling them to go home, and make sure to walk carefully in the streets as the streets were crowded with rushing people and the traffic. "You know nothing about what is happening. Keep your mouths shut," I admonished. With this, the students were dispersed in different directions. "Well, no students, I guess, means no school," I told the sisters. Instead of going home I went to the home of the Irelands since my wife was spending time on our rice farm that week. No doubt, my sons would use the no school today as a license to parade the town. Luckily for me the Irelands were all glued to their radio set when I entered. Each person appeared profoundly disturbed. Unwillingly, we began to talk about why and how did this kind of thing happen to us again. In that time my son Karbeh rushed in and almost breathlessly said, "The people are looking for you. When we went home we met Superintendent Johnny Garley and his jeep full of well-armed soldiers in our yard. He asked about you and we told him that you were at school. But he sharply replied, 'You are lying. Since your father heard about the coup he has been dancing. Now he is tired and so he resting in this house.' Mr. Garley then ordered the soldiers to search our house, and they did." He hurried away.

A few minutes following his departure, Karbeh, panting, rushed into the Irelands' home again, saying, "They are coming; I left them on our campus." What could I do, and for what were they searching for me? I had no ready answer and so I did not budge. In the meantime, Mrs. Ireland suggested that I should take cover in one of their rooms. I did. In no time the marauders calling themselves soldiers intruded into the premises of the Irelands and began ruthlessly to comb every corner

179

and nook of the home, finding me in one dark corner of a room. I was seized and handcuffed and placed in the back of a blue pickup and whisked off to the police station on Harris Avenue. When we reached the station I was ordered down, but how could I get down when both of my hands were handcuffed? They insisted. I made the attempt but to find myself tumbling over. This heartless order resulted in a serious sprain in my right foot. The handcuff was taken off and was ordered again on board the pickup and on to Camp Whisnant, an old, dilapidated, archaic military installation perched on a hill in Zwedru.

In the barrack, the victim of the Krahn conspiracy was handed over to some demon they called "Colonel Harrison Pennoh," a heartless Krahn murderer and one of the conspirators of the bloody Samuel K. Doe 1980 coup. Sitting in a comfortable cushioned chair with a bubbling glass of Club Beer in his hand looking like a tortoise's limb, the brute, the so-called colonel, shouted, "Take him away!" The next thing I saw of myself was that I was flat on the ground and was being dragged away to jail. As the guard pulled me along, some physical strength, like a whirlwind, propelled me into action and I jumped on my feet. I grabbed the belt my guard wore across his shoulders and forcefully pulled him toward me. He was startled! "What happened, Mr. Reeves?" (the guy happened to be a dropout from TWI) he exclaimed. "Tell me what I have done or failed to do. Once I am told, should I die in peace, knowing the cause of my death," I demanded. Softly my guard spoke to me, "Mr. Reeves, please leave the belt," I let go of the belt. My former student politely told me to get ahead of him. Slowly we moved into a mud-wall dilapidated country structure, where I joined seven soldiers, Major Kesselly being the most senior, and a civilian, John J. Collins, my most intimate friend in Zwedru. This was about ten in the morning. All of us sat on a dusty floor under almost a roofless house. There was no doubt that I was now confined for reasons yet to be known.

We had two guards, a Krahn and a Grebo soldier. We were under straight order not to attend the call of nature outside. Three long hours lingered on. During that weary interval I drew closer to my God by reciting my Rosary, which is often present on my person each day. At about one that afternoon, all Doe's loyalists, mostly Krahns, disappeared into the air. The barrack was completely deserted.

Seeing the scene without the seemingly hapless loitering Doe loyalist soldiers, the confined soldiers, all from non-Krahn ethnic groups, rushed out, saying that they were in charge then. With the other prisoners gone, my Grebo guard said to me, "Beta, go home." Mr. Collins was told to go home too.

This time I could not balance myself on both feet. However, I limped out with the help of John. It was physically impossible for me to walk from that point to our respective houses. What could we do? "Let us get somebody to go to my house to tell my wife to send the car," Mr. Collins advanced. A Juwle student, Alex Kyne, ran to get the car for us. Before the car arrived I suggested to Mr. Collins that we should first go to the hospital to seek medical help from the doctors. When the car came we rode straight to the hospital, passing through the vast sprawling town completely depleted of its inhabitants. The hospital was no exception of the mass desertion. Peacefully in the silence of the town John's driver drove us to my home where I disembarked. The sprain in my right leg had worsened. The driver, John's cousin, Karye, helped me by placing my left arm across his high shoulders while I limped on my right foot into my house.

Luckily my sons were home. "Please get me some hot bath," I requested the younger of the two boys. The other boy, Karbeh, was asked to tell Pastor Robert Toe of the Assembly of God Church, Kudar Bypass, Zwedru, that I was tortured and needed medical treatment. Reverend Toe is a paramedical practitioner. Before my bath was ready the reverend gentleman arrived with all the things necessary to take care of my bruised body. I was treated. I massaged my sprained foot and other parts of my aching body with the hot water. The medical treatment brought me much relief to my aching body. I ate some food and took a rest in bed. An hour later a fellow Knight of St. John International, Isaac Asibu, came in to console me. I sat up for few minutes and talked with him. Two young ladies came in after my brother left. They expressed their regrets for the maltreatment.

At seven that evening I tuned my radio for the evening news. With every Liberian no doubt hung in balance, all peace-loving Liberians glued themselves to their radio sets to get the latest news about the early morning hour invasion. Perhaps what they wanted to hear burst forth from CIC Doe's mouth: "I want to tell the Liberian people and the world at large that I am in full control of my government and my country, Liberia. I am happy to inform the Liberian people that the invasion this morning has been definitely foiled." He added, "Move about freely." At this pronouncement Zwedru went wild. The Krahns took to the streets, shouting, "Grebo people go home!" They sounded like hooligans returning from a football game. The rowdy crowd spread throughout Zwedru. The terrifyingly violent outcry engulfed the entire town. I was fully cognizant of the fact that I was one of the leading members of the Grebo ethnic group, whom the Krahns wanted out of that part of their own Liberia. My heart palpitated at the thought of our being lynched by the angry mob. The hooting of the throng galloped along the streets toward my premises. Could I run away on one foot? No way! "Cholee, you and Karbeh take and place me under the plum tree behind our house. As soon as that is done, go away from the house. Don't worry about me. I want you to live so that you will tell the story about how my life abruptly came to an end in Zwedru. Please don't think about what we have in the house. When you live, you shall be able to buy for yourselves, and perhaps better things. For me I am ready to go home to be with my God in eternity," Fatherly, I advised. In the dark night I took cover under the large cone plum tree just behind our house. Whether I was safe or not was the question. For three long hours I wearily huddled myself under the shady tree. The mad crowd did not pass our way.

At last the hooligans left the streets and my children came home. "Go to tell the sisters that I would like for them to take me onto my farm tomorrow morning," I entreated Cholee. On return from the errand, Cholee said that the nuns told him that it was risky for them to come to our house because the soldiers looking for me searched the convent this morning. They advised that I go over now. With one limping foot, how could I go to the convent? "We will carry you," in unison, the sturdy young men cried. Across their young strong shoulders I spread my arms and off to the convent we went. Cholee and I spent the night there with the strong hope that I would be taken to my farm the next day. Early the next morning the sisters had breakfast ready for me. Just before I went to the table, a friend of mine, Nelson Togba, entered. "William, I heard you were imprisoned yesterday and released later in the day. I went to your house this morning but Karbeh could not tell me exactly your whereabouts and so I came to the sisters. I am glad you are here. What do you want to do?" Nelson questioned. "I want the sisters to take me to my farm," I revealed. "No, going on your farm is not safe for you and the sisters. I would suggest I take you home until things become normal," Mr. Togba declared. The sisters were in full agreement with Mr. Togba's suggestion and so Sister Lourene drove us to Mr. Togba's residence on Kudar Bypass. For two hopeful weeks, Mr. and Mrs. Togba with their children nursed my bruised aching body. Thankful was I to God Almighty for giving me such a caring family.

Having spent two long weary weeks in the friendly hands of the Togba family, I decided to sneak out of Zwedru. Was it physically possible and advisable? On the 25th of October I directed my son Cholee to arrange for my travel through Lower Grand Gedeh into Maryland County. That whole day the gentleman did not return to tell me whether he had found a bus or a taxicab to get me away. Of course I requested Cholee to make sure of the identity of the driver. "Don't get me any car being driven by a Krahn man," I seriously advised him.

Round about nine the next morning, the stocky young man came with the message that he found a taxicab traveling to Cape Palmas. "Do you know whether the driver is a Krahn man or not?" I queried. "I did not bother to ask," my son replied to me in a matter of I-don't-care manner. In no time the driver appeared in his peugot taxicab. He walked into the Togba home, where I was standing, trying to exercise my sprained leg by walking up and down the floor. "Good morning, Mr. Reeves," the driver warmly greeted me. "How are you?" I anxiously replied.

"What is your name?" I inquired. "Tody," he pronounced. There was no doubt about his ethnic background. He was a Krahn. Here I was placed on the front page. The name Tody sent electric shock through my sprained foot and bruised aching body. It seemed that the die was cast. Surely I was now exposed to the Krahn butchers. What could I do? He then told me that if I really wanted to go, I should walk to Mr. Frank Smith's house, where he would pick me up for the journey through Lower Gedeh to Maryland County. "No, my friend, it is not possible. As you can readily see, I cannot easily walk on this foot of mine. Please come for me when you shall have gathered all your passengers for the trip. Let me wait for you here," I entreated him.

With this he went. But Mrs. Togba became very skeptical of this kind of arrangement, which appeared to prepare a booby trap for this victim of the Krahn conspiracy. Concerned, Mrs. Togba called in a neighbor, one Gboway, a Grebo man, and told him about the arrangement. In that time the driver arrived to take me away. "Wait, Mr. Reeves, let me go to find out who all are in the taxi," Mr. Gboway hastened out to the taxi. "I think it is all ready for you to travel by the taxi. Nearly all the passengers in there are of the Grebo ethnic group. Go with the taxi, you are safe in the caring arms of God Almighty. For two long weeks you have been in this home. So far nothing has befallen you. Our God is in full control of your journey and he will safely deliver you in the Grebo country. Go in peace and may God continue to protect you throughout," Mr. Gboway breathed his brotherly blessing on me. I mustered all my courage and went to the parked and waiting taxi. Limping, I reached the taxi. In the front seat with the chauffeur was a young Krahn man who came out of the car as soon as I neared it. "Mr. Reeves, I heard about the maltreatment meted out to you the other day. I find it very hard to understand why the Krahn people can be so ungrateful to a person like you who has wholeheartedly devoted yourself to educating us the young Krahn people. If you had not come here and had not generously given your precious time to us, some of us would have not received the numerous benefits of education. Through your help, I now have some measure of education and so I work for the Liberian government," my former Tubman-Wilson Institute student grievously asserted. "Never mind, my son, that gross ingratitude on the part of your blind people can in no way divert or dissuade me from my avowed social contract with my people and country. I shall continue to share generously the talent my God has graciously blessed me with," I solemnly promised my would-appear-bewildered former student. Having assured my old boy, I hopped into the taxicab.

Down the street the taxicab glided straight to Mr. Smith's house, from where we would turn right for the long pothole-ridden highway. Instead of turning right, to my amazement the driver signaled left turn, obviously heading for the main town. Certainly in the twinkle we were in the heart of town, near the motel, where the central parking station was located. The driver checked his brakes among swarms of parked vehicles. Inwardly I said to myself, "Lord, I am prepared for any eventuality. I ask you for a peaceful rest with you in eternity, if I should fall victim to the savagery of these barbarians." I waited for the taxi. During this time a group of armed soldiers came by and paid me their courtesy, "Good morning sir, Mr. Reeves." I returned their courtesy, "How are you, young soldiers?" Most of these young men were my former students from Tubman-Wilson Institute. "Oh, Teacher," Chea Kayee called, "I heard you were mistreated the other day. I went to your house but I did not find anybody to tell me where I could find you. I am very sorry for such a brutal treatment." Chea Kayee, a former student of mine, was now a member of the Honorable House of Representatives of the Liberian National Legislature. Then came a drove of Grebo women, shouting and screaming, *Teacher Reeves, never mind*. They began to shed tears. "Don't shed your precious tears. Be glad that the Krahn people say we must go home. No doubt, this implied that they know that we have home. I have a home, and perhaps a better home." For about twenty long minutes I stayed in the parked car while nearly every passerby greeted me warmly. No doubt, Teacher Reeves was a very popular teacher in Upper (and around) Grand Gedeh County as he was in the vanguard of that unabatingly and aggressively waged war against ignorance. When our driver rejoined us in the taxi, I thought it was about time we begin our journey, but instead we went on sightseeing, as it were, through the bustling city down Suah Street to Kannan Road. On Kannan Road, a very close friend of mine, on seeing me, exclaimed, "Mr. Reeves, I thought you were dead." "Well, as you can readily see, this is William K. Reeves still in his full human form," I told Mr. Harry Zelee, uncle-in-law of Superintendent Johnny Garley, who was at my throat everyday.

For about one uncertain hour for me we waited for the driver gathering gas for the trip and the return trip gas, as he said gasoline was markedly short in

Maryland. As soon as his containers were filled, the driver sparked the yellow woman and our long journey was slowly begun. It took us eight rough hours from Zwedru to Pleebo in Upper Maryland County, where we finally arrived at eight that eventful evening. On our journey I bought some fresh bush meat. In the home of a distant relative I requested for soup well seasoned with hot pepper. Charlotte prepared the soup exactly according to my request. I gulped down the soup and then later I pounced on the rice. As the soup gave me a surprised appetite, the rice lost its balance against my gobbling. In two weeks my throat had not experienced anything like that. That night too, soundly I slept for the first time in two weeks. It would appear that my arrival in a dominantly Grebo country had given me a real human touch again.

Early the next morning I took the last eighteen mile journey to the beautiful Southeastern City of Harper, Cape Palmas, Maryland County. Upon arrival at Mr. Alphonsus Nyenati Davis's home in Middlesex, East Harper, I contacted Most Reverend Boniface Nyema Dalieh, Bishop of Cape Palmas, a Catholic diocese. Bishop Dalieh, a personal friend since our grade school days, rushed at once to see his friend who had miraculously escaped the vicious plans to annihilate this dedicated teacher. Together we thanked our God for saving my life. "Well, Reeves, I am glad to see you here alive. But please find your way to the Sacred Heart Clinic tomorrow morning for examination and treatment." I was greatly thankful to the concerned bishop. I took advantage of that and for two weeks the clinic tenderly gave me its timely medical care.

Feeling well after intensive treatment, I went to Kablake to visit with my aged parents who, up to that time, did not know for sure what had happened to their son. It was believed that I was dead. When the news that I was arrested on the morning of the Quiwonkpa coup, relatives and friends and those who wished the news was not true gathered in Kablake to sympathize with my parents for the unfortunate situation. This early gathering of the people in my village, according to my father's wife Klade, disturbed my ever concerned father greatly. The young woman told me that every now and then her husband, my father, in his ripe old age, would ask, "'Don't you think that my son is dead? Why should the people gather in this number since we received the news of his arrest? Klade, I strongly believe that my son Kamma is dead, don't you think so?" my almost invalid but concerned father grievously asked.

My arrival in the village after about a month of suspense and speculation brought the old people and their relatives big relief. For my mother, as she told me, she took the whole sad news with a grain of salt. However, the reunion of the family was one of the most remembered. I stayed around, playing old baby for about two weeks and then I returned to Harper for a further medical checkup.

In the seventies my father was sick. My younger brothers at home sent me an urgent message asking me to send money in order to take our father to some hospital for treatment. The message gave me great concern but it did not move me to remit money to those able-bodied men to send their/our father to hospital. Instead of sending them money I made arrangements with a Mandingo driver to pick up my father from a point between Zwedru and Harper and bring him to Zwedru. My father was brought to Zwedru and for a month he was treated at Martha Tubman Memorial Hospital. During the one long month treatment, I pleaded with my father to spend the rest of the year with his grandchildren and me. "What are you trying to tell me? Where do I leave the village and its people our dead fathers left in my keeping? Do you want me to stay here without my wife?" my father amusingly quizzed me. To his heart, which of these pertinent questions was more paramount? Since I came to know right from wrong, my father's woman business has been the closest thing to his heart.

"May I send for your wife so that the two of you will live with us so that you will rest from the drudgery of your subsistence rice farming?" teasingly I mused. But knew the old man would not let himself down by consenting to bring his young woman over to Zwedru. "With whom are you going to leave my village and its people, the people who need my elderly advice and guidance everyday, a task no other person can adequately perform?" the former old village chief argued. He left Zwedru as soon as his medical doctor pronounced him well.

In mid-November, when I returned to Harper City, the sanitation-conscious city was bustling with commencement activities. Our Lady of Fatima High School, my dear alma mater, was no exception. This was a happy coincidence for me. About thirty short years had elapsed since I was graduated from Our Lady of Fatima High School, and I had not yet received an official invitation to attend the graduation program of the school. This time I was officially honored. As a pioneer graduate and the president of the first senior class I was singularly honored to make remarks. Among other things I said, "I am happy to be back home within these walls where education, the bread of life, is generously serviced. I want to congratulate the principal and his faculty for keeping the torch of education high aglow. On behalf of the Alumni Association of the school, without hiding behind diplomatic jargon as I am not a diplomat or a politician, I would like to note: I am not in politics but politics, no doubt, is in me. Over the years, we the members of the Alumni Association of this school find it hard to understand why the authority of the school took away our school once located at the entrance of the beautiful city of Harper and secluded it in dormitories behind Saint Theresa Cathedral, thus thwarting its public relationship to our disbelief. In this public manner, I would like, on behalf of the Alumni Association of Our Lady of Fatima High School, to respectfully request the Bishop of Cape Palmas and his education authority to reconstruct our school in a grand modern style on Maryland Avenue, the original spot. I further request, on behalf of the association, the Bishop of Cape Palmas to inform us as to how much the new Fatima High School building will cost. The Association stands ready to shoulder fifty percent of the total cost. We urge that this call will claim the immediate attention of the authorities," concerned, I pleaded.

On the 15th of December of the same year, 1985, there was a Catholic priestly ordination of Reverend Nathaniel Kwia-Wea in Pleebo, Maryland County. From Harper I journeyed with Bishop Dalieh there. The Catholic priestly ordination is always a pageant. The Pleebo ordination was no exception. Glad he was gradually increasing his number of shepherds, Most Reverend Boniface Nyema Dalieh, Bishop of the Catholic Diocese of Cape Palmas, performed the holy ceremony amongst a multitude of people who had congregated themselves in Saint Francis Parish Church in Pleebo perched on the eastern side of Firestone Cavalla Rubber Plantation. This was followed by a lavish banquet and a Grebo traditional dance called Docolor.

185

Yuletide was whispering around us in Harper, and feeling well again since that ordeal of mine in Zwedru, I thought to break away from the city life to spend quietly the annual season with my sister-in-law somewhere in the Webbo country. Two days before Christmas, I left for Gbawlake, where my sister-in-law and her husband, Charles Williams, personnel manager of a logging company back in River Gbeh in Lower Grand Gedeh, lived. The reunion was memorable as we had a jolly good time at Christmas. My next stop would be Kablake, the Gedebo London, where old age had its toll on my parents. Was there anything special in my mind for this visit again? What was it? There were many and varied problems around those old lives. One of them was hunger; poor health was another. As I saw it, old age is sickness, and so to my thinking, hunger was the main problem and that needed urgent and drastic remedy. I had enough food in Zwedru, but the long straggling distance that physically separated them from me made it practicably impossible to supply them from that distant end. What could I do to fulfill my filial duty and obligation? Before God and man, this was binding. Excuses would not help or create me a good human image toward one's old parents.

While I was awaiting the bishop's advice as to whether I would return to Bishop Juwle High School or not, I decided to make a rice farm for my father and give a strong helping hand to my sister and brother. In the meantime, I gathered the necessary tools for the rice farming in Kablake, the village my father had vowed never to be away from. In early January, 1986, I went to Kablake where my parents were battling with old age and sickness, the inevitable debilitating accessory. My father was getting too old and helpless. My mother, who was few years younger than her spouse, was also in the grips of that long-years-made commodity, which can find no willing customer to buy. At this rate my father was forced in retirement. But he had his young wife and himself to feed. Earlier my mother was driven into retirement as a housewife when her one-time beloved consort, unmindful of his sacred marital vows, deserted her.

For many years then my younger brother, seven years my junior, took full responsibility of caring for our mother. Since we are the only children of our mother, Kwee found it a pleasing and blind duty and obligation to perform. Having no girl child, our mother had thought to get a little girl of about ten to bring in our fold as my brother's wife. This, the seasoned planner gathered, would prepare the little girl as a blood member of our family, making her daughter. Wlede, the baby wife, grew happily in the tender and caring arms of our mother.

Just before my mother was forced into retirement, Wlede had reached her majority, a full-grown housewife. Seemingly my mother's dream had become a reality; she had a daughter who would attend her in her old age. But the hope turned into a sharp rejection of our mother by her daughter-in-law. Was that an insoluble problem for a woman having two able sons? Kamma, the older son, came on the scene at once to rescue their mother from the want of care, which would hasten her to early home-going. While doing the rice farming, I arranged with our mother to go live with me in Zwedru. My mother did not easily accept this timely offer as she strongly felt that I was not secure in the Krahn country. After a lengthy discussion with her, our mother finally gave in.

186

In the presence of my two younger brothers, Mudi and Kwee, our father was dying slowly under the weight of age and sickness, the deadly accomplice of old age. The village farmer was feeble but he was still obligated to take care of his wife. Must that personal duty and obligation to his wife be abrogated? Who then becomes responsible to feed his dependent mouths? There is a tree resembling a cocoa tree. It says, "When you are lucky to have an offspring, it alleviates your burden when you cannot adequately perform your obligation and duty." Our father being blessed with three sons had ready agents to whom his burden would be shifted at once. Since the two sons who resided at home with our father could not help themselves, let alone the old man, the oldest son, Kpaye Kamma, although away in Grand Gedeh County, was duty bound, according to the Gredebo tradition, to take care of his father, including those who were under the care of his father.

I remember well the kind of father he had been to us. He was, even up to his ripe old age, a responsible, loving and tenderly caring father. He fed us well. We were the most blessed family in the little village, as we were adequately fed each day. It was about time we give the old farmer his olive branch. The challenge was squarely placed on my shoulders. As I knew it, I was wholly and solely indebted to my/our father. But what could I do in the premises to adequately address the situation in which my father was then placed? No doubt, when the human body is regularly and adequately fed, it is invigorated be it old or young, thus reducing illnesses to the minimum. Therefore I must make a rice farm right here in Kablake so that my father will find something to eat everyday after the harvest. A was already in the cold water, so there was no need fearing cold. I gathered the necessary farm implements, arranged for workers for pay, and work was earnestly commenced. The underbrushing lasted for about two weeks, clearing about seven acres of fertile Gedebo land. I personally engaged in felling the trees. By the end of February, all the trees to be cut were hewed down and made ready for fire.

Just before I departed for Zwedru, late February, I told my brother and Klade, my father's wife, that as soon as the farm was burnt, Reverend Joseph Towaye would be available to share the farm among the three of them: Klade, the old man's wife, Kwee, and Jolomo, my sister taking only an acre. The proceeds from my father's farm would be equally shared between Klade and me. This I made it plain, crystal clear to Klade. My share would be kept by her until I called for it. "Kwee, on the fifteenth of March, the farm must be set ablaze. Waste no time. The earlier the better," I directed my younger brother. I promised to send them enough seed rice for planting, salt, pepper, and enough rice for their consumption during the hard farming. As I promised, as soon as I reached Zwedru, I sent enough of every item I promised. At a reception in my honor I responded to welcome statements by students and faculty. In less than a month I rushed down to Kablake to see how fast the farm work was progressing. Indeed, the true Grebo farmers were hard at it. "Please, plant no other species of rice other than LAC #23 on this farm. If the seeds I sent you are not enough, let me know now so that when I get back to Zwedru I may replenish your sowing baskets," I entreated. Returning from a brief exile in Maryland County, I arrived in Zwedru on March 3, 1986. The next day I was in school. What a rousing welcome that greeted me! For about thirty breathtaking minutes the emotion of the yelling students went on unabated. Each of the two hundred eighty-eight strong students made it his or her duty to hug my bony body. Their reception of me held me spellbound and I was completely at the loss of words or expressions.

In the old Juwle tradition, a few days following my return to the school, a well organized program was held in my honor on the palmy campus of the school. Several items of the program having been rendered, one of the favorite songs of the students, "Freedom is Not Free; You Must Pay a Price," which seemed to be their battle cry, was sung vibrantly, echoing joy for their shepherd restored to them. Two welcome statements were made, one from the student body and the other from the faculty. Both expressed joy for the wonderful care God Almighty took of me. The most expensive gift, executive trip, I ever received in my life, was presented to me. Then came the response from the principal driven out of the school and Zwedru by some criminals for five hopeless months. Among other things, I stated, "I know what was the cause I was mistreated. But it cannot be done overnight. Bishop Dalieh wants to Liberianize the schools of his diocese; that is, he wants the schools of the Cape Palmas Diocese to be headed by Liberian principals. But we are not in a hurry for that. When a Liberian is not qualified he cannot serve a principal. First of all, if you are a Liberian and you desire to serve as a principal you must get the prerequisite, academic qualification and other necessary ingredients.

In this particular case at Juwle, there is not one single Liberian teacher who is academically ready to take my place when I am gone. Often I plead with these young Liberian teachers of mine that gentlemen, forget about your domestic and get qualified so that when I am gone you will take the principalship or even while I am here you are credibly qualified I shall be happy to step down for you to become principal. I don't want to be a teacher or principal all the days of my life. The opportunity is yours. I did not buy this job or inherit it from my father. Even if I did, I have brothers who would like to occupy the position. What actually went wrong here is that the Krahn hierarchy in Zwedru doesn't want me to be the principal here because I cannot accept to be rubber stamp principal. Remotely they would run the school according to their own unprincipled thinking. Nobody can do his own thing here except if that thing is in the best interest of BJHS. They want to clandestinely install Kannoh Dobo as principal of BJHS. Under this malicious plan, the superintendent has armed his sons attending this school to terrorize the students and teachers. This is an open secret as many of you, if not all of you, have seen the deadly weapons (pistols) with Stephen and his brother Alexander. So far I know, our dear of discipline, Mr. Dobo, has all the moral and social qualifications but markedly he falls short academically. If Mr. Dobo has the requisite academic qualification I would climb down immediately for him to bring in his young and new ideas. But I am sorry Yah; our friend is just a high school graduate. Under no circumstance would Catholic Mission permit him to serve as principal of any of the diocesan high schools. The Ministry of Education, Republic of Liberia, will not condone it. Mr. Dobo teaches here because of these bookworms, the Zwedru School Sisters of Notre Dame, who nurture him everyday. This gradually qualifies him to teach in the junior high section of Bishop Juwle High School."

During July 26th break from school, I took advantage of my resting period to see whether there was hope on the farm and to see and talk with the man in charge of his father's village and its people. The legatee was in a happy mood when I met him in his galvanized zinc roof house in that serene village atmosphere. "Klade told me that our baway is over." Baway is the time when we eat one poor meal on the farm or we don't eat at all until late at night; this is hunger time, a devastating annual experience, a perennial disease that plagues the Liberian people on their fertile virgin soil. Menua simply ment that his wife began to harvest their rice, the time the villagers eat lavishly. The next day I went on the farm for my final inspection.

"Wow, wonderful," I exclaimed as I beheld the huge yield and a very large harvest we were going to have. My Lord had done it for me and my father again. Praise be to him for his good and timely gift. "Klade, I hope you don't forget. Half of all the rice on the farm belongs to me. Keep it for me," I reminded her. To my sister-in-law Wlede, I requested that she should get me one hundred pounds of the new rice from the farm so that it would be sent to me in Zwedru. With this, I trode back on duazet bus to the city of plenty. Wlede did not send me one pound of rice. Time would tell whether my stepmother had stored for me my share of the total harvest from the rice farm.

In December, 1986, a message from my father was flying backward and forward telling me that Amos of Kablake wanted to personally and physically see his son Kpaye Kamma. With the year's commencement season gone, I took the tedious ride to Kablake to visit with my "Ali." The rainy season that year had brought back the usual condition that often rendered our so-called highway impossibly passable.

My mother, upon my arrival in Kablake, without giving me Kola, the sign of welcome, revealed to me that my old father was longing to see me. Hearing this I rushed to the living quarters of the village elder. In his usual warm way, the old village chief greeted me, "Jan me ju, Tui, Blo-gba nyu." He extended his hand for a handshake. With these pleasantries done and gone, I told my father that as soon as I arrived in the village my mother hinted that you have been crying to talk with me. "I am here now; please tell all you wish to tell me.

What is it?" I queried. "I have nothing to tell you. Usually when school is closed, you come to see me. This time school was on its annual break and you had not come to this end. I was really concerned, thinking that you were sick. What I have to say is that I need clothes to wear," the old village dancer intimated. "What do you want with clothes? You don't move about any more. You could hardly leave your seat in the house. Say exactly what you need the clothes for," I pressed him. "I want to put them on when I am dead," the old Gbor member revealed. "Oh, so you need the clothes so that when you are dead you will be dressed in them?" I confronted him. "Yes," smiling, broadly he answered. "You brought us into this world. If you are dying, with whom are you going leave us?" I demanded. "No, I am not going to die; I just want clothes," he evaded. "Baa, I don't think you are telling me the truth, are you? But if you are worrying about the clothes you will be dressed in when you are dead, be assured that your black suit was made ready since two years ago. Two years ago, I became very sick, if you remember; I thought I was going to die. Knowing that there is nobody in our family to get and dress you in a decent black suit, I decided to get one for you if I would kick the bucket. I have yet to knock the bucket over, but your gentleman suit is still handy. My wife, brothers, and sister, including my mother, all know about this your well tailored suit I hope you will wear to go to glory. Don't worry. Just prepare well to meet your Lord face to face in glory," I prayed.

After the long sad conversation with my aged and sick father, it was dawned on me that my father was sick. I guessed he had seen some foreboding sign of death. He has long lived in this turbulent world. I must not take his indirect warning lightly. With this haunting me I went to Pleebo to request my cousin Emmanuel that in the event that my father should die, he should embalm the body for two weeks and in the meantime send for me. But if you the family desire to bury the Gedeh elder and our father without me, go right ahead. The joyous Christmas was spent in the clan reunion. Butter beans with dried tubedu meat, chickens, and roosters, the ones that say "D.C. and soja," formed part of the well seasoned Grebo palm butter dishes that were lavishly served amidst drumming, singing. The question of food for the old militiaman was no more there as he and his wife's attic was well stacked with the nutritious LAC #23. I was happy I did something positive for my dying father who was so concerned and responsible a father. Without asking Klade for my part of the rice I returned to Zwedru to begin work for the 1987 school year.

As I worked, and heard nothing from Kablake, although anxious about my father's poor health I took for granted that no news means good news. But on the 31st of March 1987, that bright Tuesday morning, at about seven-thirty, I arrived in school. Shortly after, I came out of my office to quickly view the campus. In that time I saw sisters Kathlyn and Lourene coming to school. As soon as they saw me they turned their backs at me. Slowly I moved toward them. Facing me they appeared to be saying something but in a stuttering way. "Mr. Reeves, Bishop says.. and...." I interrupted, "What did the bishop say?" Finally Sister Kathlyn gathered courage enough and said, "Mr. Reeves, Bishop said that your father died on the 26th of this month. He said you should rush down there at once so that you will make the needed funeral arrangement for the burial of your father." This was about five days after my father left from labor to rest. I sent for my friend Peter C. Nyepon at the Development Superintendency Grand Gedeh County. In my office the two of us wept like little children. Since in 1942 Peter and I met in school in Nyaake, Peter had been personally knowing my father whom he called his father.

At home I revealed the sad news to my wife, who flooded her room with tears. With the family halted for the time being, arrangements for our departure went in full swing. A direct bearer was dispatched to River Gbeh to my friend Charles K. Williams for some planks. Our emissary was told to take the planks to Mr. Francis T. Freeman, a casket expert in Nyaake. On the third of April we concluded our arrangements and departed Zwedru for Kablake, Gedebo.

In two weeks time the old village chief would be buried in his home village, Kablake where he longed to be. The usual rains that year created many disturbing problems, and I thought to bury father earlier would save me the frequent attacks of asthma that terrified me. I sent a special bearer to Pleebo to inform Emmanuel, the caretaker, that because of the continued asthma attack on me I would ask him to come now to Kablake for the funeral of our late father Nyanweju Hinneh. "Tell him the body was embalmed or two weeks. Today is the first day of the second week. We are not ready to bury our dear father. If he likes he may go back to his Krahn country. When it is time we shall bury the body of our father," Emmanuel averred. Because of the asthma there was no way out of the village for me. I had no choice but to wait for the appointed time. In Kablake my son, wife, and I tarried for about three suffocating weeks.

As the mourners gathered for the funeral, it was obviously demanding that more food be provided. My wife had made adequate preparations to feed as many people who would come to the funeral. But because we overstayed, we had to make on-the-spot arrangements for more food and so therefore we bought fifteen large bunches of rice. In the meantime, I remembered that I had rice with my stepmother. But I did not ask her for the rice since she was grievously bereaved for the great loss sustained; she lost her dear husband. I felt asking the lady for rice at that time would suggest that I was not thankful to my stepmother who, in a tenderly and wifely way, nursed our father in his ripe old age. I did not bother her.

As the people poured in for the funeral my father's widow was obviously pushed against the well. Food was markedly in short supply in her house. She then came to her son to see what help he could give in that line. "Please give me the nine bunches of rice I put aside for you me to feed the people who thronged the village for the funeral," the old village widow sadly pleaded. "Did you say you laid aside nine bunches of rice as my share from the farm that yielded so abundantly?" wearily I inquired. "Yes, my son, many people came begging for rice during the harvest since we were the first to harvest in this part," Kablake lamented. "But did you feed my father adequately and regularly with the rice from that farm? If your answer is yes, then have the nine bunches to feed the people who have come to sympathize with us during these bitter hours of our bereavement," I sincerely told the mourning woman. The rice had served its purpose. My father did die from hunger, a condition I feared. I had no further qualm about the rice except I got to realize that it is true that the tender mercy of a heathen is cruelty. My father's widow did not give me one bunch of rice from the farm I put so much into. Why? My sister-in-law too did not send me one cup of rice as a token of appreciation in the face of my request for one hundred cups. Why? On April 11, 1987, that bright sunny Friday afternoon, multitudes of people inundated the village for the laying out of the mortal remains of this prominent village chief.

The ceremony was a pageant. In a colorful traditional array of African dignitaries amidst drumming, horn blowing, dancing, etc., etc., the casket bearing the mortal remains of the grand village polygamist was escorted to a place specially prepared. One after the other, led by the elders of the Bodior Council, the men delivered their eulogies, followed by the members of Gbor with their fighting men. Among the many panegyrists was Charlo Musu, who among other things eloquently told us that the man Nyanweju Hinneh was not a fussy man or a troublemaker, but rather he was vocal because he never liked for anybody to trample on the rights of others. He added, "He was the most generous man of our time. The hunger of passersby will not be taken care of again as the man who sought the welfare is no more. This village will miss him. Gobajah and the whole of the Gedebo have lost a man whose loss is irreparable," Musu eulogized. My younger brother then took the stand and said, "Our father was a brave man. In his long lifetime he feared nobody." I remember once my father told me, "Kamma-o, my son, fear mouth. Nobody can swallow you alive. Be a man of your words. Always do what is right." During this ceremony at which the people of Gedebo paid their last respects to the fallen village father, I noticed some twinkling light on my dead father's face, silently resting in his lonely cell.

The next day, Saturday, April 12, 1987, the representative of the high priest (Bodior) and his elders and a throng of sympathizers assembled for the funeral service of the celebrated village farmer. Following the funeral rite the village militiaman, farmer, chief, and grand polygamist was laid to rest in the village he proudly claimed as a legacy. During the funeral I noted: In a very brief statement of the highlight of the glimpses caught here and there of my father's long life, I accounted for his life story as follows: This village lad was in the Gold Coast when the Kaiser War broke out in 1914, a war known as the First World War. Accounting to what he saw of himself, he was about twelve or more years old as he and his life-friend, Heabe Toe, were only able to take away foreign objects from the cocoa beans spread out in the sun. This was their work with the cocoa plantation employer. This somehow revealed that he was born in the early 1900s, say in 1902 or 1903. He told me that following the outbreak of that first global war, their Gold Coast employer repatriated them to Liberia. The short-lived hunt for livelihood in the Gold Coast landed them in Accra. Their hope for earning some money was dashed. Empty-handed they returned to Liberia and their village. But this did not quench their burning desire to visit the Gold Coast as soon as the war would end. They laid in wait for a long span of years. Under the watchful eye of Myer Kamma and others, at his majority, the village youth ventured out to the Gold Coast again; this time in Kumass with a logging company that lodged them in the forest for six hungry months as they found no rice to eat, rice the staple food for Liberians, especially for village dwellers. They ate cocoa yams (eddoes) and plantains. Amos served as the laborers' cook.

Born of Belloh Chowah, the scout, and Twapei Nyanweju of the Tarlo clan, in Heweke, Gedebo, the would-be village chief returned to Liberia having worked for two or more years in the Gold Coast, now the Republic of Ghana. This time around, he brought home plenty to wear and to share with his parents and relatives. Made fatherless early, the two sons born of the Nyanweju-Chowah union were fathered again by their mother's second marriage to Nagbeh Pawah, a prominent herbalist-soothsayer in the Gedebo Country. Unto that union two other children, a boy and a girl, were born. Nyanweju Hinneh was enlisted in a militia force called Yancy Volunteers. The force was named in honor of Allen Yancy, then Vice President of the Republic of Liberia and the one who was subsequently accused with his president of enslaving his fellow Liberians in Fernado Po in the late 1920s. The force steadily grew into what is called the Ninth Infantry Regiment with headquarters in the Township of Nyaake, Webbo, Lower Grand Gedeh County.

The prospective village chief took as his wives, at some intervals, Tarnu Kpaye, his first wife and the daughter of a warrior-to-be; Karley Rachor, Tuwar Tena, and Hinneh Klade. Of his four wives, one bore him no children. Tarnu Kpaye had eight and two survived: two boys, Kpaye Kamma and Kpaye Kwee. Rachor had ten and only two lived: Rachor Mudi and Hinneh Jolomo, a girl.

On March 26, 1987, the long terrestrial journey of this village master; village beautiful dancer; that grand polygamist; that strong father, who ably sought the needs of his children; village militiaman; village elder; member of Gbor; member of De-Ia or member of the Bodior Council of the Gedebo Country, and Amos and Menua as our father was popularly known and called by his contemporaries who visited along with him in the Gold Coast, came to an end. Left to mourn his loss were his two widows Tarnu Kpaye and Hinneh Klade and his sons, Kpaye Kamma, Kpaye Kwee, Racho Mudi, and Hinneh Jolomo, a daughter. May his soul rest in perfect peace and may light perpetually shine on him...Amen.. Amen.. from his ancestors.

Boniface, our son, a little less then four years old, was with us during the long waiting for the funeral of his grandfather. The rural city boy was for the first time being exposed to village life, How was his two-long-weeks stay in his father's native Kablake? From all indications one would rightly say that Boniface was well at home away from home. He found his peers in big number around the nine-hut village and he easily formed an integral part of those energy-filled kids who tirelessly roamed the nooks and corners of the one-clan village. All the men and their children, including Boniface and his father, of the village sealed under towering evergreen trees were of the Nowa-o clan or family, or Togba, or Knowan, in the Gedebo vernacular.

After listening to a local radio station (LRZ based in Zwedru) that morning in Kablake, I turned the set off and went to my brother's house to discuss some matter with him. Later I came back to our cell-called-room, where Boniface, Sophie, and I bunked every night. In that little cell I met Boniface and his throngs of his newfound friends. Boniface was trying to get the battery out of the radio set when I popped at the door. "Boniface, what are you doing with the radio?" Surprisingly I asked. "I think the battery is low or weak," Boniface answered. "I walked away, trying not to disturb the young boy trying to display his knowledge of the radio his village young rustics. Boniface's answer gave me surging admiration and envy of my son. At this age he knew about battery and radio sound. I had not the slightest idea about radio when I was about fifteen years of age. But now my son, less than four years old, knew about them. What next? I had taught Boniface to turn on and off the radio.

From Kablake to the main road (Motor Road) is a narrow path snaked through the thickets. The little boy needed somebody to carry him on his or her back or shoulders. The mother did not want to do it and I was not physically fit to carry him. How could we pull him along? His mother was leading the way and he was placed between us. All of a sudden I thought how to trick him into walking. I began: "Boniface, where are we coming from?" "We are coming from your town," Boniface hastened his answer. "My town, is it not your town too?" I fingered him. "Is it my town too?" my son asked. "Here you were born, but I was not, so how is it my town?" the boy dug in. "It is your town too since you are my son. This is our source, the place we come from," I explained. "But what were we doing in Kablake?" I quizzed him further. "One day, Ayee came from the farm. As soon as she put her load down she began to cry. Then I asked Mnoh why was Ayee crying? Mnoh said that your father died and then I said 'Oh.' After some time we came here to see the dead man,"

Boniface narrated. "Did you see the man?" I plied him with questions. "When did you see the man?" I drilled him further. "Oh, when the people were beating the drums and blowing the horns and they brought the box out. In that box I saw the man in that box and he had on clothes," laughing, Boniface said. This long, lively dialogue played the trick that caused him to walk that one-hour distance about three miles to reach the motor road. In about an hour a Zwedru-bound Suzuki Bus whisked us off to the rural city.

Chapter XXII – "Juwle Builds an Auditorium"

Before, and even now, facilities, such as desks, gymnasiums, etc., connected with smooth operation of schools, were abstract terms in the vocabulary of the students in Liberian schools. In my case, I attended an elementary school, from grade one through grade eight, in a old rectangular building with one open hall in the entire structure. All the few crude wooden benches in the school were stationed in the middle of the hall. They were used only during assembly time. Each teacher and his or her students selected a spot in the open hall for the daily recitation. The students stood on their feet during all class activities. Where the benches were placed in the open hall the teachers styled as auditorium. This gave me the early concept of the word auditorium, that important component of school facilities. I knew how to spell the word desk during my eight or more years spent in the elementary school, but did not see desk in concrete form. In reality I saw desks, modern ones imported from Western Europe, in a spacious auditorium when I enrolled at Our Lady of Fatima High School. The auditorium greatly enhanced our extracurricular activities there.

As already stated somewhere in this story, following my graduation from OLF I became a teacher in the elementary division of the school. The idea of a school having an auditorium as a necessary facility was embedded in me. In the Government School in Nyaake where I subsequently taught after graduating from college, the idea was still lodging with me passively as the basic instructional materials were nonexistent in that impoverished Liberian rural school. With a structure built for an elementary school at Tubman-Wilson Institute (TWI), where I was later transferred, the dream of even thinking about an auditorium was completely nonsensical as it was far, far from reality. But I still had the lofty idea.

In 1978 I had a happy reunion with my Catholic Mission School System, Cape Palmas Diocese. As administrator of Bishop Juwle High School, I thought I was placed in an excellent position to redream my long-buried dream. At the 1978 commencement program I told my graduation audience that there was a need for an auditorium. "During my incumbency as principal of this young promising academic institution, all of you parents and guardians working hand in hand with us here at the school must build this much needed asset." How receptive were my parent/guardian partners? It was too early to say. Time would tell.

At every graduation program of the school I reminded them of the need for an auditorium. Unfortunately for us, the country was turned upside down. All hopes, dreams, and aspirations were filtered away in the mounting, overwhelming, and devastating chaos that befell the poverty-stricken country and it people following the 1980 Samuel Doe seventeen-man bloody military coup which toppled the constitutionally elected government of President William Richard Tolbert, Jr. Like truth, suppression cannot destroy one's aspiration. Building an auditorium was my unquenchable desire. The desire was burning under cover. At the 1984 graduation ceremony, in my remarks followed by announcements, I asked in a loud and clear voice, "My dear parents and guardians and our distinguished visitors attending this remarkable annual ceremony, would you like to continue being seated in booths where you may be given an unwanted and untimely bath?

As a regular host of this auspicious annual occasion, I would not like for my guests to be treated like that. Together, let us do something. Let us build an auditorium to enhance the learning activities at BJHS and accommodate you and me at the literacy programs of the school, including commencement programs." My aspiration for building an auditorium perspired me so profusely that the droplets that fell on my student activists, notably, Alphonso Nyenuh, Mohamed Sherif, and their members of the class of 1986, especially level-headed female students like Cora Hare, Agnes Opoku, and Beatrice Hansford and their junior counterparts like Veronica Kazouh and members of her class, inundated them. The irrepressible idea became the talk of the campus. With the student activists ablaze for the construction of an auditorium, Sister Lourene Spawlding, the woman who knew no fatigue, prepared the blueprint for our dream. After knocking our heads together as to how we would generate funds and other materials for the erection of this much talked about building, a temporary plan of action was drawn up.

In the few weeks in the early school year of 1985, at our morning devotion time, on our Upon Grand Gedeh County Dry Season wither grass campus, the students raised one of their seemingly battle cry hymns:

Hosanna I build a house
Oh! Hosanna I build a house
Oh! Hosanna I build a house
Oh!
House built on weak foundation
Will it stand?
Oh no!
Stories told without creation
Will they stand?
Oh no!
Sun will shine on it, Ah ha
Rain will fall on it, Ah ha

When their melodious rendition was hushed in the air of the serene palmy campus, class after class, in a vibrant determined mood, each class pledged its unflinching commitment to supply all the sand needed for the construction of the entire building and to generate funds to defray some of the expenses that would be incurred. All in all, the students unequivocally promised to contribute at least fifty percent of the total cost of the desired structure. Fire was placed on tortoise's back. There was no turning back. Sister Lourene, the Fire Brigade, took the kick off.

The building of the auditorium at Juwle was then an open secret as the mobilization of resources was frantically and earnestly begun. Mr. William Glay, a Krahn young man and an intimate friend and staunch supporter of Bishop Juwle High School and also the victim of the building fever then gaining epidemic proportions, made a timely visit one sunny morning to the school. "Mr. Reeves, for a very long time we have been talking about building an auditorium. I guess unless we start, we will never begin. I strongly feel and urge that we should begin the construction now.

As you know, tide and time wait for no man," Honorable Glay emphasized. Honorable Glay, the newly elected member of the Liberian Legislature, House of Representatives, from Grand Gedeh County, added, " I came to tell you how prepared I am for the construction of what we want to do. I have the poles, nails, zinc, and the carpenters to build the booth where we will store the blocks as we make them." "Well, spoken, Honorable Glay. Your effort is highly commendable. My school and I are very grateful to you for giving us a push," I acknowledged with satisfaction. But I suggested that we should not use zinc to cover the roof of the booth. I explained that since the project is a self-help, to zinc the roof would be too costly. "The sheets of zinc will cost plenty. That money could buy us at least ten or more bags of cement, which I think, will cost us more money than any other material to be used on the self-help project. A local roofing material, such as mats or purport, will suffice." Mr. Glay clearly understood me and went along with my suggestion. I then promised him that I would lay our discussion before the student government and members of the faculty. In the meeting with the leadership of the student government and members of the faculty I suggested to them how I thought it would save us money if we used sheets of mats or purport, a local roofing material, to cover the roof of the booth in which we will store our blocks. This met the unanimous consent of both the student council leadership and members of the faculty. A motion for each male student to be taxed two sheets of mat was made and unanimously carried.

The following week, Mr. Glay sent the carpenters with the building materials for the booth. The students too followed suit simultaneously. As soon as the booth was finished, the students hauled mountains of sand in no time. We had yet to tap the source from where our cash would come. But we were hopeful as we were almost certain from where we would get our strong financial support. Soon or late July popped in. It was time to go on the July twenty-sixth break. A week before the Independence Day, we had recessed for the annual break.

Shortly before I went home that afternoon, I was in my office, trying to bring sanity to my desk with books scattered here and there. "How do you do, Mr. Reeves, and where do you go from here?" Sister Margaret, SSND, with her strong Swiss French accent, asked. "Nowhere, except to my home," I pointed out. "We would like for you to have lunch with us on the convent,' the sister requested. "Surely, sister, I will definitely stop by to dine with my sisters. In fact, I cannot refuse good," I gratefully accepted. At once I picked up my briefcase, umbrella, and hat and made off to the convent where I joined the sisters at their lunch table. It was spread with delicious food which sent out flavor that made the stomachs begin to send out gastric juice to arrest the food that might hit the waiting mouths.

In their usual tradition of talking while eating, of course a tradition that is not African, let alone, of the conservative Grebo, while we were nibbling, Sister Margaret left us. In no time she came back with a long envelope and handed it to me. It was fully addressed to me. I laid the envelope down on the table while I continued nibbling the palatable lunch. With the food gone, I drank some juice and relaxed; I began to chat with the sisters. I took hold of the envelope. The address on the envelope written in plain letters read as follows:

Mr. William K. Reeves
Principal, Bishop Juwle High
School   Zwedru, Grand Gedeh
County   Liberia, West Africa

    I further noticed that the stamps on the envelope were Swiss. I whispered to myself, I know nobody in Switzerland. How did my name get there? "Sister Margaret, do you know who sent the letter?" puzzled, I queried. "No, I don't know," the chuckling sister evaded. I opened the envelope to find a four digit number, two thousand dollar cheque enclosed in the letter, which read in part, "Herein I enclosed a check of two thousand dollars. This amount is for your building funds. I understand that you and your students are doing a self-help building project." Again I asked the sister, the presenter, "Who sent this money?" "I don't know," the sister reechoed. Inaudibly I questioned myself, "Does it matter to know from where or from whom the money comes? I am told in this letter the reason why this huge sum of money has been remitted to this school in need. No more questions I highly appreciate this benevolent and humanitarian gesture. I shall later write a thank you letter to the generous donor. But as the letter had no return address and the signature was not typewritten I could not send my brother-in-Christ our thank you letter. God Almighty in his own way and time would shower His rich blessing on this brother's keeper. Overwhelmed with joy, I jumped on my feet, and with an outstretched hand pointing in Sister Lourene's direction, smiling broadly, loudly I said, "Here, Sister Lourene, the huge sum of money on this cheque is for our self-help building project, the auditorium. We shall start at once making the blocks."

    During the break, the sisters went to Monrovia where they bought with the two thousand dollars the cement for our construction. Also during the short break the students busied themselves digging the trenches for the foundation of the self-help building project. The dimensions of the proposed building were one hundred twelve feet long and thirty-eight in width. Messrs. Peter Chie and Isaac Asibu were our hired construction engineer, and mason and carpenter, respectively. Each of them had but two helpers. The whole Juwle family was the helper in general. From foundation to roof level, eight-inch blocks were used. Simultaneously the mason and the carpenter worked hand in hand. At the end of 1985, the cement work had almost reached roof level. The layman's estimate put the total cost of the building at roughly forty thousand dollars. The construction was progressively on course. Were we coping with the incurring expenses for the cost of materials and workmanship?

    Oliver Goldsmith, one of the pleasing English writers of the 18th century wrote in his Collected Essays that the clergy of the churches were Ecclesiastical Beggars. We, on the other hand, were in the scholarship business. Could we be styled as scholastic beggars since we were soliciting funds from here and there for the erection of a building for a school? In the previous year, we circulated letters to some notables in and around Liberia to help finance the self-help of Bishop Juwle High School. Their responses in most cases were far below our expectation. It would appear they were not impressed with what was being done. Or was it that unfounded idea that the Catholic Church is unbelievably rich and so why should the Church or

Church-related entity solicit funds to build a Catholic school? From our meager resources, unceasingly the construction continued.

The following week found the principal riding in a duazet Renault bus, rolling over three hundred miles of potholed so-called highway linking Zwedru with Monrovia. In Monrovia, I made my first call on Honorable John P. Beh, then Minister of Internal Affairs. Luckily for me, I met Minister Beh in the corridor of his official office building. I guess it was on Warren Street. I greeted the minister and warmly he returned my salutation. "No doubt, you are here to beg me for the help your school asked for," Mr. Beh intoned.

In a very angry but calm mood I retorted, "Mr. Beh, in an absolute view, I came to remind and urge you about your duty and obligation you owe your children you send to BJHS in Zwedru. Don't you know that it is your business to send your sons and daughters to the school of your choice? In this case, you send them to a Catholic school, a school whose facilities are provided for by none other than the Catholic Mission in Liberia. As you are quite aware, those beneficial facilities are exclusively made available by the mission. These facilities are not yours, but your children immensely enjoy and advantageously benefit from them. It is then abundantly clear why it obligates you morally and socially to contribute meaningfully to improving or enhancing those facilities you did not put one black cent in for their establishment. Therefore, I did not come to beg you, but rather to remind and urge you to help to maintain those wholesome facilities by which your children are being religiously and educationally empowered." Mr. Beh snorted, "But I am not a Catholic." "You are not a Catholic and I am not asking you to become one either. But once your children attend a Catholic school, you are morally, socially, and lawfully duty bound to help the school by giving whatsoever is requested of you. Since you strongly feel that you are not a Catholic, it is not your business to give a helping hand to the school, which, in sincerity, holds partnership with you in bringing up your children sent to Bishop Juwle High School, a co-ed Catholic institution. I cannot continue to haggle with you," I rejoined.

Politely I left Mr. Beh in his ignorance and false pride, which he adamantly refused to swallow. As I saw it, Mr. Beh was sunk in ignorance and without a speck of pride in his blood. This negative attitude of his toward a worthy cause questioned his true identity with the Krahn ethnic group, a people sophisticated with pride, especially when it comes to giving to worthy causes. Mr. Beh is like a tortoise that says to its young after they are hatched, "This is your fatherland. Explore and exploit it and sustain yourselves." But how could the young do all by themselves? Mr. Beh being nowhere around yet I questioned loudly, "You are a high government official and I guess you are taxpayer too. Rather than sending your children to a mission school that gets a meager subsidy or no subsidy from your government, why do you not send them to a government school?" From all the high ranking officials from Grand Gedeh County serving in the Doe government, I received not a cent except from Mr. Shad Kaydea, a former student of mine, who donated twenty-five dollars.

According to the records of the Cape Palmas Diocesan School System, sixty-six thousand dollars, a year subsidy for a system operating fourteen schools, three junior high schools, and eight elementary schools, was given by the government of Liberia. In that same year, 1978, I read in a public record about the Liberian government subsidies given to two Baptist high schools, Ricks Institute in Virginia, Montserrado County, and Kwendu, near Tappita in Nimba County. Reportedly, Ricks Institute received one hundred eighty-two thousand dollars, while Kwendu took delivery of eighty-two thousand dollars from the Tolbert government. Half a loaf of bread was better in the Tolbert government than where there was no bread at all during the confused and despotic government of Samuel Doe. But thankful as we were, we were completely heartbroken at the unarithmetical, biased, hardhearted, and unequitable distribution of public funds in a who-knows-you society! The blatant hardhearted, uncharitable, and uncooperative attitude of the high ranking government officials from Grand Gedeh County, serving in the nepotistic government of President Doe, did not in a slightest way deter our sturdy ambition and our profound hope and belief that people who know what education, especially education seasoned with Catholic religious culture, means would continue to rally for our support to complete building the auditorium nearing completion.

It was the six week period test that morning. The students were busy writing the tests in our unfinished auditorium. On this particular day, the instructor-chairman on the administration of period tests, without the least fear about how the principal of the school would deal with him administratively, took advantage of the prevailing freedom of speech in the school in a country where all human rights were completely denied by the military dictatorship to tell the principal not to visit the auditorium while the test was on because, in his own words, "Uncle Reeves, you disturb the students. There should always be perfect silence in a room where an examination is being given. Instead of that you want to tell tales to them during this contemplative process. Please stay away." Here I was, my under man giving me order and permission to be away from my duty. With this I told the teachers that I was going to spend my free day by visiting Gbaba Elementary and Junior High School and R.B. Richardson Baptist High School, both of Zwedru. Swinging my ever-present umbrella, I went my way.

About an hour or two later, I strolled back onto BJHS campus to meet Sister Kathy all excited. "Mr. Reeves, we have been looking for you all around town. Where have you been?" Sister Kathryn breathed out. "No other place besides the two places I told the teachers I was going to visit," I noted. "In about fifteen minutes' time the United States Ambassador to Liberia will be visiting with us here in the school," the sister happily disclosed. At once I directed that our generator be sparked and our public address system be placed on the stage of our unfinished auditorium where the students were busily engaged writing the period tests and where too we would receive a distinguished visitor. A little later, after everything was put in place, a police officer rushed to where I was standing and said, "The US Ambassador and the superintendent of the county will be there in no time." Pointing in Feeney Street direction, the police shouted, "There they are!" I rushed to the entrance of the auditorium and I escorted them into the auditorium amidst the standing students. I proudly seated them on our auditorium stage.

By then, our handy teacher, Sister Lourene, had prepared items listed as program for Mr. Bishop, US Ambassador to Liberia, honoring our school with a visit.

The first item was a song, "Hosanna We Built the House," followed by a brief statement of welcome by our MC, Sister Lourene, and then another song, "Freedom is Not Free; You Must Pay a Price." The principal then made general remarks touching here and there. In part, I said, "Mr. Ambassador, on behalf of the BJHS family and on my own behalf, I welcome you into the walls of our unfinished auditorium of Bishop Juwle High School. I think it is quite convincing when our hands are firmly seen at work on the project, the self-help, for which we have been soliciting funds here and there.

Again, Mr. Ambassador, the Bishop Juwle High School family happily welcomes you for your timely visit with us in our unfinished auditorium and BJHS. In response the ambassador briefly noted, "I see here some beautiful talents in the making. You said it all in the beautiful songs so melodiously rendered by your neatly clad students. The expression, "unfinished project," is not strange in Catholic circles; for eighteen unbroken years I lived with it. No doubt, visiting with a Catholic school I would hear, 'Unfinished self-help project,' that seemingly exclusive Catholic expression, as I found your hands at work on your self-help building project, the auditorium. Therefore, the US Ambassador's Fund will give the school a financial help of three thousand dollars. I hope that the auditorium when completed will be an asset by which you will continue to develop the many talents I see here."

The ambassador's spontaneous attention was seized by the soprano vocalist, Veronica Kazouh, the 1986 junior, who led the soul-touching songs that seemed to have spellbound the diplomat. The soprano vocalist stole the US envoy away from us. On the whole Veronica is socially graceful. She brightens every corner as her laughter is contagious and friendly to the point where she seems to belong to everyone but to no one. Having made the big promise of three thousand dollars, the US envoy was about to retire when Superintendent Johnny Garley jumped up on his feet and briskly stepped on the side where I was sitting. "Mr. Reeves, I did not know that you are a politician. Congratulations for your beautiful speech. I am glad the ambassador gave your school a big helping hand," the county boss asserted. This was the very first time Mr. Garley spoke to me since he ordered my arrest on that woeful morning of October 12, 1985, the day General Thomas Quiwonkpa invaded the country. Garley's guilty conscience haunted him all those many months. Each time he saw me walking in his direction, he would divert his car onto another street in Zwedru. This did not bother me because he had nothing I wanted or needed. I was glad that he realized that William Reeves was far above his academic standing, if he had any. Only the barrel of the gun brought him where he was shakily standing. Military dictatorship had circumscribed every human institution in Liberia. Like in the previous years since the military despotism, student government in any school in Liberia could not be instituted by democratic process.

The military government of Samuel Doe demanded that student government be instituted by appointment by the school administration and not by the democratic process, elections. Circumscribed, BJHS appointed Miss Frances Harris, an unassuming young lady with contagious smiles, who with an inspirational leadership served as the first female Prefect General and the first female to head the student government. We thought to alternate the sexes. A female PG would take control of the student government. The administration had set its eyes on Joetta Pawah, an athlete, captain of the kick ball team, and a cooperative, respectful, and studious student. The administration had decided to nominate her pending her endorsement by the faculty, but up to March, 1986, she had not registered or been seen at BJHS for the school year. For our newspaper, the *Sage*, the editor-in-chief, Mohamed Sheriff, was nominated, endorsed, and appointed. All around the country we inquired about Joetta. Word came back to say that Joetta was stranded in Yekepa. The faculty requested me to write telling her that everything was well for her and that she should rush to school at once. Joetta did not show up. To our great disappointment, a sad message arrived from the would-be PG that she had graduated with a diploma in the form of a *bass drum*[11]. With this disturbing message, the faculty requested me to appeal to Mohamed to be the PG for the year. That afternoon, I negotiated the change over with Mohamed. He accepted the will of the faculty after a few minutes hushed in contemplating silence. "I wholeheartedly accept the request of the faculty," Mohamed, one of Juwle's brain trusts, declared. "Thank you, but there is something else. Since you have willingly consented to be the PG, you have to recommend to the faculty the person to succeed you as editor-in-chief for the *Sage*," I abreasted him. "Well, I think the most qualified person I know who can credibly serve as editor-in-chief of the *Sage* is Felicia Reeves of the senior class," Mohamed categorically stated. "What a nonsense! Do you mean to recommend Felicia because she is my daughter? Look, young man, be very serious. I need people who are qualified and capable to do the job so as to bring credit to the school. I think your recommendation does not represent what you think, does it?" I seriously queried. "Ah, Allah," Mohammed cried, "my recommendation is not influenced by her being your daughter but rather on her academic activities in all of our subjects, especially in language arts, in which she excelled to the very top of the class. It is upon this I based my recommendation. Quite recently, we submitted our term papers and Felicia scored the highest. Not only that, Felicia writes beautiful articles in every issue of our school newspaper, the *Sage*. Search our class records to test the honesty and sincerity of my recommendation."

I took the recommendation to the faculty. But as far as I was concerned, I would never appoint my daughter to any of the student government offices because it was repugnant to the conservative Grebo tradition. Shortly that afternoon, I met the sisters on the convent, where I disclosed the result of my mission with Mohamed. I told them that the young man had accepted the request of the faculty to serve as the PG for the year and he in turn strongly recommend Felicia Reeves of the senior class to succeed him as editor-in-chief of the *Sage*, the BJHS newspaper. This is never done in the Grebo country. We don't pour palm butter before ourselves. Pouring palm butter before oneself is called nepotism, one of our national ills that eat away our political structure. "Oh, Mr. Reeves, you are not fair to Felicia to say that you won't appoint her to a post she is well qualified for," my female instructors exclaimed. The Cape Palmas Diocesan School coordinator, Sister Raphael Ann, interposed, "Mr. Reeves, take your so-called Grebo tradition out of here.

Felicia merits the post, Felicia deserves the post." Those vocal female middle-aged American religious, who, like fellow Americans, demand equal rights with men, tried to drain every speck of my Grebo blood out of me. I had to yield to the will of the majority since I am a democrat. The next day in a full faculty meeting I delivered the message and again this time the male members of the faculty in one powerful earth breaking voice shouted, "Felicia Q. Reeves must be appointed editor-in-chief of the *Sage*. I was crushed under the will of the majority. In some form, democracy was still at work at Juwle.

Accordingly, Mohamed Sheriff and Felicia Reeves were appointed to their respective posts the next morning during our devotion time. Up to this date, my baby daughter is still wondering what had convinced that fanatic, conservative, bony Grebo traditionalist to have appointed his dear daughter. Don't forget, wise men change! On the whole, the 1986 school year was writing a memorable chapter in the annals of the school. Our one-time daydream was rapidly becoming an undeniable reality. The academic and extracurricular activities were booming as my teachers continued to distinguish themselves in their stewardship. Since the inception of the school, many expatriate teachers constituted a larger proportion of the teaching staff. The expatriates included Africans as well as American religious and US Peace Corps volunteers. Notable among the Africans expatriates, Ghanaian to be exact, were Boadu Gyamfi, a gentle, well mannered, elegantly dressed, seasoned and experienced teacher, and James Ado, a gentlemen of the first order, who spoke little but did wonderful teaching of science. Like U Thant, the silent diplomat, Ado was an exemplary disciplinarian for which the students admirably called him "*Master*," the name by which I addressed him too as he was truly a master who firmly but lovingly delivered the good.

Kannoh Dobo was the dean of discipline and the teacher often empowered by the principal to give corporal punishment to a student or students when it was absolutely required, an able chairman of Bishop Juwle High School afternoon club. The membership of this club consisted of those students who broke one or two of the rules of the school during recitation periods and were liable for punishment, but it was deferred to the afternoon. There was the Malian diplomat, Assumulo, our French instructor. He was as polished as the language he taught and a shining example to his students. There was also Moses Shannon, one of the most duty-conscious Liberian teachers, and those whom, because of limited space and time, I cannot mention individually, but all of us working hand in hand in that united strength raised the school to academic prominence.

Commencement season was peeping through the doors and windows of Juwle as the academic year, 1986, was slowly drawing to a close. At the same time, the Juwle family was contemplating on dedicating the reality of their dream (auditorium). Could the two big events be merged so that we would have one auspicious and memorable celebration? It was possible, but the preparations for the two voluminous programs were enormous. Time was not on our side as the commencement events always consisted of many activities, which the prospective graduates of any year love to actively participate in. The dedication program, on the other hand, would comprise of few items and the principal actors would be students. If we decided to postpone the dedication of the building to next year, say February, we would have no students.

The faculty, in an emergency meeting, decided to have a round table conference with the prospective graduates to see whether our suggestion for a meager portion of both important events would be agreeable to them. As you would expect, those levelheaded young intelligentsia did not want one single moment added to their time in the school. In a loud uncompromising voice they cried, "One minute more delay of our time to graduate from here is complete denial of our right to graduate this year, having successfully passed our school and WAEC examinations." They were missing the point. Their academic labor and their physical labor had earned the big events. "Stay with us for a while as we put the finishing touches to the handy work of our dream," their partners (teachers) urged the prospective graduates. Amicably a compromise was reached. Some of the activities of the commencement calendar of events included: Junior-Senior Prom, Class Day, and Seniors-at-Home with the Faculty Day. Baccalaureate and Graduation were carried over to 1987, March 15th.

By March 15, 1987, the stage for hosting the Dedication and the Graduation was completely set. On that momentous occasion the school was singularly honored by people from all walks of life; the First Secretary of the German Embassy near Monrovia, Liberia, with his young and charming American wife, high ranking government officials, church dignitaries and Most Reverend Boniface Nyema Dalieh, Bishop of the Catholic Diocese of Cape Palmas, and a multitude of well-wishers graced the history making occasion. On that festive occasion the Juwle family sincerely felt obliged to give an olive branch to the German Embassy represented by its First Secretary at the program. The Embassy significantly boosted the building of our auditorium.

The First Secretary was traditionally admitted into the Grebo Eldership with the presentation of a stool, a small, low portable chair, four yards of wax Fanti lappa, and a neatly tied necktie. So decorated, the diplomat was formally dressed as a Grebo elder and was thus admitted into the Grebo enviable hierarchy. If it is true that all the world is a stage and all the people are merely players and each man or woman in his or her time plays many parts, then let it be true with Bishop Juwle High School and her versatile, insatiable knowledge seekers. As the will was always there, our students willingly and sometimes spontaneously embraced and took every extracurricular activity that would enhance their academic activity. In this light, BJHS readily accepted the challenge to take part in a TEAM TIME QUIZ TOURNAMENT in which all the junior and senior high schools of the Zwedru School District would activity participate. As I saw it, this was a creditable and valid way of measuring a school's academic standing with other schools. And so BJHS actively participated in the TEAM-TIME QUIZ of 1986, organized by Mike Tuleh Wilson High School, an Assembly of God Mission institution.

BJHS team membership was mostly selected from the senior class of the year. The tournament, which met nearly every weekend, lasted for a couple of months. Of course as you would expect, our action lady, Sister Lourene Spawlding, organized and moderated our quizzers. Although I made it my business for the challenge to be accepted, I left the entire undertaking to the students and their omnipresent instructor. Once in a while I would ask my lieutenant, "How are our students doing at the quizzing?"

At the close of the tournament all the principals and teachers of the Zwedru

School District were invited to witness what they called their award night. I was in full attendance at the program held in an Assembly of God Church edifice, Elin Chapel, where the quizzers and their distinguished invitees were assembled. In the usual AGM religious atmosphere the program began. After rendering some items of the program, the MC announced: Presentation of Awards. Without previous notice, the principal of Mike Tuleh Wilson High School (and MC) stately and briskly walked to me and whispered, "Mr. Reeves, will you present our gift to our highest winner of the tournament?" Without knowing whom the recipient was, I replied, "Yes, with pleasure." The award was then handed me. To my utter surprise, on it was legibly written, FELICIA Q. REEVES. Inaudibly I whispered, "What does this mean?" But this principal is himself a Grebo. Does he forget, "Yon ne po au dea lo hano ge?" This time, it was not true. I was not pouring the palm butter before myself as I was no part of this organization and presenting the award on its behalf did not in any way breach the conservative Grebo mentality. With my mind clear on this I proudly moved forward to present the award to its recipient, Miss Felicia Quiade Reeves, alias Kamma Quiade. In a proud fatherly voice overwhelmed with pride and love I said, "I am singularly honored to present to you, on behalf of the organizers of this tournament, this award being awarded to you as the highest scorer in the TEAM TIME QUIZ TOURNAMENT, '86."

According to the scorekeeper, Bishop Juwle scored three hundred seventy-five points, making her highest scorer and of these points. Felicia scored half of them, thus making her second to none. I was happy that Felicia brought honor to the school, herself, me, and the family.

But something happened that year while Felicia was wearing her laurel. One day after a period test, Mr. Gyamfi, senior class history instructor, looking dejected, entered my office and ushered himself into a chair. "What is wrong, Mr. Gyamfi?" I suddenly asked. "Mr. Reeves, you know your daughter failed in this test," the teacher cried. "Who is my daughter?" I questioned the teacher. "Felicia," he lowly replied. "And so what?" I demanded. "Well, I don't know what to do," remorsefully he said. "Don't you know what to do with failures?" I queried further. "Was Felicia absent during recitation periods?" I dragged him along. "But that is not my problem. I think anybody hearing this will think that she is stupid. The young woman who memorized the whole Bible from Genesis to Revelation. The Bible is history. One logically consumes the facts as required in the study of history as well.

At the award night program of the quizzing tournament, we were told that Juwle scored three hundred seventy-five points and Felicia alone scored half of those points awarded her school. By the way, Felicia is not my daughter in the school. She is my daughter when at home with me period. But Gyamfi, do you want me to tell you to give her free grade because you say she is my daughter? Only on merit I give or promote students. Please let me out of that nonsense of that your student who doesn't represent herself," I enjoined. From all indication, Felicia was an able student. Why did Mr. Gyamfi, such an experienced teacher, talk about not knowing what to do with such an able but lazy student like Felicia? At the National Examinations Felicia met her Waterloo again. What could the school do with that lazy young woman who flatly failed to utilize fully her time and make best use of the talent God had endowed her with?

Chapter XXIII – "Glimpse of Liberia"

By the time the 1987 school year was ushered in, Bishop Juwle High School's Parent-Teacher Association, the most organized PTA in the whole of the Grand Gedeh County School System, had its Constitution and bylaws drafted under the chairmanship of Teahce Boadu Gyamfi, BJHS social studies instructor. The PTA under the presidency of Mr. Alfred Slue Barbley, a Grade Certificate holder from the Zorzor Rural Teacher Training Institute and a Bachelor's degree holder in agriculture from the University of Liberia, and his August body received, adopted, and approved the document under the Rules and Regulations governing the school.

The young man, Alfred S. Barbley, a Konobo, one of the largest sub-Krahn groups lying east of Zwedru, was the most disciplined professional teacher I had during some of my long teaching years at Tubman-Wilson Institute. Alfred was the school's registrar and teacher who introduced what he called "Happy Time," a period his students loved immensely as they made adequate preparation to meet the Happy Time each week. (Happy Time was the time in Mr. Barbley's class when the students prepared at home any question about the school or life in general and asked the teacher in his class. The students, on this day, were allowed to tell tales in the class.) Alfred had now come to serve as the PTA president in the school of his personal friend and former boss, where his three children, two girls and a boy, Alfred Junior, were students. Alfred is highly Grebo oriented because he lived in the Grebo country since his formative years up to his senior high school experience. Unlike his native Krahn, he is surprisingly and unbelievably conservative but scrupulously liberal and in a way democratic.

Konobo, according to history, was part and parcel of the onetime vast Webbo District of Eastern Province, with Tuzon in Konobo as headquarters for the government official called station master. One William Deoosthenese Farr, a former township commissioner of Nyaake, told me that he once served as a station master there. He even showed me documentary evidence. But this time my imagination failed me completely to see how he traveled through the vast wilderness with its then hostile wildlife, as Konobo is still remote and almost inaccessible by modern standards. There are also signs that the Konobo people were once an integral part of the Grebo country. Like many of the Grebo villages and towns, the Konobo towns and villages are surrounded by life trees such as coconut palms, breadfruit, bread nut trees, etc. So far as I traveled over the Krahn country I did not see such a scene. The cocoa plant is living evidence that the Konobo people had some close and long association with the Grebo people.

They served as sergeant messengers in Nyaake, the former Webbo District Headquarters. But indeed they were notorious messengers. Notable among them were Friday, alias Krakon, the tortoise shell, which his boys would beat and sing to announce his harassing arrival in a village or town; Kotofoi, or beard-bread, another nuisance, and Wau-Wau Foot. They were tax collectors who dehumanized the Grebo people and extorted their little pennies from them.

Lying far east of Konobo is a small sub-Krahn related group called Glio, situated on both the western and eastern sides of the river which forms the natural

206

boundary between the Republic of the Ivory Coast and the Republic of Liberia. On the east bank the Glio serves two political masters; on the west bank the Glio honors her one political master, Liberia, and on the east bank it is an Ivorian political entity. On whatever side you find the people of Glio, they are traditionally Grebo in their attire and customs because they were once an integral part of Webbo District.

Regardless of the long straggling distance that separated the little group physically from every known human habitation at that time, their God knew they existed. And so God, in his usual caring way, kindled the desire of somebody to bring Christ to Glio. According to the Reverend Joseph Wodo Andrews, pastor of Yancy Memorial African Methodist Episcopal Church, Township of Nyaake, Webbo, the evangelistic task fell squarely on the robust shoulders of Reverend William Taylor White. Inspired, we are told, the reverend gentleman made the historic journey without map. Judging from the geographic position of Harper to that of Glio, one would conclude that the evangelist took an unthinkably long, tedious, hazardous journey on the snaked paths through the the forest. I guess, upon his return, Reverend White told his horrible story about his ordeal in that sparsely inhabited wilderness, which made a lasting scaring memory of Reverend Andrews. It seemed that Reverend Andrews gathered that Glio was so far away and was without the limits of Liberia. He personally impressed me with this notion too. Very often Mr. Andrews would say to the girls, "You will be married to a Glioman," suggesting that once she was married to the Glioman, she would not be seen again.

Up to 1965 I did not know where Glio was. In Mr. Nayou's house in Zwedru, where I had taken up a year's assignment in late 1965, I met three young men as wards in the house. After spending about a week with them, I thought to get personally acquainted with each of them and so we met in our new family circle. Individually I shook hand with each of them and asked for his name and where he came from. David began: "I am David Brown and I am from Glio." Startled, I suddenly broke in, "Glio, did you say Glio? Wait a minute, later," I pleaded. The other two gave me their names and where they came from. "Glio is a sub-Krahn group and it lies east of Konobo and is a part of Konobo District, one of the districts of Grand Gedeh County," David revealed.

This reminded me of an incident Mrs. Golda Meir mentioned in her autobiography, entitled, My Life. During the Tubman era in Liberia, the Israeli Foreign Minister, Mrs. Golda Meir, paid an official visit to Liberia. In Liberia the foreign diplomat was assigned a Liberian female security. The episode revealed that the security lady was single (not married) and lived with her mother in Mamba Point, Monrovia.

One night the young security came home late and the old mom wanted to know why late. "These days old mom, I take care of a woman from Jerusalem. She is the Foreign Minister of Israel," the security broke loose the mystery. "What did you say, a woman from Jerusalem? Can you see her physically and can she be touched physically?" the curiosity-filled old woman dug in. In a demanding voice, she added, "Bring her here tomorrow."

The next day, according to the anecdote, with her young Liberian security lady, Foreign Minister Meir ascended Mamba Point to visit with her security lady's mother. Upon their arrival, the security lady announced, "Mama, here is the woman from Jerusalem." The story said that the old Liberian lady circled about Mrs. Meyer for three or more times before she made the least attempt to shake the distinguished visitor's hand. Did the woman from Jerusalem come from heaven? Many Christians thought that Jerusalem was in heaven. I thought so too. As I got to know that Glio is part and parcel of Liberia and so the old Mamba Point woman's curiosity was satisfied.

Mrs. Golda Meir was a star, not a meteor, in the political arena of Israel. She later became prime minister of that small powerful nation. In the Grebo estimation of woman, she cannot cut down a tree to cross a stream of water. This simply means that woman's usefulness, if she has any at all, is circumscribed in her little world, which designed her as a begetter of children. But in our own time now, women say that what we think of them is old-fashion and obsolete. To prove their case they vibrantly defy mankind in every field of human endeavor. With all those well seasoned political giants of the United Kingdom, Margaret Thatcher, the iron woman, snatched the premiership from those bellowing political heavyweights and held it for twelve unbroken years.

Indira Gandhi wrestled manfully with those haggling male Indian politicians and got elected as the first female prime minister, I think, of that subcontinent from 1966 up to the time of her cowardly assassination. In Liberia, Ruth Sando Perry would not continue to turn deaf ear to the massive destruction of our motherland and so like Eleanor Roosevelt, the First Lady of the world, she would rather light a candle than curse the darkness. Ruth lighted the candle and its glow summoned the hot Liberian warring factions to a round table conference, which calmed and restored them to sanity. Truly, women are intellectual giants as Mohandas Gandhi styled them and Oliver Goldsmith called them dangerous politicians.

The 1985 Quiwonkpa coup left us with a divided and bitter legacy as Liberians were not grouped by ethnic affiliation into camps. It was a heinous crime to belong to any of the many different African affiliation of the country other than the Krahn group. "Indigenousism" had become the rule of the day. In Zwedru, where the Grebo ethnic group formed a politically integral part of the county, the largest house owners were inhumanly marginalized. We were not even permitted to do those basic things dear to one's heart, like to eat such things as pumpkins by adding them to the ingredients of the Grebo palmbutter. We were told that eating pumpkin would breach their taboo for preventing war against them as they sensed war was impending. Ostracized as other African groupings were, the absolute-ruling Krahn severely felt the pinch of isolation.

And so Doe, the Head of State or President of Liberia, hoping to integrate Liberia again, decided to reconcile with the nation and its people, especially those in his conviction, who had been brutally and innocently murdered, whose property was looted, vandalized, or destroyed. The people of Nimba, the Gio and Mano, those industrious people, were the focus. In a seeming spirit of reconciliation, Doe mobilized the leading citizens of Grand Gedeh to go to Nimba to reconcile with our brothers and sisters, as they put it. They went. They were out there for some days. I understand the Grand Gedeans were dressed in white in "swear-in suits," the famous Tolbert national wear for this all-important historic reconciliatory conference. When they returned, a personal friend of mine and the development superintendent of the county, Mr. Peter C. Nyepon, spent the night with me but I said nothing about it. The next day, I asked him, "How did the conference go?" In a heavy political tone, he replied, "It went very well. We were able to reconcile with those brothers and sisters of ours."

"How did you go about doing the reconciliation exercise?" I fingered him further. "Well, the President told them, that is, the people of Nimba, that they should never allow a person or group of persons to use their territory to fight or wage war against the Republic of Liberia, and they too should never be part in fighting against their constitutionally elected government. In a mournful voice I said, "If you went in the true spirit of reconciliation, the government, represented by its president, was going to tell the people of Nimba that it was wrong to have so treated the peaceful, industrious, and innocent people of that county and that the government had come to apologize for the wrong done to them. In return, the people of Nimba would have poured out their hearts, that is, they would have told you how hurt they were. But instead of that way, you simply ordered them about what to do or what not to do.

There was no meeting of the minds like in contract and so there was no common ground reached in your so-called reconciliation drive. My friend, I say again, you did not reconcile with our brothers and sisters but rather you aggravated the appalling situation that tends to disintegrate the whole country and lands us into untold chaos that will destroy our national sovereignty. Their anger aggravated, manly and daring as I know them, the people of Nimba, compelled by the hard necessity, soon or late, will find the ways and means to get even with the nepotistic government of Samuel Kanyon Doe," I bluntly asserted. In a loud voice my honorable friend exclaimed that the people of Nimba did not have the courage, the ability, or capability to think about fighting against the constitutionally instituted government of Liberia. "Well, time will tell," I blithesomely calmed my friend. Since I did not know how deep his loyalty to his government was, I thought to make my position crystal clear and so I continued, "I am not praying for war. I don't know war. I have not seen war, but I read about war and its horrors. War coming to Liberia would be a tragedy which would take away from the people everything, impoverished as we are, including our lives. War is nothing to think about, but if the appalling prevailing conditions make it inevitable, then that is it! Did the Grand Gedeh County Reconciliation Conference with the depressed people of Nimba yield any fruitful RESULT?"

After the 1988 so-called reconciliation talks in Nimba, gross human rights violations were the order of the day of the Doe regime. This time power meant right as might meant right in the Middle Ages. A network of gates dotted along the dusty highway from Zwedru to Monrovia, a distance about three hundred fifty miles. On that straggling distance were found the marauders, or highway robbers, the notorious gatekeepers. Besides depriving one of his or her property, dehumanization was the last crown of the victim.

The mass failure of our senior candidates for the WAEC examinations discredited the school and its dedicated teachers beyond description the year before. However, the 1988 results restored our credibility and prestige. Our seniors came out with flying colors. Maria Tarlue and Glowon Barbley topped the class with the girls in a very slim minority. Glown saluted and Maria bid us goodbye.

Following their graduation, all the graduates, especially those who had the means to seek higher education, went to Monrovia. Maria attended a countryside university college in Bong County. Glowon and others journeyed to Monrovia to seek entrance at the University of Liberia. Unfortunately while they were still knocking at the door for admission, the savage war broke out at the very end of 1989. By the middle of 1990, the war was savagely spreading throughout the length and breadth of this country. Old and young alike began to seek refuge here and there. Glowon's church a sent a special representative to Zwedru to meet the Barbley family to see what help the church could give. For a year or so, Glowon was away in Monrovia. The church offered to send the Barbley family to Ghana through the Ivory Coast. They consented, but would they go without Glowon? The white man, the church emissary, told the family that he would search for Glowon in Monrovia and search he did. He asked the former Juwle girl to go with him to Sierra Leone from where they would meet Glowon's parents who were supposedly on their way through Glio to the Ivory Coast. On their way to Sierra Leone, they were halted at a gate manned by Krahn soldiers. "Oh, yes, so you are going with your white man to have fine time while we are battling for the survival of our dear country? Change your mind, you are not leaving this country, my dear young woman," the well-armed soldier pronounced. He continued, "Take everything out of that your fancy bag." With this, Glowon, now sobbing, said, "I am not leaving the country because of this white man. My parents have left Zwedru and are on their way to the Ivory Coast where I hope to join them." "That is a beautiful excuse, but sorry yah, you are going nowhere. Shake everything out of that bag," the young soldier ordered. He himself shook the bag and an old photograph fell down and he picked it up to find the old face of someone he knew personally. "How did you come by this? This is the picture of my former principal," the soldier revealed. Glowon, realizing that she was gaining common ground with the seemingly hostile soldier, said, "He is my former principal too. I graduated from Juwle in 1988," Glowon frankly stated. "Former students er are of Bishop Juwle High School. Certainly the old inscription on that picture is no doubt William Kamma Reeves, the no-nonsense principal." With this the soldier bade Glowon farewell and wished her luck on her journey without map.

In Ghana Mr. Barbley tried to get Glowon to a college, but every attempt failed and finally he sent her to a computer school. At the school, the former brilliant Juwle girl applied her time fully and after the required time for the course Glowon was certificated as a graduate of that institution, having distinguished herself scholastically. The institution at once employed her as a tutor while she continued to further her studies in the computer science, where she is now a computer witch.

Maria took to her young heels and found refuge in neighboring Sierra Leone. After a while she entered Njala University of Sierra Leone from where she ably earned a Bachelor of Science degree in biology. Since the senseless Liberian civil war hostilities found reason to cease, Maria Queleh Tarlue came home to a country laid waste to see whether she could further her education at the A.M. Dogliotti School of Medicine.

210

Chapter XXIV – "My Bitter Experience in Zwedru"

In the late 1970s, Charles Togbo Chie, Sr., then principal of St. Philomena Catholic Elementary School, and I were initiated into the Ancient and Noble Order of the Knights of St. John International, St. Joseph Commamdery #394, St. Theresa Parish, Harper City, Maryland County. Living in Zwedru, Charles and I were obligated to all regular meetings of the commandery in Harper.

After a large recruitment of members in order to get our Zwedru charter, in late 1988, in November, to be exact, our charter was granted and given. Accordingly, a big initiation ceremony was conducted with Kronyan Wureh as our Worthy President of Christ the King Knights of St. Jonn Commandery #467. The Sunday following the initiation, an elaborate installation program would be held in the Christ The King Catholic Church of Zwedru.

The night before the well organized installation program, I was seriously attacked by my usual holy devil, the strangling asthma. That whole night I knelt before our bed with my wife lying far back while our five-year-old son was lying in the middle. Round about two o'clock that early Sunday morning, our little son suddenly said to me, "Papa, I want to drink." Being breathlessly still, I managed and called the mother, "Sophie, Boniface needs water to drink." Sophie did not budge. No doubt she was in deep sleep and the boy hastened out to get a drink of water. Back from the water filter, Boniface took a surprising form. His abdomen was deflected like a football without air and looking breathless. I shouted, "Sophie, get up, Boniface is sick." I then pulled myself together and shouted for my son Cholee. Fighting with my faltering voice, I told him, "Run to the convent and tell the sisters to come with their car to take my dying son to the hospital." Instead of responding to the urgent call, at once the young man went about washing his face. "What is this, my Lord, what does this mean? He doesn't seem to understand me," I concluded. I left him alone. I rushed out and to the convent I ran. Don't ask me about the whereabouts of Mr. Asthma, the suffocator. My Lord had knocked that demon out of me to save my son. At the convent I pounded on the door and two sisters, Kathlyn and Peter, came to my immediate help.

Three of us jumped in the car. Before I left the house I had told Sophie to take the boy near the Police station from where I hoped the sisters would pick them up to the clinic. From the Police Station we picked Sophie and the sick child up to the clinic.

We took him to a private clinic where I thought the medical attention would be prompt and efficient. At the clinic I raised the alarm and the doctor, a Filipino, came to our aid at once. The doctor, with the sisters and my wife, incredibly began resuscitating the dying child. I could not stand that sight and so I went out. The resuscitation started about three that Sunday morning until about six that morning. I did not go near where my son was being brought back to life. When finally I decided to go where the doctor and his able aids were, I entered the room and when I entered, my son, speaking for the first time since he said he wanted water, said, "Good morning, papa." With prayer and praise sounding in my grateful heart to God Almighty, I happily saluted the boy, "Good morning Boniface, and how are you?"

Doctor Marcelio was one of our initiates and I had to attend the installation program. By seven that morning he retired to his abode to get ready for the ceremony. His wife was then in control. Early Mrs. Marcelion saw me outside and requested for my inhaler, that which I use to repel the sudden attack of the demon called asthma. Upon seeing me the second time, Mrs. Marcelino revealed to me, "Mr. Reeves, when I came in and saw your son I knew at once that he was not going to live, but now that he recognized and spoke to you is a clear reassuring sign that he lives and will live." I inquired unbelievably, "Mrs. Marcelino, is it true I was going to lose my son?" "Certainly, Mr. Reeves, but the condition has favorably changed and the good Lord has restored your son's life. Let us praise him for that," Mrs. Marcelino urged.

At about seven-thirty that morning Mrs. Marcelino discharged her asthma patient. "Take him home, wash him, feed him, and then give him this dose of medicine. See to it he takes a rest in bed for about an hour," the nurse directed.

At home the directives were followed to the letter. But instead of taking a rest in bed, our steadily recuperating son took to the yard to kick his football. "Sophie, there he is kicking his football, a true sign that Mr. Asthma has relieved him from deadly claws. We must thank and sing praises to God for saving our son from the pangs of death," I laudably urged my wife.

The formal elaborate installation program of Christ The King Commandery #467 of the Ancient and Noble Order of the Knights of St. John International was held, but I could not attend. In the 1950s Monsignor Francis Carroll, then Prefect Apostolic of Cape Palmas, felt the need to carry Christ and Education to the then remote forrest people of Tchien in Eastern Province. The Monsignor's bilingual and veteran missionary, Reverend John Feeney, SMA, with Harry Nayou, a student at Maryland College of Our Lady of Fatima and teacher of Fatima Elementary School, serving as guide and guard, penetrated the forest to deliver his religious and educational package to the people supposedly gaping for those life-giving substances, much needed for spiritual and economic empowerment. Under Father Feeney as parish priest, the school was established under the principalship of a veteran Liberian educator, Dominic Nyen Merriam, who later became the deacon in the Catholic Church. The next principal was Our Lady of Fatima High School 1958 graduate, Alphonsus Nema.

The 1958 Fatima High School graduates are one of the most academically distinguished graduates of the oldest high school in the Catholic diocese of Cape Palmas. The class I often refer to as a class of dwarfs, since many of them are comparatively short, notably among them are Alphonsus Nema, Augustine Jappah, and Patrick Smith. Alphonsus was stolen from the teaching profession and sent to Italy to pick up a degree as a medical doctor. Patrick, after obtaining a Bachelor's degree in education from Maryland College of Our Lady of Fatima, went to the United States of America from where he earned a Master's degree in economics. Augustine continued his search for knowledge after earning a Bachelor's degree in education from Maryland College of Our Lady of Fatima to the American University of Beirut, Lebanon, were he earned a Master's degree in education administration. The most prominent of that illustrious class is Luna Perry, who was popularly called Mrs. William Shakespeare because she always quoted many of Shakespeare's didactic verses.

After celebrating Christmas 1988 in the grandest style by the newly installed Christ The King Commandery of the Ancient and Noble Order of the Knights of St. John International, I carefully put away my uniform, black shoes, and other things, thinking that the Knights would not have any formal occasion until probably Easter in the coming year, 1989. I was mistaken. New Year Day was another day on which we the Knights would be required to appear formally.

On New Year Day, when I made myself ready to go to mass, to my great surprise, I would not find my black pair of shoes I had previously carefully put away. I searched, searched, and searched for it, but to no avail. Well, since I could not find my new pair of black shoes, I was compelled to wear the pair of black shoes I called "old." But I could not understand and I could not bring myself to bear the why and how my new pair of black shoes had unceremoniously left our home. Steadily the rising tension overwhelmed me as I became more frustrated. "Let me play some music, perhaps that will slow the mounting tension in me," I urged myself. Disappointedly, I could not locate my old cassette player and my new Jim Reeves cassette I bought for the season. Confusion blocked my thinking faculty as I profusely perspired. The mass time was still in my favor and so I quieted myself down to see whether the tension would take an exit. With the high tension subsided, I walked slowly to mass since the church edifice was about a stone's throw from my house.

On the twenty-seventh of December last I sent my son Cholee on the farm to get some rice thrashed and brought to town and milled so that when I returned from Grebo, where I was due for a funeral, we would prepare the two hundred pounds of rice as a package I would carry to my children in Monrovia. In the bags of rice I would conceal sliced pieces of dry meat too for the children's food, since the meat could not be taken in the open to Monrovia. The law prohibited the people, except the Krahns, from taking meat to Monrovia. Since the twenty-seventh of December last Cholee had yet to return to Zwedru.

The Knights were to meet in a formal meeting at eight that New Year evening in the BJHS air cooled auditorium situated on Feeney Street. Seven-thirty found me opening the auditorium for the meeting. Promptly at eight the meeting was convened and formally declared open. Following the formal opening I sneaked out of the meeting without a word to anybody. As soon as I reached home I went straight to bed in my wife's room. In that lonely room, without anything to comfort me, all the tension I experienced that morning began to resurge rapidly. My wife was nowhere around as she was spending the whole season with her sister in Monrovia. As she put it, "I am going to spend the Christmas season with sister so that we will drink beer."

While I was in bed, there was a knock at my door. "Who is that? Come in," I called. It was my son Cholee, just returning from the farm since 27 December of last year. The robust boy entered and greeted me. "Why do you act like a raccoon, my son? When a raccoon is asked to go to the forest, it hesitates or adamantly refuses to go, and when it is obliged, it goes. Once in the forest it does not want to hear about the young bush, and so you are. You refused to go on the farm for the rice, but then when in a firm fatherly voice I told you that you were leaving for the farm now, you had no choice but to obey your father and so you left for the farm. But look, the length of time you spent in the forest. Why?" without looking at him or in his direction, I questioned my sturdy son.

Briefly Cholee explained, "I brought in the rice this afternoon. You were not in. I borrowed two dollars from your mother-in-law to pay for the transportation." With this conversation between us, I made it no business of mine to lift my head or to look at him. I kept my head down in the dimly lighted room. Cholee left me in my restless state. The whole night was sleeplessly spent. Early the next morning, my daughter Martha came in to request for three dollars to pay for her way to our rice farm. Weak from the restlessness the night before, I fathered some strength and stood up to search for money in my pocket. I found a five-dollar bill and I handed it to the young woman. "Please give two dollars to your brother. He owes my mother-in-law two dollars," I directed Martha. Being aware that Martha finds it hard to deliver exact messages, I rushed out after her to tell Cholee about the two dollars. When I came out to the back door, I saw Cholee taking the five-dollar bill from her. This was my first time seeing the young man physically since the twenty-seventh of December last. Briskly Cholee passed by me and entered my mother-in-law's room. Out of the room, Cholee said that the old woman had given him a five-dollar bill, which he gave to the driver but the driver had no change and so the driver promised to give Cholee his change this morning. "I am going with Martha to the parking lot so that I will collect the change from Abu, the driver, and give it to Martha," Cholee narrated.

"Cholee, lose no time in getting back here. My aunt and I are leaving this morning at nine for our home in Maryland before eight-thirty so that you will carry my suitcase to the Catholic Mission. Reverend Father Hans, SDB, will drop us near our village on his way to Harper," I pointed out. With this understanding my son left. Half past eight came. Cholee had yet to return. At twenty-five minutes to nine, I took my suitcase and my aunt and I walked to the mission. Nine o'clock to the dot, the hot-tempered German priest drove us off. Early that Monday afternoon we were home in Kablake with the rest of the mourning family.

As usual, we huddled together and wept. Later, the head of the family welcomed us into the fold. The head of the family was then Yessay Nyapee.

Then next day, Tuesday, I went around the one-family village to personally greet each villager and to see how far they had gone with the preparation for the burial of old man Towaye. I saw no clothes and grave for the corpse to be buried in. The message from the family said that everything was set for burial. What happened? "I shall call a family meeting tomorrow evening," I planned single-handedly. Round about six-forty-five that Wednesday evening, the meeting was convened in Wahnyene Sedi's house, my official lodging quarters. In the meeting I told the men and women dressed in sackclothes that during vacation I do my rice farming. This year was no exception. But because of the death of our father Towaye I was to be here. According to you, everything was set for the burial, pending my arrival here. Two long days have passed since I came.

Where are the arrangements you said you made already for the burial? In a very concerned mood, I said, "As your son and now one of the elders of our family, it is absolutely necessary for me to take part physically in the burial ceremony of our dear deceased father. But as I have already told you, this is the time for rice farming. Added to this is that my son is sick and his mother took him to Monrovia where they are waiting for me so the little boy will be taken to the Catholic Hospital for treatment. He suffered from a severe asthma attack in late November last. All these must be taken care of before February ensuing. Now, if we are not ready to bury the body on Saturday, this week, I shall leave you without the body being buried. In that time I looked at my watch to know that it was news time, seven PM, precisely. "Excuse me," I said, and I went into my room to get my radio. Returned, I placed the radio on the side of my left foot. Radio Zwedru, (ELRZ) began the broadcast of the evening news.

The first news item came out. The second news item said, "One Eric Reeves (alias Cholee) was shot and killed," It went on to relay, "Eric was a student of R. B. Richardson Baptist High School, Zwedru, and the son of the principal of Bishop Juwle High School." I shouted, yelled, exclaimed, and jumped out of the meeting. Shouting to the pitch of my shrill voice, running to the place where my mother was in the house of my younger brother Kwee, away from the other huts of the small village, I met Kwee who grabbed me with all his might, saying, "Tell me what is wrong or happened that has caused you to shout?" "Oh, my dear brother, the radio said that my son Cholee was shot and killed in Zwedru," with a faltering voice I revealed the sad news. Up to then everybody in the meeting and the village grew nervously concerned, but as soon as my brother repelled me and I told him the heartbreaking story, the whole village was seized by commotion for hours. I could not believe that my twenty-year-old son, eleventh grade student, was shot and killed in Zwedru. What happened and why?

When the commotion ceased, the family elders gathered around me. "Well, I'll leave you tomorrow morning to go where they said my son was shot and killed," I told the doubly mourning family. While we were still huddling together a radiogram was brought in by a special bearer from Harper City.[12]

The radiogram came from my daughter Christiana working for Liberia Telecommunications in Monrovia, Liberia. The sad news of the death of her brother Cholee struck her, and knowing that I was down in Maryland County, she sent the urgent message through the wires in care of Mr. Alphonsus Nyenati Davis, our kinsman in Maryland County. Without delay Nyenati dispatched the radiogram by a special bearer to me in Kablake. Through the wires I had received the devastating message in Kablake earlier.

On Thursday, the fifth of January, 1989, from Kablake I went southeast for about fifty long miles to arrange for a bus to take me to Zwedru in Upper Grand Gedeh County, northwest. In Pleebo, Maryland County, I met a bus ready to ply the long potholed highway. I boarded the worn-out bus for the hard trip. On the highway I met my brother and my dead son's aunt. Both were ready to journey with me to Zwedru where my twenty-year-old dead son was lying. We huddled together in the bus as we wearily rode along.

Shortly after my brother with Cholee's aunt and I arrived, Mr. and Mrs. Alfred Barbley came in. I guess they were in eager expectation of my arrival. For a long while, Lilian and her husband tried to mend my broken heart and so before we got to know the time we were deep into the night. To cook food from that point would have meant eating in the early hours of the next day. Because of this, Lilian sent for her hot water bottle and Alfred went to buy us some bread, something just to satisfy the worms until the next day, while my mother-in-law, who was in charge of our home while I was away, sat supinely, doing nothing for the just-arrived hungry mourners. Sister Sue and I sipped hot cups of tea and nipped the bread. My brother went to bed without eating anything, saying that bread with tea is no food.

There were no signs of my son in our home. I called his name aloud but there was no reply. With tears flowing down my wrinkled cheeks, I entered their room and looked all around, only silence greeted me all round. Truly, my son was dead; he was no more! "My Lord, has sharing with people the good thing which one has become a crime in the Krahn country? For almost twenty long years I shared unselfishly my knowledge of education with the people of this place, especially people of school going age, at their request, through Professor Cyrus S. Cooper, supervisor of schools for the newly created Grand Gedeh County. Why God? Why?? Why???" lamenting, I demanded. According to information, my son's body was lying in a morgue. What happened? Frankly, I cannot answer that one million dollar question. Will the people of goodwill answer the question for me?

On our arrival that evening in Zwedru, my mother-in-law told us that when my aunt and I left for Kablake, she told Cholee that some unknown person or persons stole my old cassette player, a Jim Reeves cassette, and a pair of black shoes. According to her, my son then went to the next door neighbor's home, Robert Deh, where he met only Gaye Deh, about a fifteen-year-old boy. Cholee told the boy to deliver his father's cassette player, a Jim Reeves cassette, and a pair of black shoes. "You always steal from us. Bring those things now," my son reportedly demanded. "I did not steal them this time. Somebody stole them and brought the pair of shoes here," Gaye allegedly revealed. "Where is the pair of shoes?" Cholee allegedly questioned Gaye. Gaye turned the pair of shoes over to my son, according to my mother-in-law, and promised that he would get the other stolen items from the perpetrator(s) tomorrow.

Late that afternoon, the next day, Gaye came to our house and inquired about Cholee, according to my mother-in-law, and then she told Gaye that Cholee was around but she did not exactly know where the young man was. "Here am I," Cholee called. "My man, I am here now for us to go for the other stolen items from the guy, but I am hungry. Do you have any food here? Please give me some," Gaye begged. "Yes, I have some food, but I think it is too cold to be eaten like that. Let me warm it. In a twinkle, it will be ready for chewing," Cholee assured his friend, a disguised conspirator. After eating the warm rice, the youngsters left our house. For where, I don't know. But my mother-in-law said that she did not see Cholee again. The next morning Cholee's body was found on the Bishop Juwle High School campus. Hue and cry rained in Zwedru when the R. B. Richardson Baptist High School eleventh grade student was found dead. This was on the morning of Wednesday, January 4, 1989. How did the body get there?

On that fateful day, Wednesday, January 4, 1989, according to Gaye Deh's story aired over Radio Station ERLZ, Gaye said that that Wednesday morning he went for firewood and there he saw his dead victim (Cholee), who, he said, drove him away from the bush. When he came to town he could no longer hide the heinuous crime he had committed against humanity the night before. He told the mystified radio audience that he and his elder brother Boy Deh had taken the body of Cholee in a wheelbarrow to where it was found. According to him, when they emptied the body out of the wheelbarrow, it made a groaning sound. This alarmed them because, according to them, it meant that their victim was not dead. With this, according to Gaye, he drew his .38 Smith Calibre pistol and shot my son in his leg. Again, there was another groan. This time the elder brother took the pistol and leveled the gun and shot Cholee in the head, which bullet found exit through Cholee's left eye. I guess then the victim breathed his last and gave up the ghost. The police then arrested, charged, and sent the heartless juvenile criminals to the Palace of Correction.

That night of Friday, January 6, 1989, my wife and children arrived from Monrovia. Saturday morning I found, on entering the room where once my dead son slept, that there were no signs of his clothes, including his school uniform. I called Karbeh, his elder brother and one of those arrived from Monrovia, and I asked him, "Karbeh, where are the clothes for your brother?" As I continued to search around, I discovered on the wall outside footprints, a sign that some person had climbed on the wall into the room and, no doubt, had made away with the clothes and perhaps other valuables. With this, I went to the police station to inform the police about this disheartening discovery. The officer investigating the case told me that he would take care of that aspect of the case. Later in the day, the officer came to our house to tell us that he had obtained a search warrant to search the house of Mr. Robert, whose sons, Gaye and Boy, were charged with the murder of Cholee.

According to the investigating officer, three different times he searched the culprits' father's house and each time he found nothing. On his fourth search trip to the house, as soon as he entered the house, Mr. Deh dashed a bundle of clothes at the officer. "Here is a bundle of clothes. I don't know who brought it here," Mr. Deh declared. This obviously connected him with the crime being investigated. Therefore, he and his wife Esther were arrested and placed behind prison bars.

My people, the Grebo, called at our house in large numbers. Each expressed his grief and sympathy for the death of our son Cholee. I reminded each group that visited with us that we were not in the Grebo country, but rather we were in the Krahn country. Our tradition in dealing with such a case could not constitute our reaction here. The least institution of such a measure according to the Grebo tradition would mean an untimely annihilation of our kind here. The heavily armed Krahn soldiers seen in every corner and nook of this vast rural city implicitly tells the story of what awaits us if we dare to do our Grebo thing here. "My son, certainly, would die one day and perhaps this is the day. For the death of this little boy, let us not risk our lives. The sacrifice is not worth making," I strongly warned my bitterly grieving ethnic group.

Before I arrived in Zwedru everything was in place for the burial. My friend, Peter C. Nyepon, had prepared a black suit in which Cholee would be buried. Friday Doe, a nephew of mine and an executive of the PTP Logging Company near Zwedru, made available a beautiful wooden box called casket in which Cholee would be laid for his eternal rest. A crude tomb was in the making, too.

On the sixteenth of January our family decided to bury our son. While a Requiem Mass was being put in place at Christ The King Catholic Church in Zwedru, I received a verbal message from the police authority in Zwedru saying that the Government of Liberia was sending a team to pass a postmortem examination on my son. Can you imagine the bitter angry mood that surged in me on hearing from a government, an irresponsible government, to put it the humblest way. The body of my son was discovered dead on the morning of January 4th. Today was the 16th of the month! The hopelessness and the don't care attitude and the complete discriminatory complacency of the Doe government were glaringly clear. "As you can see, the priest is about ready to begin the funeral mass. The body is here. If you need it, have it, but you shall not return it to my house or the church. Pass your autopsy as it may please the government and do with the body what further thing you want to do with it, if our government thinks now she is obliged to do what it wants to do. Fine. I have nothing against it except that once the body is given to you, you shall not return it to the family," angrily I pronounced. The oligarchic government of Doe, truly a government by few as only his ethnic group rules Liberia, did not bother itself about a dead Grebo man, Cholee. Cholee was laid to rest in the new Zwedru cemetery.

The police investigation about the death of my son revealed that the pistol used by Gaye and Boy to silence my son was brought to Zwedru and was left there by one Gbeku Wright, a top Krahn security officer assigned to the Executive Mansion. Why he carried it there or why he left it there, the worried public was never told. But the most baffling thing is that Mr. Gbeku Wright, a Gbobo Krahn, a sub-Krahn ethnic group from where President Doe belongs, was never summoned or investigated by the Zwedru police or any other branch of the law enforcement agencies of Liberia. The WHY is the ONE-MILLION-DOLLAR-QUESTION that Doe left for his cohorts to answer.

The open complacency of the Doe government in this case impelled my daughter Felicia to write an open letter, telling the reading public how brutally her dear brother was murdered in cold blood by a Krahn family in Zwedru and questioning the Government of Liberia why in a don't care fashion they neglectfully failed to probe into the cause of the untimely death of her brother and a young promising citizen of the Republic of Liberia. The government did not budge. But strongly we hoped and believed that God Almighty in his own time would redress the grievous situation.

A day or two after the burial of our son, Honorable Johnny Garley, superintendent of Grand Gedeh County, came to our house to express his condolence for the irreparable loss we sustained. "I am very sorry that I could not come while the body was here," in a very sad tone Mr. Garley expressed his condolence. "But Mr. Garley, since your wife came, you came too because the two of you are one. However, I am glad that you have come to reinforce the sympathy your wife conveyed on behalf of you and herself," I sincerely acknowledged. In a very concerned tone Mr. Garley observed, "Mr. Reeves, I am very surprised that the Grebo people I know very well are acting so supinely about the death of your big boy. I find it hard to understand why the Grebo people have yet to act according to their tradition in such a case." "But Mr. Garley, you have said it all. This place is not a Grebo country. We are sojourners here. The Grebo tradition you talked about has precedence only in the Grebo country, not in the Krahn country. The Grebo people are law abiding citizens; we don't take the law into our hands. We shall remain law abiding citizens. As you know, or perhaps you don't know, nearly all the churches here in Zwedru are pastored by Grebo clergy. In short, the vast majority of the Grebo people residing here are Christians. As Christians, we unreservedly adhere to what the Holy Scripture teaches: "Vengeance is mine and I shall repay." We as Christians believe and know, according to the Holy Bible, that only God has the exclusive right to redress us when we are arbitrarily or inhumanly treated. I am very surprised that you the superintendent and your ethnic group see my son murdered in cold blood and up to now you pretend that you don't know what happened. Why should you talk about the Grebo tradition, which, in this case at bar, would lead to violent assault upon the culprits in this kind of heinous crime? You have come in disguise to encourage my people to take the law in their hands so that your heavily armed soldiers, already deplored in every part of Zwedru, can massacre the grieving Grebo people? I say a categorical no to your sinister web. Grebo people don't act rashly. Soberly they act. We will not lynch your heavily armed soldiers on ourselves in any way."

Following the burial of our son, my wife and I with our little asthmatic son went to Monrovia to take our new asthmatic patient to St. Joseph Catholic Hospital, where a treatment would be prescribed by a medical doctor. We arrived back in Zwedru after staying about a week in the nation's capital.

1989 was a woeful year for me. Zwedru, I grievously felt, was very unwholesome for me to live in again. However, I was still actively involved in the everyday administration of BJHS and with the Program Advisory Committee of Radio ELRZ. But deep down in my sad heart I was quite aware that my family and I were not secure anymore in Zwedru.

With this perturbed feeling of insecurity I experienced yet another devastating blow. On the afternoon of the sixth of May, 1989, my wedded wife deserted me. "What is this?" I queried myself to the hearing of no one. "Well, she once told me that her marriage to me was singularly her choice and so perhaps her leaving me is exclusively her choosing. What shall I do?" pondering over my plight I asked. I comforted myself, "That doesn't matter much. My first wife left me with our four children and took the wings of the morning and flew to what they called "freedom."

During the July 26th break I went to see my sick mother in Kablake. Message reached me, saying that the old woman had tripped and suffered a dislocation of her ankle. In the village I found that the story was true. However, I was happy that she was slowly but steadily recovering. My mother told me later about the drugs Cousin Emmanuel often treated her with. After a day or two in the village I went to Pleebo to buy the drugs. Cousin Emmanuel dispatched one of his aides to take the drugs to my mother and administer them. I celebrated the Independence Day with Emmanuel and his large family in Hospital Camp, Firestone Cavalla Rubber Plantation in Gedetarbo, Maryland County. From Pleebo I went straight to Zwedru.

Of course, before I left Kablake I told my mother that I would return to Kablake on the 23rd of August ensuing just to see how well she would be improving.

In early August, the Joint Faculty of the Zwedru School System met in a meeting to plan for the coming Liberian National Flag Day, August 24th. At the meeting I was elected chairperson for the committee on Ways and Means for the celebration. Having accepted the chairmanship, I informed my fellow teachers that I would not physically celebrate the day with them but I would insure that everything would be in place before I left for Kablake for a visit with my mother being haunted by old age and sickness. I hoped to leave on the 23rd of August, but unfortunately that bright Saturday morning, Sisters Loreene and Kathlyn drove to my house. As soon as I spotted them from inside my house, I came out to greet them, but instead instead of turning towards me to answer me they turned their backs at me. This always suggested to me that they had some sad news for me. I went closer to them. "Yes, sisters, what is strange?" I hit them hard. "The Bishop says..The bishop says..The bishop say..au da.. we must tell you that your...he says we should tell you that your mother died yesterday in your village and you should lose no time to go there," they finally broke words. "Oh God, my mother yesterday," I cried. This meant that my mother died on the 18th of August since today is the 19th. Inwardly I asked God, "Why is it that you are being so cruel to me this year? Early this year you snatched away my robust twenty-year-old son. Why?" I questioned my God. I assured myself, "One thing, God cannot give you a burden that you cannot carry or bear. Let His will be done." I was deeply hurt by the homegoing of my dear mother. I thought I was going to meet her alive in Kablake to learn from her rich storehouse of Gedebo tradition and stories. Her concern for my well-being unceremoniously left her this time, my God. The prolific gospel singer in the Gedebo vernacular was no more!

Lonely, I departed Zwedru for Kablake, the spot of my roots. In the Catholic Mission station wagon jeep I placed the casket in which to bury so loving and caring a mother and other items for the funeral. I had planned that my mother would continue to live with us in Zwedru until her God would summon her home, but the negative behavior of my wife toward my mother turned my plans upside down for my mother. The disobliging, hostile, and uncaring act of my wife came about one afternoon. I came from strolling about in town. At our home I met my mother sitting under a tree at the back of our house. She appeared so dejected and so I slowly moved toward and sat with her under the leafy almond tree. "What happened, Ayee, that you are unusually quiet?" I asked a sad looking old woman, seemingly nearing her eighties. "Nothing. I just feel like enjoying the cool air under the tree," the granny replied. To me the answer was evasive but there was nothing to argue about. I broke the silence when I began to tell her about an incident that happened in my school the other day, but then suddenly I asked, "Where is Sophie?" She pointed to Deh's house, the house nearest to our house. I said nothing further about Sophie, my wife.

After a short while, Sophie came from Deh's house and joined us under the tree. "Where are you coming from?" after Sophie told us the time of the day, I questioned. "From Deh's house and why do you ask?" Sophie angrily snatched back. My mother broke in, "Sophie, people who and their husband are always in a quarrel, you should not visit their homes because anything bad from there that comes against your husband the public will conclude that you are part and parcel of that happening. You know very well that Deh and his wife don't like my son, your husband." "And so you and your son sit under this tree to discuss me?" shouting to the pitch of her voice, Sophie asked and resentfully walked away. She could not listen to reason anymore. From that moment, Sophie did not want to see the very ground my mother walked on, let alone, the presence of my mother in our home. With this kind of hostile attitude toward my mother on the part of my wife, I was compelled to send my mother back to Kablake where I hoped her son Kwee, my younger brother, with his wives and tons of children would give their mother and grandmother their tender care. If you read this story carefully, you will get to know that my mother's motherly advice and warning to her young daughter-in-law were like prophecy. The Deh family brutally killed my son Cholee.

Chapter XXV "War Looms over Liberia"

In early 1989, I had a dream. It was like a vision. I saw in a circle in the sky soldiers wearing fez caps with long black tassels and their guns hung on their backs. They were dressed in the old Frontier Force style. They said nothing but they were all hanging in space over Zwedru. The next morning, I called in my friend, Mr. Peter Nyepon, and I told him what I saw in my dream. I told him, "To me, this was a foreboding, a sign of war in the making." No, William, my feeling is that the soldiers were parading," Peter rejected. "Do soldiers parade in the air?" I questioned. Each of us strongly held to his interpretation of the dream. About two weeks later, the same dream occurred to me again. I summoned Mr. Nyepon to inform him about the recurrence of the ugly dream. "Brother, as I told you before, I dream but I don't make dream my master, but if a dream is repeated to me in a short time, then I am greatly concerned because I then believe that something is afoot and this particular dream is no exception. I seriously think that some undesirable event is in the making for this country. But I know one thing that I am going to do for myself: I am going to make two rice farms next year—one here in Zwedru and one in my home village, Kablake in Maryland County. He shouted that that would be straining on me. "Well, when the war comes and I am driven out of here I will go nowhere else but to my village. With my rice farm there, I will have adequate food to eat and be more secure," I explained my stratagem. On December 24, 1989, that Christmas Eve, BBC, the window on the world, announced that a rebel organization calling itself NPFL (National Patriotic Front of Liberia) had attacked Liberia at a town called Boutou in Nimba County. In its reaction, the Government of Liberia called the attackers bandits who would soon be destroyed.

The following year, 1990, I went about making my two rice farms, one in Zwedru and the other in Kablake. In early March, 1990, schools in Zwedru, especially Bishop Juwle High School where I was principal, were in full swing.

One day a political officer at the US embassy near Monrovia flew into Zwedru, according to information, to brief US citizens, including the Catholic nuns and US Peace Corps volunteers, in Grand Gedeh County. They met in their meeting. When the sisters returned from the meeting, they stopped by my office and casually said to me that there was nothing serious about the meeting. "Don't worry," they assured me. I said to myself, "But this is my country, I have nowhere to go whether it is hot or cold. I don't care what it is, I must stay." The US Peace Corps young volunteer serving Juwle entered my office and said to me, "May I sit down, Mr. Reeves?" "Oh yes, Paul, sit down. This is your office. You don't have to ask permission from me to sit in your own office. After sitting down, he pulled his chair closer to me and said in confidence, "The political officer from the United States embassy near Monrovia informed us that the NPFL rebels have infiltrated every part of Liberia. Right near us in Tapita, we were told that there are two hundred fifty well trained and well equipped rebels whose target is Zwedru. And because of this war hanging over the country, we the US Peace Corps volunteers are asked to leave the countryside for about two weeks. We were informed also that we will be sent to Ghana where we will spend two weeks watching to see whether the prevailing situation in Liberia will not deteriorate. If it escalates, we shall not return to our respective stations, but rather we will go back to the US and then this will mean my goodbye to you, Mr. Reeves. I will always remember you well; you were my real papi, to speak your dialect. With this Paul Steinberg left me, and up to date he has yet to return to Liberia, a country now completely devastated by the war that drove our partners in progress out. Will Paul return to Bishop Juwle High School once in the unknown future? In early May, 1990, the war was closing in on us in Zwedru. Everyday the soldiers, that is, the Armed Forces of Liberia (AFL) detachment in Zwedru went to the war front and they came back each day with their trucks loaded with household things such as dishes, etc., and food stuffs, such as bunches of rice, etc., plus sheets of zinc, cows, goats, and sheep. I don't know whether these things were captured from the enemy and were called the spoils of war which are often accrued to the victor.

From the war front one day, Colonel Joloka, the detachment commander, went on the air, that is, over Radio Station ELRZ to tell the bewildered citizens that they were attacked seriously. We all wondered what he meant by seriously. But unconfirmed information said that they had lost about forty men and several were seriously wounded. With that disturbing information, the Catholic schools in Zwedru met in a joint faculty meeting to see what we could do in the alarming situation. We decided that in as much as the war was on our threshold, we would like to close the schools at the end of the month and I was told by the faculty to inform the bishop about the time we decided to close the school temporarily because of the impending war. Accordingly, I directed the sisters to inform the bishop about our temporary plan. In reply, the bishop in a point blank statement told us that we were not going to close the schools at the end of the month, but rather he was directing us to close down the schools that week, Friday the 25th of the month (May). And so on that Friday, the 25th of May, 1990, the schools were shut down temporarily. In the bishop's message about closing down the schools, he added that he was going to place a truck at the disposal of those of us from outside of Zwedru to take our leave of Zwedru immediately after we close the schools. He further directed that William Reeves, the principal of Juwle, must be the first to get on board because he knows his standing with the Krahn people. Because of what the bishop said over the air, he gave a verbal message to the driver of the truck to personally deliver it to me. The driver did. "Mr. Cooper, when you go back to the bishop, tell him that William Reeves says that he does not have coward's blood in him. If he can remember well, I come from a distinguished line of warriors."

Evacuation continued, but I went on my farm as I thought Doe was ripe for shaking. In no time he would fall or give in so there was no sense in leaving Zwedru with my rice farm unfinished. I couldn't give up life like that. With the school closed my earning was put to a halt. If I abandoned my rice farm, that would mean I abandoned my whole life, no maintenance and no sustenance, and so I stayed on in Zwedru. But the bishop's message kept coming, saying tell that bony Grebo man to come home. I don't want to be held responsible for his death in Zwedru. I paid no attention to the unmanly cry of the bishop, but on the 29th of June, 1990, I came from the farm to Zwedru to see how the town was looking. This time again the catholic priest told me that the bishop told him that the truck he was sending would be the last time and he was not going to send it again and that the priest should make sure that I was on that truck. This time, I yielded and went with it. But when we got into Lower Gedeh, I told the sisters with whom I was riding in their car to stop. I came out of the car and pulled out my suitcase and said to the sisters, "I'll see you in Zwedru sometime, I am going to spend some times with my friend, Moses Sloba, the paramount chief of this area."

With Moses I spent five days, then I decided to go to an old schoolmate of mine in Fleroke. With him, he and I went to a paddy rice farm right beside the highway leading to Zwedru. One day my nephew Friday Doe, working for a logging company, PTP, in Jarkake met me and became very bitter about my being on the roadside leading to Zwedru. As he put it, "You are well-known by these Krahn people and they are hunting for everybody, including you. If they find you on the roadside, most certainly, they will snatch you off and it would mean death. While can't you come with me in Jarkake that is off the main road?" The next day he came for me and I went with him to Jarkake. On the 16th of July I decided to go back to Zwedru with Mr. Jeffrey Seidi, the manager of the company, to their abandoned camp just seven miles outside of Zwedru so that I would visit my rice farm. I went with him and when we reached his camp he gave his car keys to his driver to drive me to my farm eight miles away. I spent one whole week planting eddoes, plantains, potatoes, etc. My children in Monrovia had complained that the country rice cost them more to prepare, and so I decided that since the country rice which I had in abundance could not help them, I would plant those things that could substitute for the rice.

According to my request to my nephew before I left Jarkake, he was to pick me up on the 23rd of the month. Exactly on the 23rd of July, about ten that morning, his pickup braked in front of my house on the farm. After eating, we left the farm for lower Gedeh, passing through Zwedru the then deserted city. On the 24th of July, the next day, I left for Maryland County. As soon as I reached Maryland, it was learnt that all highways and roads in the country were not passable because of the rebel activities in the country. After spending a week or so in Harper City I went to my own village in upper Maryland. This time I was a village dweller again, but the village was not the way I knew it before. My parents were no more there. My father had died about three years before and my mother about two years. I went there without a single member of my family, family in a western sense. My estranged wife and child had fled to lower Gedeh and the rest of my children were in Monrovia. Such was a lonely life in my home village.

One morning I looked at my palms and I said to my God, "What will you find for me to do here? You know I am sickly and now I am away from all good medical facilities, what shall I do if I am attacked by this dreadful asthma? No doubt, this will spell death for me. What shall I do? I have no employment now, and so it goes without saying that I have no income. But I need to do some work in order to live. I strongly feel now that it is a necessity that I fully return to the soil. Before I was a Saturday rice farmer, but now I better get engaged in full time farming, but will my frail health permit me? God, this is your one-million-dollar-question."

I remained in the village and I got involved in doing something with my hands. I first started to make a garden, to plant eddoes, but there were many goats and sheep in the village. I needed to make a fence around the site before planting the crop. If not, the plant would be eaten up as soon as I put it into the ground. To prevent the intruding animals, I made a fence. The eddoes were planted and around the fence I planted butter beans.

One the 29th of November, 1990, I resolved to go into rice farming. This seemed funny to my villagers and so they asked me in a very scornful way, "How can a single man, this is, a man without a wife, successfully cultivate a rice farm?" I told them, "Don't worry, you will definitely see it done by a man without a wife."

Let me trace 1990 a bit backward. At the end of August, I was short of some provisions. My radio set and torch light had run out of battery and so I went to Harper to see what help the bishop could give me. Usually I lodge with my cousin Alphonsus Davis in his Middlesex home in East Harper, but this time I was told that the Davis family had gone to a town in the countryside, I guess, to hide their heads from the flying bullets and so therefore I became the guest of the bishop in his mansion also in East Harper. The bishop adequately supplied my needs.

One afternoon, a Catholic priest who was on his way to travel to America was caught in the war in Monrovia, but later found his way through the Republic of Ivory Coast to Harper. Upon his arrival, Father Frank told his horrible story of his ordeal to us at the bishop's house. Bishop Dalieh then told him that he would like for the priest to tell the story of his terrifying ordeal to the parishioners of the St. Theresa Parish tomorrow at mass. The next morning, Bishop Dalieh and I went to mass where the priest narrated his bitter experience of his narrow escape: "In a jeep driven by the bishop on our way home to his house in East Harper, just at the intersection of the road going to Harper airfield and the other going to the bishop's house, we met a child soldier who said to us, 'Halt!' and then added, 'The commander say you must come just now!' The bishop turned to me and asked, 'Will you come with me?' 'No,' I told him. But he said, 'It is drizzling, will you walk under the rain?' 'It doesn't matter; I just don't want to be involved with the Krahn soldiers who think that the Grebo people are no part owners of our native Liberia.'

Just as I was entering the bishop's house I looked behind me to see the bishop's jeep being driven by himself followed by a pickup load of heavily armed soldiers. The pickup was earlier seized from the Catholic Diocese of Cape Palmas. With this I rushed into the house to secure my little provisions the bishop provided me with, as I knew the Krahn soldiers were marauders in army uniform. On my way out, I met the soldiers in the bishop's dining room where the uncouth soldiers were shouting at the bishop, 'Open the doors!' They rushed here and there, searching for what? The bishop was lucky that the contingent of armed men was under the command of a non-commissioned Grebo officer who ordered the soldiers not take away property of the bishop except what was reported that the bishop had. According to them, the information they received from some unnamed source in Harper was that the bishop was the agent of Charles Taylor, the insurgent and leader of the rebel organization called National Patriotic Front of Liberia that had infiltrated into every part of Liberia. Bishop Dalieh, we were told, had received arms and ammunitions for the Taylor-led rebels and was requested to place the mission vehicles at the disposal of the Taylor rebels when they show up in Maryland County. Also, according to the information, Bishop Dalieh used the mission radio to communicate with Taylor everyday. 'The order is,' Sgt. Wallace reminded the soldiers, 'seize any radio, arms, or ammunition you might find in here. Besides those, don't touch any other property of the bishop.' They searched and found no trace of guns and ammunitions, except the mission radio set, and that was seized and taken away with the bishop to the barracks."

The bishop did not come back to his house until about two that afternoon. He came with some people for lunch and together we ate lunch. "Well, Reeves, it was your plan to leave today. I was going to drive you to Pleebo myself and then you would take a bus from there to your home. But presently I am not in the mood to drive. I will ask my driver to take you to Pleebo." This was on the 31st of August, 1990. Immediately, the driver and I left for Pleebo where I spent the night. Early Saturday morning, the first of September, I rode with the market women from Pleebo to Karloke. From Karloke, with my bag on my back I made the three hour trek to my village.

At about six Tuesday morning, September 4, 1990, my brother woke me up saying there were alarming sounds of guns in the Karloke area. "What must I do with sounds of guns?" sleepily, I questioned him. He said, "But the sounds are strange and I guess it is the war we have been hearing about." I said, "If the war is here, what do you think we should do now?" I collected myself from my mattressless bed and went into the bathroom. While there, I heard a thunderous sound from the Karloke area. The problem was, how were we going to know exactly what was going on in such a distant place with no means of modern communication? There was nobody to answer such a pressing question. But later in the day some young men mustered the courage and went to Karloke to find out what all the shooting was about. They returned to say that it was the NPFL rebels that attacked the government soldiers at their checkpoint in Karloke, leaving six government soldiers and two civilians dead, including a woman killed in the cross fire. Truly the wildfire of war had engulfed Maryland.

I continued to live some kind of a life in the village. I was lonely but I was not sad. I was not happy either as I tried to live my life the way it was. Sometimes, the going was tough, but one good thing was my poor health showed some sign of improvement. For money, I had an adequate sum of money but what was gradually depleting my coffers was I had to exchange JJ (the Liberian currency) with CFA (the Ivorian currency). I remembered once I had no soap, kerosene, etc., and everything was out. With the little money left in my pocket I became parsimoniously prudent. But I needed those things that were of necessity to my well-being. One morning I realized without those things I was going to face serious health problems. I cried out, "Oh my God, where shall I find money to meet the necessities of my displaced life?" And then I thought for a while. "Oh yes, way back in this village my father taught me something and I am going to use it to make money to buy things I need." And what was that? That old village militiaman taught me how to make mats, the kind we sleep on. And so I took hold of my cutlass and right behind one of the huts in the village there were plenty of the leaves used to make mats. I cut as many leaves as I needed. As I was cutting the leaves, everybody in the village became concerned and began to murmur among themselves, "But what is he going to do with them? He doesn't know how to make mats. Perhaps he knew it before, but he has been away from the village for rock of ages. Does he still remember how to do it?" Sooner or later, they would find out that their question would be answered in a spectacular affirmative. As soon as I finished cutting those thorny leaves, I hauled them under the eve of the house. With my sharp penknife I cut the thorns off, put them in the sun, and by three that afternoon, they had withered to satisfaction and I rubbed, folded, and stocked them over fire in the hut. A day or two following, I hauled them down and rubbed and wove them into mats—two mats. That week Thursday some young women were going to Grabo in Ivory Coast to sell each for five hundred CFA each. I made two other mats for the same price. Laboriously and earnestly I earned CFA one thousand five hundred, the money that bought me plenty of the things I needed: a liter of kerosene, two pair of battery, laundry and bath soap, etc. Certainly I dropped my bucket where I was and it was filled with refreshing cold water.

Afterward I told the villagers that if they would only make use of what they know and can do, they would make better living. They were worrying, or least they were feeling funny that something I was taught to do when I was about eight years old, I could still do it after about fifty long years. They forgot to know that anything that is learned and mastered is yours for life. My making the mats was the impressive evidence.

On the tenth of September, 1990, when I was sitting down thinking about my new village life, a radio announcement over BBC said that President Doe was captured by the Independent National Patriotic Front of Liberia (INPFL) headed by General Prince Johnson. I was very sad that Doe had lost his young life. On the other hand, I was happy as I thought it was the end of the bloody civil strife. In no veiled terms, Charles Taylor had told the victimized Liberian nation that he would kick President Doe out of the Executive Mansion. Taylor did not, but evidently Doe was dead and out. The broad road leading to the Executive Mansion was then wide open for Mr. Taylor to march and occupy the place he wanted at the expense of the precious blood of Liberians and their sovereignty. But instead of that, Mr. Taylor drilled another wedge into the Liberian nation by putting more than half of the little West African nation under his exclusive and unlawful rule.

1991 found me a busy rice farmer, this time a full time rice farmer. My labor was not in vain at all. My rice farm yielded plenty; in other words, the harvest was very large.

In December, 1991, I was asked to attend a workshop, a development workshop of the Catholic Diocese of Cape Palmas on the Catholic Mission in Pleebo. This workshop was to draw up strategy for the reorganization of the diocesan schools of the Cape Palmas Diocese. At the end of the meeting, I was named on the committee to make on-the-spot assessment of all the schools within the Cape Palmas Diocese. With me on the committee was Sister Marilyn Singh. A two-person committee, we in person visited all the schools of the Cape Palmas Diocese except that of Zlehtown. Early in January, 1992, we reported our assessment findings to the ad hoc school committee of which we were part. After the committee report I went back to the village to plant some cassava and other crops.

Chapter XXVI "The Diocese Reassigns Me"

On one bright morning in February, 1992, while I was sharpening my cutlass to carry on some improvement in my garden in the village, a special emissary from Bishop Dalieh arrived in the village. "I am here to summon you, oh no, to arrest you as the bishop told me to bring you alive or dead, as he urgently needs you at his diocesan headquarters in Harper City," Edward Smith, the bishop's messenger asserted. "What is happening in Harper? What does the bishop want of me, a desperately displaced man in this isolated village almost short of every necessity of wholesome life?" I seriously demanded. A life friend and my spiritual leader was in urgent need of me, according to Mr. Smith. To my sense of patriotism it was like a clarion call to active teaching duty again and so I was pulled away from the village and to Harper I went.

In Harper I met Most Reverend Boniface Nyema Dalieh, Bishop of the Catholic Diocese of Cape Palmas. "Nyanbeju, Blobaa, welcome to the City of Harper, County of Maryland, Republic of Liberia, West Africa," my old friend sweetened me up with those high honor Grebo expressions. "According to our reorganization plans for the diocesan schools, we need to many, many ground works before we can open the schools. Presently the Christian Health Association of Liberia will conduct a Trauma Healing workshop for our teachers and prospective teachers of the diocese and I would request you to coordinate the workshop. It will last for about a week. By the way, it seems that two persons of those to conduct the workshop know you personally as they have been asking about you, a Deana Isaacson and another lady," the bishop tried to beat up my interest for his workshop. I accepted.

During the workshop the bishop named and appointed me principal of Our Lady of Fatima High School, my dear alma mater in Harper City. This time the bishop happily succeeded in getting me to accept the principalship of the first senior high school in his diocese, which runs four senior high schools and a number of elementary and junior high schools which dot here and there in the counties of Grand Gedeh, Sinoe, Grand Kru, Maryland, and River Gee. Several times the bishop requested me to take the administration of Fatima. "This is the school you graduated from. Don't you think it is a big honor and pride to administer your dear alma mater?" the bishop cajoled. Often I told him that it was not my desire to leave my place near the water to go live on the hill where there is no water. "The School Sisters of Notre Dame who are members of my staff here at Bishop Juwle High School treat me like a blood brothers and the members of African staff honor me like a patriarch. With these generous men and women you want me to go live in isolation?" But this time when the senseless, so-called Liberian civil war drove me out, I acquiesced to his standing request because as Captain William D. Johnny of the Ninth Infantry Regiment once observed, "Necessity compels a free man to be a slave." I had no choice this time but to accept his so-called honorable position.

After the workshop there was no time enough for me to return to Kablake. In March, I was actively engaged in the onerous task of school administration in a war-torn country. This time school administration had more problems than ever before, as nothing was adequate in terms of instructional materials and absolutely necessary equipment for the smooth operation of schools. The prewar salary structure was far below the galloping high costs of living in our war ravaged country, Liberia. With the economic power of the whole country in shambles, how could we ably address the appalling dehumanizing situation? Our Lady of Fatima High School was no exception, but comparatively she was a have in a country where the masses of the schools were have-nots.

In addition to being principal of Fatima, I was serving also as coordinator of the Cape Palmas Diocesan School System. This was the work of the ad hoc Education Committee chaired by me. From March, 1992 to October, 1994, the schools all over the diocese, except that of Zlehtown, Gbarzon District, and Grand Gedeh County, having been reorganized, operated smoothly, that is, classes were conducted regularly, teachers were paid regularly, although the salaries were meager as they could not commensurate with the rocketing costs of living. With strong hope of better tomorrow, we were manfully coping. But sadly in mid October, 1994, a hot warring faction calling itself Liberian Peace Council (LPC) overran Maryland Country and drove us into exile in neighboring Republic of La Cote d'Ivoire, where I painfully tarried for fifteen long unbroken months.

In the Ivory Coast I settled in the Prefecture of Grabo, a growing countryside town nestled beneath towering hills covered with evergreen trees. Grabo is about sixty kilometers away from Tabou, perched on rocky hills overlooking the Atlantic Ocean and the headquarters of the region. It was strange and sad to experience in that region dominantly inhabited by the Grebo ethnic group of the Ivory Coast, the kin of the Grebo ethnic group in Liberia, to note that we were never treated like brothers and sisters by our Ivorian counterpart. To add insults to injury, our kins often referred to us as THOSE WHO RAN AWAY FROM WAR, the expression intended to ridicule us.

Long before the Liberian civil crisis, these Ivory Coast brothers and sisters of ours lived practically at the expense of the Liberian Grebo taxpayers. For example, their minor health problems were treated at the Webbo Health Center, located in the Township of Nyaake, Webbo, and the major ones calling for surgical operation were ably handled at the J.J. Dossen Memorial Hospital, Harper City. Such operations included hernias, hydrocele, elephantiasis of the scrotum, etc., etc., etc. These are the same people today who did not have name for us and could not permit us the disease-ridden refugees to attend their so-called hospitals and clinics infested with mosquitoes. But as God would have it, I was quite aware that I was outside of my country, and if I had any pride about myself, this was the time to swallow it and live the kind of life my God was providing me there. On the whole, as I observed it, the whole world was deceived during the onslaught of the Liberian refugees into the Ivory Coast. The octogenarian, Houphoute Boigny, the president of the Ivory Coast, told the listening world that Liberians running away from the war in Liberia would be treated as friends and brothers by the people of that sisterly state. The Liberians would be catered to as they would be housed by their Ivorian brothers and sisters. The hoary president emphasized that there was no need for refugee camps. The papi lied to the world. As soon as the misery inflicted Liberian refugees settled in those privately owned houses, each landlord or landlady demanded rental fee from each refugee who was said to have been fraternally housed. From where would a miserable refugee find money to pay rent? And rent we paid until some refugees in the countryside and even in Tabou decided to build some structures for themselves. And so was our plight with our kins and our next-door neighbors, the people of the Ivory Coast.

My worst experience came about when my younger brother was very sick in Grabo and I decided to take him to Tabou for medical treatment. It was during the heavy rainy season (October), the same we have in Liberia about the same month. The dirt motor road was scarred with potholes everywhere. In a duazet Renault bus on our way to Tabou, the bus jumped into a hole and bounced up and an iron bar in the bus lacerated deeply above my brother's left eye. Everybody in the bus was terrified, seeing the blood gushing from the emaciated refugee. I calmed them down although my brother was still bleeding almost profusely. "When we arrive in Tabou we will just take him to a hospital, where, I hope, he will be taken care of, with the bus owner being responsible to settle the bill with the hospital for the treatment," I solicited. But sadly to say that when we reached Tabou and we disembarked, when I requested the driver and his mates to take my brother to the hospital, they inhumanly disobliged. "We cannot take him to the hospital. You take him there and bring us the bill," they uncompromisingly declared. "There is nothing wrong with what you are suggesting, but the hard fact is that this is my first time in Tabou and the next barrier is that I do not speak or understand your language, French. Please help me. Don't let my sick brother die here for the want of care," I begged.

While I was humbly pleading and appealing to their consciences, the driver with his mates drove away from my sight. I took the case to the Transport Union. "Take your brother to the hospital and bring us the bill and the union will compel the bus owner to pay the bill," the union followed suit. Luckily for me, a fellow Liberian refugee, a physician assistant, a indigenous man of mine, suddenly appeared one the scene. Almost at the brink of bursting into tears, I narrated my story. "Come with me now, I'll take care of him," Nyanye Musu, J.J. Dossen Memorial Hospital health worker in Harper, Maryland County, Liberia, relieved me.

All was not bleak in the Ivory Coast. There was a young medical doctor, Yassi Modeste, who took special interest in me, a very sickly man. Each time I went to the hospital, he would see to it that the drugs he prescribed for me would be made available always. By this special attention I was well taken care of in a country where refugees were not considered as human beings. But William Reeves was in the humanitarian eye of Doctor Modeste and for this I was sincerely grateful for his filial care.

In early 1994, while I was still in Liberia, I requested Bishop Dalieh to allow me to go to Ghana for treatment of my failing eyesight. The bishop consented and placed a four-door pickup at the disposal of some parishioners also seeking medical health in that distant country. Through Tabou we left for Abidjan on our way to the Republic of Ghana. Later that afternoon, we departed the Ivorian-Ghanaian border for Ghana. With Edward Smith, the chief mechanic of the Cape Palmas Diocese, in full control of the wheel, we embarked on a one hundred forty-two kilometer journey to Tarkaridi, Ghana. At about ten o'clock that night, we landed at a gate manned by military personnel in Tarkaridi. We were briefly questioned about our destination.

"We are going to Accra for medical attention," Smith told the soldiers. "Come with us," the soldiers ordered. With them we went to a place that was, surprisingly, a military installation. There we were told that we would not be allowed to continue our journey but rather we would be sent back the next day. Impulsively, we asked, "Why?" The rebel factions of your civil war are in a peace conference here in Ghana. Hoping to bring peace to your country, the Ghana government learned with dismay that some Liberian refugees here in Ghana are planning to kill one of the rebel leaders, Charles Taylor. It is because of this we received strict orders to send back immediately any and all Liberians wanting to enter our borders. Tomorrow you shall be escorted back to the borders and across," the looking no-nonsense soldiers pronounced. We were quartered at Charge of Quarters' cells. In reality we were prisoners, and virtually we were! Thick army blankets were given us. My eleven-year-old son and I cuddled together for the long, weary night in a cell swarmed with mosquitoes.

My daughter Felicia in America had adequately provided for the trip and so I thought to take her baby brother along, but unfortunately, the next morning our official escort ordered us to load our baggage onto our pickup. One of the soldiers took the front with Mr. Smith, the seat I had during the journey. I was then ordered to get in the back of a military vehicle in which the commander of escort positioned himself in the front seat. "I am sorry; I cannot ride in the back of a truck to travel over the one hundred forty-two kilometer distance. I cannot compromise my health. I am an asthmatic person and riding in the back of a truck over that long distance will spell death for me even before we reach the end. Let me ride in our pickup and you escort us as you wish," I vigorously stressed. With this, I was given a seat with the driver of their truck, where the commander of the escort had seated himself. Was I second in command then? At the borders the soldiers went through the exit and entry procedures for us, both on their side and the Ivory Coast. As soon as that was done, we were on our way back to Liberia.

Although I was refused entrance into Ghana because of the so-called rebel factions' meeting in Ghana, I still had reason to visit that West African country from where my father accumulated many of his lofty ideas about good living. My father was a lover of good food. Each time he enjoyed such a dish, he would make an expression that did not sound like our native dialect. Beaming with broad smiles after drinking some water, he would splash the water from his mouth and then would say loudly, like a libation, "Wyame wo soro; ena me wo jem." Since in the conservative Grebo tradition, children should only be seen and not heard, I could not ask my father what was he talking about. But one day, full of curiosity and eagerness, I ventured to inquire, "Baa, what does this your favorite expression mean?" In the manor of gratified achievement, the one-time employee in the Gold Coast said, "Well, you have to go to Down De Coast to learn the people's language, I mean the Fanti people. My son," he continued, "it pays to travel. Truly, the language is strange." he added, The Fanti man says and I say with him in that strange language, 'God is up there and I am down here,' meaning, as God is God up there so he is a man down here." In short, this mortal Fanti man thinks and believes that he holds equal rank with God. Of course, my father's fantastic stories about the Gold Coast knew no end.

His description of Accra was far beyond my youthful imagination. The distance he said Accra covered mystified as there was nothing in my infantile memory I could associate with his description. Our own village, Kablake, had about twelve habitable huts at that time. The largest town, Worteke, in the whole of the Gedebo group, had about one hundred huts. The old Gold Coast worker's dimensions of Accra seem to suggest that Accra took in the complete length and breadth of the Gedebo country. "One town?" inwardly I questioned. Greatly amazed by this amazing fact, I wondered whether I could one day visit Accra or the Gold Coast, now the Republic of Ghana, for that matter. My father's other wonder was of a store, which he called Kingsway in Accra. His description of the store again was a mystery for my infantile imagination. All these interesting but baffling stories surged in me a burning desire to visit the Fantiland.

My Gold Coast educated elementary school arithmetic and English teacher, Mr. Peter W. Kun of sainted memory, a native of Betu in Grand Kru county, Liberia, added to my storehouse of stories from the Gold Coast. Teacher Kun told us, my classmates and me, that Accra and London in England were on the same latitude. And so when it was twelve o'clock midday in London, it was twelve midday in Accra. The time in London was announced by the booming of a clock called Big Been at Westminster Abbey and that of Accra was announced by the booming of a cannon.

Some time in late 1994, I heard a live interview by BBC Question Box, Robbin White, over Network Africa. The man being interviewed was Ephaim Kwaku Amu at his home in Peki Avetile, a celebrated ninety-five-year-old musician and rediscoverer of African Heritage. With a horse and sinking voice, Dr. Amu narrated his stories about his African lifestyle and work as a musician. Again, there was another urge for me to go Ghana to see this world-famous African musician physically in his hometown.

The silly so-called Liberian civil war had finally driven me out of my motherland into the Ivory Coast in mid-October, 1994. I took refuge in the Prefecture of Grabo. Sooner or later my eyes began to bother me. Inquiring about from where to get medical help for my eyes, I was advised to go to Accra, Ghana. "Ghana again, will I be admitted this time?" I cried. "Well, I'll try again" I urged myself. On the second of January, 1995, the trip having being adequately provided for by my daughter Quiade, I boarded the bus for Abidjan on my way to Ghana.

My first night in Ghana was spent in a Liberian refugee camp called Bujumbura. The next day I found myself on the way in search of my friends, Mr. and Mrs. Alfred Slue Barbley, Liberian refugees from Zwedru. I was told that they were living a few kilometers outside of Accra, the Ghanaian capital. At twelve midday my guide, Miss Dekontee Tarlue, a former Bishop Juwle High School student now a refugee in Ghana, and I arrived at the site called Square, where the imposing, majestic, towering telecommunications building stands. This time, the twelve midday was announced in Accra by a bellowing siren instead of a cannon as my teacher told us it used to be, a progressive and positive step forward from the colonial period to independent nationhood. On hearing the siren I shouted, "What a wonderful and happy coincidence." I continued, "Teacher, your story told us is as true as you told us." But there was no way I could verify the coincidence whether the Big Ben with its mighty pendulum struck at the same time. In the meantime, we stopped at the telecommunications building and briefly I announced my arrival in Ghana over the telephone to my daughter Felicia in Elizabeth, New Jersey, United States of America

From the Square, my guide and I traveled on a bus going to Nsawan. Midway between Accra and Nsawan, we disembarked near a village called Kutunse, where the Government of Ghana has its satellite station. Within that vicinity the Worldwide Church of God has its retreat camp. Here Alfred and his large family were housed and hospitably, adequately, and regularly maintained by the gracious and caring church. In this wholesome surrounding I met my personal friends, Alfred and Lilian Barbley with their happily growing children, all refugees from Zwedru, Liberia. The reunion was the happiest during the ugly and silly war that destroyed our onetime land of peace and love. As a concrete sign of welcome by the Barbleys for their old friend, a huge drake lost its head. One thing was certain at last; I was in this famous Down De Coast or Gold Coast, now the Republic of Ghana, a full-fledged independent West African country, after many, many years of British exploitative rule.

In the Gold Coast, could I in reality see Accra and other sites in my father's fantastic tall tales about Accra and its environs? A few days following my arrival in that culture-conscious country, I visited many parts of that vast, densely populated city. From my personal estimation, my father's dimensions of the Ghanaian capital fell far below mine. His much-talked-about Kingsway Store did not look like anything that much according my father's description of the store. It was just like any ordinary Lebanese store in Liberia. In mid-February, 1970, in New York City, United States of America, I shopped at a store (Macy's) said to be the largest in the world. I guess this experience of mine destroyed the supposed vastness of the Kingsway Store as seen by the old Gold Coast worker, who gloried in his experiences he vicariously shared with me about that former British colony.

Having physically seen Accra and the much-talked-about Kingsway Store, I was then thinking about when to journey to Peki Avetile to visit the grand old teacher, musician, and the rediscoverer of African Heritage. One night while my eyes and attention were glued and focused on the television screen, a cortege rolled in: a funeral procession of Dr. Ephraim Kwaku Amu. The veteran teacher I thought I would be blessed to talk with personally was being escorted to his eternal resting place. No doubt, I was out of luck. The renowned African musician's family and their home were still in Peki Avetile, but the reason for my planned visit was shattered by the death of my African hero.

Since Ghana, unlike Liberia, is one of the African countries where the "book people" write about themselves or others, I surmised that I would, while in Ghana, find some literature on Dr. Amu. After Dr. Amu's funeral, a day or two following, Teacher Amu's dismissal from the Presbyterian Akropong Teacher Training College was dramatized on the television screen. The glimpses gathered from the drama about the rediscoverer of the African Heritage enlightened and enkindled my desire to search around for information about the shining life of my honorable African. Luckily for me, Dr. Amus's biography, written by a learned retired journalist, Fred M. Agyemang, was on a bookstand in Accra. Alfred bought me a copy.

In a day or two I devoured the one hundred and ninety-three page well-written biography of the teacher-catechist and African musician, giving me a clear insight into how the trained teacher-catechist of the Presbyterian Church of Gold Coast rediscovered his African heritage and promoted it at all costs. Indeed, from his biography by versatile Mr. Fred Agyemang, a teacher, writer, and journalist, I wish I could relive my youthful days so that I would learn to recourse to my/our beautiful African culture, which I love beyond mere description of words. This is my fond reason why I thought to seize the glimpses of the noble African lifestyle of Dr. Ephraim Kwaku Amu, the African, thinking that someone might find interest in reading this, my obscure life story, and get inspired by the flashes of Dr. Amu's African way of life.

Ephraim completed his four year teacher and catechist training course at Abetiff in December of 1919. The work of a Presbyterian teacher-catechist in those days, according to Mr. Agyemang, could be described as between that of an ordained pastor and a teacher-evangelist. It was one of teaching, preaching, and living a life of good example in the school, in the Christian community, and in the town or village. In this expectation the Presbyterian Church authorities consecrated Amu and his classmates. It is said that from then on a teacher-catechist could eventually be ordained as a minister of the Gospel in the church after a minimum of fifteen years service as a catechist. My source said that Kwaku began to nurse this secretly in his heart as his life's ambition to become one day an ordained minister in the church.

Mr. Agyemang observed that the prospect of Mr. Amu's going to church someday in his indigenous African attire had earlier attracted, agitated, and challenged Amu a great deal. Amu thought and urged that it was more hygienic, more suitable, and more convenient than the warm European clothes with starched collars and tightly knotted neckties, which every teacher-catechist was obliged to wear either for preaching or on special days, like Good Friday and Communion service days. Amu further expounded that the African cotton dress which could be washed every week had the additional advantage of allowing for more circulation of air. The whole idea of a European type of dressing in the warm tropics did not make sense to cultural avant-garde Ephraim Amu.

The way Amu saw it, to preach in a long black European ministerial gown sort of separated a minister socially and culturally from the indigenous members of his African congregation. Our teacher-catechist would like as a minister to take up the children in his arms and embrace them. If, in so doing, Amu argued, his tropical cloth got soiled, he could easily wash it, but in the long black seemingly untouchable sacerdotal Geneva gown and white starched front strips, few ministers would attempt to or think of lifting children of the congregation in their arms, let alone, embrace them, being more careful of their gowns than to let the children come unto them, in the manner of Jesus who hugged children to his breast in his work day dress.

One day in 1931, when it came to his turn to preach, Amu decided in his zeal to match conviction with action, to go in his African attire. He conducted the entire service of liturgy, reading of scriptural texts, calling of hymns, preaching the sermon, prayers, and benediction in his African attire. This caused quite a stir. Amu was acquiring the image of an iconoclast more so when this coincided with his development of the construction and use of indigenous African musical instruments:

234

flutes, drums, etc. He had crossed the Rubicon. With his conviction matched with his action, Amu was finally dismissed. For me, Amu's dismissal was glorious because he was sacked for what he believed was the right thing. I think it was the late American Human Rights activist, Dr. Martin Luther King, Jr. who said that he who does not have a cause to die for does not worth living.

It would appear that the western missionaries had determined to rob the whole of Africa of its *Africanism*, of the unique things that make her *Africa*. Long before the Western missionaries came to these beautiful shores of Africa, the ethnic group called Grebo in the Grebo country in Southeastern Liberia were ardent and steadfast worshippers of many idols which the missionaries called gods, but they steadfastly and unequivocally believe in *One Supreme God*, gloriously called *Nyansowa*. Perhaps the Grebo group was not Christian, but their belief in that One Supreme Being was unchangeable. This vast ethnic group had its own God-given identity, culture, customs, and traditions. I suppose those foreign missionaries came to Christianize the already faithful worshippers of God Almighty. But instead of preaching the *good news* of how and why Jesus died on the cross to redeem mankind from sins, they stealthily imposed their culture on us, kicking off our African *uniqueness*.

Now as before, the western world always grades us Africans below the normal human living standards. Writing comparatively in his poem entitled, The Traveler, Oliver Goldsmith, one of the most notable 18th century English writers, told the literate world that the Africans were naked and were panting at the line. And so the missionaries came with huge consignments of wearing apparels as one of the baits to lure the Africans to accept Christianity. As token for the acceptance of the Christian faith, the Africans (Grebo) were given those oversized frocks, coats, trousers, shirts, etc., etc. Our freed brothers and sisters from the United States of America and elsewhere, bearing their acquired culture, felt compelled to stick to to their alien culture because the Grebo had stupidly relinquished his culture.

In the Grebo country, the wearing of a Kwi lady dress suggested that the lady who wore the western style of dress was literate. The "Suku Marys," those converted to the Christian faith, saturated Eastern Province and Maryland County. Reverend Joseph W. Andrews, now resting with his God in eternity, told us an interesting story about those many unlettered women. He said that in the early 1920s when he was in school, it was common to see those gaily dressed women in their oversized frocks, superfluously dressed, attending literary programs. According to him, as they came in, each was given a hymnal. Those 'Suku Marys" pretended singing with their hymnals turned upside down. Through this, illiteracy blossomed and prospered in both Maryland County and Eastern Province.

My whole belief was that only literate women in Liberia wore dresses, except the Suku Marys, whose conversion to the Christian faith had dressed them in borrowed robes, which in turn culturally misplaced them.

In the sixth grade, for the first time in my life, I saw some handwriting of a woman dressed in African costume, commonly called "lappa suit." This young woman came from Togoland in West Africa. She wrote in the copybook of my classmate Felicia Gadegbeku. Seeing the strange handwriting in her exercise book, I suddenly asked, "Feli, whose handwriting is this?" "The woman you saw sitting with me in our house the other day," Felicia replied. "Are you saying it is the lappa woman's writing?" I fingered her further. "Yes, that woman is a college graduate," my classmate asserted.

As ignorance blurred my thinking, I was not convinced and so the next day, to find out one way or the other, without any yardstick, I went to the home of the Gadegbekus to personally talk with the African lady. How could I determine whether the lady had attained that level of education since I was just a sixth grade student? Luckily for me, on reaching the Gadegbeku home, I met Old Man Gadegbeku himself. In a whispering tone, pointing in the direction of the young Togolese lady, I asked the old sage, "Is that lady educated?" Proudly the old man replied, "Yes, she is my niece and she is a college graduate." "And she wears lappa?" ignorantly I queried. "But, Rees, don't you know that that is the African dress?" the old man enlightened me.

Somewhere in the 1970s, US Peace Corps/Liberia cited me to a workshop held at Kakata Rural Teacher Training Institute. Many people in education in the country were in attendance. On the day of the workshop the participants were assembled in a classroom on that campus. Having seated us, the convenor requested that one of us should take the marker to jot down the points to be discussed. The first to volunteer was a US Peace Corps female volunteer but she was rejected on the ground that the workshop was a Liberian workshop. A Liberian lady, with a ready smile, well proportionate, gaily dressed in what they called "flamingo," volunteered to do the writing for the workshop. With her headtie sweeping the ceiling of the room, our young Liberian lady took possession of the marker. At once I sucked my teeth at her as the sign of scorn for her. I turned my back at her and inwardly I derided, "Liberian women like this empty bluff. I hope she will not disgrace us." Thinking with Hardcastle in Oliver Smith's "She Stoops to Conquer," I added, "What superfluous silk she is wearing!"

Evidently, to me, this was a clear manifestation that educated Liberian women had begun to think African as they gradually were recoursing to their culture, dressing the way an African lady should. I had no idea who this our workshop volunteer was. Secondly it was strange, very strange, for me to have seen an educated, very educated Liberian lady. Dorothy Musleng Cooper did not deserve my seemingly unreasonable scorn. Efficiently, legibly, and correctly Musleng jotted down the workshop points for discussion. Unknown to her, she captured by admiration and love for her. For the first time in my life I boldly grabbed a strange woman's hand and asked her, at our tea break, to sit with me at the same table so that I would personally talk with her. Dorothy and I sat together as close as two peas in a pod and conversed during the whole period of the break. Before the break ended, I mustered yet another courage and said to her, "Dorothy, without reservation, I admire and love you for all you stand for." I drew more tightly my manhood cap and added, "I have not seen or met so educated a Liberian woman as you. I wish I could meet you every now and then," I sincerely implored.

I did meet Musleng as frequently as ever, as both of us were working for the United States Peace Corps/Liberia Education Training Program. She was my director and I served as her site administrator in Zwedru, Grand Gedeh County. She was my constant example I cited for my female students to emulate.

Exploiters of Africa came (and still come) in different guises. The missionaries under the guise of the Good News about our risen Lord Jesus Christ told us, "Close your eyes and let us pray." As we closed our eyes and prayed, our riches, including our rich culture, were stealthily snatched away. Paradoxically, Africa is but the richest continent under the sun. According to Oliver Goldsmith, "Man's best riches are his ignorance of wealth." I guess, no doubt it guarantees one's happiness and security. Attracted by this great wealth of Africa the exploiters descended on us in unbelievable numbers.

The missionaries, especially the Penecostal missionaries, built what they called Bible Institutes in Maryland County and Eastern Province, Grand Gedeh County, where they taught illiterate adults how to read the Holy Bible. To my mind, the Holy Bible is the hardest and most complicated piece of literature, written by those learned and inspired men of God, to comprehend. It takes a highly trained person to understand the Bible and to interpret it. These illiterate adults without any formal literary background learned how to read the word of God and to preach it accordingly. How possible is it? This results in the funny and misleading interpretation of the Holy Scriptures. For example: St. John 14:I, "Let not your heart be troubled, ye believe in God believe also in me." Hear the shocking interpretation of that passage by our illiterate Bible readers: "Don't drink cane juice. No woman business." How and why? This spreads ignorance and increases the mockery of the Gospel.

I had come to Ghana for many reasons: a visit with the venerable rediscoverer of African Heritage and musician, Dr. Ephraim Kwaku Amu, my failing health, especially my eyes, and some of the sites my father's stories made historic in and around Accra. I also intended to inquire whether there was any possibility of a hospital that could rid me of my hernia with little or no cost to the penniless refugee like me.

For about two long weeks the Barbleys and I had narrated our respective sad stories about our refugee experiences. Comparatively, mine was more bitter than the Barbleys." In the Republic of the Ivory Coast, where I was residing, the inhuman treatment by our kinsmen and kinswomen, with whom their grand old President Houphey Boigny told the anxiously listening world that we would be at home away from home, humiliated us. This was a blatant lie the president told just before he left this turbulent world for his eternal rest.

In mid-January, 1995, while I was still with the Barbleys in Ghana, Alfred had gathered that an eye clinic, the Christian Eye Clinic, Cape Coast, Ghana, had an excellent reputation for the treatment of eyes. Going to Cape Coast would mean tracing my steps back to the Ivory Coast border from whence I came. This would also require extra money from the stranded refugee's no-money pocket. "I shall call my daughter Quiade over the telephone and request for more money as it is a must that I take care of my ailing eyes." With this, Alfred and I journeyed to the Cape, where the heartless African kings sold their brothers and sisters into slavery and from where the slave traders exported their purchased laborers.

237

The Christian Eye Clinic delivered well its service of examination and treatment of my eyes. The total cost for transportation, to and fro, examination, treatment, and lunch amounted to sixteen thousand cedis. Roughly that was a little less than ten US dollars. That did not put an extra hole in the refugee's pocket.

Having received the satisfactory attention from the Christian Eye Clinic, I then exclusively devoted my time in acquiring information about the Ghanaian world, especially their world of education. Eagerly I read their brief history of education and other stories about their colonial past and nationhood. They all charmed me considerably. While the Liberian nation, the oldest African independent country, was counting her empty years of independence in no concrete terms, the young Ghanaian independence was being measured in concrete terms, in what the nation had industriously, economically, and politically achieved during those short years of independent nationhood. The way I saw it, their education system and public life were systematized.

On reading about their education, I discovered that during their colonial period educational opportunities were in abundance. This was the time many Liberians, including my father, in search of livelihood, visited the Gold Coast, now the Republic of Ghana. What troubled me was why my father did not grasp the golden opportunity of learning how to read and write. According to my teacher who taught me in the elementary school, he obtained his education in the Gold Coast when he was also in search of his livelihood. But, I guess, that young conservative Grebo man (my father) said to himself, "This book business ebe good for my man pekin; ebe my son will learn nam." No doubt, my father was thinking with the old Grebo King Freeman who told the missionary when the missionary advised the old king to put away all of his wives and marry one woman according to God's law, "That law ebe good for my man pekin, not for me. Put away all but one? Who will take care of the abandoned ones? God telling we, he say we must be kind and love one another," the African sage revealed profound knowledge of the holy book.

I wanted to take one stone to kill many birds. With the help of my former student, Adama Campore, serving as my guide and interpreter of French, I visited Lome, Togo, the native home of many of the leading men of the Township of Nyaake, Webbo. In late January, 1995, Adama and I boarded a bus for a ride on the ninety-five kilometer distance between the Ghanaian capital, Accra, and the Togolese capital, Lome. In Lome, we shopped for a few hours and we also strolled around to catch glimpses of some of the landmarks of that clean West African city. I noticed that the Togolese people were more friendly and more accommodative than their Ghanaian counterparts. My visit to both Ghana and Togoland had given me a brief insight into the ways of life of these two West African nations whose nationals migrate every now and then to Liberia for a greener pasture. In the meantime, the sponsor of my health-seeking journey to Ghana, my baby daughter Felicia, insisted that I should spend more time, say a month or two, with the hospitable and generous Barbleys. Generous and caring as they were, it was well known that they were refugees. "Why should I double their trouble?" I questioned Felicia, the little girl who wanted to demand that the hoary-haired man accept every suggestion of hers. But this one was vehemently rejected in no uncertain terms. Financially, I was beholding to her, but I am the papi. On the 30th of January, 1995, after barely a month's stay in Ghana, I returned to the Prefecture of Grabo in the Ivory Coast, where I tarried for the rest of the gloomy year.

238

Chapter XXVII "My Return to War-torn Liberia"

The demanding and sometimes sensible voice from Elizabeth, New Jersey, United States of America, sounded once more, "Since you uncompromisingly refused to spend a few months with your friends in Ghana, would you be willing to go to Monrovia where, I sincerely hope and believe, your children will take care of you when you are hospitalized and operated on?" Felicia pushed me against the wall. "Would my children take care of me while they were busy with their enticing and bustling city life?" I would like to know, but I had no choice as Felicia was my only financial and moral support at the time. Facing this hard glaring fact, I conceded. In early December, 1995, I packed my scanty belongings in preparation for my departure from Grabo to Tabou for my unwilling return to my war-ravaged country, Liberia. In mid-December, 1995, Felicia sent me two hundred US dollars to transport me by bus from Tabou to Abidjan and by air to Monrovia, the devastated nation's capital. From San Pedro I bought my air ticket on the seventeenth of December. The next day, at ten that night, I boarded the bus for Abidjan. To see me off was my then ten-year-old son Boniface. At the bus station my son suddenly asked, "Papa, will I never see you again?" The question went deep into my heart. "Yes, Boniface, you will see me again, the good Lord being our keeper," I assured my baby son. During my four long, weary year stay in Monrovia away from Boniface, his pricking question silently repeated itself a thousand times a day.

Throughout the long lonely night of my bus ride to Abidjan, I felt desperately sick. At many of the checkpoints, I could not get down from the bus to present my pass to the authority. A young Liberia traveling on the same bus helped me all along. At about five that morning, we safely arrived in Abidjan.

"Mr. Reeves, where are you going to wait for the plane?" my young Liberian anxiously queried. "On the airfield, I suppose," I coldly replied. Seemingly concerned, my son warned, "No, Mr. Reeves, if you do, all of your things will be stolen from you. I'll take you to my brother's house. I guess you know him. He is called Ambrose. Don't you know him?" my son pleaded. "I think I do. Is he not Ambrose Weah, a onetime teacher at the Zwedru Multilateral High School?" I shrewdly guessed. "Certainly, he is," the young man assured me. With him I went to his brother's house, where, surprisingly, I received a very warm welcome of hospitality by Ambrose's girlfriend who introduced herself as my daughter Felicia's friend. Secured, I relaxed for one or two hours before my young friends escorted me to the Ivorian International Airport, where we waited almost indefinitely until about twelve-fifty that sunny afternoon. At one we boarded the aircraft and precisely the air monster ascended into space. At two-twenty, that bright sunny afternoon, the flying lizard touched down on the James Spriggs Payne Airfield in Monrovia, Liberia, where, seemingly all the hungry people were hovering around. Completely I was confused on seeing the multitude of people probably on a looting spree. But swiftly a former student of mine at once led me out of that hurly-burly and whisked me off in a chartered taxicab directly to my daughter's office at the Liberia Telecommunications Building at the corners of Broad and Lynch Streets in Monrovia.

The reunion was memorable. This was the second time my children and I, excluding Felicia, were meeting since the senseless so-called Liberian civil war. Again I was with my children. God had wonderfully secured us from the nationwide carnage and mayhem.

It would appear that the Wilton Sankawolo-led Council of the State Interim Government of Liberia was loosely together. On the whole, as I keenly observed, the rebel leaders and Liberians in all walks of life were yearning for peace. The rebel leaders, now members of the Interim Government, sparked the weary hearts of the Liberian people with the high hope that slowly but steadily peace was in sight. But the without-principle behavior of power-oriented Taylor during the long wearisome peace process appeared to have no foundation in reality. The war-torn nation hung in the balance. Was my expectation unwarranted for the few-months-old interim Sankawolo Government? I am always an optimist and a Christian who does not allow himself to jump at conclusion rashly.

My January 19, 1996, arrival back in war-ravaged Liberia after languishing in the bigotry of the Felix Houphoet Boigny Ivorian Government for fifty hopeless months could lead a hapless soul to act impudently. But optimistically I looked on passively, while I busied reuniting myself with found sons, daughters, relatives, friends, and loved ones in and around Monrovia, where the homeless, hungry, sick orphans numberlessly abounded.

My first call was at the Dugbo Law Offices headed by the learned jurist, Counselor Frank W. Smith, Johnson Street, Monrovia. Upon inquiring about my elderly friend I was told that my Ator, because of ill-health, had not come to the office for about two weeks. "Well, I must find him at his residence when I get someone to give the direction to his house," I assured myself.

In late January, one solitary night, in the Frog Valley, in the estate of one Sante, where my daughter Christiana was renting, Christiana rushed into my room to relay the sad news just announced about the death of Counselor Frank W. Smith over some radio station in Monrovia. That self-taught wizard of law had been seized by the cold hands of death. The Grebo Blogba had lost a true son. The loss sustained by this vast ethnic group would be irreparable for untold years.

About two weeks following his demise, the mortal remains of Counselor Smith were released by the St. Moses Funeral home. The counselor was regally dressed in the robe of the kind the associate justices of Liberia wear to adjudicate cases in the Supreme Court of Liberia. But I could not understand and by which I was perplexed was for the first time I saw a dead man wearing shoes. Yes, on Counselor Smith's feet was an expensive pair of black shoes. Inwardly I questioned, "What is a dead man doing with shoes on his feet, an expensive pair, too? A whole one night wake keeping was conducted with the St. Moses Funeral Home singing band in full attendance.

As we huddled together in deep sense of Grebo mourning, it was also another golden opportunity of meeting relatives, friends and loved ones, and unprecedented reunions never experienced since the ugly Charles Taylor war, a war of personal willful revenge against the very government he was one of the leading members of who openly and brutally deprived the country and its bewildered people of their rights and property. It was during this time I met the daughter of my distance relative who suddenly asked me, "Uncle Reeves, where is my mother?" For sure, I did not know where her mother was. "Well, I cannot tell you exactly where your mother is. However, I left your mother on my farm in Zwedru. Before I left Zwedru I appealed to her that we should go back to our home in Gedebo but she totally refused, saying she had no close relatives in our home. She added that all her children were in Monrovia and, according to her, it did not make sense going eastward. With this, I reluctantly departed Zwedru for the Grebo country, having assured her I will take care of her as before, but to no avail," I narrated.

As Gertrude listened to my long story, I noticed that her countenance was gradually sinking into sobbing. "But, Gertrude, wait a minute, let me tell you what I learned about the situation in Zwedru in early 1995: a new hot warring faction, calling itself the Peace Council of Liberia, fiercely attacked Charles Taylor's rebels in Zwedru. According to the story, some of the inhabitants of Zwedru fled into neighboring Tapita, Nimba County, while others founded refuge in Tabou in the Ivory Coast. I personally met many of those who went to the Tabou region, but your mother was not seen and so I presume that she must have gone to Nimba. It is my strong belief that she is in Nimba," I speculated. But suddenly I added, "Since you young women travel more freely in war-devastated Liberia, I would ask you to go to Nimba in a diligent search for your dear mother." Gertrude nodded her head but made no verbal expression that she would search for her mother in Nimba. With this we parted from the funeral of Counselor Smith. This was mid-February, 1996.

In Frog Valley, Gay Town, Old Road, Sinkor, I continued to live some kind of way. In desperation I constantly lived as it would appear that my onetime useful and dutiful life had no direction again. My ill health was getting graver every day, but my children and my adopted son, Counselor Fredrick Doe Cherue, steadfastly continued to pay my increasing hospital bills. My doctor, Walter Brumskine, had advised me that I would undergo surgery on the 8th of April, 1996, a day following Easter Sunday.

It was Palm Sunday, the 31st of March, 1996. When I returned from the 10:30 mass, I met a young man said to be the son of Gertrude Wesseh, my niece. Slowly in a quivering voice the young man began, "Uncle Reeves, I came to tell you that our mother, your cousin, Targba Wreyah is dead." He continued, "the body is at the St. Moses Funeral Home in Gardnerville, Monrovia," That afternoon my daughter and I went to Duala, a suburb of Monrovia, where Gertrude resided.

Mournfully Gertrude told the story about the death of her mother as follows: "As you directed, I went to Tapita, Nimba County, in search of my mother. After a hard two days trucking on an almost no-road, I reached Tapita, Lower Nimba. I met my mother in company with her paramour in the home of a caring Tapita family. When I entered, my dear mother did not, though quite awake, even know that someone had entered, let alone, recognize who had entered. In a low voice, I called but she made no reply. I then placed my right hand on her shoulder, asking her, "Ayee, don't you know me?" After dimly looking in my face, my seriously sick mother smiled and said, "Oh Gertrude, my child," and then she broke down in tears. Bitterly we lamented, mama and I together. "I have come to take you to Monrovia, where your daughter Etta, my younger sister, prepared a whole house for you." "Yes, take me and my friend to Monrovia, my mother sadly pleaded. I stayed on for about a week, thinking that my sick people would gather some strength after nourishing them regularly with all the food I could get in Tapita. A week later I made arrangements with a truck driver for our journey to Monrovia. Of course, the long week feeding program served no useful purpose. However, with the arrangement in place, we departed Tapita. Between Tapita and Saclepea there was a dilapidated bridge. When we reached the bridge the driver requested that all the young people aboard should come down while the sick and old people should remain on the old truck. I descended, including the other able people. We crossed over on the other side of the bridge, waiting for the duazet truck to creep across successfully. To our utter surprise the bridge broke and the truck and every thing on board was sunk into the large body of water below. My mother and her friend were no exception. All had met their untimely death," Gertrude concluded her sad story. "No doubt, Gertrude," I sighed, "in sight of port sank many a vessel fair." The wake, without the body, would be held on that Friday (Good Friday), the fifth of April. Some Grebo women including my daughter and me went to the wake in Duala that Friday night. We spent the whole night at the wake.

But the week before, it would appear that the war-devastated country and its besieged people were being squarely placed on a time bomb again. According to news reports, there was a shoot-out in warlord Roosevelt Johnson's yard one night and reportedly the shooting left one man dead. Reports had it also that intransigent rebel leaders Taylor and Kromah, now members of the interim government under the chairmanship of Professor Sankawulo, were demanding that Teacher Johnson, a teacher turned general, be brought to justice as Liberia was and is a sovereign state and as such law and order must prevail. Johnson must be arrested and tried in the court having competent jurisdiction. The reports added that Taylor and Kromah were mobilizing their killer armies which arrogantly and adamantly they called government forces to arrest Johnson. The tension in Monrovia was moving at a strangulating speed. The demand of these two fiends posed many and varied political and legal questions:

1. Was there any army for the interim government, and if so, under whose command was this interim government army?
2. Was the defense of the country in the hands of warlords who insurgently, maliciously, and wantonly burned the sovereignty of the Liberian nation?
3. Was a warring faction amenable to other unlawful killers?

These and many were and are the protruding and glaring questions the sorrowing silent majority was asking and demanding the answers to from those unconstitutional power seekers. The impotent Sankawulo interim government sat supinely while Kromah and Taylor openly and arrogantly usurped his power.

Saturday, that woeful morning, while we were returning from the wake, unknowingly to us, the taxicab in which we were riding drove us as far as 15th Street in Sinkor to be told not to move any further. "Your lives will be in danger, if you go any further," a police officer warned. "There is a fierce battle going on between the combined Kromah and Taylor forces and Roosevelt Johnson on 19th Street," our friend revealed. About face we turned and our understanding taxi driver took us back to the Freeport on Bushrod Island. From there we took another taxi to the Red Light in Paynesvillle. Things appeared normal all along and so we gathered in another taxi to take us to our home on Old Road. At an ECOMOG checkpoint in Oldest Congotown, a suburb of Monrovia, we were told by the officer at the checkpoint that we should disembark from the taxi. "No car is allowed on this road. If you want to go on Old Road, you can try by foot only," grinning, the officer ordered. Unhappily we disembarked and on our feet we jumped. For about two or more hours we tramped to reach our home on Old Road. Between 11:00 and 12:00 that noon we were home.

At about three that afternoon, Monrovia was ablaze as the battle raged on Nineteenth Street. Kromah and Taylor virtually declared war again on the war-ravaged people of Liberia. The fleeing throngs inundated the suburb. Hastily, my children and I gathered some things and joined the people having no definite direction of where they were going. But where were we going? Wearily we journeyed somewhere, and after about an hour's trek, my children and I hid our heads from rattling bullets in Clara d'Almeida's house in Oldest Congotown, where we languished for three hopeless days.

The attempt-to-arrest-Roosevelt Johnson war went on unabatingly, but the actual battlefield was away from Old Road and so we took courage and came home. The war dragged on into the heart of Monrovia where it became more intensified as it laid waste to lives and property as Johnson was manfully determined never to submit to his fellow murderers, whose insurgent arrogance had failed them to see first the mote in their wanton killing eyes. I guess, no one attended that sunny Easter Sunday of April 7, 1996. Easter, an annual Christian festival in commemoration of the resurrection of Jesus Christ, this the core of the Christian faith. But, no doubt, all Christians fervently prayed on that day, imploring God to save them from the flying bullets.

For about a month, the war to arrest Johnson raged on in Monrovia. Under the able protection of his butt-naked fighting men, General Roosevelt Johnson took refuge, according to news reports, in the US embassy near Monrovia and subsequently left the country. A new interim government was set up again to see whether under the new leadership led by former Grand Cape Mount County Senator, Mrs. Lue Sando Perry, sanity would be restored to Liberia and Liberians, especially the warring factions. Hopes were high.

A pot calling the tea kettle black, Charles Taylor said that the Doe government was rampantly corrupt and had devastated the country and its people. On a Christmas Eve, the 24th of December, 1989, Charles Taylor, an alleged fugitive from law, an embezzler of huge sums of money from the broke Doe government, viciously attacked the peaceful people of Liberia, declaring in no veiled terms that he had come to overthrow the corrupt Doe regime. To me, the Doe government grossly underestimated this manly declaration of war of Mr. Taylor.

From Butuo, Nimba County, Charles Taylor and his supposedly well-trained militiamen besieged the whole country in no time, and so in a little less than a year, on October 10, 1990, CIC Doe was captured and subsequently killed by independent militiamen under the command of Prince Johnson, according to news reports.

The Doe government had fallen. Doe was no more. Charles Taylor's desire was met directly or indirectly. It was then Mr. Taylor's lot to occupy the Executive Mansion and take effective control of the Liberian government. Instead of this central move, Mr. Taylor clandestinely moved to Gbarnga, Bong County capital, where he established his self-styled "reconstruction government." From this point, the hardhearted rebel leader and his cohorts inhumanly continued to pillage the country and its bewildered people. The brutish rebel leader established what he called the National Patriotic Reconstruction Government, a division of the war-ravaged country that brought untold miseries and hate among the various ethnic groups of this small West African country and the oldest independent nation on the vast African continent. With this wedge of belligerence placing each ethnic group on warring camps against each other, Liberia is no more a place where once Freedom raised her glowing form. The burning question the silent majority of the devastated people of Liberia are asking Mr. Taylor is, "Mr. Taylor, why did you establish a new government in Gbarnga when the Liberian government you fought violently to control had fallen by the death of President Doe?" Like the silent majority of the violently dislodged people of Liberia, here I have a problem with Mr. Taylor.

The way I saw it, although I do not believe in violence, I strongly felt that our country was being poorly managed by this bunch of highly illiterate blind leaders headed by CIC Dr. Samuel Kanyon Doe. Doe, without the constitutional means, toppled the constitutionally instituted government of President William Richard Tolbert, Jr., and Taylor not being clothed constitutionally to take control of Doe's government did not legally abrogate any rule between usurpers, as "thief from thief makes God laugh." But why did Taylor run away from the Liberian government seat, his political heart's desire?

For seven unbroken years Charles Taylor and his henchmen destroyed our country, driving ever well meaning Liberians out of their one time useful lives. Personally, this senseless war changed my lifelong commitment of remaining a teacher as long as I would live in this lawless world. As I live now, I painfully and regrettably feel that I have not won the crown of success in the field of education, where I diligently and sacrificially labored for thirty-eight selfless years.

Chapter XXVIII "The Political Gear of Liberia"

In July of 1964, what were called provinces in the hinterland of Liberia were given county status. They would now be integral parts of the body politic of the Republic of Liberia. The provinces were comprised of districts controlled by district commissioners, while each province was administered by a provincial commissioner. The legal system of the provinces was a set of rules called Interior Regulations, completely different from the legal system of the Liberian Republic. Until 1944 or round about that time, the provinces and their dominant inhabitants, the indigenous people or the aborigenes, or the Lords of the Land, styled by the freed slaves from the United States of America who settled in the Grain Coast, as *Native People*, were no part of the body politic of the Republic of Liberia.

On his political platform for his bid for the presidency of the republic, former associate justice William V. S. Tubman promised to unify and integrate the entire country by allowing each province one representative in the Liberian Legislature. Tubman won the presidential and general elections held in 1943 and was accordingly inaugurated in January of 1944. Counselor Tubman did not lose any time in implementing his platform, especially the part that called for the integration of the provinces. The law integrating the provinces was enacted, passed into law by the Liberian Legislature and was approved by the president. Accordingly, elections followed for the election of the first indigenous representatives from the three provinces. In Eastern Province, my home province, the honor and luck fell to my indigenous man, Daniel Poo Derrick of the sub-Grebo ethnic group called Gedebo.

Finally, when the provinces were totally admitted into the body politic of the Republic of Liberia in 1964, they were proportionately given representation in the Liberian Legislature. Grand Gedeh County, the former Eastern Province, had its political aspirants for both the Senate and the House of Representatives. The two districts in the then Eastern Province, Webbo and Tchien Districts, shared the seats for the Lower and Upper Houses. In Webbo District, my home district, our aspirants for the Senate were Honorable Moses P. Harris, Honorable Joseph Itoka, Counselor Lewis Karbeh Free and General Harry K. H. Carngbe. Four strong, well known people were contesting for a single Senate seat. What a fight!

In Nyaake, the Webbo District headquarters, the political storm began to rage among the hotheaded aspirants as the citizens began to take cover behind their respective aspirants. Personally and unreservedly I camped with hopeful General Carngbe, a man widely honored and respected for his stance regarding the brutal activities of the commissioner and his messengers and soldiers against the NATIVE PEOPLE. Carngbe tramped over six hundred miles to bring to the attention of the government in Monrovia the brutality meted against his people by the district commissioner and his instruments of brutality, the soldiers and messengers. The going was tough but I steadfastly stood by my fellow NATIVE BOY, Harry K. Hne Carngbe.

In a political meeting, all the citizens of the district, particularly those of the Township of Nyaake, Webbo, assembled to listen to those ambitious to represent them in the Liberian Senate. The meeting was presided over by the district commissioner,

Honorable Edmund B. Gibson. Each aspirant briefly told us why he thought he would be the right choice of the people to represent them in the Liberian Senate. While these old political promises never kept were being pronounced, the commissioner received a radiogram from the President of Liberia. In part, the radiogram read, "The Senate seat for Lower Grand Gedeh County is one. I heard that four distinguished sons of the Webbo District are vying for this single seat. I would ask them to let one of their number get it." The commissioner put it to them and they requested us to excuse them for thirty minutes. "We will allow sixty long minutes," the commissioner told them. With this, we grouped ourselves on our various political camps outside of the meeting place.

When the contestants returned, through their spokesman, Counselor Free, one of the aspirants, they told us, "We would rather have the party machinery (True Whig Party) to decide for us than to choose among ourselves." To the party machinery we were obliged to go. Each aspirant provided the means of transportation and off we went to the party hierarchy in Harper City, Maryland County, where the President of Liberia (William V. S. Tubman) was spending his Easter holidays.

In our meeting with the President, House Speaker Richard Henries and Senator James N. Anderson (Maryland County), Senate Protempore of the Liberian Senate, the President asked the chiefs and people of the Webbo District who was their choice for the Liberian Senate. Paramount Chief Coffee Steme, the headquarters paramount chief of the Webbo District, said that they the chiefs had not chosen anyone yet. "You as an individual citizen, whom have you decided on?" the President fingered Paramount Chief Steme. "Not as yet, Mr. President," the old chief evaded. The question was then cast to the citizens in general. "Since these ambitious aspirants came around, Mr. President, we the citizens of the Township of Nyaake choose aspirant Harry K. H. Carngbe. We cannot allow a man like Moses Harris to represent us because he does not know us and he has not shared in our hard times and troubles in the Webbo District. Lewis Free took away all his indigenous people from the Webbo District and brought them to Tchien District to prospect gold for him. Tchien is his home now and those are the people he shared his wealth with and those are the people he should represent. Honorable Joseph Itoka is our own man but he is too old to represent us in that August body. We know he served your government faithfully and you cannot forget him and so we beg you, Mr. President, to give him what an old person like him deserves. Mr. President, since this political battle began, our political hen has been sitting on the eggs. It has hatched the eggs and the first chick that came out cried out vocally, 'CARNGBE! CARNGBE!! CARNGBE!!! CARNGBE!!!!' We want Carngbe, I mean, we need Carngbe to represent us in the Liberian Senate," Mrs. Eliza Collins of the Township of Nyaake, Webbo, emphatically and factually narrated. Mr. Felix Itoka, the son of aspirant Itoka, then told the party Standard Bearer and his hierarchy that his father served the Liberian government for seventeen unbroken years and the man with such an experience should represent his people. The young citizens of the Township of Nyaake were now on fire calling aloud their spokesman, the skinny language arts teacher at the Webbo District School, William Kamma Reeves. The president's security made way for me to get before the president. "If we do not give this Senate seat to General Carngbe, we will be worse than the dog that bites the hand that feeds it, Mr. President. Are we interested in the number of years a man served his government or what he has actually done with those years, Mr. President? That is, what quality of service it was; what good his service brought to his people in a given community; his contribution for the welfare of all. Honorable Itoka's service in the government, as we know it, was his personal accumulation of wealth which benefited nobody outside of his little clique. Mr. President, this Senate seat for Lower Grand Gedeh County belongs to Harry Carngbe. If we don't give it to him, we will be worse than the dog that bites the hand that feeds it. Carngbe is one of us. He knows our pains; he shares equally with us in everything: sorrow, joy, pain, etc., etc., etc... When the soldiers drive us out of our villages, Carngbe is with us in the open where the towering trees canopy us. When the soldiers brutalized us with the butts of their old rustic Belgian rifles, he calls on the Government of Liberia to see the dehumanization of his fellow NATIVE PEOPLE. Harry K. H. Carngbe is the man, the only man who can ably represent us in the Liberian Senate. Mr. President, let us not bite the hand that feeds us. We are not dogs. We are human beings, rational human beings," I reminded the President.

The party hierarchy gave us the choice of the majority, Harry K. Hne Carngbe. Back to Nyaake we went that night of the resounding victory for a NATIVE BOY on his way to representing his people. The next day was the party convention where our aspirant would be nominated as a candidate for the Liberian Senate for election. Multitudes of people came to the convention to see their overwhelming choice, Hne Carngbe, nominated. My father, although his Gedebo chiefdom was no more of the former Eastern Province, now Grand Gedeh County, came to see and congratulate the man who saved him from going to jail for not performing militia duty after he became a town chief.

Mr. Isaac S. Tanwin, secretary to the supervisor of schools for Grand Gedeh County, no doubt, was so impressed with my verbal strongly worded statement that he thought that a young man like me could never in his human form so bravely address the President of Liberia. It must be that I was well tutored and undoubtedly equipped in African science. Since my father lives, Mr. Tanwin was with the strong conviction that my father had thoroughly washed me in African black magic. At the True Whig Party convention the next day, Mr. Tanwin met my father and said to him, "Your son is a first class wizard. No doubt, you taught him well. From the way he spoke before the President of Liberia, I gathered that he was not alone; he had some kind of magic power on him." "I don't know what you called witch. I am not a wizard, neither is my son. I taught him to speak the truth always and once he spoke the truth, he should never, never be afraid of anybody, high or low. This is my principle and this is what I instruct my children with," my father elucidated. General Carngbe was nominated as the sole candidate for the Senate seat for Lower Grand Gedeh County.

"Nobody can swallow you bodily, my son. When you say what is true and factual, say it without fear," my father often told me. And so I learn to speak what is true always. Once I have truth on my side, I fear nobody. I look unblinkingly in your face and tell it the way I know it. My instruction from my father is well buttressed by this passage from the holy Scripture: The Epistle of St. Paul to the Galatians chapter 4:16- "Have I therefore become your enemy because I tell you the truth?"

In our brother district, Tchien District, now called Upper Grand Gedeh County, the political battle was fiercely raging. The front runners were Professor Cyrus S. Cooper, then assistant supervisor of schools for Grand Gedeh County, and former road overseer David Towah. The Old True Whig Party held fast to its unprincipled tradition of selecting people who are not the choice of the majority and are completely non-productive in such a public place to be nominated for the Senate or the House of Representatives. Over Professor Cyrus S. Cooper, completely illiterate David Towah, who often said, "I speak fifteen percent of English and I understand sixty percent of it." Students of arithmetic want to know what happened to the balance twenty-five percent of his English language? Towah was chosen by the party over Professor Cyrus S. Cooper to represent the people of the newly created County of Grand Gedeh in the Honorable Liberian Senate, where Standard English is in vogue for the transaction of business. Here we are now part and parcel of the total body politic of the Liberian nation. But this kind of political maneuvering will definitely not benefit us as our unlettered representative brags about his understanding of the King's language fosters no hope of true representation.

What disquiets me in the Liberian politics since I became a member of the literary world is the passage in one of the preambles to the 1847 constitution of the Republic of Liberia, which says, *"We were without representation....... and we were taxed without our consent."* If this is what the freed slaves experienced in the United States of America, taxation without representation, and they exercised it over the indigenous people in the hinterland and parts where indigenous people resided in Liberia for a heartless period of about a century before giving the Lords of the Land what I call "eye servant representation" as the only political party, the Grand Old True Whig Party, literally handpicked those to represent the Lords of the Land in the legislature, people highly illiterate so that they would be there just for being there's sake, is a farce. For instance, in Eastern Province, a man, Daniel P. Derrick, without formal education, was handpicked over Reverend David Toe, a graduate from an academically renowned institution in Liberia, the College of West Africa. They placed the juicy sugar cane on our shoulder while they and they alone suck the tasty juice. What a nominal representation! Then nineteen or more years following, the provinces were declared "counties" and the same handpicking, seemingly a Liberian political tradition, continues as a devastating result. Actually, the voice of the masses of Liberia has yet to be distinctly and demandingly heard in the Liberian National Legislature. What a political gimmick!

One hundred and fifty or more years have come and gone since Liberia became an independent sovereign State. What we have done with those blessed God given years since independence is simply to count them on our fingers without our pointing to anything concrete as a sign or example of our independence. Once a veteran politician, Karyee Farley, Putu Chiefdom, Grand Gedeh County, speaking at a political rally where he was canvassing for the paramount chieftancy of the Putu Chiefdom, lashed out at his political opponent, incumbent Paramount Chief Brown Kwia, "This man, your paramount chief, is the laziest man in our chiefdom. He cultivates no rice farm to produce rice to feed his family. Loitering about the town with his arms clasped behind his back and with plumes stuck in his hoary hair, your paramount chief is no good example to our young people." The best example of political power is what it can do for the people who give the power. In short, he added, "Power lif for hand and not lif for muf." It would appear that the Liberian political power lives in the mouths of those who govern without working to improve the lot of the governed. What shall we do?

Chapter XXIX "Epilogue and Recessional"

Throughout this autobiographical narrative, you read many words written to convey my innermost thoughts to you. A word, be it spoken or written, always has something to do with the person who speaks it or writes it. There are power and inspiration in a human word. Through it we feel contact with living persons. I have no doubt, therefore, that you feel the embracing contact through the inspiration of the human word which leads you from sentence to sentence and from paragraph to paragraph.

Every human being starts as a *Tabula rasa* (a smooth tablet without impressions on it). If the Latin quotation above holds true, then perhaps the truth contained therein speaks doubly in my case as I came from a village where life was so circumscribed that it would appear that there was no life at all; a kind of vacuum, it seemed. Coming out of that stagnant environment to a western styled school in that rustic village enclosed atmosphere, it appeared that even the *Tabula rasa* was not there.

The exposure, from the onset, I bitterly experienced with the very physical absence of my parents' love as I had to live with another family away from our village. To me, this was a betrayal of my youthful days. However, the new experience in the school, my first encounter with a woman (my teacher) dressed in a dress completely different from my mother's or any other village woman's dress, and learning the names of the letters of the English alphabet created a standing excitement for me. This summoned in my courage and understanding. Buttressed by these supporters of learning, I gradually expelled ignorance and knowledge progressively and aggressively took the salute.

Reverend William Taylor White had come to the village during the feast of the birth of Jesus Christ to fish for more members for his newly organized village church of the African Methodist Episcopal Church Denomination in the Gedebo country. Obviously it suggested that the reverend gentleman would rather begin his membership drive from the grassroots. And so with artificial bait in his hands, he went with Pastor Moses to the waterfront where the nude village boys had gone to bask in the bulging creek. The box of candy in his pious hands as his bait to fish for members for his Tenzonke congregation, Reverend White, in a seemingly tantalizing way, invited the timid looking boys to share the candies if they would attend school in Tenzonke, their home village. Without feeling any tinge of obligation or commitment and without any awareness I accepted the candy with the lifelong condition attached. In addition to this, later in the day, Elder White revealed that the recipients of the sweet candies were also obliged and committed to becoming followers of Jesus Christ in the African Methodist Episcopal Church Denomination. *Tabula rasa*, I accepted both.

Without any formality, I was already a follower of God as my parents repeated before me several times each day acknowledgement of some good the good Lord had done for them. Again, unknowingly, I walked with God. My father also taught me how to count in the English numerals orally. In short, my parents firmly laid my foundation in the Christian faith and the way of the western school. As I know it now, being a Christian and being educated are both lifelong commitments. To steadfastly embrace all well, one must stand tall all the time. As you may have observed from reading this story by a man from Nyaake, the author fearlessly battled with keeping the faith and studiously and diligently to being kept in the number of the lettered. Fidelity into a commitment requires constancy, courage, dedication, perseverance, and some heroism. As you read these pages, no doubt, you discovered these sterling qualities displayed.

The Christian philosophy of life is defined as sharing, especially of self, a sharing that hurts and can be a cross. I had long wished to become a lawyer, an international lawyer, or a medical doctor. It was my burning desire to find my way to Germany, the country that Grebo man believes is the most meticulous manufacturer of commodities in the world, after completing high school by being employed on board a ship in the Ivory Coast. I was reliably informed that ships carrying produce from the Ivory Coast to Europe hired laborers to that effect. When employed in that fashion, I would stow away as soon as the ship would anchor in any German port. But the prerequisite, high school education, had yet to be obtained as I had no money to do the first thing first to set me on the path to Germany. The will was still bulging, but was the way there too? Without high school education the will was sadly blocked. What could I do?

In the holy Scripture it is said, "Seek ye first the Kingdom of God and all its righteousness and all other things will be added unto you." And I think education, like righteousness, should be sought first. Once obtained, it will foster your ambition in whatever field you desire to pursue. As I saw it, my ambition to become an international lawyer or a medical doctor was hanging in balance as the prerequisite, high school education, had yet to be obtained. The way was not there as I had not the means. When the golden opportunity finally knocked at my door, it came with an attached "condition," "We are offering young men the opportunity to attend our high school (Our Lady of Fatima) and upon completion they will teach for us the number of years they spent in the school," the Catholic Prefecture of Cape Palmas announced.

With mixture of pain and happiness I wholeheartedly seized the glorious opportunity and I unwillingly gave up my previous heart's desire, regrettably holding onto TEACHING as a HARD TIME or NO WAY SUBSTITUTE for my heart's desire. But later did I happily realize that if my desire of wanting to become a lawyer or a medical doctor was or is to serve humanity, then I was still in the GIVING LINE, a nutritive substitute that gives copiously to all seeking help without any cost to them, directly or indirectly, a profession that gives the total person to those being served and the mother of professions. Realizing the massive need for this sacrificial but noble profession, I unreservedly decided to cast my lot with the GRASSROOTS, the grownups. With these, over the years, I shared my total self.

Here I dropped my bucket to fetch water for the thirsty for thirty-eight unbroken years. I had vowed to remain a teacher as long as I would live to serve humanity. But in the succeeding years, disruptive political storms rocked our country. An uneducated, immature, seventeen-man military junta unlawfully seized power and toppled the constitutionally-elected government of President William Richard Tolbert, Jr. The aftermath of the coup held the Liberian nation and its people hostage.

Eventually the country lost its peaceful direction as the entire country was in turmoil. In that chaotic state the country relentlessly struggled to survive, while the Doe government administered the affairs of the country nepotistically. For instance, of the thirteen political subdivisions (counties), six were manned by people of his ethnic group.

It is said that a teacher's role in society is assessed by the possible impact of the quality of his life and teaching on his students, his community, and his generation[13]. I guess the assessors of the quality of my life and the impact my teaching made on my students, my communities, and generation will do themselves justice to make the assessment earnestly.

It was on that bright Christmas morning in Tenzonke, a remote village nestled under towering evergreen trees, in the then abundant rice producing Gedebo Chiefdom in the then Eastern Province of Liberia, in the presence of Presiding Elder Reverend William Taylor White of the Cape Palmas District of the African Methodist Episcopal Church and the Village Pastor Moses Challaba Yessay, when I unconsciously accepted the call and challenge of becoming an educated man. This lengthy life story of mine, I hope, depicts exactly, one way or another, how I live or whether I measure up to my calling and challenge according to the way I live. Shortly, I suppose, I don't know 'when' or 'where' the tolling church bell will be saying, "Lord...Lord...," and the kettle drums in unison will be asking, "I wonder what he did?" while the bass drum will unhesitantly answer the protruding question... "He talked...he talked...he talked too much..."

Appendix

About ten years ago I earned a Bachelor's degree in Education at Maryland College of Our Lady of Fatima, Harper, Cape Palmas, Maryland County, Republic of Liberia. Obtaining this degree did not suggest an end to my learning but rather an end to begin. This was only a little preparation – a very small preparation – comparatively, for a sacrificial but noble profession that I had embarked upon for four years previously before obtaining a degree in it and for it.

Since my early elementary school days I found English, which is actually a second language for me but surprisingly was never taught to me as such, the only subject among the many subjects of the school curriculum to be the one I desire the most. Being in love with this, so to speak, throughout my school days, including college, it was in English (literature, composition, etc.) I saw my own initiative at work. Consequently, I was graded among the doing-wells but never the-best in the class.

Subsequently, when I left high school, I became a teacher in the elementary laboratory school for the university college of which I am an alumnus. This served as a wholesome laboratory as I put into practice what I had gathered from my professional courses in education taught by those under whose direct supervision and guidance I was fostered during practicing periods. The subject engaged in most of the time was English, the subject I love to teach. How well, I do not know but most of my students say I do a good job at it, but I am Hard.

In 1959, the year I left college, the Liberian Department of Education requested me to teach language arts in the Annual Teacher Vacation School, Webbo Center. A program geared toward the upgrading of in-service teachers academically sponsored jointly by the United States of America and Liberian Governments. Since then I regularly serve as an instructor at that center where the teachers meet every January for some academic and method courses. Besides this assignment, I am full-time teacher of language arts in a government junior and senior high school. Tubman-Wilson Institute is the only senior high school in the newly created county of Grand Gedeh, a county rich in fertile, virgin land area but sparsely inhabited and markedly short of qualified teachers. In this poorly staffed school, I teach.

But I am aware that if you keep giving and do not get anything in return, you will soon have nothing. With this hard fact facing me, I requested the Department of Education on several occasions to grant me a foreign scholarship so that the more academic preparation I would get the more help I could give to their program of upgrading my colleagues who were and are still in dire need of this academic assistance.

Every day the need for upgrading myself spoke defiantly for itself. That the department never granted this request, which would yield mutant benefits for both the grantor and the grantee, is the question that boldly glares in the face of the department.

Each day as I pondered seriously about how to improve myself so that I would continue to serve as sunshine in others' lives, I murmured to myself, living in hope, one of my favorite poems, the first stanza I quote below:

Serene I fold my hands and wait
Nor care for wind nor tide nor sea
I rave no more 'gainst time nor fate
For lo, my own shall come to me.

As I hold these lines to be self-evident, I made no fuss about my getting a scholarship. But, as you know, a man's earnest purpose is like a cork that when submerged under water comes up on the surface as soon as it is released; I knew deep down in my yearning heart that the time would come one day. God in His good book promised that those who seek would find. As He is faithful to His promises, so my faith in this direction was never dying. At last this glorious and challenging opportunity, the long awaited time, came for me to make the much desired educational tour of this beautiful and affluent country with its altruistic and affable people. The opportunity is mine now; let's see how much use I shall make of it. Well, time will tell.

It was in June of 1969 that my department of education was writing the names of those teachers to participate in the International Teacher Development Program. On hearing this, I told the department, as Abu Ben Adhem told the angel, "Write my name too as one who wants to improve himself so as to help others." And lo, after the names were written and sent to Washington, D. C., for scrutiny I suppose, the Americans wrote my name first on the list, providing to me that even those distant people knew my burning desire.

Until I was officially informed I was not sure that I was going to be accepted, knowing that, as Oliver Goldsmith puts it, "No one is sure of his dinner unless he has eaten it." As you and I know, this is especially true in a democratic society where nobody has absolute right to anything. Eagerly but patiently I waited for the GREEN LIGHT.

Although this educational tour offers no academic award, yet there are some educational benefits, personal experiences, which over the years have been accepted as the best teacher. So here am I! The opportunity and challenge are equally mine. Let us see, with the protruding eyes of opportunity and challenge focused on me, what good can be mustered out of this educational tour. ARRIVAL

It was just like a dream. At 8:00 a.m. (5:00 a.m. U.S.) that early Sunday morning, August 31, 1969, we landed on the Kennedy International Airport amidst swarms of airplanes.

Disembarking, we were led into a terminal that my whole thinking refused to believe was the work of mortal man. Gazing at the many attractions that naturally caught my eyes, we wandered about the spacious and roomy building for entry procedures.

Surprisingly to me, a young white lady standing in one of the broad doorways inquired audibly, "Who is Reeves, a passenger from Liberia?" The question was so direct that I was left with no choice to deny my own name but to say, "Here am I." She then with a warm broad smile of welcome presented me a long envelope on which were written the names of Liberians grantees, "What does this mean so early?" I whispered to myself. I handed the envelope to Mrs. Cooper, our leader, who

254

opened it and read the letter enclosed in it. Among other things, the letter said, "If you are jammed let me know at once." Relieved we continued out tramping through the building, the feeling of being in a foreign country had already dawned on us as we experienced the chilly air unfamiliar to us in Liberia.

Having gone through these formal entry procedures in the Pan-American Air Terminal, the airline by which we came, an arrangement was made for us to get to the National Airway Terminal. But as each person carried his/her own load, we were a bit late in getting to the place where the bus was. This was our first experience that time means much here.

We then hired taxicabs that took us to our next terminal. After delivering our luggage to the transit station, we were told to make our exit through Gate 7. We were on the march again. Through the endless corridor we staggered, gradually losing hope that we would ever reach Gate 7 as it seemed to be moving away from us the closer we thought we were. At last we captured Gate 7. There we waited for our next air trip to Washington, D. C.

Our flight to Washington, D.C., was wonderful for two good reasons: (1.) the attractive, beautiful countryside greeted us below, and (2.) the congenial, beautiful stewardesses who were not coy in sharing with us the undying smiles from their thin lips. The two-hour flight was just like a fleeting moment to me. To my disappointment, in a twinkle of an eye, the plane touched down on the Washington, D.C. airport. As those angel-like creatures hissed the words, "Goodbye, come again," in the exit, we unwillingly descended the aircraft.

ORIENTATION

Monday, September 1, was a national holiday (Labor Day) for our host country. Our orientation was begun on this day too. That morning we were informed that at 1:30 p.m. chartered buses would pick us up at the Dodge House, the hotel in which we lived in Washington, D. C., for a visit to many important places in and around Washington, the nation's capital. This included memorials and graves. Thinking with Oliver Goldsmith, I asked myself, "What do monumental inscriptions inspire?" I pressed farther, "I hope these American people will not waste my precious time here with things like looking at monuments and the like." The places visited included the following:

1. Lincoln Memorial
2. Tomb of the Unknown Soldier
3. The Kennedy's Graves
4. Jefferson Memorial
5. The Shrine of the Immaculate Conception
6. The Marine Monument

After that long four-hour trip, which seemed as brief as fifteen minutes, came the time of subjective as well as objective assessment of the visit in terms of educational values, if there were any, since my primary concern here is education. To begin with, these monumental inscriptions do inspire plenty! First of all, I realized that the United States recognizes the talents of each individual citizen, and if these talents are extraordinary ones, she preserves them as securely as possible so that they will serve as some source of inspiration for the oncoming generations. These are gathered, as I observed, and reserved from all the contributing factors that have made the United States great and affluent at home and abroad.

As I stood gazing at the imposing statue of the historically famous Thomas Jefferson, the man whose mighty pen and ingenuity laid down the ideal principles of democracy in one of the greatest documents ever written by mortal man - the American Constitution - I began to murmur those historic independent..." In short, the statue vividly brought to my mind the work of this world famous figure.

Abraham Lincoln, whose bow tie appeared to be askew and whose statue is by far less imposing that the statue of Thomas Jefferson, essentially believed in the dynamic principles laid down in that historic document, and because of this firm belief, like Pope Gregory the VII who hated iniquity and therefore died in exile, Lincoln was murdered. There was another source of inspiration. The Guards of Honor at the Grave of the Unknown Soldier tell also that no job is mean in this country. A soldier is an honorable man too.

The next day at the Department of Health, Education and Welfare Building, at 10:00 a.m. precisely, the participants assembled themselves according to program in a spacious, beautiful auditorium where we were officially welcomed by the following dignitaries: Mr. Robert C. Leestman, Associate Commissioner for International Education, presiding; Honorable Robert Finch, Secretary of Health, Education and Welfare; Mr. Peter Muirhead, Acting Deputy Assistant Secretary of Education; Honorable John Richardson, Jr., Assistant Secretary for Education and Cultural Affairs, Department of State.

Later in the day, after a break, the most humorous and the most to the point speech was delivered by Mr. Thomas E. Cotner, Director, Division of International Exchange and Training International Studies. This was the formal introduction of the program. In no veiled terms, the able speaker candidly described what our many and varied experiences would be like at the end of this tour. To be frank, I think, my colleagues and I enjoyed the talk of this man the most because he receive the loudest and longest ovation from us.

At 2:00 p.m. on the same day each university group had its first session with the Program Officer. In the Regional Office Building in Room 5636, the group officially known as the Indiana University Group, met a gracious, ever-smiling, beautiful young lady. As she hissed the words of welcome through her thin, smooth lips, Miss Patricia Simmons, our program Officer, greeted each of us warmly as we filed through the door. Seated in cushioned chairs, the members of the group listened attentively to the program specialist whose catching eyes seemed to be focused on every person at the same time in the room as she briefly outlined the program for the group. As much as I wanted to look around to see the attractions in the room, her presence pulled me away like a giant magnet. At the end of the day I said to a friend, "Don't you agree with Gandhi that women are intellectual giants, having observed our Program Officer today?" Every day of the Orientation I had to meet this impressive and charming lady who was very fast becoming an integral part of our

256

activity in this bustling city.

Day in and day out we attended, listened to lectures about American culture, education, people, family, economy, government and what not. These lectures were given, most of the time, by American intellectuals. The Principal idea behind these lectures, to my mind, was to present to us, their guests, America as a whole. Obviously these men and women are learned in their various fields of occupation, and they definitely knew what they were talking about and how their cases were being presented to their attentive judges, this time of facts instead of law. Wonderful was their regular quotation of some famous authority! "No doubt," I said admirably, "These people drink deeply in this business." I admired their full reliance on the authoritative sources which made their talks more witty.

These talks were followed or interrupted by questions, as each speaker proposed, you would expect from such a select group with many varied cultural and education backgrounds, many interesting and intricate questions arose as those grantees sought clarification of the precarious knowledge they had previously gained about the United States through reading some biased and unbiased writings.

As each speaker resigned the platform, it was interesting to see the group during breaks broken into units of two, three, four or even more, discussing the highlights of the speaker's speeches. This was a scene of heated debates as those who did not agree with certain points or where they felt the speakers were evasive in their answers to many pertinent questions while his supporters revealed more facts upon which they sought more reliance. This was the order of the day.

Our visit to the United States Department of State brought the Liberian visitors in contact with a one-time teacher, career diplomat and a man ripe with age. There were many sources of confusion for me during the orientation, but the most striking was the one I experienced when we dashed along the brilliantly lighted corridors of the fantastic building where we met the one-time teacher.

As we moved along the many endless corridors of this majestic building, most of the time I forgot where I was or my reason for my being there. But as soon as we came in personal contact with this man, his very presence arrested my wits and put them at parade rest! Attentively we gazed at this man with unquestionable knowledge of the many education problems facing the underdeveloped or the developing countries, the African ones in particular.

Patiently and in a tender fatherly tone, this venerable man explained the United States Policy about education in foreign countries. Every word that came through his sighing lips emphasized the sincerity of the help his government is wiling to give to any country desiring to boost its educational development. My thoughts ceased to wander about at this learned man led me into thinking seriously about our main purpose in the United States. This concerned humanitarian is Dr. Trucelda.

Our sightseeing continued down the Potomac River. Sailing in a boat on a river is quite and excitement, but this excitement was heightened when we reached the wharf of Mount Vernon. There we ran into an old teacher again who briefed us about the site we were about to visit.

Mount Vernon is the place George Washington, the father and first President of the American nation, lived. With no guide leading the way, we ascended the hill, stopping first at the tomb of the late man rich in high titles, General, Father, and the President.

On arrival at the tomb, a visitor experiences some high honor hovering around the tomb of the late Chief of Staff as the two starry flags seemed to be beckoning to the visitor, "Come up here to see the final resting place of a man whose earnest and brave struggles have made what we represent." With this symbolic gesture from the waving flags we marched majestically with pomp and pride of ambassadors going to present their letters of credence to the Chief Executive.

This time we were only roving ambassadors so instead of making any formal appearance or being accorded the formal protocol, we were shown where to go. We began our journey around the compound of George Washington at Mount Vernon, Virginia. As we were gliding through the historic site, I said to myself, "This man died about two hundred years ago, but he still lives." With opened mouth, I gazed at the various stations where George Washington had his mortal hands at work. While I was in the present, I was looking at the very far distant past. "What has rendered this man immortality?" I questioned myself inaudibly as I filed through the thick crowd. To my mind, as I saw it, there is something spectacular about the American way of life. The spontaneity and willingness of the American to always put himself in the sacrificial position just to do good to friend, a neighbor, a community or a nation is one of the most striking characteristics I observed about him. Suppose the association of the lady volunteers who organized themselves just for the preservation of the home and tomb of George Washington, General, Father and President of the United States of America, had not given themselves selflessly, what would have become of him and this place?

Halted by the red sign "Don't Walk" on one of the busy streets in Washington, D.C., I could not help but whisper this to a fellow grantee from some faraway country, "But don't you think our mission explores more of the American life than an ambassador extraordinary and plenipotentiary accredited to this country?" I guess an ambassador having this highest place of the diplomatic mission, is never given the slightest opportunity of seeing more than two or more rooms in the White House, the official residence of the President of the United States. Well, we had!

The tour through the White House gave us another insight into the American public life. Our guide, a well-uniformed police officer, Needham by name, ably gave us the history of the building and the significance of each room visited. Suddenly I remarked to one of my colleagues who seemed to be putting his words together to make the same observation, "These Americans are well at home with their history." To me the Americans believe in living in the past while they breathe the present breath of life. In other words, they preserve the past in some concrete way; for example, the dishes used for state dinners given by preceding Presidents are carefully stacked and placed on well-built shelves. Today a child of this generation can see a concrete sample of what dishes were used when President So-and-so lived in the White House. This is a democratic way of keeping the taxpayer informed too!

From the White House our tour took us across the street to a fabulous building called the Executive Office Building. We were seated in a spacious room breathing the air of some historic significance. Indian Treaty Room is the official title.

There, two high-ranking government officials briefed us about the functions of the Executive Branch of the United States Government. As usual, questions period followed. Government officials to answer questions about their government, what did you expect? As the questions from this seemingly interested group were being shot at the officials, they made quick, brief, evasive answers, the type diplomats make.

The visit to these public buildings revealed to me some deep impression that the United States Government no doubt has some duty and responsibility to the people for which it is instituted. All long, the will of the people, the will of the majority, that is, was the paramount objective of the functions of the government. And this seemed very true as every move of the functions of government was made accountable to the people. In this respect, I think, the people are truly fee and independent in their democratic society because one writer says and I say with him that when the transactions of the government are not made known to the people their safety and liberties are insecure.

Americans crave for and demand Freedom for every aspect of their life. But what disappoints me is with all the panegyrics about their freedom and liberties, looking closely at the American society, one discovers the opposite.

A get-to-know-each-other party was held in our honor in the Dodge House. (This was intended for this and just what it did.) But this did not meet the Liberian expectation of such a unique occasion. (However, one should be thankful to a generous friend for whatsoever he gets from him because it is not what we get but the intention with which it is offered that matters.) Happily we met our new friends and were appreciative of our hosts' effort.

The series of lectures came to a close when we attended the one entitled, "Race Relations in the United States." The programmed lecturer did not turn out, but a timely substitute, who, although I have nothing with which to compare the two of them entertained us with exactly what we expected. He did what we called in Liberia, "He ate the crab without being ashamed of its crackling sound of its shell; or he ate the bull without being afraid of its blinking eyes." Dr. DeMartin unearthed the truth and the hypocrisy of the American society, which acts like guano abroad.

Perhaps it is an exaggerated statement that Americans are great lovers of their neighbors. Yet to some extent it is not. But what bothers me is when one looks closely at the American life, there is a marked hypocrisy. The late President John F. Kennedy once said, when he visited the Berlin Walls, "Although Democracy is not perfect, we don't have to build walls to keep people in it."

Hypocrisy is like a two-tongued man who says one thing and means the opposite. According to what the United States says she represents and believes speaks so eloquently for the reason why many countries of this turbulent world find beckoning hope in her. As we know, the United States has a democratic form of government. One of the many reasons why many countries choose that form of government is that it fosters individuality. Every human being is unique in himself and anything that tends to destroy that uniqueness is bitterly frowned upon.

So far as we know today, the United States is the father of democracy and one of the super powers of the world. America preaches the principles of democracy everywhere and these include EQUALITY, JUSTICE and what have you. How are they preached, by precepts or examples? They should be preached with double sway…both precept and examples…anything other than that is hypocritical. But when you turn the other side of the coin, you find frustrating, glaring evidence that the United States does not practice these principles of their chosen form of government at home. Why?

The Negro, a term which the white man uses to imply inferiority for this race, was imported from his fatherland as slave here to work on the American cotton plantations which laid the foundation of America's greatness and affluence today.

After many years of hard slavery, these less graded human beings were set free. For hundreds of years they had been separated from their fatherland, so it sent without saying that they had no home again but America. From that time up to now the black man lives in America. But what surprises me and by which I am perturbed is that all the lectures about American economy, culture, education, etc., revealed no contributions made by black man in America. Even the devil in hell would be ashamed to tell this willful lie that one who worked on plantations, fought in defense of the country in two bitter and devastating wars and now in Vietnam, built roads and gave rise to prosperous industries, drove trucks and practically did and is doing everything possible to boost every phase of the American life has not contributed to eh society of which he is an active member. What shall we do? The black man is even denied a place on the printed page except when he is ridiculed and degraded. This is shameful and does not become any person or nation that believes and stands for what the United States preaches about – DEMOCRACY. How can then American be great lovers of their fellowmen when they hate the very ground on which their blood, black brothers walk?

Dr. De Martin was the crowning glory of the Orientation lectures. A black man himself, Dr. Martin, without trying to be what he is not, presented the Race Relations as plainly and painfully as he could. Victim of the mad prejudice, Dr, Martin told us the sufferings of his fellow black Americans in words which adequately painted his pictures. These stories have become our everyday life as the mass media of communications throughout the country told the shameful stories of the unreasonable denial of the rights of JUSTICE and EQUALITY to the black man in America.

After listening to Dr. Martin's speech about the black man's plight in the United States, certificates were given and we repaired to the beautiful garden of the International Center for a Garden Tea Party in our honor.

With Americans, it seemed, no occasion is formal but this party was formal. Our hosts and hostesses were formally dressed. The distinguished invitees were no exception.

As soon it was time, serving everything available for the party started without any opening of the party. This was very strange to me because it was unlike any party I attended in Liberia. As we got served with some juice and some other foodstuff, we engaged ourselves with talking with strange people, people we had not met before. Amicably we mixed and a strong air of friendship hovered around.

One of the great many things I admire about the American is hi thrifty way of handling money. I sensed further that perhaps the man of plenty is given more because of his thrift.

Some of us from developing countries thought the party like something given in honor of a four-year-old child's birthday. Why so? In many of these have-not countries vast sums of money are un-prudently spent for expensive drinks just for entertainment of this kind. No wonder things needed for these countries are never taken care of! I must add here that the party served its purpose and that was it!

At home I enjoyed reading the U.S. Affairs in Time Magazine. Our visit to the Capital was a special opportunity for me to see in reality the scene and actors of where the people's representatives plead the just cause of their respective constituencies and nation.

Our guide, and active middle-aged woman, led us through this magnificent and fabulous building, and each room, like the police officer at the White House, as we made a stop in a room our guide briefed us about its significance. To be frank, most of the time I did not understand what the guide said because the marvelous walls mystified me. Of course what really mattered to me was to see the rooms, because maybe there would never come a time in my life to behold these walls naturally. As you understand the significance of each room remains but the chance of getting there is not in your hands.

The oval room was empty. It seemed that the August body was not in session that day because of the death of Senate Minority Leader Dirksen. This is the chamber of the U.S.

We moved across to the chamber of the House of Representatives. Fortunately for us the honorable ladies and gentlemen were in session. Of course their number was not the one I saw on the printed page before. However, while we were sitting in this stadium-like room, we had the opportunity of listening to one of their number, a gentlemen from New York State, presenting his views about why the ELECTORAL COLLEGE SYSTEM should be abolished so that the people of the United States will elect their President directly. All around were seated voters or taxpayers who came, I guessed, to see whether their elected men and women were well fulfilling the mission of representation.

At the Supreme Court building I was fascinated by the photographs of the distinguished justices (living and dead) of the United States' highest tribunal, the final resort for justice. As I gazed at the high walls, my mind's eyes and ear began to see and hear the rap of the judge's gravel…Order…Order…it went and suddenly another voice that loudly said, "May it please your Honor," the learned gentleman who has just resigned the floor… abruptly came…Order…Order. Don't ask me what did the guide say about the Supreme Court Chamber. I said I was dreaming.

We had visited the headquarters of the three coordinating branches of the United States Government. What a breathtaking descending order it was! Up to then wee had no definite or concrete knowledge about the basic unit, the family, that has made the existence of the government possible. But we were told we would see it and for a time being would also become a part of it.

So our Orientation period came to a close with the hope that we had some useful gist of American life to rely on for happy stay and safe travel in the United States.

DEPARTURE FROM WASHINGTON D.C.

The 11th of September was exciting and boring. It was exciting only when we made visits to some important places: boring because we had run out of patience with the city's numerous broad streets, the cars that swarm them, the glaring red signs, Don't Walk, and especially with it s overflowing population of the people of my color. We had come to the white Man's country to see him. Seeing black faces everywhere you turned in that vast city was somewhat frustrating and disappointing to me!

Finally we got out on September 12. This time the American forgot his self-esteemed punctuality. The chartered bus arrived fifteen minutes behind scheduled time (7:30 a.m.). The whole delay cost us forty-five useful minutes! With our countless baggage placed on the bus, our elderly driver took full possession of the wheel and off we went.

All along the broad freeways, Maryland-Pennsylvania, the driver, obviously with the history of the important places at his fingertips, gave us a network of knowledge of the countryside. His telling of the stories about the important places along these superbly built highways, seeing the long cornfields that sketch the way and the fat grazing domestic animals, arrested my attention and made the long journey interesting and short.

That part of Pennsylvania through which we came looks much like Whoyah in Barrobo, Maryland County, Liberia. Just to tease those who inhabit this region, people say to them, "God made your home on a Saturday." This implies that since Saturday is the last day of the working week, everybody seems to be in such a hurry to get his work done. And so they think that God was in such a hurry that He left behind rocky hills in every corner of that region. But, unlike the people of Whoyah, the rocky hills mean no obstacle to the Pennsylvanians. Everywhere you see the unbelievable signs of the conquest of nature.

At last our long trip landed us in Pittsburgh, Pennsylvania, Renaissance City of America, as it is proudly called, for night stopover.

In Liberia, it is widely held by our unlettered brothers that books do not lie. This is just what they know without any proof. But in some cases these are some willful lies told in books, especially newspapers and magazines. In Washington, D.C., we were given some leaflets that told the fussy story about the renaissance of Pittsburgh. Most of the time I am a Thomas so I waited to see for myself whether all this fuss existed in some visible form to convey fully the meaning of the word "renaissance" as Webster or Thorndike defines it.

With no past knowledge about this city and desiring to know whether its developments and improvements merited the word renaissance, I had this problem. How to begin my argument put me in a straight jacket! On arrival in that beautiful city with its network of bridges, I marveled at the work of the mortal hand and literally had my mouth wide open as I said. "Marvelous! Marvelous!"

The bus dropped us at the Pick-Roosevelt Hotel. With all the warm friendship prevailing in my group, there was no way by which I could forget and stop thinking about my young wife and our growing children, whom with this "book business," I felt were being unwillingly deprived of a sincere paternal love. In order to pacify myself, I sat in my hotel room and began to whisper to my glamorous waist consort by means of my magic pen. I briefly accounted for the day's activity and told her my whereabouts.

To sleep in a hotel again would really double my trouble. I was homesick. I said to myself, "These Americans who pretend to be busy doing nothing make life not worth living to me here. I need someone to talk with in order to lift away my worries," I added.

"Pittsburgh, Pennsylvania, I recalled, "is the place where the Joneses, my warm American friends (White Americans), live." Luckily for me, I had their most recent letter with me. I hurried out of my silent room into the elevator. In the lobby of the hotel I found a public telephone.

The public service telephone system is just like a visit with a witch doctor. In order to speak to the operator to tell you your fortune, so to speak, you have to knock to her door with ten cents. I inserted the ten cents and dialed "0". "Hello, may I help you?" the sweet voice from the other end politely inquired. "Yes, please," I said eagerly. I then read the Joneses' address and in a twinkle of an eye I hear Mrs. Eleanor Jones' voice saying, "Is that William Reeves?"

After a hearty exchange of friendly greetings she said she would pick me up in an hour's time.

I did not go back in that silent room again until Milton and his wife and their baby in her arms came to take me away.

The reunion was the happiest in my memory! My wife with an American family began. But this, to me, was not because Milton and Eleanor had lived in Liberia and wanted and did treat me like a Liberian family would. For example, they gave me plenty of rice and eggplant typically cooked in Liberian way but without hot pepper. In reality this was an American home equipped with appliances foreign to me.

As quickly as possible, the Joneses and I tried to review our past experiences about the school system we were actively involved in and the community life as Milton projected the slides showing me making a brief statement about Liberian Decoration Day at the tomb of the late Honorable Deh Suah, the second man to represent the indigenous population in the Liberian Legislature, the then Eastern Province, now Grand Gedeh County. The atmosphere was purely Liberian as we sipped away Scotch. To our surprise, we were deep into the night and so we bid each other good night.

After a hearty breakfast with Milton (he prepared it while his wife was still asleep. I hope this kind of freedom for women in America should find no foothold in Liberia) he drove me to the hotel to join my friends for the continuation of our journey.

At 8:00 a.m. we were on our final leg of the journey. This time the driver was by far much younger than the previous entertaining, fatherly one who made the long, hard journey interesting. Instead, this one was the extreme opposite in every detail.

At last we happily reached our destination, Indiana University, Bloomington, the home of Hoosiers. On hand to greet us was our most venerable coordinator, Dr. Willis P. Porter, Professor of Education, Indiana University.

In a brief remark of welcome to this group of eleven different nationalities,

Finnish, Peruvians, Jamaican, Costa Rican, Indians, Turks, British Hondurans, Chilean, Thais, Hong Kong, and, or course, Liberians. Among other things, Dr. Porter told us that our dormitory was a second United Nations in which he was quite sure we would feel at home during our stay. A few words of instruction followed and the keys for our respective rooms were given. Each person struggling with his/her baggage got the help of the never-refusing elevator, which took him safely to his floor.

THE DORMITORY

This is a fourteen-story building, called Eigenmann Hall, named for the first dean of men of the university. The building houses more than thirteen hundred students-graduate students.

Shortly after we were housed, it was time for supper. With my dining hall ticket handy, I joined the processions. This brought into my mind Bon Pour Day in Firestone, Liberia, where the employees line up for their monthly or weekly rations.

For several years I was a boarder. Did living here mean following the hard routine of boarding life? I was too old for that! But when I met those men and women in line, I said if these people can stand the life, I will too. Life here is not as I thought your own time is your time.

Like the Krahn tribe in Liberia, the Americans will not speak to you when they do not know you. This obviously presents an unfriendly attitude on their part. Hasty judgment would undoubtedly reveal that the Americans are not friendly. But rash judgment should not be part of any educated man, especially a Christian.

Fanatically the American does not want to be "involved." In Washington, D.C., we wanted to know why do the Americans seem not to notice anybody? The answer came like an electric shock the first time the question was asked. The respondent was somewhat careless with his language, which, if quoted directly or indirectly, will stain my unbiased report. However, at another time the question was answered in a gentlemanly way and straight to the point. We were told that Americans fear lawsuits, if, by chance, they stop to talk with someone who is a criminal, they might be charged with him. And furthermore, they have no time to lose. But a group of dignified people like us coming into the dormitory could be criminals, too, for which nobody noticed us?

The next day Mr. Hana, Graduate Assistant to Dr. Porter, took us on a walking tour of the vast campus.

Our first plenary session was held on Monday in Sycamore Hall, South Jordan, as well as all plenary sessions, during which time Dr. Porter outlined briefly the plans three-month stay in the university.

During what was considered the academic phase of our program here at the university, our time was occupied with many activities. Besides attending our regular classes, we attended seminars on Mondays, Wednesdays and Fridays. At these seminars we listened attentively to the coordinator or some professor of some field of specialization.

The seminar room was the center where many feats of knowledge were displayed. Dr. Porter, himself a well-seasoned educator of the highest grade revealed unbiasedly the educational practices of his country and compared and contrasted with to some satisfying degree of authority. Our principal concern here was Teacher Education.

Mr. Dinesh Joshi of India and Miss Marjorie Myers of Jamaica, both of our group, whose questions unveiled their high standing, rich experience in the field of education, stimulated the group to discuss lengthily their common problems of education.

At one of our regular Monday sessions, an elderly, retired university professor, Dr. Robert A. Johnson, told us about the old and new American farming methods. In order to see what he meant by this, he invited us to his time-worn-out farm. There he showed us the simple machines his grandfather used as a farmer about one hundred years ago.

Later in the afternoon we paid Mr. Deck, a multi-farmer, a visit. We had questions to ask about the way the American farmed a hundred years ago and how he does it today. The heavy machines were the medium of explanation, especially the one that literally sucks the milk from the fat cows that came in willingly.

My reaction here on the whole was a bitter frustration that crept through me. I began to wonder thoughtfully about what specific ideas I was gaining to adapt to my immediate need, since the most primitive simple machines are not available to the masses of our farmers in Liberia. It would appear that we are away one hundred years from what is considered the most primitive now. Of course we are, to face the hard fact!

One day a professor came with two students from the department called Crisis Biology. I have not seen a man who produced as concrete examples to illustrate his points of argument as this professor did.

This issue treats about AIR POLLUTION and POPULATION EXPLOSION around the world, especially in the underdeveloped countries. The two students – an American, plump, energetic, the full sign of excellent health and physical fitness; the second a Filipino, the true symbol of malnutrition, skinny, emaciated and physical unfitness, but this hungry looking girl was well at home with what she had to us about the appalling population growth and the various methods by which it can be controlled. "Our world is finite," the little girl ably began, "and the rate at which the population tends to grow, we will sooner or later be out or everything." According to her, statistics reveal that every second there are 3.9 births; 1.7 deaths; 132 births a minute; 19,000 a day; 72,000,000 a year. At this fantastic rate of growth of the world population, it would appear proper to devise means whereby this alarming growth would be curbed. But looking at it from the other angle, if I were an island, I would never jot down one line of note about this threatening disaster which is starvation serving as a means of massacring the inhabitants of the finite world because my country is sparsely inhabited. If we could devise artificial means that will produce babies as fast as sheets of paper run out of a duplicator, Liberia would have sufficient land still to contain them. But the question is – what would they subsist on? Already Liberia does not produce enough to feed her very thin population.

Let us say in the year 2008, when the population of Liberia will be twice the present one, what will be the plight of the people living in this evergreen country that boasts about its virgin, fertile soil but experiences virgin hunger each year? The

265

question of population growth control should therefore, be of personal, community, national, and international concern.

Man's own knowledge or quest for knowledge will end his life in this turbulent world tragically.

The pollution of air comes form many sources we learned. One of them is DDT, which we know as a friend of us who live in mosquito-infested countries in Africa. Surprisingly, we were told that DDT is A DOUBLE AGENT. It is true that it gets rid of mosquitoes that carry malaria which plagues Africa, but at the same time this gets concentrated in food and becomes harmful. As it reduces the number of malaria carriers, mortality rare is also reduced, which brings about the threat of population explosion! The manufacture of this chemical is being banned here in the United States.

The knowledge of air pollution is amazing and disastrous. Let me illustrate: In 1950 I was in the 7th grade. One day we went in hygiene class. That portion of the lesson for the day told us how to take care of our bodies – what to eat and drink or what not to and drink. Among the many things the text stressed was that one should never drink form a creek that is still and this was the point the teacher emphasized, too. Having had this lesson, I was sent by the principal to a distant town, eight to twelve hours walking distance, for by the principal to a distant town, eight to twelve hours walking distance, for kerosene. On my way I found every creek was sealed up as a new highway was under construction. Imagine a boy hiking that distance without a speck of water on his tongue! This experience landed me in the hospital where I remained for several weeks.

Let us think with Oliver Goldsmith for a moment. Goldsmith says and I say with him, "Man's best riches are his ignorance of wealth." Perhaps if we stop thinking about danger, it will not come to us. Or as a former U.S. attorney general puts it, "To anticipate violence is to encourage violence." If all the things around us, which make life worth living, are said to be polluted, then why not get out of the world?

This interesting lecture revealed also that excessive consumption of starchy food without the supply of other kinds of food which, blended together, will develop a sound, healthy body, results in blindness. The lecture pointed specifically to the wholesale type of foodstuffs being supplied by American Cooperative Relief Everywhere (CARE) to hungry African countries, especially Liberia, where he said the rate of blindness is very high. This appalls me! What shall we do?

My regular courses, methods in teaching English on both Junior and Senior high school levels, were conducted by Dr. I. Strom and Dr. Vernon H. Smith.

I feel strongly that I was worn out, that my methods were seemingly out of date, so my enthusiasm was overflowing to attend those courses. Ten years had lapsed since I left college. Deep down in my heart I realized I was getting to be a teacher of eh "old school," because I had not gone anywhere so as to bring my methods up to date.

At the Education Building, Room 124, that night (the 15th of September, 1969, to be precise), I met the aging professor, Dr. I. Strom. I was in the class before she came; but to my astonishment, she seemed not to notice the presence of a new and strange student.

Dr. I. Strom was the teacher of methods in English for graduate students, while Dr. Vernon H. Smith conducted the methods in English for the undergraduate students. I audited both courses, which to a considerable degree overlapped each other, except that each professor's approach differed markedly from the other's. The presentation in each case left a disheartening frustration. As a result I sat in class most of the time like a dummy. It was nothing better than what I learned years ago.

The names of the books to be used for the courses were given. We were asked to buy them. As soon as the books were obtained, each person was assigned a book and was required to report to the class the author's ideas of how to teach English in high school. This was the approach of Dr. Strom.

This was ably done by each assigned student, but what really bored me was that these assigned authorities read were never in agreement with any one idea except that all had students to teach. I was shocked when one of those authorities defines a sentence as a group of words between a capital and the last punctuation mark!

Dr. Smith's approach was different and, to me, this was more meaningful than the other approach. Here a book assigned to a group of students-discussion groups, led by their given leader. These smaller units of this class met to discuss the main points of the book as outlined by the leader. I was also placed in a group. The members of my group, in fact the members of the class, except my fellow-grantee and me, were undergraduates who had no classroom experience as teacher.

One thing I was aware of was that I came to observe and not infuse my ideas that were worn out by my thirteen unbroken years of teaching experience. Of course those young ladies recognized my association with them.

These enthusiastic young readers ate up every book assigned for reading and discussion. I admired greatly their voracious reading habits and the sharp comprehension of those girls. I just could not understand how they read. Here I realized that those girls were not superior in one way or the other except that they had been exposed to books since their early school days and even I had no doubt that they knew about books before this time. But, still to my judgment, this is not the basic reason. From the beginning, these children were taught the correct habit of reading by people who have this useful habit themselves.

THE NUCLEUS OF THE AMERICAN SOCIETY

"I am Jack Block, the father of Janis, U.S. Peace Corps Volunteer in Liberia," Mr. Block told me in his first letter to me. This was a letter of introduction and invitation received from this loving and cheerful American family. According to the letter, the Blocks were to meet me on the I. U. (Bloomington) campus for our first meeting and a get-to-know-each-other lunch. On the 25th of October, Mr. and Mrs. Block, with their 14-year and 16-year old towering sons came to see their skinny Liberian friend.

Both of gracious professional standing, the Blocks met me with all cordiality and friendship, which endeared them to me at once. At some downtown Bloomington restaurant, the Blocks lavishly entertained their daughter's Assistant Principal. It is worthy of note that, during this month, too, I received a letter, which painted a very rosy picture of her life in that West African nation. In part, the letter said, "I have conquered my trouble with malaria. I have become very Liberian, as I put plenty of hot pepper in my soup. I wear lappa nearly. The people call me by the Krahn name they gave me. I also try to speak the dialect. I am very happy!"

It seemed that the Blocks had substituted me for their daughter. Another invitation for a visit with them in their home is South Bend, Indiana, followed the lunch. I accepted.

Four days later Mrs. Block, with hr college-going daughter, Malinda, drove to Bloomington to pick me up for a long weekend visit with them. On our way to South Bend, Mrs. Block intimated that a teacher in a Catholic high school in Misawaka, Indiana, had requested her to ask me whether I would be willing to talk to her sociology class. For thirteen unbroken years, talking with children has become my second nature. For almost three months, I had not done this, and I was already feeling that I was not living my full life. Wholeheartedly I seized this opportunity.

On that cold Friday morning of October 30th, Mrs. Block drove me to the school. My hostess; a cordial, unassuming, beautiful, young lady, Miss Kathleen Surges (now Mrs. Edward Kinley), welcome me warmly and briefly introduced me to her robust students.

Briefly I told the eagerly listening students about the organization of the American Colonization Society which led to the founding of Liberia. This was followed by a question and answer period. I never saw youngsters so greedy for knowledge as those healthy American boys and girls. Questions came from all the corners of the spacious room. This was a big surprise to me. During the many years of my teaching experience, my children would accept without question most of the things I told them in class. Most of the time the Liberian students act like the students in Goldsmith's "Deserted Village".

> And still they gazed
> And still they wonder grew
> That one small head could carry
> All he knew.

But these frisky American children act the opposite. They wanted to know everything by way of question.

A few hours after I went home, I phone the teacher requesting written comments about my talk from the students. A few days after I returned to Bloomington, a pregnant envelope landed in my mailbox. In that fat envelope, I found about seventy pieces of paper. For the first time in my life, I had the rich experience of seeing myself through the unbiased comments of those high school boys and girls.

Why do the Liberian schools boys and girls act so irresponsive in class? From my personal analysis of the problem, I realized two things:
1. language barrier and very limited vocabulary, and 2. no adequate information on any given subject because of limited reading materials.

THE PILGRIMAGE

The 17th of December (1969) morning found us hurrying up with our heavy loads to the native-refusing elevator for our departure from our UN-like dormitory and Indiana University, Bloomington campus. In a matter of minutes, the spacious lobby of the dormitory was crowded with those loads. Shortly a bus arrived, and we unwillingly left Indiana University and our dear dormitory where we had made ourselves quite at home.

Our first stop was Chicago. As we rode thru the U.S. Breadbasket, the eyes were naturally caught by the black, apparently fertile soul. This made it quite understandable why the country produces enough to sustain herself, taking advantage of her rich soil and the technical know-how. Smokey Gary, Indiana, told us that America is a highly industrialized country too.

Crime infested Chicago, which hosted us for four days, spoke eloquently about the United States as a leading industrial power. But our stay in this vast, smoky city was not a happy one. Of all the major cities in the United States, Chicago is the only city widely covered by Liberian newspapers. Mostly they told of the high rate of crime committed there. In our YMCA hotel, a man, thirsty to commit crime, forcibly gained entrance into the room of our assistant coordinator and chaired him brutally. On hearing this sad news, I told my roommate, "It is true monkey cannot hide its black hand." From that day the feeling of insecurity haunted us.

When we were in this city, we visited many places of interest. The Museum of Science and Industry was our first stop. Here my keen observation led me to think that one could learn more zoology in this one section of this tremendous building without wasting his time in a formal school.

There is also a possibility of becoming a geologist, a miner, or a sailor by merely making an educational tour of the building. The ingenuity of the American people to recreate nature in a building impedes my thinking!

At the planetarium we were led into the heavens while we remained seated. Gazing at the man-made heavens clustered with brilliant stars, we learned about the biblical fact told about the birth of Christ. What really impressed me beyond reasonable doubt was that, in spite of all their inventions, discoveries, conquest of nature, and their last feat (and the greatest of all to my mind), the landing of a man on the moon, most Americans have undying belief in Christian faith.

On the 21st of December, we were very happy to leave Chicago because the feeling of insecurity crept on us every minute of our stay. Glad we did! At the train station (Northern Pacific), the rush for departure from Chicago was unimaginable. It seemed the thick population of Chicago was on an evacuation schedule as the crowds wound their way to the numberless coaches of the waiting train. Finally, we settled down and the monster glided along like a woman eight months gone!

This experience was as exciting as wearisome. But nothing was more seeing the conquest of nature by the Americans and their unbelievable ingenuity. Their railroads and highways through those bare, Rocky Mountains registered a special respect and high honor in my admiring heart for them.

In God's good book, it is said, "Sow and ye shall reap." This I had not given any serious thought. But since my arrival in this country, I realized the full meaning of this aged biblical passage. Back in Liberia, my friendship with the United States Peace Corps volunteers I knew personally was warm, enviable, and surprising to my fellow Liberians. This is the friendship that has paid me the highest dividend! It made me paramount chief in the United States. My bosom friends, Mr. and Mrs. Milton D. Jones, Pittsburgh, Pennsylvania, arranged for me to live with a family in Washington State where we were scheduled to spend Christmas.

At the train station in Seattle, Washington, another American City which sharply depicts the American ingenuity, I met, on arrival, Mr. William L. Bates of 317 Avenue B, Snohomish, Washington, who came willingly to take me to their beautiful home where they are rearing their four college and high school going children. The husband is editor of Snohomish Tribune and Mrs. Bates is Chairman of Snohomish City Planning Commission. With this distinguished, hospitable and solicitous family, I spent four luxurious days, including Christmas day.

The network of bridges in San Francisco, California, found me, upon arrival, completely mystified! How in the name of goodness man could have ventured out to display so wonderful an engineering feat! In order to comfort myself, grinning, I said, "The Americans glory in building bridges."

My friends, Mr. and Mrs. John R. Bachert of 3385 Sacramento Street, San Francisco, California, had written me a letter requesting me to lodge with them during my three-day stopover in San Francisco. This was another reunion I was eagerly looking forward to. John, his wife, Marjorie, and I had taught together in a junior high school in Nyaake, Webbo, Grand Gedeh County, Liberia.

About fifteen minutes after we arrived, John picked me up at the hotel where my friendless friend was to live. Can you imagine how John and I hugged each other?

The returned U.S. Peace Corps volunteers are the only awakening hope for Liberia's century-old relations with the United States. It is disturbingly and dishearteningly surprising that most Americans have little or no knowledge about Liberia, despite Liberia's historical ties with them. I am not living in despair! The Peace Corps boys and girls try now to revive this century old relationship as they identify themselves with us here in the U.S.

It seemed that it is quite true here in the United States that old age, which lessens our vigor, increases our desire to live more. In Los Angeles, California, in a place called Disneyland, grownup Americans pretend to be little children as they play with toys. This is very fascinating, but there was more to this. As we traveled around Disneyland, we would soon discover that it was also a land of history as we sailed in the steamboat and saw the life of the American Indian portrayed along the banks of the rivers. This experience thrilled me. The educational value is immense!

Here in Los Angeles, our warm, altruistic friends, the Americans, lavished us doubly with their hospitality again. A hospitality group in that city arranged for a sightseeing trip around the city. I had not seen people like the people of these United States who selflessly put themselves in a sacrificial position just to accommodate some friends form faraway lands. Besides what they gave us collectively, each individual citizen made another sacrifice. So it was in Miss Leslie Priest's case, a high school senior of 39959 Franklin Avenue, Los Angeles, California, when she drove us around in her own car.

Our trip around the city landed us in what they called Marine-land. Here the American imparts tricks to animals and fish to act like human beings.

Our journey form Los Angeles to Austin, Texas, was brutal! Can you imagine seeing someone sitting in one position for about seventy-two hours? But my burning desire to see and live for awhile in a state of my political hero, Mr. Lyndon B. Johnson, gladdened me and to some extend took extent away the pain I experienced in this sedentary position of hard riding.

After two nights of hard and wearisome riding in the Greyhound bus, we arrived in Austin, Texas, state capital, on Sunday morning, January 4, 1973. At the bus station, our Texas coordinator, Dr. Severo Gomez, and his staff members greeted us warmly and loaded our luggage on their cars. We were housed at the Commodore Perry Hotel.

As soon as our handsome coordinator had done everything for our happiness in the hotel, he invited us to join him and his staff at some restaurant that evening. Dr. Gomez picked us up at the hotel and off to the party we went. At the dinner we chatted as we ate away the delicious food.

There were many wild tales told me about Texas and its people long before my coming to the state. As you can imagine, I had my eyes wide open to see those things and people in reality. Among many things, I was told that the friendship here was much warmer that in any other state of the Union, but I would not be able to understand these warm and cordial friends because of their unusual intonation. Yes, truly, the friendship is warmer and more cordial; but, as you know, good stories tellers generally season their stories with pleasing lies in order to add some entertaining flavor to them. I understood my friends quiet well.

The next day we were privileged to attend a Texas Education Board meeting. As we filed through the door, with Dr. Gomez leading the way, the warm expression of welcome was seen in each corner of the room filled to capacity. Our formal introduction by Dr. Gomez seemed to have conferred upon us full citizenship of the State of Texas. Mr. Hubert Wilborn, Texas Education Board member from Amarillo, assured me that in Panhandle I would feel quite at home.

The Board of Education, whether state or local, (in most cases, as I was told), is composed of members elected from all walks of life, who serve without compensation.

During the lively deliberation of this selfless body, there was nothing more striking to me than the case of a teacher who was dismissed by a local school board because he wore a beard. Both the local school board and the dismissed teacher were represented by counsels. After a few minutes of argument from both sides, there was a motion to affirm the dismissal of the bearded teacher. This motion to my mind was a travesty justice and one that tended to undermine the democratic way of life. But just before democracy crumbled, there was some fast thinking man was saved our cherished institution. This reversed the decision and the State Board ordered the local board to pay the teacher for the full term of his contract with them.

That afternoon we met with Dr. Gomez at the Texas Education Agency Building where he briefed us about the educational polices of the State of Texas.

Wednesday found us riding on the treeless plains to Houston, Texas. This was a sightseeing trip to the Astrodome and NASA. On our arrival at the Astrodome we bought our tickets for admission into the monst6rous building. As we entered the oval stadium, our guide told us that this was the 8th Wonder of the World. Definitely,

271

I observed, the engineering feat is super, but I could not grade it as a wonder. Perhaps what would make it a wonder was I paid one dollar to see my own African mahogany. NASA did not offer me any excitement as I thought. On the whole, the day was not well spent.

On Thursday, we were honored, by attending Texas School Administrators' meeting. There again I saw the American democracy at work. Two members of Texas lawmaking body came to brief these administrators about what this August body was doing about the education of the people of Texas.

THE COMMUNITY ASSIGNMENT

This was the core of the entire program. Here I saw the very foundation of everything that makes the American society. The main reason for this phase of the program was to observer the many facets of community life including the public school system.

My assignment took me to Amarillo, Texas, under an ever-joking boss, educator of high standing, solicitous host and a Henry Cardinal Newman gentleman. This is Mr. David C. Austin, Director of Secondary Instruction, Amarillo Independent Public School District. The Program called him my contract man.

As I understand the word observation I know what to do. But afterward I found that the meaning of the word could be carried out in two ways and so I worked out two modifiers to spell out my task; passive and active. Passive observation would place me in a sedentary position with any group of people to look on. Active observation would land me talking with the group. In this situation I was asked to talk about my home country and so briefly I gave the historical and geographical background and this was followed by a question and answer period. With my objectives clearly outlined to myself, I embarked upon this assignment, with Mrs. Beth Jones, Mr. Austin's secretary, in charge of appointments.

My first visit took me to Fannin Junior High School, headed by Mr. A Lehman Gregg, a reserved, soft-spoken gentleman. The night before, Mr. Gregg met me at the Austin's. At his school the principal showed us his facilities, which his spacious and roomy school building contains. Many junior high school visits followed this one.

Mrs. Hazel Black Davis, wife of a retired college mathematics professor, niece of U.S. Supreme Court justice, coordinator of English, Amarillo Public School System and also teacher of English at Tascosa High School, made arrangements for me to visit her senior English class. Long before this Mrs. Davis had met me several times in the administration building where we had talked about my formal written report which was then being typed by Mrs. Jones and Mrs. Clara Griffiths. According to Mrs. Davis, Mrs. Griffiths had told her that she (Mrs. Griffiths) was enjoying reading my written expressions of my impressions and comments about America and Americans. So she made it her point to read them too. Having read them, Mrs. Davis automatically became my able salesman while Mrs. Griffiths continued to be my industrious advertisements agent.

Finally the day came for me to visit with Mrs. Davis. My chauffeur, Mr. Austin, boss turned servant, drove me to the school. There I had the pleasing time of

272

talking with those energetic young American question boxes. Back in the administration building after the visit, Mrs. Davis showered me with all the epithets that possibly ranked me second to none in the teaching profession. She told the story with the strokes of her arms. As Lincoln says, "Everybody likes a compliment." I am no exception. I appreciated her compliments so lavishly paid me and thanked her for them but deep down in my heart I knew I did not merit many of those compliments.

It seemed she wanted to know whether somebody else shared her glorious thoughts and expressions about me, so she requested those greedy knowledge seekers (her students) to write exactly what they thought about my presentation to the class. They wrote and the comments were sent to me. They gave me the qualities that make a mortal man perfect. Again, I learned what others thought of me. The one that really reminded me of my origin was the one that called me "Mr. William K. Reeves, Civilized Savage." This student apologized for this title but it was nothing offensive to me. She simply told the truth and she added this was one of the points that impressed her most. This was the active observation because from the talk I observed their reactions.

From Austin, Texas, to Amarillo I had the distinguished privilege of riding with Mr. Laycock, director of Texas Education Agency Regional Service Center in the Panhandle, and Messrs. David Cole and Paul Hilburn of the same service. After sometime in Amarillo, I was invited by this center to attend their staff meeting. Mr. Hilburn picked me up at the administration building. Patiently I listened to their lively deliberations. After the meeting Mrs. Edith Smith invited me to her office. Mrs. Smith is a staff member and consultant of English. This was the first time and the only experience of what they call team-teaching. Mrs. Smith wanted to know how I teach English. I presented orally my lesson plan. She then told me how she did it when she was a regular school teacher. Our final analysis proved we had many things, if not all, in common. I was quite satisfied, knowing that an English consultant and I shared similar views. This, to me, was a wholesome assuring sign that only facilities limited the Liberian teacher. In fact this was the thing I enjoyed the most because Mrs. Smith wanted to know how I did it and if there was need, she would advise. To me this made her title more meaningful.

"Arrangements for you to live with six different families are complete now," wrote my contact man, Mr. Austin. These arrangements were exciting and strangulating but I was grateful. Knowing what my life would be like I came to Amarillo with a feeling of warm friendship sparked of my Mr. Austin's personal letters to me. But as a poet puts it, "In sight of port sank many a vessel fair," so I did not live with all of my hosts and hostesses. The ones I lived with were Mr. and Mrs. David C. Austin, Mr. and Mrs. Arthur Champion, Mr. and Mrs. David C. Stults and Mr. and Mrs. Philip Jones. To these gracious, solicitous, hospitable people I say thank you. Those who willingly opened their doors to me but did not get to bear this burden deserve and honorable mention too. They are Mr. and Mrs. Griffiths and Mr. and Mrs. Jackson. To them I say thank you too.

My visit with Mr. Bunch, Principal of Hamlet Elementary School, stood more prominently. There in this school I noticed some rare human trait in the principal and the angel-like students. The thing that really impressed me about Mr.

Bunch, a tall, heavily set man, was his very fatherly touch and human gentleness with the little ones. As he and I strolled in the corridors any child who called to him he would call by name too and would take some of his busy time to stop and listen to this child. Another thing that moved me was the children's spontaneous friendship with me. Into this picture come clearly Anmy Burds, Paul Harris, Mike Johnson and Vaughn Worcester, the sixth grader who requested me to join him, his classmates and their young, charming teacher, Mrs. Nash, for lunch. This 12-year-old boy showed me that he loved me as he presented me his pen adding, "Mr. Reeves, this is the sign of friendship and expect me in Liberia as soon as I am old enough." A girl of my dear color said, "Come again to read my composition."

"One of the great traditions of Texas is hospitality," writes Texas House Speaker Mutscher. This great tradition has less meaning to people who read it. My time in Amarillo was spent in gracious hospitality as each person I came into contact with tried to give up his/her own money just to please a man from some faraway land so that he would feel at home away from home. Mrs. Nell Dunn, the lady in charge of the snack bar at the administration building, did something extraordinary to me in this respect. For the first time in my life I ate cake at the persuasive urging of this lady with her contagious smiles.

Well, I came, I saw, but I cannot say I conquered. However, I think, I have gathered enough good and useful ideas which have definitely broadened my outlook primarily on education and some things of life in general. As the protruding eyes of challenge and opportunity are blinking at me, the only thing that bothers me now is, will I be put in the situation where I will put into active use some, if not all, of these ideas mustered here in a very Liberian way?

The Americans are diligent observers of the niceties of life as each time they talked with you before leaving they would say, "It was nice meeting and talking with you." This I admire and will try to acquire and so I say now, "Thank you, it was nice of you to have invited me and to have shared with me your manifold blessings."

-William K. Reeves

NOTES

[1] What has become of learning.

[2] Richard Nixon. The Six Crises.

[3] "Kwi" is a word coined by Liberians and it means a western kind of anything: food, clothes, or what have you. Kwi food means western food, not African or Liberian.

[4] Macbeth III. ii. 16-17

[5] Here "augured" means predicted or foretold.

[6] To "cross" a worker means to deny that worker of credit or pay for the day he worked.

[7] Sore corners are found at the corners of the human mouth. This is the local name given to a diseased mouth.

[8] Atina is a word derived from the Kru dialect and it means, "This is our time."

[9] "Je bor dor" is a Liberian expression meaning "girlfriend."

[10] No, she did not brandish anything but rather she thought shouting my name loud would beat me off.

[11] "Bass drum" is pregnancy. Instead of graduating from high school, she became pregnant. The pregnancy is the diploma.

[12] What has become of learning.

[13] I taught in three different communities, Harper in Maryland County, Nyaake, Webbo, in Lower Grand Gedeh County, and Zwedru in Upper Grand Gedeh County. Zwedru took the lion's share, twenty-two years of my thirty-eight years in the active service of my country

Cheif Musu

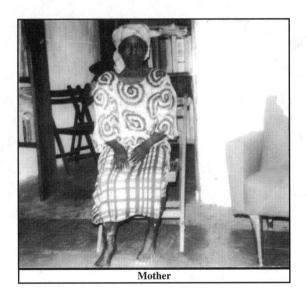

Mother

BJHS Faculty

Writing

William Boniface Peter

Brother and Sister